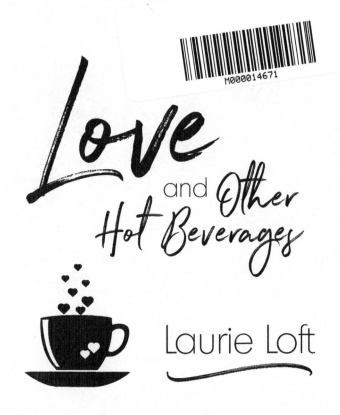

Love
and Other
Hot Beverages

Laurie Loft

M000014671

Love and Other Hot Beverages

Laurie Loft

RIPTIDE
PUBLISHING

Riptide Publishing
PO Box 1537
Burnsville, NC 28714
www.riptidepublishing.com

Love and Other Hot Beverages
Copyright © 2017 by Laurie Loft

Cover art: L.C. Chase, lcchase.com/design.htm
Editor: May Peterson, maypetersonbooks.com
Layout: L.C. Chase, lcchase.com/design.htm

ISBN: 978-1-62649-597-5

First edition
July, 2017

Also available in ebook:
ISBN: 978-1-62649-596-8

For Stan, who makes me hot beverages.

Table of Contents

Chapter One

Office Boy

The office boy smiled at Todd. "That coffee's shit."

Hard hat under one arm, Todd stared at the coffeepot in front of him. He waited impatiently for the drip to stop, conscious of several teammates waiting their turns. They jostled one another as they laughed and joked. The men with their hard hats seemed to take up more space than necessary in the confines of the mobile office. Todd itched to get his coffee and get out into the fresh air.

"You look like someone who would appreciate good coffee," the boy continued, and Todd knew a fishing query when he heard one. What the boy meant was, *You're gay, aren't you?* Because everyone knew that gays liked gay coffee. Todd tried to remember the boy's name. They all called him *office boy*.

"I like shit," Todd said with a feral grin. "Keeps me awake. Keeps me from falling off buildings." Todd was not interested in having his cover blown. Passing for straight among a gang of construction workers was easy enough if you watched yourself, and that meant not watching any cute office boys. He reached for a cup, but the boy handed him one first, his tanned fingers brushing against Todd's.

He's shorter than I am. Not many guys were. The one who had broken his heart had been four inches taller than Todd.

"I know a good place to get real, honest, quality coffee, not the sludge they keep here," the boy continued. Apparently, Todd's feral grin was not scary enough or het enough. "I don't mean like Starbucks—a local coffeehouse. It's real nice, *lo prometo*."

"I'm allergic to coffeehouses," Todd said. "Step inside one and I'll need hospitalization."

It was in a coffeehouse that his heart had been broken.

The cozy New York coffeehouse had seemed innocuous enough. And then there had been one Vivian Oscar Stanton-Owens, a young man of only eighteen who had so adorably crushed on Todd. Todd should have known better—he *had* known better—but, flattered by the attention, had thought, *Give the kid a thrill,* and then had fallen for him like an idiot. There in that cozy coffeehouse, Todd had lost his heart and had it handed back to him like so much old coffee grounds.

Todd poured, staring at the brown liquid and not allowing his eyes to flick toward the boy even for a split second, definitely not noticing his dark-sienna hair and how it curled against the back of his neck.

"I'll bring you some good coffee tomorrow," the boy offered. "I only buy fair-trade beans. I grind them fresh each time. And I use spring water and a French press."

That's all I need, another kid with a crush. "I prefer this shit." Todd threw the coffee back like a slug of whiskey, scalding his entire mouth and throat so that he was unlikely to taste anything for days. Adjusting his goggles over his eyeglasses, he turned and exited the mobile office with a manly, het swagger. He forced his mind away from the lingering impression of alluring deep-brown eyes.

Atop the Gimondi Brothers' scaffolding, Todd indulged his favorite fantasy. Looking out over the ground below, he imagined a slight figure in bright colors picking his way across the lot, shading his eyes with his hand, squinting up at the crew. In Todd's mind the light gathered around this figure, haloing the white-blond hair, and Todd imagined how his heart would seize up, how he would trip over himself getting to the ground. He would fling his hard hat aside, run to the figure and halt, perhaps an arm's-length away, noting the look of mingled hope and apprehension on his—on Vivian's face.

Todd would have to swallow hard. "You're here . . . You came all the way to Denver?" Viv would nod and smile, and Todd would clasp Viv to himself, and the hell with all construction workers and all heterosexuals and all the world, because Todd would kiss Vivian in full view against the backdrop of the Rocky Mountains.

Some mornings later, the crew gathered around a hole while the foreman decided what to do. They stood, a study in casualness, arms crossed or hands on hips. *How many laborers does it take to look at a hole?* Todd wondered. He dragged his eyes from the dirt to gaze at the mountains. He was still a flatlander, easily mesmerized.

"Good morning, men."

Todd turned to see that the office boy had approached on silent cat feet. A chorus of unintelligible monosyllables answered.

As he unscrewed the lid of a thermos, the boy piped up: "Payroll's done early, so pick up your checks at lunch if you want." Cheers sounded. Gus, a grizzled man next to Todd, clapped the boy on the back, causing him to spill whatever he was pouring into the lid-slash-cup. The boy held the dripping cup away from himself, letting the liquid dribble onto the dirt. The aroma of good coffee reached Todd.

"Oh, sorry, Sebby," Gus said.

Sebby. That's his name. What kind of name is that?

"It's okay. Here . . . hold this?" Sebby offered the thermos and cup to Todd.

Annoyed, Todd accepted them. Sebby pulled a bandanna from his pocket, then took hold of Todd's wrist and wiped the cup. Sebby's fingers pressed firmly on his skin. Todd ground his teeth, not wanting to pull away and get coffee-splashed. After wiping every possible microbe of coffee from the outside of the cup, Sebby let go, fingers stroking Todd's wrist in a familiar manner as they slid off. "Try it."

"You letting him try your private stash? How come *he* rates?" Gus laughed.

"You're welcome to try it too, Gus," Sebby offered.

It did smell tempting. "Give it a go, Gus. Good coffee gives me the runs." Todd pushed the coffee at Gus, turned, and stalked off.

He imagined he could feel Sebby's eyes on him and found himself trying to remember which jeans he'd donned that morning. He had to fight to keep from touching himself to check.

"Yeah! Paid early! Office boy does it again! Hand me that three-quarters," Dean, one of the pipe fitters, said.

"He actually *does* the payroll?" Todd asked, passing him the requested tool.

"Yeah. Whatcha think he does?" Dean grunted with the effort of tightening the bolt, lying in an awkward position, his arm extended to reach into a tight spot.

"I thought he just handed out the checks."

"Naw. He's an accountant or some shit."

An accountant. If that was true, then Sebby had to be older than Todd had first thought. If he had an associate's degree, he'd have to be around twenty. "How long has he worked here?"

Dean shrugged. "He was here when I got here, and I been here off and on for two years. Another year and I'll make journeyman."

Around twenty-two, then.

The lunch siren sounded, and the crew swarmed down to the ground. Some men headed to the local diner, while others ate in their cars or near the scaffolding or sprawled on the ground. Todd sat in his rusty old pickup with the windows rolled down. Since the Vivian incident, he'd been living with his older brother, Lloyd, and his sister-in-law had packed a lunch for him. He unwrapped it and opened a book: *The Inimitable Jeeves.* There was nothing better than a Wodehouse book when one needed cheering. The breeze ruffled his sweat-damp hair as he chuckled at the exploits of Bertie Wooster.

A shadow fell across his book. Todd glanced up.

"Coffee?" Sebby asked. He leaned his forearms on the open window so that his hands were inside Todd's pickup. One hand held a styrofoam cup.

Todd's smile emptied itself. "I told you I'm allergic to the good stuff."

"I know. I brought you the bad stuff." Sebby wiggled the cup a little, and Todd took it.

"Oh . . . well . . . thanks." He sniffed it and grimaced. The earlier whiff of Sebby's quality beverage made the office shit smell even worse.

"You like to read," Sebby observed.

Todd nodded. "And you're blocking my light."

"What is it you're reading?"

"A spy novel. W.E.B. Griffin." Todd knew W.E.B. Griffin to be a manly, het writer because his brother read him. Todd took a gulp of coffee and couldn't help making a face.

"You take it black, don't you? I've never seen you put anything in it."

"It tastes more gawdawful than usual. But I like it that way," Todd hastened to add.

Sebby leaned in, and Todd leaned away. "You don't like that coffee," Sebby said in a conspiratorial tone. "Taste mine. I won't tell."

Hello, innuendo. The corners of Todd's mouth twitched, and he forced himself to frown. The boy's voice was as smooth and sweet as café au lait.

Todd wondered if Sebby tasted like his good coffee.

"What kind of name is 'Sebby'?" He put as much scorn into his tone as he could muster.

"Sebastián. My momma was Mexican. But my dad thinks 'Sebby' is easier to say."

"Sebastián," Todd repeated, and his tongue went numb. It was a beautiful name, and Todd wanted to say so. Instead, he drank his coffee.

"What kind of name is 'Todd'?" Sebby shifted, turning to the side and tilting his head back. Sunlight fell on his face, and Todd saw that his brown irises were sparked with tiny gold flecks.

"It's, ah, I don't know. It means 'fox.'"

"Fox on the run." Sebby flashed Todd a smile before turning and walking away. Todd spent the rest of his lunch wondering what that remark might mean.

Chapter Two

Love Is Gross

"*U*ncle Todd? Why don't you like girls?"

The voice drifted down out of the semidarkness, and Todd gazed up at the slats of the bunk above him. The youngest of Lloyd's three sons had been kind enough to evict his stuffed animals from his bottom bunk in order to accommodate his unfortunate uncle, and these after-dark heart-to-hearts were becoming habitual. "I like girls fine. My best friend is a girl."

"Yeah, that girl that was here with you." Holly, Todd's best chum since they had both fallen in love with the same guy in ninth grade, had accompanied Todd and provided moral support on the road trip from New York to Denver. Quitting a job and running away was bad enough, but if not for Holly, he didn't know what he might have done.

"But you don't *date* girls. You date boys. Maybe if you dated girls, you wouldn't have got your heart broken."

Todd chuckled. "Ryan, I assure you that men who like women get their hearts broken just as often. It's a part of life, and rather unavoidable."

"Well, I'm not gonna get mine broken. I'm never gonna be in love. Love is gross."

"An elegant philosophy and one that I cannot condemn."

Todd crouched alone, goggles atop his hard hat on his head, pretending to wipe dirt from his eyes. On a construction site, no one saw this as either suspicious or unusual. Unfortunately, Todd's hands were grimy, and he was quite handily accomplishing the supposed cause of his pretended activity.

"Coffee?"

The gentle voice made him glance up. Of course it would be Sebby standing over him, offering a cup and an expression of detached concern. Todd grabbed the cup and gulped. A rich and aromatic liquid went down his throat before his sense of smell alerted him. "Motherfuck," he sputtered.

"I sneaked the good stuff on you, yeah. You gonna knock me down?"

Todd shook his head and went back to wiping his eyes.

"There's an eyewash in the office."

"No . . . thanks . . ." He gulped the coffee again and grimaced. Swinging the cup in an arc, he threw the rest of it out, painting a parabola on the ground in front of him.

Sebby *tsk*ed. "What is it with you and the coffee? Was your last boyfriend Juan Valdez?"

Todd raised his head and glared at him.

Sebby *tsk*ed again. "You're a mess. Come on into the office, Todd. That's an order." He turned and walked off. After a moment, Todd got to his feet, his knees creaking like a ninety-year-old's. He hurried to catch up with Sebby, who paced across the site.

"Fox on the run," Sebby said.

"Ah, what?"

"You're on the run from a love affair gone bad."

A consternated Todd had no reply.

"You don't have to talk about it. It's just, um, you're pretty pitiful, you know."

Pretty pitiful, Todd thought, privately enjoying the alliteration.

They reached the mobile office, and in they went, the screen door banging behind them, and they were alone.

"Clean up." Sebby pointed at the sink. "I'll get the eyewash."

Todd set aside his hard hat, goggles, and eyeglasses. He tore off a fistful of paper towels and wetted them in the sink. The cold water refreshed him as he buried his face in the wet towels and wiped away the grime.

"Lean back over the counter."

Todd jumped. He hadn't heard him approach. "What?" He began finger-combing his hair. *I have helmet hair. Sweaty helmet hair. And that makes my hair look a dark, icky blond, and why do I care what I look like?* He gave his hair a final fluff. "What?" he repeated.

Sebby tossed a cloth towel to Todd, raised a plastic bottle, and shook it. "Eyewash. Lean back over the counter."

Todd reached for the eyewash. "I'll do it myself."

Sebby held the eyewash out of reach. "You can't. Lean back."

"How do you mean?" Discomposed, Todd did not know how he could lean backward over the narrow counter.

"On your side. We'll get this eye, then the other. The wash needs to be able to run out, and you don't want it all over you. Move over." Todd did so. Sebby washed his hands, snatched the towel from Todd, and demonstrated the correct position, leaning half over the counter, pillowing his head on the folded towel. "See? Now you."

Todd did as instructed. Sebby rested a cool hand on Todd's brow, smoothing back his hair. Todd shivered and closed his eyes.

"Hello, Toddfox, eyewash requires eyes to be open?"

Todd opened his eyes. Sebby's face was very close. Deep-brown eyes looked into Todd's blue ones. "How old are you?" Todd asked.

Sebby straightened. "Twenty-five."

"Twenty-*five*?"

"I know; I should staple my driver's license to my forehead. And you're twenty-three until September twenty-second, and your middle name is Marvin. Now, ready?" Pressing gently on Todd's head, he bent over him again and brought the plastic bottle close. "Open wide." Having said this, he thumbed Todd's eyelid and released the eyewash. Todd flinched, but the wash flowed soothingly into and out of his eye.

Sebby released him, and Todd blinked. "You snooped in the office records," Todd accused.

"I *am* the office. Please turn over."

Bemused, Todd shifted to his other side. The angle was different, and Sebby pressed up against Todd's back to again smooth his hair away and direct the flow of the eyewash. Todd lay there, all awkwardness. How long had it been since anyone had touched him with affection? *You're exaggerating. Ryan hugs you. Donna is always taking your arm or ruffling your hair. Jesus, even Lloyd's been known to do the macho shoulder squeeze.*

"You're done. Better?"

Todd wiped his face with the towel and straightened, blinked myopically. "I believe so. Thank you."

"Your eyes are red."

"Dust."

"Coffee. Will you please try my coffee? I've been making it for you every day, and you keep turning me down and dumping it in the dirt. And it's expensive stuff, and I labor over it."

"I tried it," Todd protested, adjusting his eyeglasses, followed by his goggles. "It didn't suit me."

"Liar."

Todd hesitated. He couldn't remember why he had declined in the first place. "Very well. In my weakened state, I cannot refuse."

Chapter Three

Days Since Last Accident

Something caught Todd's eye, pulling his gaze from the mountains. Far below, he spied Sebby emerging from the mobile office, and his heart gave an unfamiliar little skip-hop. It was break time. Some of the men preferred to rest where they were, others headed for the ground. Todd took his time descending from the partially completed building.

"Hey, French Press," he said in greeting as he reached the ground.

Sebby grinned, and a tiny crease with a perfect pinprick appeared in the middle of his left cheek. *He has a dimple!* Todd stared as Sebby poured from a thermos and pressed the cup into Todd's hands.

"Well? Are you going to drink?"

"Er—yeah." Todd inhaled the rich aroma, sipped, and swallowed. What could he say to keep that smile on Sebby's face? His wits failed him. All he could think about was reaching out to touch that small indentation. "Mmm."

The grin grew; the dimple deepened. "That's all you've got to say."

Todd sipped again. "Mmmmm," he elaborated.

Elegant eyebrows went up.

Todd considered. "Ah . . . thank you?"

"You're welcome."

Looking down from the scaffolding and scanning the site for the small figure of Sebby and his thermos at break time became habit to Todd.

"What is it with office boy always bringing you coffee?" Dean wanted to know. They were all taking a breather, sitting in a loose group high above the ground.

Todd shrugged. Sometimes the best answer was no answer at all.

"Office boy wants to suck his cock!" said one of the journeymen. There was general laughter. Todd was accustomed to this sort of talk. It was a mystery to him, but straight men seemed to find nothing more hilarious than homoerotic humor.

"He'll just have to get in line. Behind all you homos," Todd said. There were shouts and more laughter demonstrating that Todd had scored a point.

Todd gazed at the mountains, seeing instead Sebastián's face and that smile. What would it be like to kiss it, the dimple? It was so small, would his lips even feel it? He imagined poking his tongue into it; that could work.

If Sebby was smiling when Todd kissed him.

"Hey, Zorro," Sebby said as Todd reached the ground.

"Zorro?" Todd considered slashing a *Z* in the air, decided against it.

"*Zorro* is Spanish for fox." Sebby poured a cup from his thermos and handed it to Todd. Their hands brushed.

"I didn't know that." Todd felt inordinately pleased by the nickname. "In French it's *renard*."

"You speak French?"

"*Mais oui*." The memory pricked his heart like thumbtacks. He and Vivian had nattered on in French almost as much as they had in English. He watched while Sebby offered coffee to the others. They stood or sat in groups, drinking coffee or smoking. Todd kept a decent distance between himself and Sebby, who showed no inclination to close the gap.

"Fuck! Fucking shit, oh fuuuck!"

Curses could be heard minute by minute from anyone on the crew, but something in the tone of this one made Todd turn toward the yell. He spotted Rob, a welder about Todd's age, holding his arm up and staring at it as if staring would stop the bleeding. Drawing a hissing breath, Todd hurried to his side.

"Shit! Fucking fuck, I caught myself on a sharp!" Blood soaked the side of Rob's shirt and pattered on the planks.

A gray curtain dipped over Todd's eyes, and he had to avert his eyes. "Ah . . . you need to get to the office. There's first aid shit in there. Come on." Todd swallowed, took hold of Rob's good arm, and pulled, breathing through his mouth to minimize the coppery smell. Todd towed him toward the office, giving thanks that at least they were on the ground level. The earth swayed a little. *Think about something, think about anything: coffee.* He imagined the aroma of good, strong coffee, and the ground righted itself. They made it to the office.

Sebby applied first aid with the casual skill of someone who has seen dozens of similar injuries. "It's not as bad as it looks, Mr. Clumsy. But you do need stitches. Todd, drive him to the hospital?"

Todd lifted his head from his knees. "Me?"

"I can't leave the office. See, he's patched up, no more blood, this'll hold him for a while." Sebby erased the number twenty-three from the board, which read: *Days since last accident.*

Todd tried to gather his wits. "I— All, all right."

Sebby peered at him. "You don't look so good. I'll get someone else. Can't risk you fainting behind the wheel." He pulled out a cell phone, dialed, and spoke briefly. "Gus'll be here in a sec. He's an old-timer, so he's seen plenty of worse stuff. Hey, don't worry, Robbie." Sebby patted Rob, who appeared petrified. "A few stitches and you'll be fine. Todd, though, I don't know. I think he's traumatized. He'll need weeks of therapy to recover."

"Oh, thank you *so* much." Todd dropped his head back to his knees.

Rob laughed, a shaky, forced laugh, but a laugh nonetheless.

Head down, Todd's thoughts strayed to Vivian. Viv had once hurt his arm and needed a blood transfusion, and he had looked so pale and ethereal in the hospital. The realization left him shaken that now no one was likely to call him if Vivian were hurt; no one would even think to call him. No one thought of him at all.

Gus left with Rob in tow, and Sebby presented Todd with a cup of coffee. "No smelling salts, but maybe this'll work just as well."

Todd accepted the cup but kept his head down. "That was humiliating."

"Ohhh, very. You'll need even more weeks of therapy to get over the humiliation." He commenced rubbing Todd's bent-over back, up and down. It was soothing and somehow familiar. "Seriously, Zorro, don't worry about it. I've seen burly construction workers drop at the sight of blood, and you at least walked him to the office." He continued to rub Todd's back.

Todd closed his eyes. It was all he could do to keep from wrapping his arms around Sebastián and pressing his face against him. *Jesus God, just to hold someone, just to be held.* Instead he wrapped his hands around the coffee cup. "I'm a tower of strength, I am."

Chapter Four

Get Laid and Get Out

Up in the unfinished structure, Todd crouched over a stripped screw, trying to get it loose. A twinge in his shoulder made him wince.

"Office boy wants you."

Startled, Todd looked up at Dean. It was several seconds before he realized the words were not a sexual reference. "Ah . . . did he say why?"

"Paperwork or something. Here, I'll get that. We got a special head for it."

Todd stood and stretched, working the kinks out of his shoulder. "You going back down?"

"Naw."

Todd was nervous at the thought of being alone again with Sebastián. "Anybody else going down?" He caught Gus looking at him. "You going down, Gus?"

"You need help with your paperwork?" Gus said. "ABCs giving you trouble?"

"No, it's . . . Office boy scares me." Todd tried to laugh it off.

The lines of Gus's face settled into a frown. "I'll go with you."

They reached the ground, and Gus began to lecture. "You have no call to be rude to Sebby, Addison. He's a good kid. The guys may joke about him, but they like him. He's kind of a mascot. You treat him good or I'll know the reason why."

Todd swallowed hard. "No, sir. I didn't mean—"

"There's nothing wrong with gays. They're good at what they do." Gus left him at the mobile office, turned, and headed back across the site.

They're good at what they do? Todd snorted, knocked on the door, and entered.

Sebby, seated at his desk, looked up from the computer. "Zorro!"

"You wanted me?" Todd said and then bit his tongue. *Jesus, more unintended innuendo.*

"Yes," Sebby said in a businesslike tone. "Have a seat."

Todd did so. He threw one arm over the back of the chair and crossed his ankle over the opposite knee.

"I'm worried about you, Todd." Sebby put his fist under his chin and regarded Todd with professional concern.

"I apologize. I'd no intention of causing you worry. I assure you I've suffered no permanent damage from my fainting spell the other day. As long as no one bleeds in my vicinity in the near future, I shall make a full recovery." Todd hid his nerves behind a confident smile. His instincts told him he was about to be propositioned.

"Coffee? I just made it." The familiar thermos stood on the corner of his desk, and Sebby poured two cups. "I'm worried about where you'll get good coffee from if something should happen to me. You can't or won't make your own, and you have this life-threatening coffeehouse allergy."

"Is something going to happen to you? I'd just have to go back to the office shit."

"*No más.*" Sebby shook his head. "I feel responsible for your coffee needs."

"What do you propose, then?"

"You need to learn to make good coffee yourself. Come over to my place and I'll teach you to French press."

More innuendo. Todd opened his mouth and shut it again. *It's too soon, I've just met him, and I'm not ready to move on . . .* "Okay."

Sebby looked like he'd missed the last step of a staircase. "Okay? Really?"

"Really."

"I thought you'd say no."

"Evidently, you were wrong."

"It took you so long to say yes to my coffee. I thought you'd play harder to get."

Todd gave Sebby a severe look over the rims of his glasses. "Sebastián, is this why you had Dean fetch me from all the way up there on what will someday be known as the ninth floor?"

"Look, um . . ." Sebby turned away and shuffled some papers on the corner of his desk. "If I'm making you uncomfortable, I'm, um, I didn't mean to. It's not like sexual harassment; I mean, technically, we don't even work together. So, you know, if you don't want me hitting on you, nothing will happen if you turn me down. You'll still get a paycheck and whatever."

Todd put a shocked and hurt look on his face. "Are you *hitting* on me?"

Sebby regarded Todd over his shoulder.

In a wounded tone, Todd said, "I thought you were going to teach me this French press out of altruistic concern for my coffee needs."

Sebby laughed, an unself-conscious burst of sound. "I don't usually invite guys over."

"I can see that you are unskilled in the art of flirting."

"I mean, I usually get them to invite me somewhere. But you're different, Zorro. You are stiff-necked." He stepped behind Todd and placed his hands on Todd's neck. His thumbs on either side of Todd's spine pressed firmly upward.

Todd stiffened at the familiarity of it. How many times had he massaged Vivian's neck when he'd been ill? *This is what it feels like from the other side.*

"You're tight," Sebby said. He kneaded Todd's neck and shoulders. Todd found himself relaxing into Sebby's hands, until the sound of feet mounting the steps of the mobile office made him tense up, and Sebby moved away.

Todd was surprised to learn that Sebastián owned a small house in the Capitol Hill neighborhood. Sebby provided him with detailed directions for finding his place.

"And here's my number, so just call me if you get lost. Maybe I should come and pick you up? That would be easier. Or you could just follow me home." Sebby batted his lids and smiled, and *God, that dimple*. Politely finishing dinner before nabbing him would take self-control that Todd was not sure he had.

"I want to look my best for this coffee instruction, not arrive covered in dust and perspiration. I'll go home and shower and change first."

Sebby slid his hand down the length of the inside of Todd's arm before lacing his fingers with Todd's. He tugged, and Todd looked down at him, and Sebby looked up at Todd. Todd's breath caught, and he leaned closer.

Sebby said, "If you decide not to show, that's okay. I'll understand."

Todd blinked. "Why would I do that?"

"You best know the answer." And Sebby let him go.

Todd went home to shower and change. He pulled into the driveway of his brother's suburban four-bedroom home. Wiping his palms on his jeans, he made his way to the kitchen. He'd been living with his brother's family for a couple of months now and had rarely missed an evening meal. Donna, his sister in law, stood at the stove. Lloyd was bent over, rummaging in the refrigerator.

"I won't be here for dinner tonight. I'm going to a friend's."

Lloyd straightened. Donna looked up from whatever she was stirring. "Oh, you have a friend?" She sounded thrilled.

"Yeah, just someone from work, ah . . ." What was he doing? This was family and they accepted him. "It's a . . . ah, a date."

"That's great!" Donna said.

"You're dating someone from work?" Lloyd's forehead broke into furrows. He closed the refrigerator and tossed a bag of carrots on the counter. "You sure that's such a good idea?"

"Considering whether or not something is a good idea has never stopped me from doing anything. Having said that, I will further say that I believe it to be an excellent idea."

Donna turned off the burner, moved the pan, and came forward, still clutching her spatula. "Why wouldn't it be a good idea?"

Lloyd ripped open the carrot bag. "Sooner or later he'll get outed. If he's gonna be seeing someone on a regular basis that works where he works."

"Is it going to be regular?" Donna asked.

"I apologize, but the hard drive on my crystal ball was downed by a vicious virus," Todd said. "As soon as prognosticative capabilities are restored, I'll let you know the exact duration and intensity of this particular affiliation."

They blinked at him.

"I mean, dear people, I do not know! How can I know if it's going to be regular?"

Lloyd shook his head and commenced chopping carrots. "It better not be. Just get laid and get out."

The idea of treating Sebby in such a manner filled Todd with self-loathing. "That's not how I roll."

"'That's not how I roll'?" Lloyd guffawed. "Where are you getting this?"

"Look, I gotta get ready. Any other advice you'd like to offer? Of the useful variety?"

"Don't go empty-handed." Donna pointed her spatula at Todd. "Bring something."

Chapter Five

Cat at a Mouse Hole

The house numbers ticked by till he came to the right one, but instead of turning in, Todd drove past the house and around the next corner and parked at the curb. He couldn't stop thinking of Vivian, and that was hardly conducive to a successful first date. Todd gave himself a shake and sat straight up. *I might as well go home. He said it was all right if I didn't show.*

Reaching to put the truck in drive, it occurred to him that Sebby had known Todd would feel this way. Todd drummed his fingers on the wheel. He thought of Sebby's hair and how it curled at the back of the neck. He recalled Sebby taking his hand and looking up at him. He remembered Sebby's smile and how he had almost kissed him.

Todd put the pickup into gear and drove around the block.

Sebby opened his door before Todd reached it, beaming like a flood lamp. "Toddfox! Come in, come in! *Mi casa es tu casa.*" He held the door and stepped aside. "You look nice."

"Ah, thanks." He followed Sebby through the house to the kitchen. "Mmm. Smells wonderful. Oh, here, I brought this." Respecting Donna's advice, Todd had stopped and bought a baguette.

"Thank you!" Sebby laid the baguette on the counter. "I want to show you my home."

Chattering, he took Todd's hand and led him through the house, which was filled with collectables and glassware of all colors and descriptions. The word *eclectic* came to mind, though the place was neat as any pin Todd had ever poked himself with. It was a quick tour, and Sebby didn't even linger in the bedroom but instead drew Todd through the rest of the house and back to the kitchen.

"You like my place?" Sebby tilted his head to the side. The bright lighting in the kitchen picked out the gold in his eyes.

Todd squeezed Sebby's hand. "It's perfect. Charming. As are you. Did you know there are gold flecks in your eyes?"

Said eyes widened. "No?"

"Has no one ever told you? I noticed it in the sunlight, but it's evident here as well, where your eyes catch the light. It's like . . . It reminds me of . . ." Todd hesitated. "Have you ever taken a tour of a gold mine?"

"Of course. In these parts? Who hasn't?"

"You've seen those souvenirs they sell? The little vials of gold flakes suspended in solution?"

"My eyes are like little vials swimming with tiny gold flakes?" Sebby's smile broadened, and the dimple appeared. Todd's stomach tightened.

He raised his free hand to touch the indentation, which disappeared as Sebby's expression sobered. Todd's fingers brushed Sebby's face where the dimple had been.

Sebby took a breath. "You want to kiss me. I wish you would."

Todd stroked the side of Sebby's face, smoothed his hair behind his ear, and brought his fingers to Sebby's lips. "I hardly dare. You're too sweet; you'll disintegrate, leaving nothing but a sticky spot on the floor."

Sebby laughed, and Todd moved, pressing his lips to the dimple, but Sebby's face had already smoothed out again. Todd was both irked and charmed; it was a tricky thing. Kissing was apparently serious business to Sebby. "Smile for me."

Sebby smiled uncertainly, not enough to bring out the dimple. Todd felt like a cat at a mouse hole ready to pounce at a glimpse of prey. "Um . . . bigger . . ."

"Bigger?" Sebby's eyes went wide and baffled; his face fell into a frown.

"Smile bigger? I like your smile. I . . . love your smile."

Understanding dawned. Todd caught the dimple this time, kissed it, poked his tongue into it, and Sebby squirmed. Todd's hand went to the back of Sebby's neck to hold him still, and he moved to kiss Sebby's mouth gently, as though disintegration were a real danger.

All too soon Sebby pulled away. "First things first: you must have coffee. I'm sure you need it. Can you go even one hour without?"

Todd endeavored to catch his breath. "I'm able to go long periods of time without many things. It's merely that I don't like to."

Sebby tittered. "Come here, I'll show you my French press."

"Whyyy does that sound so suggestive?" With his eyes following the swing of Sebby's hips, Todd allowed himself to be towed to one end of the galley-style kitchen where an old-fashioned coffee mill stood with a bag of beans.

"It's best to grind only the amount you need for the moment." Sebby scooped beans into the mill. "Turn the crank," he instructed and, placing Todd's hand on the knob of the crank, guided his hand in wide circles as the crank turned in a plane parallel to the floor.

Todd closed his eyes and inhaled the fragrance, feeling Sebby's hand on his, Sebby's arm against his.

"Now, open the drawer." Todd opened his eyes as well as the drawer of the mill, wherein rested the fruits of their labor. "And that goes in here." Sebby spooned the grounds into a small glass pitcher with bright-red trim. "Now the water." He added hot water from a tea kettle. "And we let it steep." He placed the lid on the pitcher. A long stick with a knob on the end projected straight up from the top of the lid.

Todd cleared his throat. "For how long?"

"Two or three minutes for extraction of the essential oils. I know you like yours strong, so we'll wait three minutes."

Sebby turned away to set a timer. He bent his head, and his hair fell away from the back of his neck. Without stopping to think, Todd placed a kiss there, to the creamy-brown skin where his spine emerged from his collar. Sebby trembled and pressed back against him, and Todd's arm went around Sebby to pull him even closer. He nuzzled into Sebby's dark curls, breathing in his scent, like spicy coffee, as if he'd bathed in it, and perhaps he had. He kissed his neck and his hair and murmured his name, *Sebastián*, and then the timer sounded, and Sebby moved away and slapped it off.

"Now we . . . Now the French press." Sebby took Todd's hand again and guided it to the lid of the pitcher, to the stick with the knob. He closed his hand over Todd's. "This is . . . the plunger or the piston. You must push it all the way down, slowly and smoothly, all in one motion, and the rod must remain straight up, or the coffee is ruined." He put pressure on Todd's hand and, slowly and smoothly, together they depressed the piston.

It was a long time before they had either coffee or dinner.

With morning light glowing red through his eyelids, Todd half awoke, steeped in drowsy tranquility, and eased closer to the warm body next to his, nuzzling the soft hair. His eyes fluttered open. The hair in front of his eyes was dark brown, and he recoiled. The brown head lifted, and Sebastián's face appeared. Time and memory unwound like thread from a spinning spool. Todd drew a swift, deep breath.

"Todd? Something wrong?"

"No . . . a dream . . . falling. I was . . . woke up suddenly." Todd ripped a hand through his hair.

Sebby eyed him. "It's disorienting, waking up in a strange place. You don't remember where you are . . . who you're with . . ."

"Sebastián. See? I remember." Todd lay back and threw an arm over his eyes.

"Shh, Todd, for a moment you thought I was *him*. It's all right. It's natural. It doesn't hurt my feelings." A hand brushed his arm where it lay across his eyes, a tentative touch. Todd didn't move, and the hand commenced to stroke his arm. "Now, if you refuse to drink my coffee, that will hurt my feelings; if you grab your clothes and take off in your truck, that will hurt my feelings, but it won't hurt my feelings if you need to cry a little."

Todd fisted his eyes. "Sebby . . . oh, Sebby, I'm sorry. I am not a fun date."

"Toddfox, how can you say that? You just need coffee. Wake up and remember how much fun you were." Sebby's fingers moved down

Todd's arm to his chest and traced idle patterns. "Guess what I'm writing."

"Ah . . . what?" Todd dropped his fists and moved to sit up.

Sebby pushed him down. "Don't look! Guess what I'm writing." His finger continued moving on Todd's chest.

"You're writing something?" He tucked his chin and tried to see.

"No! Cover your eyes again." Sebby reached and put his other hand over Todd's eyes. "You're supposed to try and feel what I'm writing."

Todd put his hands over Sebby's hand. "Ah . . . is it my name?"

"Score one for Todd. Erase erase erase." He rubbed his hand briskly over Todd's chest. "Now, guess again." He resumed writing.

"It . . . has an *O* . . . 'Fox'?"

"Good! Erase erase erase."

"You're making this too easy."

"Always wanting a challenge, no?" Sebby's finger moved quickly.

"I didn't get it. Do it again," Todd demanded, and Sebby complied. "It has an *F* . . . You're not doing the same word again, trying to trick me?" Sebby's finger moved, and Todd, concentrating, began to laugh. "'Fuck'?"

"Thought you'd never ask." Sebby's hand swooped south, Todd yelped, and that was the end of that game, though the beginning of the next.

After a late breakfast, Todd took his leave, needing to process and regroup. He felt as if he'd cheated on Vivian and felt guilty for mistaking Sebby for Vivian. No reasonable list of facts could assuage Todd's guilt—that Vivian had ended their relationship, that Sebby understood and didn't seem to take it personally. It seemed to him that he had hurt two people.

How did I get myself into this? I was going to be anonymous, I was going to keep away from cute boys, I was going to work and sleep and be with family, and grieve, and that was all. Todd pulled into the next convenient parking lot and dialed his best friend and confidante, Holly.

"Todd-o! Why don't you call more? Geeze, I've been worried. You've called me like once since I drove down there with you."

"Holly, sorry, ah . . . everything's fine. I saw that you called. I should've returned your calls. I've been in a fiendish funk. I didn't want to speak with anyone who . . . who knew Viv." Todd scrubbed his hand over his forehead.

"That makes no sense. Someone who knows Viv knows what you feel like. And, I don't know, life has to go on, even if it isn't going on the way you want it to."

"I know, you're right, and . . . I sort of met someone. I had a date. Last night." He winced, anticipating a squeal of delight, but Holly answered in cautious tones.

"Ohhh, Todd. Are you ready for that?"

Todd sagged with relief. He hadn't realized how stressed he was by people telling him he needed to get over it and get back out there. "I don't know. I thought it went well, but then— Now I've had second thoughts. I feel guilty."

"You can't help how you feel, but what do you have to feel guilty for?"

Todd tangled his hand in his overly long hair. "When I woke up this morning, I was with him, and I reached for him, and it wasn't Vivian, and it was like a nightmare."

There was a pause. "You slept with someone on the first date?"

"Will you *listen*? It's not as though I just met him. We've spent time together at work, and then he invited me over, and, yeah, I slept with him. Don't lecture me. And now I feel guilty." Todd sighed. "I don't know. Maybe I shouldn't be with anyone. It's hardly fair to Sebby—that's his name, Sebby—if I'm in love with someone else. And what if Viv changes his mind? What then?"

There was a longish silence. "He's not going to change his mind."

"I know that, I *know* that. But what if he did?"

"If he did, then . . . he'd be being capricious, and you shouldn't get back with him, because he'd just dump you again. Is that what's stopping you, just that you feel like you should wait around for Vivian? Because that's messed up."

"I'm not, no. I didn't mean that—I don't know what I mean. Jesus, I don't know anything."

"Okay, okay, um, forget that for now," Holly said. "What's he like? What'd you say his name is? And is he— I mean, how old is he?"

"Twenty-five. Sebby. He works in the office where I work, and he's little; Holly, he's shorter than I am." He paused. "Do you know, I don't think I've ever been with anyone shorter than I am?"

"That's because he'd have to be a hobbit, and they're scarce in the New World." She laughed.

"Har, har. Yeah, and he's cute. He has this dark-brown hair that curls a little and big brown eyes, and when he smiles? A dimple appears. At work, he kept bringing me coffee and trying to get me to talk to him, and, in point of fact, I wasn't nice, but he was persistent, and he's patient and adorable, and he was understanding and sweet and not even upset this morning when I leapt out of bed with fright at the sight of him."

Holly's voice became the one reserved for cooing at puppies. "Awww, Tooodd."

"What?"

"You like him!"

"Well . . . yes . . . I . . . Did I neglect to mention that?"

"You did neglect, and it's kinda an important point." Holly reverted to a brisk tone. "Sebby sounds nice, and I don't think you should, you know . . . miss out on a possible opportunity, when it's someone you like."

"Perhaps I'm uninterested in such opportunities."

"Nooo, I think you're scared. That's what I think. But it's supposed to be a little scary and weird and uncomfortable and exciting; it always is, don't you think?"

Todd thought this over, drumming his fingers on the steering wheel. "So . . . I should see him again."

"If you want to. Do you want to?"

"Yes, but—"

"But what?"

"What if I'm bad for him? What if I'm . . . just bad for people in general?"

"Todd, holy crap. Having one relationship not work out doesn't mean you're bad for people in general. Good grief." She growled.

"I'm afraid of hurting him; he's the sweetest thing. He doesn't deserve someone who will fuck up his world. I th—"

"You're allowed to seek happiness, Todd-o," Holly interrupted, and he could hear the frown in her voice.

"Constitutionally I am guaranteed that right; yes. That's not the point."

"Well, to me it is."

"I should call him. Or text him. Or something."

There was silence on the other end for several seconds at this swift turnabout. "Um. Okay."

"I left rather abruptly. I'm afraid I may have worried him." Todd fretted and chewed his tongue.

"Okay . . ."

"I just, I like him."

"Okay . . ."

"I'm going to text him. Ah . . . thanks, hon, I'll call you later?"

"Promise?"

"Stick a needle in my eye. Bye. Thanks. Bye."

Todd screwed up his face and considered what to text. Everything sounded stupid. He decided to call instead. His hand felt slippery. He forced himself to loosen his grip on his phone.

"Hello?"

Todd ungritted his teeth. "Hello, French Press; it's I, Todd."

There was a pause. "Todd? Not Todd Addison. He's busy all day helping his brother with the yardwork."

"Ah, but he's a speedy worker and has finished already and would like to take you out this afternoon if you've not already made plans."

"Get over here and we'll talk about it."

"I, well, I wanted to, ah, make my reservation with you, so to speak. I'll go home and change first, freshen up, then I'll come fetch you, shall I?"

"No. Get over here now."

"But—"

"I think you want to. Am I wrong?"

Todd gave up. "No, you're not. Very well. I'll be there."

Chapter Six

Slasher Sectary

"You were gone almost the whole weekend!"

This accusation proceeded in injured tones from the mouth of an angry eleven-year-old. Ryan had come bounding out of the house almost the second Todd's pickup pulled into the driveway. He leaned against the driver's side door as if intent on preventing Todd from exiting the vehicle.

"I'm here now," Todd pointed out. "Do you want to do something? Go to a movie?"

"It's too late for a movie!"

"Too late for a matinee, but we can catch the evening showing."

"There's nothing I want to see, anyway."

"Let's do something else, then. Bowling? I'll even spring for chili dogs."

Ryan ducked his head and scuffed his foot in the gravel.

Todd continued to wheedle. "Nachos, for good measure. You cannot say no to nachos. I know this and you know this, so you may as well announce your surrender now."

"Mom probably won't let me," Ryan mumbled.

"Leave it to me. Your mother has a soft spot where I'm concerned, and I guarantee you that fifteen minutes after I get in the door, you and I will be on our way."

As predicted, Donna relented. Kenneth asked to come with them. Todd deferred to Ryan, not wanting to ruin an uncle-nephew outing by adding an additional nephew, but Ryan was delighted that his older brother wanted to come. Christopher protested at being left behind, and so the four of them piled into Todd's pickup.

The conventional wisdom of dating dictated that he hold off on calling, so Todd compromised by texting instead.

French Press! It is I, Todd.

A minute or two later the response came: *Is this the Todd who made beautiful love to me a few hours ago?*

Todd grinned. *How many Todds do you know?*

Too many to count. I guess you'll go back to being all awkward tomorrow.

No. What? Am I awkward? No. I will not be awkward. Yes, I probably will be awkward.

Don't worry. I won't out u.

Todd hadn't thought about it. *I'm not worried about that.*

It's OK. We can fuck in the office and no one will know.

Todd stammered to himself. *That is a rather disturbing mental image.*

Not what I was going for. LOL. Todd imagined the sweet, ingenuous sound of Sebby's laughter. *It's so easy to unnerve u.*

I beg your pardon? I have nerves of steel. LOL.

OK if I bring lunch for u sometime? If u don't want to I understand.

Coffee and now lunch. People will talk.

They'll say I have a crush. Just frown at me and no one will think bad of u.

"Sebby," Todd said, aloud. He almost decided to call after all. *It isn't that it's bad. I don't think that. You don't think I think that?*

When can I see u again?

You'll see me tomorrow.

Not what I meant. Don't be mean.

You will see me tomorrow, and we can make plans then.

Ur going to make me wait allll night? Ur mean.

Todd gave up and texted the first thing that came into his head. *Very well, after work tomorrow, would you like to go bowling?*

There was a pause before the response came. *I don't think so?*

Okay, not bowling. Would you care to take in a movie?

The response took longer, but Todd could almost hear the enthusiasm. *There's an old theater downtown that shows classic films and I'd love for u to take me. They're showing Texas chainsaw massacre.* Another text followed: *The original not the horrid remake.*

Todd pursed his lips, consternated. *Sweet Sebby is a slasher sectary?*

Slasher secretary? What's that? Chainsaw is a classic film, it's exciting and also existential. Todd had begun a reply when the next text came: *Oh I forgot ur squeamish. It's OK, I'll go with friends. U and me can find something romantic. U like romantic?*

No, a sectary: it means a zealot, a devotee, a fanatic.

LOL. U like words. Y r u in construction?

Construction guys can't like words?

U know your way around a site, but u don't belong there. Ur a word sectary. So y r u there?

Todd was not ready to have this conversation. *It's temporary. I am in limbo, as it were.*

Bc of what happened. Your love affair.

Todd chose his words carefully. *Because I don't know what I ought to do.* He immediately followed with another text: **what I want to do.*

Sebby replied, *I know what I want to do and who I want to do it to.*

"To whom I want to do it," Todd said, and winced. He and Vivian had been in the habit of correcting one another's grammar. *Tomorrow and tomorrow and tomorrow. A thousand times good night!* he texted. He was mixing his plays, and Viv might have called him on it, but Sebby did not.

His last action before going to bed was to stare at Vivian's name on his cell phone, or rather his pet name, Vivid. He realized he should delete it. He decided he would. First thing the next day.

Chapter Seven

Paperwork

"How was the big date?" Dean asked.

Todd's smile was genuine. "Pretty goddamn awesome."

"Sweet! So she was hot? Did you get some?"

Uncomfortable with this line of questioning, Todd just smirked. *Let Dean draw his own conclusions.*

Some days later, it was particularly warm, and Todd removed his hat in order to wipe his forearm across his brow. He was tired and grubby, and a dip in a pool might have been preferable to lunch, were he given the choice.

"Hat on till you're out of the hard hat area, Addison," Gus ordered. Todd replaced his hat until he was across the site and in his truck.

"*¡Oye, Zorro!*" Sebby leaned into the open window of Todd's truck. "Too hot for coffee?"

"Never too hot for coffee." Todd accepted the proffered cup. "This is a . . ." He looked into the oversized cup and back up at Sebby. "Iced coffee? You're amazing, French Press." He gulped the cold beverage, and it was close to the most delicious thing he'd ever tasted. He leaned his head back and closed his eyes.

"These are Thai spring rolls. You eat them cold."

Todd felt a nudge and opened his eyes to see a plastic container being shoved at him.

"There's peanut sauce for dipping. So . . . you know. Let me know if you like them." Sebby rapped his knuckles on the door and turned to go.

"Sebastián? Won't you join me?"

Sebby turned back, glanced around. "Are you sure?" Todd nodded. Sebby smiled and then bopped around to the other side of the truck and climbed in, slamming the door and bouncing a little. "This is the first time I've been in your truck."

"Hopefully not the last." Todd ripped the cover from the container. "Did you make these?"

"Of course. They're refreshing on a hot day." Sebby took the container from Todd and parceled out spring rolls. "We have to share the dip." He slid toward Todd along the old truck's bench seat.

Todd was conscious of Sebby's body so near and his dimple, just within kissing distance. Sebby was neat and clean and made Todd more aware of his own sweaty state. "You may not want to sit so close. It's a hot day and . . . I'm hot."

Sebby rolled his eyes. "I knooow what you're trying to say. No, I'm not used to sweaty construction workers at all, no." He edged a bit closer.

Todd's nerves were doing the Lindy Hop. To distract himself, he dunked a spring roll and took a huge bite. It was refrigerator-cold and his eyes widened. "Mmm."

"No double-dipping," Sebby said.

Todd felt a hand on his thigh, just resting there, and suddenly he could think of nothing except the fact that there was a hand on his thigh. He stuffed the rest of the spring roll into his mouth.

"Tell me about *him*." Sebby's hand moved up Todd's thigh.

Todd inhaled a bit of spring roll and was seized by a coughing fit. He tried to suppress it, which made it worse, so he gave into it, coughing, wheezing, eyes watering. Sebby eyed him. A swig of coffee and Todd caught his breath. In a strangled voice, he said, "I don't want to talk about him, I'm trying to forget about him."

"And doing such an epic job of it. You never talk about him, and it isn't natural. Sometimes you have to talk to forget. Like emptying the garbage." His hand inched up Todd's thigh.

"I don't . . . It's not . . . Discussing one's former paramours with one's current paramour is a *faux pas* I don't intend to make." He moved his leg away a bit, but Sebby's hand followed, moving ever-so-slightly inward.

"Is that what I am? Your paramour?"

"Yes! My—my paramour. Sebby, don't."

Sebby's hand curved toward Todd's inner thigh. "Tell me one thing about him, just one thing."

"Ah, God," Todd remarked under his breath. Then aloud: "He was eighteen . . . is eighteen."

Sebby's hand stopped. "Ahhh."

"Ahhh, what?" Todd said, irritated.

"The young ones. They break your heart and teach you humility." He raised a spring roll, took a bite, and chewed meditatively.

Todd shifted, unsure if he wanted Sebby's hand to continue its progress. "I don't think the age thing was the whole thing, but are you saying you had . . . did you have a younger love?"

"Who hasn't? We all do it when we're young, and we all fall for them when we're older. I had many older lovers and broke all their hearts. I didn't mean to, but I did."

"We . . . *we* who? Homosexuals? I never did. I've never broken anyone's heart."

Sebby laughed. "Oh, Toddfox, you're so naïve. I don't know about straight people, maybe they do the same thing. But tell me, Todd-who-has-never-broken-a-heart: when you were young, did you never date someone older than you?"

"Of course . . . often. But they were all casual affairs. I never got close to anyone until Viv—" Todd made an annoyed sound in his throat. He hadn't meant ever to mention Viv's name to Sebby, ever.

Sebby patted Todd's leg. "They were casual to *you*; you *told* yourself they were casual so you had no guilt when you left them."

It was like looking at one of those optical illusions where a stack of three-dimensional cubes abruptly seemed to be sunken in instead of sticking out. He tried to swallow a glob of half-chewed spring roll.

Sebby regarded him with concern. "*Ay*, now you're thinking you must hunt them down and apologize. I didn't mean to make you feel guilty. Don't you see? What goes around comes around. You did it to others, and now it was done to you. The universe, fate, no?"

Todd stared straight ahead through the windshield, seeing nothing. For once Sebby had read him wrong. The thought uppermost in Todd's mind was not the wrong he might have done to others, but that perhaps Todd had meant no more to Vivian than the men from Todd's youth had meant to Todd.

"Now you're sad. I'm sorry." Sebby petted Todd's shoulder and peered into his face.

Unblinking, Todd shook his head. "I think you're wrong. Viv . . . Viv loved me. We'd planned to marry . . ."

"Marry?"

"We had rings and everything." Todd gave Sebby a twisted, wry smile. "I still have them—both of them. He gave me mine back, but I kept his."

Sebby's eyes were huge and pained. "I'm sorry, Todd."

"I mean that I don't think it was the way you paint it." He hunched his shoulders in a painful shrug and turned away. "Maybe it was. I don't know anything anymore."

"I'm sure I'm wrong. *¡Dios mío!* I shouldn't talk so sassy and rude. Shh . . ." Sebby squeezed Todd's leg. Todd leaned against the door to keep himself from leaning into Sebby. "I'm going back to the office, and there's still this paperwork you've never completed. I'm going to get it out. You finish lunch and then come straight to the office. *¿Entiendes?*" There followed a gentle stream of Spanish, and Todd was lulled in spite of himself. "Okay? You'll come into the office. Okay?" Sebby's grip tightened.

Todd nodded. "I will, yes. I'll be there in a few." He tried to smile, but his face would not respond. "I'm all right. I promise I'm not going to sit and weep. I'll finish eating and I'll trot on over there."

"Good." Sebby moved away and was out the door all in one smooth motion, and the loss of physical contact was like a blow. Todd watched him walk away, and it was strange, it was so strange, to want someone so much who was not Vivian.

Todd entered the mobile office, his stomach full of spring rolls, his head full of nagging voices. The window air conditioning unit hummed, and a chill settled on his skin. A boilermaker stood hunched over Sebby's desk, grimacing while Sebby pointed with a pen. Sebby looked up. "Those forms are on the table, Todd." He gestured. "Leonard, do you want privacy? Should I tell Todd to come back?"

"No, it's not a big deal."

Todd seated himself at the table, setting aside his hard hat and goggles, and bent his head over the forms. Nearby were two pens and two sharpened pencils. *Emergency Notification.* Todd listed his brother first and his mother second. *Physician.* Todd hadn't tried to find one since he'd moved. He left it blank. His pen tapped, and he listened with half an ear to Leonard and Sebby.

"I'm short right now. Can't you take out less now and even it up at the end of the year?"

"No, we have to take out the court-ordered amount. I'm sorry, Lenny."

Todd glanced over to see Sebby patting Leonard's hand, and hid a smile behind his papers. The way Sebby mothered the men on the crew was endearing.

Eventually Leonard agreed that Sebby was doing his best. Sebby followed him to the door and shut it behind him before returning to stand behind Todd and slide his arms around him, leaning his cheek on Todd's head.

Todd put a hand on Sebby's forearm where it rested on his chest. "I gotta finish these papers."

"I'll just stand here while you do that." He squeezed Todd. "I don't want to go out tonight."

"No?"

"I want us to stay in. So we can talk. You can't talk at a movie. Or snuggle." He nuzzled Todd's hair, and Todd was comforted, but he couldn't help thinking that it probably smelled like the inside of a helmet. "Come straight to my place. Do you like baths?"

Confused at the change of subject, Todd stammered. "Do I what?"

"Some manly men refuse to take baths; it must always be a shower. But you may have noticed my beautiful claw-foot tub, and you can soak in it, and I have fizzy bath balls."

"Bath balls?"

"You drop them in the water and they go *foosh* and they make you tingle all over." He ran his fingers up and down Todd's chest. Todd fidgeted and bit his lip.

"You're telling me I smell bad."

Sebby nuzzled again into Todd's hair and then his neck, and spoke with his lips just below Todd's ear. "I'm telling you I want you to come straight to my place, not go home first. And have a nice, relaxing bath, and I'll even join you, if that's okay."

"Oh, that would most definitely be okay."

The afternoon crawled by, but the day was over at last. Just to remove his hat and feel the breeze ruffling his damp hair was bliss. Todd climbed into his truck and cranked the air, aiming all the vents at his face. Leaning back and closing his eyes, he pulled his shirt up to let air pass over his itchy skin, feeling achy and so grimy and slimy that he was considering the possibility of heading home for a pre-bath shower, when a knock on his door startled him. There stood Sebby with a knowing smile. Todd opened the door, and Sebby shoved a handful of folded papers at him.

"You forgot to take your copies. Do you forget things you're supposed to do, Todd?"

Todd accepted the papers. "Ah. N-o . . ."

"Good. Then drive slow so I can have a few minutes to get things ready." He rapped his knuckles on the door and walked away, and Todd watched him go, noting the roll of his hips and the bounce of his hair at the back of his neck. *I've got it bad.* The thought scared him a little.

Chapter Eight

The Face of My Charms

*H*e drove slowly as instructed. Sebastián opened the front door as Todd came limping up the walk. "Poor Todd, you're a mess. You might as well jump straight in the bath."

Todd ran his fingers through his matted hair and edged past Sebby. He toed off his shoes and shuffled to the bathroom and paused, confounded, in the doorway. Candles were burning on the shelves and windowsill and glowing on the sink and the back of the commode. The high-backed claw-foot tub had been filled, and candles floated, flickering, *in the water*.

"Jesus. You didn't have to—"

Sebby's voice came from just at Todd's shoulder. "But I wanted to."

"I can't believe you went to so much trouble . . ."

Sebby drew his hand down the inside of Todd's arm and took Todd's hand in his. "It's only a few candles."

"A few? The Denver denizens will suffer a Sebby-sprung candle shortage." He raised Sebby's hand to his mouth, kissing the knuckles before removing his eyeglasses. The room blurred into a mix of colors and hazy candle nimbuses. He peeled off his sticky, clinging clothing and dropped it in a heap.

"That was an elegant striptease, Zorro. I'm breathless."

Todd threw him an embarrassed grin before leaning over the tub to swish his hand in the water. He thought he looked good; the weeks of construction work had turned him into something of a hardbody, ridding him of the extra fat that had accumulated during the year or so of desk work and infrequent exercise. There was a sudden wish that Viv could see him now, see his flat stomach and rounded biceps.

But Vivian had liked him the way he'd been; maybe he would not approve.

Stepping over the high sides of the tub, he nudged the floating candles aside and sank down into the hot water with a long sigh, then ducked under and came up dripping. The back of the tub sloped just so and fit against him, warm below the waterline, cool above. After long moments, he realized he was still alone in the tub and opened his eyes to see Sebby, wearing only a pristine, white towel around his waist, about to attack with what appeared to be an oversized chunk of shredded wheat.

Todd sat up straight. The water sloshed around him. "What is that?"

"A loofah. It's organic and biodegradable." He dipped the shredded wheat in the water, squeezed something greenish onto it, and brought it close to Todd, who grabbed Sebby's wrist. The shredded wheat dripped green.

"What are you doing?" Todd demanded.

"What d'you think? I'm going to wash you."

"Oh, no, French Press. If there's any washing to be done, I shall do it myself."

"There *is* washing to be done, and I want to do it."

"But . . ." Todd hesitated, still holding Sebby's wrist. "You wash my back, I'll wash yours. That's how it works. Get in here." He made as if to pull Sebby into the tub with him, but Sebby crouched down, and the tub's high sides gave Todd no leverage. "But you said you'd join me!"

"I never said I'd join you *in* the bathtub. Now, this is my bath and I'm the boss of it, so you're going to let me wash you." Sebby wrinkled his nose, looking up at Todd from his crouch. "Unless you want to jump out and put those nasty clothes back on before I've had a chance to wash them. Oooh. That wouldn't feel nice at all."

Todd hesitated. "What am *I* supposed to do?"

"Relax. Enjoy."

"I cannot just sit here and allow you to be my bath boy."

"Why not?"

"Be . . . because . . . because . . . it doesn't feel right."

"Why?"

Todd squirmed as though someone were restraining him rather than the other way round. "Because I just sit here and do nothing and just let you . . .? No, I can't do that."

"Todd, this is uncomfortable and you're hurting my arm."

Chagrined, Todd released him. "I'm sorry."

Sebastián bounced to his feet and stepped around to the back of the tub, behind Todd. He put his hands on Todd's shoulders, pulling him till Todd reclined against the slope. "You weren't hurting me. I just said that so you'd let go." He ran his fingers through Todd's wet hair. "I want to wash your hair. That's very sensual, you know, someone washing your hair. Won't you let me?"

Todd's breathing grew ragged. "All right. But only if you—"

"No, no bargains," Sebby interrupted. "Just let me." He continued running his fingers through Todd's hair. "Aren't you used to someone taking care of you? Manly Zorro, all independent?" Holding Todd with one arm, he commenced to scrub Todd's chest and abdomen in slow up-and-down strokes. The loofah was pleasantly abrasive, and an herbal fragrance arose, but Todd felt awkward and stiff.

"Sebastián." Todd placed his hand on Sebby's arm where it lay across his chest. "In point of fact, I am much too needy, as has been pointed out to me emphatically and often."

Sebby raised Todd's arms one by one and washed beneath them, ignoring Todd's cringing. "Shh. Will you relax? This is nice." He moved around the tub and washed down the length of Todd's legs. "Tell me something else about *him*." He lifted Todd's foot from the water and scrubbed it with something that Todd could have sworn was a rock. Sebby glanced at Todd through his eyelashes. "What's he look like?"

"What does it matter?" Todd watched as Sebby rubbed the rock between each of Todd's toes before lifting the other foot. "Wouldn't that be easier if you were in here with me?"

"Maybe, but I want to pamper you a little. You had a hard day working in the hot sun while I sat in an air-conditioned office. And it matters because . . . Tell me what he looks like and then I'll tell you why it matters."

"Office work is not necessarily invigorating and stress-free." Todd was so uneasy with this treatment that he rashly promised, "Tell you what, French Press. Climb in here with me and I'll tell you everything you wish to know."

Sebby's musical laugh bounced around the room. "You're crafty like a fox trying to get your own way, but, okay, I give. Let the water out, rinse the tub, and fill it fresh. I'll be back in a minute."

Todd watched him go, enjoying the contrast of the white towel with Sebby's brown skin. He pulled the stopper by its chain. Standing in the draining water amidst bobbing candles, he draped a towel over his shoulders, retrieved his glasses, and amused himself by inventorying the bath products on the shelf behind the tub. There was tea tree shampoo, mint shampoo, sugar cookie shampoo . . . he'd counted six different varieties when a brown and white bottle caught his eye. *Spicy Cappuccino*, the label read; it was coffee-scented shampoo, and Todd's heart lurched like a drunken frog, knocking into his rib cage and rebounding to cut off the breath in his windpipe. He tilted the shampoo bottle; it was barely used. The natural conclusion was that Sebby had bought it in order to permeate himself with the scent of coffee, and Todd recalled how he had imagined that Sebby had bathed in coffee. No one had ever, to Todd's knowledge, gone to such trouble to get him into bed; it was the most endearing thing, and he wanted to crush Sebby to his chest and cover him with kisses, or sweep him off his feet and carry him off into the sunset. Smiling, he replaced the bottle behind the multitudes before rinsing the bathtub as ordered and starting the water.

Sebby reappeared with a bottle of wine and a plate of grapes. He stopped in the middle of the room and narrowed his eyes at Todd. "What?"

"What? Ah, nothing. What, what?"

"You're giving me a look."

"This?" Todd beckoned and attempted to strike a classical pose, like a towel-clad Greek statue. "This is my come-hither look." Standing in the tub, hot water splashing out of the tap and rising around his shins, he held out his arms to Sebby, who set his things aside and came into Todd's arms. With Sebby on the floor and Todd in the claw-foot tub, Todd was a foot taller. Even though he was slightly taller than Sebby anyway, the extra height felt strange and good to Todd, who was accustomed to being the shorter one in his relationships.

"You smell good enough to eat and drink." Todd pulled Sebby tighter and caressed his neck and back, relishing the feel of the smooth skin. "Get in here already."

Sebby sighed and rested his cheek on Todd's chest but remained where he was. "What happened?"

"Ah?"

"I was gone a minute. I come back and you're all different."

"Sebastián. I, ah—" Air swirled in Todd's mouth. "I, ah, I want you." He moved his hand in lazy circles over Sebby's back.

Sebby stretched beneath Todd's touch and uttered a different sort of sigh. "Mmm. You can have me. Oh, the water!" Sebby pulled away to shut off the faucet. He plucked the extinguished candles out of the bath.

Todd removed his towel with a flourish and flung it aside. He reclined in the water. "Todd-in-a-tub. Everyone wants one." He beckoned to Sebby.

"But I'm the only one who's got one." Sebby stepped back and lifted the bottle and corkscrew. "It's Pouilly-Fuissé. It's French. I thought you'd like French."

He bought me French wine? Todd had never been more tempted since the day he had given it up. "My sweet, I regret to inform you that I do not drink. Sorry. I, ah, should've told you sooner."

Sebby cocked his head to one side. "You don't drink. You mean ever?"

"You needn't abstain because I choose to."

"Well . . ." Sebby began inserting the corkscrew. "If you're sure it won't bother you?"

"I'm sure."

The cork came out with a satisfying pop. Sebby removed his towel and hung it, before pouring a glassful of sunny gold. "Okay, then, make room." He waved his free hand at Todd. Todd grinned and spread his legs, but Sebby shook his head. "No, no, I get the back. Scoot forward."

Todd's eyebrows lifted. "You want the back? Okayyy." He moved as ordered, and Sebby rolled his eyes.

"That wasn't any kind of hint, and I wasn't talking about sex. I meant I still have to wash your hair."

"Of course. But aren't you forgetting something?"

"I am?" Sebby paused. "Oh, sorry, you need a beverage. Mineral water?"

"Water, water everywhere, and not a drop to drink. But I wasn't referring to a lack of potables."

"Oh, do you want coffee? I should've known. I can make you some. It'll take a few minutes." He turned to go.

"Sebby! Everything is perfect. I do not want coffee. However, I believe I was promised fizzy bath balls?"

"Oh! *Dios mío*, I was forgetting." He turned his back and opened a drawer, and Todd watched how he bounced on the balls of his feet as he rummaged, and how his gluteus muscles contracted and relaxed. "Hm, there's lavender, basil mint—that one has little seedy things in it—ginger cranberry, tropical breeze, almond . . . What sounds good to you?" His chin touched his shoulder as his head swiveled to regard Todd.

Todd blinked and refocused on Sebby's face. "Ah . . . the last one."

"That's my favorite." He tossed a brownish thing like a tennis-ball-sized SweeTART into the bath.

It bobbed, submerged, and began to effervesce. Todd viewed it with suspicion, but Sebby climbed in behind, holding aloft his glass of wine, and sank into the water, legs on either side of Todd. Todd leaned back, and Sebby put an arm around him, resting his other arm on the rim of the bathtub. Todd's head nestled on Sebby's shoulder. Tiny bubbles caressed his skin. He could feel Sebby's cock against his ass, and he wiggled just a little.

"Don't do that." Sebby kissed Todd's hair. "We're going to sit here, and you're going to behave."

Todd petted Sebby's knee. "For how long?"

"For as long as it takes."

"As long as what takes?"

"For you to feel better."

"I feel better." Todd endeavored to stroke Sebby's knee in the most erotic manner possible. Maybe he would forget that Todd had promised to tell him everything he wanted to know.

"Good. Do you like the bath ball?"

Todd considered. "I feel as though I'm being percolated."

Sebby nuzzled Todd and laughed softly in his ear. "Always with the coffee." He stretched, and Todd, feeling Sebby move against him, suppressed a groan. "Now I'm going to feed you grapes." Sebby presented one to Todd's mouth.

"You are an evil tease."

"It's only teasing if you don't follow through."

The grapes were fed to him in silence one by one, and each burst in his mouth with refreshing sweetness. Todd made an effort to relax, allowing Sebby to feed him and letting his thoughts wander. After a time, he decided to speak before Sebby asked. "He's tall. Skinny. Blond. Green-eyed. Fair, Irish skin." He waved his hand in a circle at his face. "And pierced. He has piercings." He accepted another grape and sucked on it.

Sebby's chest lifted and deflated with a sigh. "That's good."

"What?"

Sebby drained his glass and moved to refill it. "That he doesn't look like me. Some will try to be with a person who is like their ex. Maybe they don't even know they're doing it. And if I looked like him, I'd worry that's the reason you want me."

Todd ruminated on this. "Suppose the opposite is true? What if I've subconsciously gone looking for someone as *unlike* Viv as possible? You're small, brunette, and tan all over." He drew Sebby's hand to his mouth and kissed his fingers.

Sebby pulled away. "I don't like that thought."

Todd sat up and half turned, took Sebby's hand and earnestly protested, "It isn't true. I wasn't looking at all. You found me. And I tried to resist you and could not. Cannot. I am defenseless in the face of your charms." He pressed a kiss into Sebby's palm.

Mouth quirking in a half smile, Sebby gave Todd's face a little push. "Hair. Turn around."

Todd obeyed, and Sebby drew Todd back to rest against him. "Close your eyes." Sebby removed Todd's eyeglasses. Water trickled over his head. Sebby's fingers worked shampoo into his hair, one hand lifting his head forward to get the back, massaging his neck and scalp. Todd went limp, and Sebby let his head loll against Sebby's chest while he kneaded his scalp, briskly and then slowing, drawing his fingers through Todd's hair in long, gentle sweeps. Water trickled over Todd's head once again, and it was done with such care that no bit of soap strayed into his eyes or down the side of his face. This seemed to take a long while, and then Sebby's arm went around him, a hand smoothed his hair, and Sebby's lips were at his ear, speaking his name. "Todd."

He felt breath on his skin and pressed himself back against Sebby, tilting his head and arching his neck. Todd's flesh ached with the expectation of being kissed. Sebby lifted a foot and hooked a leg over Todd's. He drew the foot along the inside of Todd's thigh to his crotch, kneading and provoking a groan from Todd, who reached back to push Sebby's face into his neck. Still, Sebby did not kiss him; he turned his face to the side. Frustrated, Todd tried to sit up, but Sebby hooked his other leg over Todd's, pinning him. An arm looped over Todd's elbow and held him with surprising strength. Todd struggled experimentally; Sebby's hold tightened. Todd was helpless unless he wished to grapple in earnest. His chest heaved in ragged breaths.

"You're defenseless in the face of my charms," Sebby murmured. He kissed Todd's neck from ear to collarbone.

"Sebby, please, Sebby, oh God . . ." The kisses were maddeningly gentle in comparison with the tight hold, and Todd knew Sebby was being careful not to leave any marks, but he wanted Sebby to leave marks, wanted to feel Sebby's mouth sucking hard, bruising him.

Sebby's foot moved against Todd's hard cock, and was he being jerked off by a foot? It was so odd that he laughed a little, a shaky, breathless sound, and Sebby made a pleased noise and let him go.

The water sloshed in a mini tidal wave as Todd rolled over and wound his arms around Sebby, one hand in his hair so as not to knock his head against the tub. He pushed his tongue deep into Sebby's mouth, tasting the illicit French wine. Rubbing Sebby's back, he moved his hand down and down, and ran his fingers into the crack of his backside.

"Todd, now . . ."

"Condom?"

"There." Sebby gestured, and Todd disengaged to grab a condom and lube. He took a good, long look at Sebby, lithe and glistening, letting his desire build.

"You're making me hard, just looking at me." Sebby tugged on Todd's cock. "You can have the back now."

They rearranged themselves. Todd pressed first one finger inside, then two. Sebby whimpered.

"All right?" Todd asked, anxious.

"*Sí*, yes! *Es bueno.*"

Todd eased Sebby backward into his lap, penetrating him carefully. Sebby moaned and pushed himself down on Todd. At first it was awkward, Todd pulling Sebby's hips down while thrusting upward. The water sloshed and splashed around them, and as they settled into a rhythm, Todd reached around Sebby's waist to grasp Sebby's cock and stroke him root to head in rhythm with their thrusting. He kissed Sebby's back, fastened his mouth on a shoulder blade, and sucked hard, the way he had wanted Sebby to kiss his neck. Sebby made noises that were becoming familiar, and Todd let go of restraint and thrust madly as Sebby shuddered and came, muscles contracting in orgasm around Todd, who thrust once more, twice more, and came in a heady rush like an ocean breaker lit by the setting sun.

In the cool of the evening, they ate a leisurely meal on the back deck looking out on Sebby's treed yard, and afterward went for a stroll around the neighborhood, Todd having borrowed some sweats and a T-shirt. He took Sebby's hand in his as they walked, and Sebby appeared both pleased and surprised. Some of the neighbors were out walking their dogs or puttering in their yards, and they nodded or waved or greeted Sebby by name. The late evening was spent drinking coffee and cuddling on the sofa—Todd leaning back against Sebby, Sebby cradling Todd to his chest—and Todd somehow found himself talking of Vivian.

He told Sebby how sweet Viv was and how quick-witted; how Todd still thought of Viv as pure and innocent even after having carnal knowledge of him; how protective he had felt; how Todd had never gotten over their age difference; how Todd had hurt him with his moods and fits of temper; how he had worked to be better, but Vivian had been unhappy and had put an end to it. And as he talked and Sebby listened and petted and made noises of sympathy, Todd felt his soul begin to lift and uncurl, like the leaves of a neglected houseplant upon receiving its share of water. He thought for the first time that his heart could heal, that he could put it behind him. That he could love again.

"*Tsk*. It was your fault, how it went wrong?"

Todd nodded, still lost in his epiphany.

"You're pitiful. It takes two to ruin a good relationship."

"Not always."

"And so *he* was perfect and did no wrong, *he* never hurt you or led you down the path with promises he couldn't, wouldn't keep. He didn't seduce you with his youth and beauty, oh no, it was you the whole time." Sebby huffed, and his arms tightened around Todd.

Surprised and amused at Sebby's indignance, Todd raised Sebby's hand to his mouth and kissed his knuckles. "No, you were right all along. He was young, just young, and it was wrong of me to put so much pressure on him, to expect forever of him. No, I hold nothing against Viv, and you mustn't either." He opened Sebby's hand and kissed his palm, and Sebby's fingers stroked his jaw.

"You think a lot of *him*," Sebby said in a wistful tone. "My work is cut out for me."

"Ah, and quick and thorough work you make of your work. And now, I've kept my promise, and in return I ask that you tell me something of your last love."

Sebby laughed and pushed Todd away, dove at him, winding his arms around him and burying his face in Todd's middle. "I had a boyfriend who liked feet." Sebby rolled back, rested his head in Todd's lap and lifted his leg, waggling his foot in the air. "And mine are pretty, yes?"

"Indeed." Todd eyed the shapely foot and noted the upside-down V tan line created by the regular wearing of flip-flops.

"He would do the pedicure thing, but instead of a pumice stone, he'd rub my feet against his beard stubble." Sebby giggled.

"You are making that up, Sebastián!" Todd said, incredulous and fascinated.

"Nooo, I swear. And he always wanted me to make love to him with my feet. I did learn a few tricks." He cocked an eyebrow at Todd. "Most boys, I've found, do like it at least a little."

"Ahem." Todd's face warmed.

"He was always with the lotions and treatments, and he made me wear special socks to keep my feet soft, and I could never go barefoot, even in my own yard, because I might step on something, and then he didn't want me to wear sandals, because other people'd see my toes." Sebby laughed, and Todd watched the play of the dimple. He trailed his thumb over Sebby's smiling lips. Sebby looped an arm around Todd's neck, pulled himself up, and kissed him, quick and hard little kisses followed by tender and lingering kisses, followed by deep and passionate kisses.

In the late evening there was leisurely sex and then sleep, and in the morning there was hurried sex and then breakfast, and then they both left for work in their separate vehicles, Sebby leaving fifteen minutes later than Todd to be sure they didn't arrive together.

Chapter Nine

Bourgeois

Reaching across the table of a secluded booth, Sebby fed Todd bits of tandoori chicken before looking at him through downcast lashes and saying, "What did you mean the other day?"

More days than not, they had lunch together, leaving separately and meeting up somewhere they were unlikely to run into other members of the crew. Todd paused in the act of licking Sebby's fingers. "Could you narrow that down?"

Sebby dropped his chin. "I heard you tell Gus you're only staying through the season and you don't want to apprentice."

Todd squeezed Sebby's hand in both of his, messy Indian sauce be damned. "Has this been eating at you for days? You could've just asked me."

Sebby did not return the hand squeeze, but neither did he withdraw his hand. He glanced up at Todd and then away, his eyes roaming the room. "I'm asking you."

Todd hesitated, but it was clear that whatever he and Sebby had was more than a fling, and Todd felt that if he was going to sleep with someone on a regular basis, he owed that person the truth, insofar as he was capable.

"You've noted before that I don't belong in construction."

Sebby nodded.

"You've surmised correctly; I don't. But . . . it's comfortable. I admit that I ran away, and . . . my life plan was shredded like so much old paper money, and I needed something to do while I pulled myself together. Perhaps I wanted physical labor so I would be too tired to think at night. And being out of doors is revivifying to the soul.

I can't bear the thought of being imprisoned behind office walls the day long."

"What did you do before? You never said, and I checked your job app, and it's not on there."

Todd ground his teeth. He chewed his tongue. He bit his lip. "I listed my construction experience. I used to work construction with my father. It's how I saved money for college. But in New York . . . I worked in fucking advertising."

Sebby's eyes opened innocently wide. "So, you advertised for prostitutes?"

"I . . . har har. No, I wrote ad copy and thought up concepts and shit."

There was a glowing smile. "I can see you doing that, writing and putting things together, you'd be good at that, and you're talented with words."

Todd dropped Sebby's hand, grabbed at wadded-up napkins, and swiped ferociously at his own fingers. "I can do other things, goddamn it! I am not married to my profession; I've many options available to me!"

Sebby's expression went quiet and closed. "Don't snap at me, Todd."

"Sorry." He didn't feel particularly sorry.

"I can tell that you're really not mad at me, you're mad at someone else, probably *him*, so I'm not taking it personally. I never said you couldn't do other things, but someone else said that to you?"

"He implied it. Fucking hell." Todd threw the wad of napkins atop his plate of food, having lost his appetite.

Sebby handed Todd a lemon-scented wet wipe, keeping one for himself. "You said you didn't hold anything against him."

Todd said nothing. He tore open the wipe and scrubbed his hands.

"I guess you said it because you'd just had a good fuck and were feeling at peace with the world."

Stricken, Todd drew in his breath and stared.

"There's still time left." Sebby leaned forward across the table. "We could fuck before we go back. Will that help you feel better?"

Todd's mouth worked, but no sound came out.

"Or I could suck you off. Would that do just as good?"

"Sebby!" Todd couldn't tell if Sebby was teasing or in earnest.

"How often does it take? Is once a day enough? Do you need it morning and night? Morning, noon, and night?"

"Jesus. You make it sound as though I'm using you . . ."

"Aren't you?"

"No! I . . . Perhaps I am." Todd leaned back and slumped. He thought of how he had told Holly that he was bad for people, that he didn't want to fuck up Sebastián's life.

"You think you're using me," Sebby said.

"I don't know. Perhaps."

"You don't like me at all?"

"I like you a great deal!"

"Then you're not using me."

If this was logic, it was of a form unfamiliar to Todd. "The fact that I like you does not, in and of itself, preclude the possibility that I am using you."

"It's a *fact* that you like me?" Sebby's mouth curved, his dimple making an appearance, and Todd's stomach tightened.

"As opposed to hypothesis or theory? Sebastián, I . . . Of course I like you! I—" Consternated, Todd stopped. How had the conversation progressed to this point? "You—you—" He sputtered. "You are just impossible."

"Awww." Sebby looked as if he wanted to climb into Todd's lap. "You're so sweet when you say things like that."

"Ah . . . I didn't mean to snap at you."

Sebby nodded. "I know. Now, tell me, Todd. Tell me everything he said. Just get it out and you'll feel better. And I'll feel better."

Todd's throat closed up; he tried to swallow.

"Tell me," Sebby insisted. "Don't choke on it."

"He said we wanted different things, that I wanted a nice home and a good income, and 'there's nothing wrong with that,' but that he wanted to volunteer in a third-world country or join the Peace Corps, and Sebby! We'd been together for months, and this was the first I'd heard of it, on the cusp of being dumped! He'd never once mentioned volunteering or wanting to, never once! And he accused *me* of wanting to be domestic, *me*! *He* proposed. *He* pushed to move in with me, and I contended he must have his own life, his own place. But do I get credit for my restraint? I do not."

"He sounds . . . young."

"And he tells me, he says he's anticapitalist and *I'm* bourgeois because I'm in *advertising*. For God's sake, everybody advertises! The fucking Peace Corps advertises." His voice fell into singsong sarcasm. "'Toughest job you'll ever love.' You know, some ad man thought that up."

"He hurt your pride. I'm sorry. Did you tell him? What you just said?"

"I was too busy begging him not to leave me. Jesus, what a loser."

"Loving doesn't make you a loser." Sebby reached for Todd's hand, and Todd let him take it. Staring off into space, Todd continued.

"I told him . . . told him if he wanted to go, I'd go with him; I told him I wasn't married to advertising; I told him I'd do anything, I didn't care what we did. And he said that was the problem, that I'd be doing it for him, that I'd never think of it on my own."

Sebby squeezed Todd's fingers. "Would you have?"

Todd had been over and over this in his mind, so many times that he was sure he'd worn a groove clear through the surface of his brain. "That is not the point! The point is that I was willing to be flexible, to consider other possibilities. I mean, no, I wouldn't have thought of it, but so what? Any person that you encounter may put new ideas into your head. But, Sebby, I was trying to be a 'nice young man with prospects'! For his sake! And then he shoots me down for being just that."

Sebby stroked Todd's rough hand as if it was made of velvet. His eyes watched the movement of his own fingers as he spoke. "If you're not going to stay in construction and you don't want to go back into advertising, what are you going to do when the season is over?"

Todd took a deep breath and wrapped his fingers around Sebby's thumb. "I've applied to the Peace Corps. I've sent in my recommendations. I've spoken with a recruiter. I'm waiting for my interview, and if they'll take me, I plan to join." He stared at Sebby defiantly.

A troubled look came over Sebby's face. "The Peace Corps is a big commitment."

"It is."

"You'd be gone for, what? A year?"

"Two years. Plus three months for training."

Sebby hesitated, and his mouth worked. "I'm just asking. Why? Do you want to get out of the country; is it not big enough for the two of you?"

Todd growled in the back of his throat.

"You're trying to prove something to him, I think. D'you think that'll win back his love?"

Todd's face went hot, then cold. "I'd be gone for over two years. And either I'd be over him by then, or . . . Viv would be almost twenty-one. He . . . will have matured."

"I understand, but those aren't the right reasons for going into the Peace Corps. Do you think they are? The Peace Corps is for helping people, and you'd maybe see poverty or injustice or disease, many sad things. Your reasons, they're selfish."

Todd waved this away with a broad gesture, nearly sweeping his water glass from the table. "What difference do my reasons make? If I do see those things, maybe I'll learn something. I need to gain perspective; perhaps then my pain won't seem so great."

"You want to put your pain in perspective." Sebby considered this. "Why don't you volunteer here? There're so many things you could do: teach English as a second language, help adults learn to read. There's no need to be so drastic."

Letting go of Sebby's hand, Todd knuckled his eyes. "But I'm not myself anymore: I don't act the same; I can't think the same; I just— I— What am I supposed to do?"

Todd felt a nudge and opened his eyes to see that Sebby had moved to sit beside him. Sebby brushed his fingers over Todd's cheek before taking his hand. "You have the world around you. You're young and strong and healthy. You can do anything. What do you want to do?"

Todd regarded Sebby's hand in his own. He noted the long, slender fingers, the rounded fingernails, the pink half-moons, the soft fingertips, so unlike his own broad hands, which were blistered and calloused, the nails split and broken and bruised with labor. "I don't care what I do. I just want Viv back. There, I've said it."

He tried to drop Sebby's hand, but Sebby wouldn't let go.

"If I could get him back for you, I would." Sebby laid his cheek on Todd's shoulder, and Todd's stomach was lost to butterflies and confusion.

Chapter Ten

Diminutive

"You're seeing an awful lot of that kid."

Todd rocketed to his feet from where he'd been crouching pulling weeds. "Kid?! He's *twenty-five*, Lloyd!" He hurled the trowel away. It landed soundlessly on the thick lawn.

Lloyd shrugged, not looking up from adjusting the dial on his fertilizer spreader. "You guys are kids to me. You're my kid brother."

"Apologies. I'm a little sensitive regarding age scenarios." He fetched the trowel and went back to digging.

"I'm just saying. You can't keep this up and not get outed."

"Yeah."

"What's his name again?"

"Sebby."

"Sebby. What kinda name is that?"

"It's a diminutive of Sebastián, which is a Spanish name. His mother was Mexican." Todd smiled to himself, thinking how appropriate the word *diminutive* was in the case of Sebby, who was himself so diminutive. He cleared his throat. "I was thinking . . . if it's quite all right with you and Donna . . . I'd like to invite him over for the Fourth. If you wouldn't mind." He had never brought a boy home to meet any of his family.

Lloyd frowned. "Yeah, that'd be great, we'd like to meet him. But if you're inviting him over, that means you're getting serious."

"No. I just want to spend the Fourth with him, and I want to spend it with my family. I don't think we're serious. I just got out of something serious. It would be a mistake to get right into something serious."

"You're trying too hard to convince me. Look . . ." Lloyd gave the dial a final tweak and straightened. "You oughta find another job."

Todd could see where this was heading. He tossed a weed into the bag and moved to the next one. "I'll get around to it. When the season's over."

"I wouldn't wait that long. Why don't you try to get a real job, one in your field? Before the gang figures out you're gay and decides to hold a blanket party."

"A what?"

"That's what they call it in the Marines when a guy in the unit won't behave. In the middle of the night, they grab him, roll him up in his blankets so he can't see what's happening, and beat on him." Lloyd mimed rolling his arms and then clutching one hand as if holding something and pounding on it with the other.

"Jesus!"

"Construction guys are basically the same as Marines. They want to think it, anyway."

Todd couldn't imagine Dean or Rob or any of the crew being so homophobic as to want to hurt him. "Lloyd, I appreciate your concern, but when did you last work construction? When were you last in the Marines, for that matter? Twenty years ago? Things are different now; people are different, more progressive and tolerant."

Lloyd set off across the yard with the spreader. "It's the same guys working construction. They're just twenty years older."

Todd spoke to Holly about the situation. She thought that quitting a job so soon after quitting another job would look crappy on a résumé. Todd speculated that he did not need to include construction work on his résumé. Holly pointed out that gaps had to be explained.

Standing apart from the crew and sipping coffee, Todd spoke to Sebby in a low voice. "Lloyd thinks I should quit."

"I would miss seeing you every day."

"You don't seem surprised."

"If you don't want them to know . . . then, yes, you should quit."

Todd eyed the group over the rim of his cup. If he thought his coworkers wouldn't mind, why was he going to so much effort to appear straight? Partly, he thought, it was habit. Growing up in a small Minnesota town, it had been years before Todd had come out even to his closest friends, and during summers spent working construction with his father, Todd had become used to hearing gay slurs.

College in the big city of Minneapolis had been a different world, multicultural and diverse. He'd found a freedom he'd hardly dared imagine. Nature had taken its course, and Todd fit himself comfortably into the Minnesota queer culture, but summers meant home, meant working construction, meant pretending to his parents that he had a girlfriend, meant shame and guilt and inward seething. What a relief it had been when he acquired a real job in the city, an internship in a fun and fascinating field, where he could be himself. The occasional visits home had spaced themselves further apart as time went by, and though he'd come out to his father, his father had forbidden him to tell his mother. *"You'll break her heart."*

So why had he put himself back into a hated situation?

Chapter Eleven

Tongue-Tied

Sebby cajoled Todd into watching a scary movie. They cuddled together on Sebby's sofa, sharing a bowl of organic popcorn. "It's an old one. I promise there's not one single drop of blood in it, but it's very scary, about a haunted house. It's one of my favorites."

"Very well, but I warn you I'm prone to screaming."

"Oooh, I love screamers." He poked Todd's stomach.

Soon after the opening credits Todd let out a yell. "That's Riff!"

"Shhh. What's Riff?"

"Riff, Riff! From *West Side Story*!"

Sebby scowled in thought. "I don't know that movie."

"Good Lord. Your education has a monstrous pothole in dire need of fill." Todd could not resist breaking into song. He turned toward Sebby, flinging one arm and one leg away from the sofa in a dance pose as he belted out the Jets song. Sebby's eyes went wide with alarm, and he leaned away from Todd, who jumped up from the couch and into an impromptu and energetic rendition of the gang dance. He punched the air: *pow pow pow*!

Sebby clearly did not know what to make of this display. He smiled uncertainly. "You're a Jet, but I'm the other team? I'm Latino."

Todd plopped next to Sebby on the sofa. "Romeo and Juliet, that's us. But the Sharks were Puerto Ricans, not Mexicans. Play on! Riff was in *Seven Brides for Seven Brothers* as well as *West Side Story*. I thought he only did musicals!"

The movie played, the drama unfolded, and Todd grew increasingly uneasy. The tension onscreen grew, and he clutched Sebastián more and more tightly. As the screen characters huddled in the dining room while an unseen entity pounded down the hallway outside, Todd hid his face in Sebby's hair and prayed for the film to end.

At last it was over. Sebby sat up and stretched. "Very scary, yes?"

"Who enjoys this sort of thing? What is *wrong* with you?"

Sebby laughed, shut off the television, and stood up. He stretched again, like a languid cat. "It's the feeling of fear when you know you're safe. Adrenaline. It's fun to be scared." Taking Todd's face in his hands, he pressed his lips to Todd's temple.

"You're insane if you think that's fun." Every one of Todd's muscles had tied itself into a granny knot.

Sebby insinuated himself into Todd's lap. "And when you get so scared and tense, then you need some release, no?" He sneaked a warm hand under Todd's T-shirt and stroked his abdomen.

"They need to burn that house to the ground," Todd said with feeling.

"It's not a real house." Sebby put a finger under Todd's chin, tilted his head up, and placed a kiss on his throat.

Absently rubbing Sebby's back, Todd gazed at the ceiling. "You have decorative moldings. Similar to what they had in the film."

"Not so similar." Sebby pressed his face insistently into Todd's neck and drew Todd's hand to the inside of his, Sebby's, thigh.

"You can see faces in it if you look."

"You can see faces everywhere, if you look." Sebby squirmed. "Don't you wanna go to bed?"

"All right. Yes." Todd allowed Sebby to hop up and lead him down the hallway, up the narrow staircase, and into the bedroom. "Leave the light on?"

Sebby beamed, and Todd was distracted by his dimple; he pressed his lips to it, poking his tongue into it as had become his custom. Sebby stepped away to peel Todd's shirt up and over his head and came back to run his hands down Todd's chest.

Todd pulled Sebby close against himself, relishing the feel of Sebby's shirt buttons pressing into Todd's bare skin. He smoothed his hand down Sebby's back, over the curve of his buttocks, and between Sebby's legs from behind.

"Oh! Oh-oh-oh, Todd!" Sebby tangled a hand in Todd's hair, and they shared a deep kiss. Together, they shuffled to the bed. Todd dropped his pants and pushed Sebby, fully clothed, onto the mattress.

Todd stood up straight and examined Sebby consideringly. "Prepare to be—" He stopped and turned. "What was that?"

Sebby blinked. "What? What's what?"

"I heard something." Todd nodded toward the bedroom door.

"Shh, there's nothing. It's an old house, it creaks." Sebby unbuttoned his jeans and began to slowly unzip. "*Ven aquí. Bésame.*"

Todd couldn't concentrate, and every little noise unnerved him: the wind in the trees outside, the house popping and settling. His head crawled with the sounds and images from the film: the faces in the wallpaper, the statues that appeared to move, the unintelligible voices muttering in the night. Finally, Sebby propped himself up on his elbow and tapped Todd's chest in exasperation. "*Dios mío*, you're never allowed to watch a scary movie again. You're no good to me at all until daylight now, are you?"

Todd felt ridiculous. "Oh, well . . . I wouldn't say I'm no good, but, very well, yes, I'm no good. Sorry, French Press."

Sebby rolled out of bed and shut off the light. He let out a long sigh and settled himself against Todd, idly running his fingers over Todd's chest.

"I made you watch the movie, you told me you don't like horror, so it's my own fault, and anyway, what do you think I am, insatiable?" He laughed and patted Todd over his heart. "Next time we'll watch that dance-fight movie."

"*West Side Story?*" Todd cleared his throat, and struck by inspiration, he softly started a bit of *West Side Story* lyrics, switching out *Maria* for *Sebastián*. He repeated the name in song multiple times, his voice rising in crescendo: "Sebastián . . . Sebastián, Sebastián, Sebastiáááán!"

Sebby fell into helpless giggles, and Todd relished the sound and feel of his laughter and how it seemed to thrill through both their bodies.

"You're sooo silly!" Sebby laughed some more and then sighed, and Todd sighed.

"Sebastián."

"Yes?"

"Sebastián," Todd repeated, "do you know, when first you spoke your name to me, I wanted to tell you that it was beautiful? But I was tongue-tied."

"I knew you were. But I didn't know that's what you wanted to say." He paused and then said breathlessly, "Tell me now."

"Sebastián." In the darkness, Todd imagined Sebby smiling, and trailed his fingers over Sebby's face. "Your name is beautiful, and it suits you. If the angels had presented you to me and I'd been given the task of choosing for you an apt appellation, I would have searched and studied and worn myself to tears, and not found anything more perfect than *Sebastián*."

A held breath was released. "Oh, Todd. How can you say things like that with a straight face?"

"Because I am sincere."

In turn, Sebby's fingers stroked Todd's face. "Maybe it isn't straight. I should turn on the lamp."

"Straight jokes aside, I assure you that my face is straight as a Kansas horizon." He paused to kiss Sebby's fingers. "Would you prefer I didn't say such things?"

"It's so hard to take you seriously, sometimes. I don't know if you're joking, or . . . exaggerating, or . . ."

"A gift for exaggeration is prized among ad men, Sebby." He repeated the diminutive. "Sebby. Such a suitable sobriquet: Sebby." He laced their fingers and nuzzled his face and neck. "Sebby."

Sebby's breathing quickened. "Stop. Stop saying my name or I'll die."

"Now who's exaggerating?" Going in for a kiss, Todd was taken aback when Sebby moved as neatly as if he had dropped into another dimension, disengaging his hand from Todd's and sliding across the bed, turning on his side, away, and dragging the blankets with him.

"Stop talking. Um, just, um, leave me alone for a while."

Todd sat up. "What's wrong?"

"I'm fine. Leave me alone." Sebby curled up like a pill bug. Todd could feel the curling up as if all the air in the room were curling up around Sebby in sympathy, leaving Todd nothing to breathe. Todd went over the conversation in his mind. They had been laughing together and sharing a tender moment . . .

"S—" Todd started to say his name and stopped. "Sweetheart, do you want me to go?"

"*No*," came the emphatic answer. "Stay here, just leave me alone."

"I'm . . ." He knew he must have said something hurtful, but he couldn't for the life of him figure out what it was. "I'm sorry? I didn't mean to . . ." There were additional curling-up noises. "I'll leave you alone, if that's what you want, of course. I'm sorry. I . . . Can I have a blanket?" The bedclothes rustled, and a balled-up blanket hit Todd in the chest. Todd reclined and arranged the covering, berating himself for getting involved with someone when it should be evident that all he was capable of was hurting people. He threw his arm over his face and considered what it might be like to be alone forever, before finally reaching out and gingerly placing a hand on what might be Sebby's shoulder. Whatever body part it was shrank from the touch.

"*¡Chingados!* Leave me alone, I mean it."

Todd lifted his hand. "At least tell me what's wrong," he pleaded.

"I just, I can't talk right now."

Everyone needed space, but this was clearly a reaction to something he had said or done, and he itched to pull Sebby to himself and make it all better—literally itched as if he'd rolled in poison ivy. He lay back and folded his arms, stuffing his hands into his armpits, biting his lip, rewinding and replaying the conversation.

The silver lining on this cloud of relationship doom was that the present difficulties crowded out the fears the movie had inspired, and it wasn't long before he slept and slept hard, and he did not awaken when Sebby draped himself on Todd and pulled blankets over the two of them.

Chapter Twelve

A Greater Variety of Recreation

"*D*o you care if I fuck other boys?"

A stone dropped into Todd's stomach, and his head jerked up as if by counterweight. In Todd's experience, when someone asked that, it was already too late.

They were eating dinner out on the deck, watching the birds flit to and from the bird feeder. His eyes sought Sebby's, but Sebby's were trained with studied indifference on his salad as he nudged aside a crouton and forked greenery into his mouth.

"Is this a hypothetical question?"

"So far."

Todd pushed salad around on his plate. "I . . . When I'm in a relationship, I tend to be monogamous, but I suppose I needn't require the same of you."

Sebby speared a carrot and dipped it in his vinaigrette. "So you don't care?"

Todd fidgeted. "If you want to sleep with other people, you will, whether I want you to or not."

"So you don't want me to?"

"We haven't made a pact as far as exclusivity; I've no right to ask it of you. If you want to see other people, though, I would appreciate a courtesy notification."

"So it's okay with you if I do?"

"'Okay' being an inaccurate term of description, I would say that I don't wish to limit you if you desire a greater variety of, ah, recreation . . . but . . ."

"I don't want to if it's going to bother you."

Feeling put on the spot, Todd laid his fork down and ran his hand through his hair. "Bother me . . .? I can live with it; it won't make me angry. I surmise it would mean that we see less of one another. Also, I doubt that I would see anyone else even if you choose to . . ."

Sebby met his eyes, his expression unreadable. Todd's own face must have shown his distress, but Sebby dropped his gaze and went back to his salad.

Todd swallowed at nothing. "Do you . . . have someone in mind?"

Sebby shrugged. Todd stared at his salad. He, himself, was not exactly a bohemian. Perhaps Sebby found him dull. "Were you wanting a, you know, a threesome or something?" He dared a glance at Sebby.

"Is that what you want?" Sebby asked, placing an asparagus spear on his tongue.

"No! It's not what I want."

Sebby's head lifted, and his eyebrows arched at Todd's tone. "What do you want, then?"

"I don't want you to want anyone else, but if you do, I can adjust, I can accommodate, I—" Sebby's expression softened, and it struck Todd that Sebby was trying to squeeze some sort of declaration from him. "I don't want you to be with anyone but me. I could bear it if I had to, but it would like to crush me with sadness."

"*Querido.*" Sebby pushed aside his plate and hurried around the table. He eased himself into Todd's lap and buried his face in Todd's neck. "I don't want to crush you."

Todd laughed in unalloyed relief. "You oughtn't plop your ample bottom in my lap like that, then," he said with an exaggerated groan. Sebby swatted at him, and he wrapped his arms around Sebby and pressed his face to Sebby's hair. "My beautiful one, I want you all to myself."

Chapter Thirteen

Overreacting

The morning of the Fourth, Todd arose early to help get ready for the party. Preparations continued until around ten o'clock when Lloyd gestured to Todd, who followed his brother outside. It was shaping up to be another gorgeous Colorado day, with a baby-blue sky and a hint of a breeze.

"How soon you looking at getting your own place?" Lloyd asked, squinting up at the sun.

Taken by surprise, Todd stammered. "Well, ah, to be honest, I've not given it much thought. I'm enjoying staying with you. I don't know that I—"

Lloyd interrupted. "You got a boyfriend now, and maybe you want a place you can take him."

"Sebby has a place. I suppose I've not felt that I need my own place. Nor had I planned to remain long in Denver." Todd kicked at a sprouting weed. "I'm sorry. Am I in the way? Have I overstayed my welcome?"

"Not the point. A man your age should have his own place. That's all. Now, what's up with your finances? You're making good money. We aren't charging you rent. You're socking it away, I hope?"

Here it comes. "Some of it, as much as I'm able. I still have student loans and . . ." He hesitated.

"Yeah? What?"

Fuck. "I'm still paying rent on my New York apartment." Todd lifted his chin.

Lloyd's eyebrows made as if to fly right off his face. "But you brought all your stuff! You said you were gonna sublet it. It can't be that hard to get rid of a place in the . . . whatever part of New York it's in."

"The East Village. Ah . . . no, I chose to keep it."

Lloyd's cheeks puffed out. He blew out a sigh and gazed into the distance. "It's sitting there empty? That's a dumbass thing to do. You'll be liable if some squatter gets in there."

Todd ground his teeth and said nothing.

"You don't still think you'll go back? If you do, fine, get back there. Get your job back, get a different job, whatever. But you don't hold on to a high-rent New York apartment for sentimental reasons."

"High rent? Hardly that." Todd had shared an apartment with a coworker for several months while searching for a suitable one-bedroom or studio of his own. He had wanted a place where he could feel comfortable bringing Vivian. When he had finally found one, it was going to be a surprise. Todd had planned to christen the place with cupcakes and sex, but then Viv had dumped him . . . "I kept it against the possibility that I might choose to return. It was worth a few months' rent to preclude having to go apartment hunting all over again." Todd ripped his hand through his hair and noticed how long it was getting. He was surprised that Lloyd hadn't mentioned the fact that he needed a haircut. How many times had he heard that from his father over the years? *Get a haircut, you look like a girl. No one'll hire a damn hippie.*

"Okay. I'll buy that. But by now you should know what you're doing. You going back?"

Todd dropped his eyes.

Lloyd rested his hand on Todd's shoulder. "I'm glad you're not. That kid was bad news; he messed you up. If you were going back to him, I'd try to talk you out of it. I know it's hard, but you're getting along. Huh? And, you know, I like having some family in Denver that isn't Donna's family." He squeezed Todd's shoulder. "You need help dumping that place?"

"No. I know what to do. And as soon as that's taken care of, I'll think about looking for something here." *If I don't join the Peace Corps.*

There followed a flurry of last-minute cooking, cleaning, and setting up of chairs before guests began to arrive. Entrees in hand,

Sebby showed up, and Todd introduced him to his family. While Todd hovered, Sebby found places to set his food and went to work helping Donna to arrange and unwrap things, as if he'd grown up in her kitchen.

First chance she found, Donna pulled Todd aside and murmured, "I love him! He's adorable."

Todd beamed in flustered pride.

The men gathered around the grill while the women and Sebby worked on arranging and setting up. Todd dithered before joining the men in their cloud of smoke, lighter fluid, and charring meat.

Evening arrived. Someone produced a guitar and began running through Neil Young tunes. Todd was on the point of joining the singer when someone mentioned the *1812 Overture*. "With cannons, even. Somehow timed with the fireworks, but it seems like, I dunno, how could they?"

Todd's head turned. "How could who? Is there an Independence Day performance of the *1812 Overture* scheduled?"

"Yeah, downtown. With fireworks. That's what I was saying: you can't time fireworks to music, you can't."

Todd questioned the speaker and determined that an orchestra would be performing Tchaikovsky's *1812 Overture* on the lawn of the State Capitol, complete with cannon and accompanying fireworks. It was scheduled to begin at ten that evening. "Sebby, we should go! Would you like to?"

"Of course. I love fireworks."

"There's fireworks closer to home," Lloyd said. "And going downtown'll be a nightmare. The crowds, the parking."

Sebby assured them that if anyone knew how to maneuver downtown, he did.

"I think we'll brave it," Todd said.

"Take me!" Ryan clutched Todd's sleeve. "Can I go?"

In the end, Ryan and Todd climbed into the pickup, while Sebby drove his own vehicle, as the fireworks were near his home. Eventually the three of them were seated on a blanket on the capitol lawn. Thousands of people were spread out across the area on blankets or lawn chairs, waving sparklers and American flags, wearing glow sticks around their necks and wrists. Sebby leaned back against Todd, and

Ryan leaned against both of them as the music swelled, the cannons boomed, and the fireworks opened overhead like sea anemones. The acrid smell of the pyrotechnic smoke reached them, and they *ooh*ed and *ahh*ed with the crowd. Todd stared up at the sky and thought, *This is what it's like to have a family.*

As they gathered their things, Ryan bounced around like any kid who'd had too much junk food and stayed up too late. "That was *awesome*, Uncle Todd and, um, Sebby. That's the best fireworks I ever seen. The music was, like, so whoa."

They made their way down the sidewalk as the crowd separated and streamed away into the tributary roads. To keep from being separated, Sebby took Ryan's hand in his and placed his other hand on Todd's shoulder. As they drew farther away from the capitol, the crowds thinned and Sebby let go of Ryan and hugged Todd from behind. Impulsively, Todd tossed the blanket to Ryan and reached around behind himself for Sebby. "Hop up."

Sebby laughed, put his hands on Todd's shoulders, and vaulted onto his back, winding his arms around Todd's neck and giggling as Todd grabbed his legs and staggered. Ryan shouted with laughter and shoved at the two of them with his blanketed arms. "You're gonna fall over!"

"Ryan, dooon't," Sebby wailed. Todd ran a few steps and regained his balance, Sebby shrieking the while.

"Isn't he heavy, Uncle Todd?"

"Incredibly so," Todd groaned.

Sebby swatted at Todd.

"Look at the little faggots!"

The voice was just another noise in the crowd, and the words might not have even registered with Todd, but he felt Sebby tense. Sebby patted Todd and said into his ear, "Todd, let me down." Todd let go and turned to see who had spoken.

"Hey, little faggots! That your faggot-in-training?"

The street was well lit, and Todd spotted the offender among a group of clean-cut college boys, who ought to have been making Faulkner jokes in the library rather than faggot jokes on the street. None of them looked as though he would survive a good jab to the nose. Sebby drew Ryan under his arm. "Just walk away. We'll lose them in the crowd, come on."

Todd stayed where he was. "My boyfriend and I are indeed fags, and one might with accuracy apply the word 'little' to any of us. However, your last comment requires an apology, and this I demand."

That set some of the college boys to laughing, though a dark-haired one spoke up from the back of the group. "Sorry. He didn't mean anything."

"The hell I didn't!" A boy with shining blond hair grinned at Todd.

"Shut it, Josh." The dark-haired one smacked the insulter in the back of his head, and the insulter turned and shoved him. The dark-haired boy held his hands up. "Whoa, chill."

"Todd, come *on*." Sebby tugged on Todd's elbow, and Todd acquiesced. They walked quickly, but the voice came from behind them again.

"Woo woo! You need a fucking *straw* to go with that shake!"

Todd's stomach ground on itself as if he had swallowed stones. He would have halted, but Sebby's grip pulled him along. "Ignore it, just ignore it, just ignore it." Sebby quickened the pace, and the three of them threaded their way through various couples and families, Sebby repeating the words like a mantra: *Just ignore it, just ignore it, just ignore it . . .*

"Hey, kid, you better come with us if you want to stay *virga intacta*. Unless it's too late. They fuck 'em young."

Todd shook Sebby off. "You two go on ahead." Sebby made a small sound of protest, but Todd turned to face the gaggle of well-fed college boys. "I am in awe of your misuse of Latin. You are a discredit to your institution of higher learning. On behalf of my nephew, who is too young to defend himself, I must insist that you apologize."

"You're defending your *nephew*?" The blond one snorted and called after Sebby and Ryan. "Kid, I recommend you sleep with both hands over your ass."

Rage swelled, crowding rational judgment back into a small and ignored spot in Todd's mind. That Ryan should be made to hear such a thing! "Much as I dislike fisticuffs, I'm willing to thrash you if you refuse to apologize." Todd was ready to get his head punched, though he thought he could give a good accounting of himself, enough that the young man might think twice before harassing gays in the future.

The dark-haired boy put a restraining hand on his friend's arm. "He takes it back. Josh, drop it. There's cops everywhere just looking out for this kind of shit."

"Let 'em look. They'll probably join in." He moved closer and loomed over Todd, who dropped into a boxing stance. That set the group to laughing again. Passersby gave the scene a wide berth.

"*Todd.*" Sebby's sharp cry rang out. "Get over here. Now. That's an order."

"Yeah, *Todd*, your wife's calling you. He doesn't want your pretty face messed up."

"If you don't get over here, I'm leaving and taking Ryan home!" Sebby's voice was barely on the right side of panic.

Todd hesitated. He straightened up. His fists itched for contact with the creep's jaw, but the thought of Sebby explaining Todd's whereabouts to Lloyd and Donna, and the brouhaha that would result, made up his mind. He locked eyes with the insulter. *Josh*, he remembered. He smiled and took two careful steps backward.

"I'm afraid I must take my leave, Joshua. But I stress: never confuse a homosexual with a pedophile. I love my nephew and would never harm him or allow another to do so. And thus I require an apology."

"He's sorry," repeated the dark-haired one. "I, uh, apologize on his behalf."

"You don't do shit on my 'behalf'!" shouted the agitator.

"Accepted," Todd said. "As for a faggot-in-training, Joshua, I'd be happy to take you on, if you're interested. We begin with the Seven Habits of Highly Effective Fags, the first habit being: never let a homophobe become comfortable with his homophobia."

Todd turned on his heel and sauntered off. His body was primed, half expecting an attack, but only sputtered insults followed him and soon faded as he left the group behind.

The door of Sebby's car flew open as he approached, and the overhead light showed Sebby behind the wheel and Ryan in the backseat. He climbed inside, slammed the door, and was attacked by a frenzied Sebastián.

"Are you all right? Todd, are you all right?" Sebby's hands flew all over Todd's body in the most nonerotic fashion imaginable.

"I'm fine, no broken bones. Only my pride was hurt, and I soothed it by means of a few choice words." He tried to pull Sebby closer, but Sebby moved away.

"We're getting out of here. We'll come back and get your pickup tomorrow." The car jumped into gear, and Sebby laid strips of rubber making their getaway. Perhaps a mile went by before he pulled into a parking lot, empty but bright with security lights, and pressed trembling fingertips to his eyes.

Todd held out his arms for Sebby. "French Press, I'm sorry you were frightened." He hugged Sebby and felt his embrace returned, but a moment later Sebby's palm connected with the side of his face, and his head rocked back.

"Jesus!" He raised his hand to his cheek and stared. Ryan whimpered.

Sebby retreated. "Don't ever do that again! If you ever do anything like that again, I'll...!"

Todd blinked. "W— But— Ah . . . I didn't do anything."

Sebby's voice quavered on the verge of tears. "Walk away, I told you to walk away! You could've been hurt, Ryan and me could've been hurt, you put us all at risk for the sake of your silly pride."

"I was *protecting* you! I told you to go on. I kept them occupied." He rubbed at his face.

"I don't need you to protect me! You couldn't just ignore them? All we had to do was walk away!"

"Can we go home? I want to go home!" Ryan cried.

"Oh, Ryan. Baby, I'm sorry." Sebby put a hand out to stroke Ryan's hair, but Ryan recoiled.

"I'm not a baby! I want to go home! Uncle Todd, let's go home!"

"We will, Ryan, we'll go home." Todd twisted toward the backseat and reached both arms to Ryan. "Everything is all right, my lad. An idiot yelling homophobic slurs. Nothing more." He comforted the clinging Ryan for several moments before turning to Sebby. "Sebby, I owe you an apology. And you as well, Ryan. I didn't mean to frighten you so."

Sebby launched himself at Todd, who squeezed his eyes shut in case another slap was forthcoming, but Sebby clutched Todd's shirtfront and pressed his face into Todd's neck. Muffled words emerged. "I was so scared, Todd, so, so scared. I called 911, but nothing was really happening. I mean, they don't send a policeman just for fucking-around talking, and I was about to lie and tell them someone was being beaten, but then I just yelled for you and you came."

Todd petted him and murmured into his hair. He wondered what was behind Sebby's reaction, which, to Todd, seemed all out of proportion to an incident that had involved only the trading of insults. The trembling eased, Ryan fidgeted in the backseat, and Todd patted Sebby and sat him up.

Sebby drew a deep breath. "Let's go back and get your pickup. It's getting so late. We don't want to have to come back in the morning."

"Sebastián, you're distraught, and I'm uncomfortable with you driving in such a state. If you want to go home, I'll take you there before I take Ryan home."

"Then I won't have a car if I need one! No! I'm fine. I can take care of myself. I've been doing it since before you showed up!"

Todd bit back the harsh words that tried to escape. "*Please*. I'm sorry for upsetting you. I'm sorry that I didn't listen. Please don't go home angry, I beg you."

"I'm not angry, Todd!" Sebby's tone belied his words, and Todd arched his eyebrows. "Okay, I'm angry a little, but mostly I'm upset, and I just want to go home and have a drink and go to sleep. *By myself*."

Todd was not a person who was much desirous of solitude, but he respected the idiosyncrasy in others. Or tried to. "Very well, but—"

Ryan whimpered again, and Todd decided the discussion must wait. He reached to touch Sebby's face, where his dimple would be if only he would smile, and Sebby took hold of Todd's hand and pressed it closer.

"I was so scared," Sebby whispered.

When Todd and Ryan arrived home after midnight, they found Donna and Lloyd waiting up. Todd relinquished Ryan to his parents and went to the bathroom. He texted Sebby and made certain he was home. When he returned to the living room, he knew he was in trouble. Lloyd regarded him sternly, and Donna with wide eyes.

"Go to bed, Ryan," Lloyd said. Ryan left, throwing anguished glances at his uncle, and Lloyd indicated that Todd should have a seat. Perching on the edge of a chair, Todd leaned forward, clasped hands between knees.

"Ryan told us what happened," Lloyd said.

"I was going to tell you. It was nothing serious."

"We don't want you and . . . Sebby . . . taking Ryan out anymore."

Todd rolled these words around in his head. "W-what?"

"Ryan's eleven," Lloyd continued. "He doesn't need to witness a hate crime. Especially one that involves his own uncle."

"At no time was there any danger of *that*. The most that might have happened was a few punches getting thrown, and I did manage to avoid it."

Lloyd folded his arms. "You're playing down the situation, but Ryan's upset. It's clear there was more going on than you'll admit. Besides, the fact is, if Ryan's out with a gay couple, he could come up against homophobia at any time."

Donna put her hand on Lloyd's knee. "*You* can still take Ryan out. We're not forbidding you to see him. But we don't think it's safe for you and Sebby, as a couple, to—to take Ryan places. He's just too young. This thing scared him."

Todd's mouth opened and shut several times before any sound came out. "But nothing *happened*!"

Lloyd folded his arms. "I don't call that nothing. Sebby called the cops?"

Todd wrung his hands. "Sebby . . . he seemed to be more . . . afraid . . . than the plight warranted."

"You're saying he overreacted."

"In a word, yes."

Donna and Lloyd looked at one another. After a moment Donna spoke. "But, honey, what we hadn't thought of before is that something *could* happen. There's a lot of hatred out there against gays. It's not your fault, but it's there. Ryan's our son. Our number one job is to protect our kids."

How many times in one season could a man's heart be broken before it crumpled like a dry husk? "You're just giving in to homophobia! Many circumstances incite hatred. Suppose I were straight but involved in an interracial relationship. Would you hand me the same conditions? That Ryan might be in danger because some white supremacist could take offense?"

Donna blinked rapidly, but Lloyd shrugged. "Maybe," he said. "But, anyway, that's a hypothetical."

Todd bolted from his chair and paced across the room, gesturing madly. "So is my whole life. If I someday take a spouse, you're saying my husband and I can never take Ryan to a ballgame, to a movie, to the fucking mall."

"*You*, just you, can take him wherever you want to, honey," Donna reminded him.

"It'll be different when Ryan's older," Lloyd said. "Right now he's too young to understand, and we don't want him exposed to that kind of crap."

"Please respect our wishes," Donna said. "If you ever have your own kids, you'll understand."

Todd stopped in the middle of the room. "If I draw out your assertions to their logical conclusion, I and my husband should never take our own children anywhere as a family. No family vacations, no family trips to play minigolf. *No fucking family*."

Donna appeared stricken, but Lloyd remained unmoved. "It's true that your kid would face a lot of prejudice. It'd be tough for him, and you should think about it real hard before you have any."

"No worries," Todd said. "Right now I'm thinking that I would never be so cruel as to curse my children with a family." He strode across the room toward the front door. "I can't stay here, can't live with you, knowing you feel that way. I'm out of here. As soon as I can swing it."

"Honey!" Donna was on her feet and across the room. She attempted to hug Todd. "We don't want you to go! Ryan's nuts about you, so am I. You're overreacting."

Todd laughed again, the sound so hollow that he impressed himself. "The strangest thing of all about this entire night is that I appear to be the only individual who is *not* overreacting."

He shook her off and, as he exited the house, heard Lloyd say, "Let him cool off."

Todd slammed the door, climbed into his truck, slammed the truck's door, and dialed Sebby on his cell, hoping he was still up.

"It's my fault," Sebby said, after Todd related what had passed.

"No, it isn't! What is?"

"Ryan. He thought you were going to beat them all down. He wanted to watch. But I freaked, and I made him scared." There was a pause, and there were noises in the background, familiar. It took Todd a moment to place them as the sounds of the grinder.

"Are you making coffee?"

"Yeah. Ryan, he, you know, thinks you hang the moon. Every night."

"What I wouldn't give at this moment for some coffee."

"Todd, you're avoiding."

"Avoiding? I? You're the one who refuses to admit that there is a reason behind your overreaction to tonight's incident."

"I had a friend who was beaten. Satisfied?"

Todd had expected something like this. "Sweetheart, I'm sorry. Was he all right?"

"No. And what you did was foolish. Standing up to a group of men all by yourself . . . You think you were being heroic, but it was just stupid. Violence doesn't solve anything."

Todd drummed his fingers on the steering wheel. "I cannot say that I agree. Many issues in our world are resolved by violence, and there are times when backing away from a fight would be morally wrong. Sebby, your friend, did he . . . was he killed?"

"No. What was going to be *resolved* if you got put in the hospital? Whatever in the fucking world makes you think you can take on six men? I wouldn't even bet on you against *one*; you used to box, you told me, but when was the last time you actually hit a person?" Sebby paused for breath.

"That's not important. What's important is that there is a sort of person who believes he can with impunity badger homosexuals, that we cannot or will not defend ourselves. By putting up a good fight, even if I come off the worse, I make that person consider his folly before he attempts the same again, thereby having saved a future homosexual from suffering said oppression." He continued in a bantering tone, "You are so convinced, are you, that I couldn't thrash six men? Ryan had faith in me."

There was an exasperated sigh, like white noise through the cell phone. "How would it be for Ryan to see you beat up and bleeding, spitting teeth, falling in the gutter?"

"Sebby, my love, is that what happened to your friend?"

"No. You can't change those people's mind by fighting them! Six of them. *Dios mío*, you're like Don Quixote, fighting windmills, only not windmills."

Being compared to Don Quixote delighted Todd more than it ought. Though he was sure Sebby didn't mean it as a compliment, he held his cell as if it were a microphone and sang the opening lines of the title song of *Man of La Mancha*, about being Don Quixote.

Putting the phone back to his ear, he heard Sebby's muffled laughter, and his heart lurched sideways. "What say I come over there, French Press?"

"Toddfox, it's so late, and still I'd say yes, but poor Ryan is probably crying his little eyes out, and you should go talk to him."

"Shit. What, Sebastián, am I to say? I can't stay here any longer, after what they said. Fucking hell."

"Your brother and Donna, they don't mean to hurt you. What I think is, it'll blow over. Everyone overreacted, and now you're overreacting. After they think about it, they'll realize they're being silly." A sentence or two in Spanish followed, soothing as a lullaby, and it occurred to Todd that Sebby was probably right.

"Okay, French Press. Sebby, I . . . I am fond of you."

"I know, Todd."

"And I'm sorry that I frightened you."

"I know."

"At times, I am not . . . the most prudent prune in the prune jar."

"I know that too."

More than coffee, at that moment Todd craved the feel of Sebby's skin next to his own, and he almost said so. "Well . . . good night. *Buenas noches, mi chico.*"

"*Buenas noches*, Todd."

Todd stared at his phone in his hand, and then he kissed it. *I am kissing my phone,* Todd thought, and he grinned. He got out of his car and drew in lungsful of sweet night air and realized three things. One, he had not gotten the story out of Sebby of whatever had happened to his friend. Two, the moon appeared to be full. Three, he had called Sebby *my love.*

Todd entered the darkened bedroom quietly, against the possibility that Ryan might be sleeping, but Ryan spoke up as soon as Todd closed the door behind him. "I was listening. I heard everything you said."

The conversation with Sebby was fresh in Todd's mind, and it took a moment to realize that Ryan was referring to Todd's conversation with his parents. "Thank Christ. That relieves me of having to relate it to you."

"So I guess you came back to get your stuff."

Todd threw himself facedown onto the lower bunk and hugged his pillow. "Why? Tired of me, nevvy?"

"You said you were leaving. You're not leaving?"

"I talked to Sebby, and he convinced me that I was acting impetuously and that this entire thing with your parents will blow over. Therefore, no, I'm not leaving. Unless you're kicking me out."

"I'd never do that. Um, I'm sorry, Uncle Todd. It's all my fault. Are you mad at me?"

"What? Ryan, my lad, nothing is *your* fault." Todd rolled over and lifted his legs, placed his feet on the bottom of the bunk above, and pushed, giving his nephew a few jostles. "If anything, the fault is mine for not walking away."

Ryan made no comment on the jostling. "You did walk away, though. I mean, um, it's my fault that I told my parents and now they're all mad."

"Nevvy, if you hadn't told them, I would've told them, and then they would've questioned you, and the end would've been the same. Besides, they aren't angry. They're worried."

"I wasn't scared at first. But then I thought something bad might happen. But nothing did, so. Those people were just yelling mean things. Did you break up with Sebby?"

"Why would you think that? No!"

"But he *hit* you!"

Todd had quite honestly forgotten it. "If you call *that* a hit. Ryan, every man gets his face slapped now and then. It's proof of one's manhood."

Ryan's voice was puzzled. "Why?"

Todd grimaced and jostled Ryan again. "I was being flippant. Ah . . . Sebby slapped me because he was in an agitated state due to having been frightened. Not that I endorse hitting one's significant other—in fact, quite the opposite—but . . . I understand that there were extenuating circumstances, and I forgive him."

"Oh. Did he say he was sorry?"

Todd's brow wrinkled. "No . . . he did not."

"Uncle Todd, is Sebby kind of like a girl?"

Todd coughed. "Ahem . . . what makes you say that?"

"Well . . . he stayed in the kitchen with the moms, and he's kind of pretty like a girl, and he got scared like a girl, and the way he hit you was kind of like a girl."

"Out of the mouths of babes." Todd heaved a sigh and wondered why it fell to him to explain these things. "First of all, you are stereotyping females. Secondly, some men tend more to the effeminate, just as some women tend more to the masculine. There isn't necessarily a dividing line between the genders, is what I mean. Ah . . . rather, there is a line, but it's often blurred." Todd despaired of making any sense and went back to jostling Ryan with extra gusto.

Ryan let out a muffled yell. "Quit it! But I'm glad you're not leaving."

Chapter Fourteen

Skin

Todd's Peace Corps interview was a devastating disappointment. The recruiter asked about any relationships Todd might have and how they might be affected by a long absence, and he told her he'd just ended a relationship. She excavated the whole Vivian story out of him. She told him that it was not a good idea to make such a decision at such a time and that they'd be happy to interview him again in six months if he was still interested.

"She was doing her job, then, wasn't she?" Holly said.

"Interfering busybody," Todd grumbled.

"Well, I'm glad. It's a dumb idea. Geeze, Todd."

Todd did not tell Sebby about his interview. He was afraid of hearing *I told you so*, and, moreover, afraid of hurting Sebby's feelings. Todd's aggravation at the recruiter gave way to despair. What was he going to do with himself for six whole months? He didn't know if he could stand it.

Todd wandered into the mobile office on the construction site. Even though he knew it was no longer his place to worry about Vivian, he couldn't help wondering whether Viv was all right, whether anyone was caring for him properly. Did Vivian regret giving Todd up now that he no longer had Todd's hands for back rubs, Todd's voice for reading aloud, for singing him to sleep? Not that it mattered. Even if Vivian did miss those things, time was passing and he would stop missing them; Todd would be a memory, an indiscretion of Vivian's youth.

From behind his desk, Sebby gave Todd a searching look.

"Do you want to do lunch?" Todd asked dully. He plopped into a chair.

Sebby tilted his head and regarded Todd, and then came around his desk, slid into Todd's lap, and rested his forehead against Todd's. "There's lots of things I want to do."

There were footsteps outside, and Sebby rose from Todd's lap and stepped aside as the door opened.

"Gus, Todd doesn't feel good. He's going home sick," Sebby said.

Startled, Todd glanced up at Sebby, who moved behind Todd and placed a hand on Todd's neck. One finger went inside Todd's shirt collar and stroked. Todd tried not to move like a cat under his hand.

Gus glanced at Todd. "Yeah, s'fine. Sebby, I need to know where that order of aluminum coil is at."

"It's going to be late. I called this morning and bitched at them, and they said they'll get it here day after tomorrow."

"Damn it. Guess that'll have to do," Gus said.

Todd got to his feet. Never had he used a sick day on false pretense. He walked to his truck, wondering if he should just sit there for a bit and then return, saying that he felt better and would not need to go home after all.

Sebby appeared and tapped at his door, a small, metallic sound. He offered Todd a key. "Go to my house. Okay? Wait for me. I'll be so happy all day just thinking of you at my house." Dimpling, he gave Todd big eyes, and how could Todd say no? Besides, the thought of crawling between cool, crisp sheets and sleeping the afternoon away, of being awoken by Sebastián easing in beside him, smooth and perfect as a new bar of soap, was too lovely to resist. He took the key.

By the time Todd had driven the distance to Sebby's house, he was seized by the idea of using the afternoon to do something nice for Sebby. He could wash dishes, sweep or vacuum, mop the floor, clean the bathroom . . . One by one he considered and rejected ideas as he examined each room in Sebby's house and found them all pristine. Perhaps he could try to cook something, but when he hunted in the refrigerator and cupboards, he could find nothing he felt capable of preparing.

Having secured a box of soy crackers, Todd took a seat on Sebby's deck and munched, looking around the shady yard. The grass was overlong, and that decided him. He crossed the yard to the shed and found a lawnmower. It was a pleasant task, and he enjoyed the alternating sun and shade on his shoulders, the thrum of the mower, the tang of cut grass. At the rear of the yard was a small vegetable garden with thriving tomato and pepper plants, and Todd picked the ripe items and carried them to the kitchen. He cleared a patch of crab grass and reseeded the patch with grass seed from the shed. He filled the bird feeder and repaired a loose step on the deck.

Just as he was finishing the step, he heard a car in the driveway and started. He'd meant to have something special ready for Sebby's return. Instead, he'd let time get away from him and now here he was, grimy.

"Tooodd?" Sebby called through the house.

"I'm out back!" he yelled. Sebby appeared in the doorway. "Sorry, I meant to get cleaned up before you got home." Todd brushed his hands off, wiped them on his jeans, ran his fingers through his hair, realized that he was getting dirt in his hair, stopped, and smiled sheepishly.

Sebby came out on the deck and stared around wide-eyed. "Toddfox. What've you done? I thought you'd sleep or watch TV; I never meant for you to have to . . . Oh, you mowed my lawn? You . . . What'd you do?"

"I hope that's quite all right? If I overstepped my bounds, I apologize. It's— Oof!" The air was knocked out of him as Sebby, in effect if not by design, tackled him into the mown grass and covered his face with kisses. Todd cringed, sure that he tasted of soil and grass and sweat. He started to put his arms around Sebby and stopped, for fear of dirtying his good clothes.

"Todd, oh Todd, you didn't have to do that!"

"It was my pleasure. Sweet, let me up. I'm dirty. Let me go wash."

"No, no, put your hands on me. Get me dirty."

Charmed, Todd laughed and wrapped his arms around Sebby, who nestled his head below Todd's chin. Todd nuzzled the soft hair. The sweet smell of cut grass rose around them, and Todd wondered if he could ever mow a lawn again without thinking of this moment.

"Todd, oh Todd, you didn't have to do all this. You're so good to me. I would've let you fuck me anyway."

Appalled, Todd protested, "I did not tidy your yard in expectation of getting laid. I did it because it made me happy to do something nice for you."

"Everyone does everything to get laid, don't you know that?" He buried his face in Todd's neck and kissed him over and over. "It was so nice. Todd, you didn't have to. Todd, oh Todd, oh *Todd*." His arms tightened convulsively.

Chuckling, Todd whispered, "Stop saying my name or I'll die."

Sebby went still, and Todd, regretting the words, slid his fingers under Sebby's curls at the back of the neck and pressed him to his chest. He kissed the top of Sebby's head. For long moments, Sebby permitted this, but then he raised his head and regarded Todd. The late afternoon sun streaming through the branches of the trees backlit him, and Todd drew in his breath at the beauty of Sebby's dark hair feathering into a golden nimbus.

"I'm sorry about that. It's just, that night, you kept saying it, um, and it seemed so intense, like serious, and it was a little scary."

"I'm a frightening lout, I am." Watching the play of light, Todd ran his fingers through Sebby's tresses. "But it's fun being scared, remember?"

"It's fun being scared when you know you're *safe*," Sebby corrected him. He dropped his eyes and laid his head again on Todd's chest.

Todd continued stroking Sebby's hair as these troubling words sank in. "You aren't safe with me? You don't know you're safe?" Sebby didn't answer. He sneaked a hand under Todd's T-shirt and traced circles around Todd's navel, but Todd felt this was an important point. He took hold of Sebby's hand and draped one arm around his shoulders. "Wait, Sebby . . . are you afraid of me?"

There was a long pause. Todd waited.

Finally, Sebby spoke. "I think, Todd, that you might go back to *him*. I don't want to get too attached. If he invited you back, I think you'd leave me and go."

Todd was struck silent.

"You love him so," Sebby said with a wistfulness that squeezed Todd's heart. "You talk about him like he's an angel that some old artist should carve in stone."

This was so similar to something Viv had once said that Todd was mightily annoyed. "He isn't so great."

"*Ha.*" Sebby's back jumped under Todd's hand with the force of his exhalation. "Maybe not, but you think he is, and is there anything you really like about me? Tell me one thing, just one thing you like better about me than him." Todd felt the held breath as Sebby waited for an answer, and he spoke the first words that came into his head.

"Well, you're here, and you haven't broken my heart."

"Ohhh." It was a drawn-out sigh. He raised his head and kissed Todd with exquisite tenderness, as if Todd's mouth were yet wounded by Vivian's kisses. Todd tangled his dirty hands in Sebby's hair, and it seemed he felt a thrumming, an echo of the lawnmower's vibration. Sebby paused and looked Todd square in the eye. "That line is going to get old, you know, about your broken heart."

"And so I use it sparingly, *mon cher*." He smoothed his hands down Sebby's back and tugged at his shirt till it came free of its tuck. "Anyway, it's not so broken now."

"*Oh, querido.*" This utterance was a whisper against Todd's lips.

Todd insinuated his hands under the cotton, loving the smooth, supple feel of Sebby's flesh. "Your skin," he began, and stopped.

"*¿Sí?* My skin?" Sebby arched his back and regarded Todd expectantly.

"Your skin. Smooth and perfect as a new bar of soap. I cannot get enough of it." He caressed Sebby's back, allowing his fingers to dip below Sebby's waistband to touch the curve of his rear. Sebby tensed and molded himself to Todd. "It's, well, to be honest, it's . . ." It felt disloyal, and Todd had to swallow and clear his throat. "It's much nicer than his skin." Todd's face flushed. Through no fault of his own, Vivian was layered in scars: some smooth and pale, some ridged and hard, some gouged and hollow, and it was the simple truth that Sebby's unblemished hide was more attractive to a detached observer. Todd waited for the gods to strike his head with lightning for this temerity.

"Tch. *Mi chico tierno.* You don't have to. I was silly to ask. Silly and childish. But I love that you tried." He kissed Todd again and nestled against him with a sigh. The sun warmed him, and the mown grass cushioned him, and Sebastián was compliant in the circle of his arms, and the sensation was so unfamiliar that he had to think about it before realizing he was happy.

Chapter Fifteen

Rosencrantz and Guildenstern

I'm becoming utterly too fond of Sebby, Todd texted Holly.
See? You CAN get over Viv, she replied.
Maybe. He sent her a photo of Sebby.
Yikes, he's really attractive, she texted. *What's he see in you?*

One evening, near dark, Todd returned to the construction site and mounted the steps to the mobile office. Sebby had texted that he was working late. "Thought I'd keep you company," he said to Sebby's startled look. "I could even help. I promise you, I balance a mean spreadsheet." He dropped into a chair at the table.

"Keep your *patas* off my spreadsheets." Sebby sighed and regarded Todd, chin on fist. "I can't concentrate on my numbers with you here. I'll finish up tomorrow." He began shutting down.

"How validating it is to be the man who can distract you from your love of numbers." Todd stretched and flexed his biceps.

Sebby did not appear to notice. "I'm hungry. Did you eat yet?"

"I ate, but I will gladly eat again."

Sebby stood and came around his desk. He looked sidelong at Todd as he thumbed a stack of papers. "What about this weekend?"

"Yes. I am sure I will eat again this weekend."

"No. I mean I want you to meet my friends, and will you go with me to a party thing?"

Meeting Sebby's friends could be a significant step in their relationship. But why was Sebby avoiding his eyes? Todd slid from the chair and went to Sebby's side. "A party *thing*? Pray do elaborate, Sebastián."

"It's like a dinner party or get-together, and they said I have to bring you or I can't come. They want to meet you. I think they're a little suspicious . . ." Sebby tapped his finger against his chin and frowned. "They don't even want me to bring any food. They said just bring 'this Todd.'"

"Fear not, I shall charm them and set their minds at ease." Todd took Sebby's hand in his and put an arm around his waist and led him in a graceful turn. "Will there be dancing at this gathering?"

"Nooo, Todd, dancing? What are you talking about? It's dinner." Sebby pushed at Todd but then clung.

"Aw, sweetheart, are you nervous to have me meet your friends?"

"Aren't *you* nervous? It's just, they don't always like my boyfriends. I want them to like you."

"What's not to like?" Todd cupped the back of Sebby's head and kissed him.

Sebby melted. "Mm. Kiss them like that and they'll like you pretty good."

It was a longish drive from Sebby's home to the suburb south of the city and closer to the mountains. When Sebby led Todd into his friend's house, Todd felt as if he'd strayed into a ski lodge. The entrance opened with no preamble into a brightly lit great room with a ceiling that seemed to be at least three stories above their heads. A staircase to one side swept up to a second-story landing that looked over the great room. The rear wall was floor-to-ceiling windows framing a stunning view of the Front Range of the Rockies.

Their host, a tall man of about thirty whom Sebby introduced as Ethan, appeared puzzled when Todd was presented. "You're Todd?"

"Todd, rhymes with God," Todd affirmed, gripping Ethan's hand, and Ethan grinned as if UPS had just delivered an unexpected package on his doorstep.

Sebby took Todd around and introduced him to a few people, at which point a blonde girl pulled Sebby aside, and Ethan took over the introductions. Repeatedly, upon being informed that this was "Sebby's boyfriend, Todd," the same surprised and pleased look came over their faces that had come over Ethan's. Todd concluded that they had been expecting something different and that, for whatever reason, they were glad to have their expectations contradicted. What had Sebby told them about him?

After dinner, Todd found himself seated on a sofa near the windows between two young men who, at first glance, appeared to be twins, but upon closer examination were revealed to be men who were fairly close in appearance and who had done everything they could to look alike: same styled brown hair, same artfully applied eyeliner and faux beauty spots, same pierced nostril, same tight plaid pants, and even the same mannerisms in their speech and gestures. Each sat like a reflection of the other, one leg folded under so he could turn toward Todd.

"So you're Sebby's boyfriend," said the one on Todd's left, Barry or Lawrence; Todd had already lost track of which was which.

"How much of his boyfriend are you?" asked the one on Todd's right, tilting his head and placing a forefinger against his lower lip.

"*Very* much," Todd said.

"So no playing?" said the one on Todd's left, placing his hand on Todd's shoulder.

"None whatsoever," Todd said.

"All work and no play makes Todd a sad boy," said the one on Todd's right.

"It's sad," the first one pouted.

"Sebby should let you out sometimes."

"Like tonight."

"You'll get stir-crazy."

"It's not healthy."

Todd's head moved like that of a tennis spectator as he tried to keep up with this dialogue. "Ahhh . . . if you gentlemen will excuse me?" He attempted to rise and was pushed back by two arms. Ping and Pong, as Todd had begun to think of them, leaned closer. Ping looped one arm around Todd's elbow and Pong rested his knee on Todd's thigh.

"Maybe he's already stir-crazy."

"I think he is."

"Would you feel better if *we* brought it up to Sebby?"

"We'll tell him we like you."

"He'll be glad. He wants us to like you."

Ping nuzzled Todd's ear. Todd flinched away, which sent him nearer to Pong, who nuzzled his other ear, humming breathily. "Sebby told us you like to sing."

"We can sing . . . into the right microphone."

"Ah . . . I'm sure you can," Todd said.

"We like a big microphone," Ping said.

"It doesn't *have* to be big," Pong retorted, placing a hand on Todd's chest.

"No . . . it doesn't *have* to," Ping agreed, placing a hand on Pong's hand.

"Are they trying to seduce you?"

Todd looked up with relief at the arrival of Sebby, who stood with hands on hips and eyebrows raised. Todd opened his mouth to say that indeed they were, and would Sebby please save him.

"We like him," Ping said.

"He has our seal of approval." Pong shifted his hand in order to pat Todd's chest.

"We didn't get to seal him yet, though."

"So, can we?"

"Todd's conservative," Sebby said, "so you won't get anywhere with him." He paused as if in thought. "But you're welcome to try." He smiled and walked away.

"Hey!" Todd protested.

"See?" Ping moved closer and smoothed his hand over Todd's chest with renewed enthusiasm.

"We told you he wouldn't mind." Pong smoothed his hand in a motion mirroring that of Ping's.

"He'd like it, even!"

"He wants you to be happy."

"We're not trying to steal you." Something wormed its way under Todd's ass.

"'Cause we wouldn't." Ditto something else.

Todd plucked their hands from his chest, one hand in each of his own. "Charming as the two of you are, and tempting as your offer is, I must confess that I am a one-man man." He raised their hands to his mouth and kissed them, pressing his lips to both at the same time. Identical regretful sighs came from Ping and Pong.

"So gallant."

"Oh, Sebby's just *got* to share."

Disentangling from the two, Todd felt as though he were escaping from a pair of octopi. He almost expected to hear giant kissing noises as their tentacles came free of his skin. After giving them a small, formal bow, he made his way to Sebby, who was pouring himself a glass of wine. "*Pardonnez moi, mon cher,* but what's the big idea, leaving me in the nefarious clutches of Ping and Pong?" He drew Sebby's arm about his own waist, feeling the need to reestablish who belonged to whom.

"*Ping* and *Pong*? That's not nice. Don't you like them?" Sebby squeezed Todd with the arm, his other hand being occupied with the wine.

"I feel fortunate that they've been declawed or I should never have escaped unscathed. Seriously, what?"

"You don't think they're sweet? Poor Todd. I told them you wouldn't want to."

"So you get credit for being generous with your friends and I get credit for being loyal, is that it?"

"It wasn't a test, if that's what you're asking." Sebby took a long sip of wine and glanced at Todd sidelong. "You really don't want to?"

"Is Sebastián in the habit of loaning out his boyfriends? Seriously. Seriously, *what*?"

"Mmm . . ." Sebby made a stalling noise into his wineglass. His eyes wandered around the room before coming back to Todd. He moved closer. "Don't ask questions if you won't like the answer."

"W— But— Ah . . ." Todd blinked. He blinked again. "What?"

"We're all friends here, and Barry and Lawrence, well . . . they're kind of a special case."

"Yeah, I can see that!" Todd reached for a bottle of mineral water. He fiddled with the lid, unscrewing it and then screwing it tight again. "Sebby, did we or did we not have a conversation regarding exclusivity, wherein you gave me the clear impression that you did not want me sleeping with other boys? And wherein I *thought* I gave you likewise?"

"That's not exactly what I said." Sebby rubbed Todd's back and peered anxiously into his face. "Are you mad? Are we having a fight?"

"Am I mad that you're pimping me out to your friends?"

Sebby set down his wineglass and put both arms around Todd. "Is that what it seems like to you? I'm sorry, it's, um. It's, um." He rested his forehead against Todd's shoulder. "Some of my boyfriends before—"

"Sebbyyy, you're monopolizing the new guy!" A tall, redheaded woman, perhaps in her late twenties, appeared and separated the two by hugging Sebby. "Mmmuh! Sorry I missed dinner." She extended her hand to Todd, who shook it. "Hi, I'm Becca, and you're Todd. Sebby told me how he totally stalked you down." She grinned, displaying crooked teeth, and wrinkled her freckle-sprinkled nose. "Who do I have to fuck to get a drink?"

"Not Todd." Sebby's remark was said under his breath, but Todd heard. Sebby looked over the wine selections and poured Becca a glass of burgundy.

"There wasn't a great deal of stalking to be done," Todd said.

"Yeah, 'cause you're easy. He told me that too. Ooh, you know what I like." Becca accepted the glass of burgundy and half drained it in one go.

Ethan appeared at Becca's side. Putting an arm around her waist, he plucked the wineglass from her hand despite her protesting groan. "Honey, you better watch that. Come sit with me awhile. Sebby, Wayne wants to meet Todd; would you mind taking him upstairs?"

"Okay." Sebby took Todd by the elbow and led him away. "Wayne doesn't like being around people?" Sebby explained as they mounted the wide staircase. "I mean, a lot of people all at once? He doesn't like it. He gets, like, claustrophobic. So, he'll say he has work to do, but, it's just that he doesn't like so many people. All at once. Um, sorry?"

"Sorry?" Todd slid one hand up and down the smooth, varnished railing.

"You're mad. 'M sorry."

"No, no. Not mad. I would say, confused. Overwhelmed?"

Sebby turned, one step above Todd, which made him about two inches taller, their heights reversed. "You're going to dump me."

"*What*? I most certainly am *not*." His inner self said to reach out and take Sebby in his arms, but his outer self was angry and wanted to turn on his heel, stomp down the stairs, and call a cab.

"You're maaad. I don't want you to be mad."

"Let's just go see whozisfuckface." Todd moved to the side and trotted up the stairs, leaving Sebby to trail behind him. Todd stopped at the head of the stairs. A long, slim table displayed a collection of porcelain figures alongside framed black-and-white photos of Ethan with another man. The landing led off in either direction.

"This way," Sebby said in a subdued voice. He gestured to the left. "All the way down at the end."

Moving at a quick march in the direction indicated, Todd reached the end of the hallway, took his best guess at one of the doors, and knocked.

A startled voice answered: "What?"

Sebby appeared at Todd's side. "Wayne? It's Sebby. Sorry to bother you, but I want you to meet Todd? Are you too busy?"

"Oh. Sebby? Ummm, sure. Sure, come in."

Sebby opened the door, and Todd's eyes were drawn to the only light in the room, which emanated from the several computer screens at the workstation, where a balding man sat, his eyeglasses opaquely blue in the light. He was turned toward them, hunched over, his clasped hands between his knees. "Hi."

"This is Todd. Todd, this is Wayne. He's Ethan's husband."

Wayne shrugged, scrunching his shoulders to his ears and dropping them. "Sorry I wasn't downstairs. I have this deadline. Sebby talked about you a lot, though."

"So I've been told," Todd said. He felt Sebby wince. "What sort of work do you do?

"Web design. I just freelance. I used to have a real job, but Ethan saved me from that." He smiled, an expression so quickly gone that Todd almost wondered if it had been there at all.

"You've enough to keep you busy? These days when everyone gets free sites with templates? It seems that anyone can make a website with little to no experience. I'd think that has cut into your business." Todd moved closer to get a view of the screens.

"It hasn't. The templates you're talking about are more for personal use, and some small businesses try to use them, but they find out pretty quick how limiting they are. And SEO is quite difficult. Besides, if you want to look professional, you gotta hire a professional."

This agreed with Todd's own philosophy. The same principle applied to businesses that created their own advertising: to an experienced eye, the difference was obvious. "I've done a little bit with web design. I'm not a designer myself, but I worked alongside web designers when I was in advertising."

Wayne nodded, bluish reflections glinting from his shiny scalp. "Advertising plays a big part in what I do."

The two were soon deep into a discussion of their respective professions and their intersections. Todd had limited technical ability but knew enough of the lingo to put Wayne at ease, and in no time Wayne was demonstrating his intricate setup and showing Todd his work. Todd directed him to some sites on which he had worked in the past, and Wayne was impressed. "I could put you in touch with some people, if you want. If you're looking for work."

"Hey, Wayne. You found a playmate." Ethan entered the room carrying a glass of wine. "I thought I'd bring you a drink and get you alone."

Wayne jumped as if he'd been caught with his hand down Todd's pants. "No! Just—just talking shop. Todd, this is my husband, Ethan. Oh, you met him. Of course."

"I should go. Sebby's probably bored." Todd looked around, and it hit him with ice-down-the-back suddenness that Sebby was gone. "Where's Sebby?"

"Downstairs." Ethan nodded toward the door. "There's still a few people left, but not many, if you feel like coming down, Wayne."

"No, no, no, I got sidetracked, and I have to finish this." Wayne turned his back and hunched over his keyboard.

How long have I been in here? "Wayne, thanks for showing me your work. I hope we can speak again, and I'd be interested in learning more about the contacts you mentioned." Wayne nodded without looking up. Todd left the two of them together and hurried down the stairs, where he was waylaid by a glazed-eyed and slurring Becca.

"You're nah gonna fuck BarrynLawrence? Why naaaah?"

Todd took a step back from the drunken woman. He peered around for Sebby. Despite the crowd having thinned, his whereabouts were not apparent. "I don't believe that to be any of your business."

"Buuuh, lookathem." She waved an arm, and Todd's gaze followed her gesture. Ping and Pong stood, arms entwined in a fluid pose reminiscent of the Three Graces, except that there were two of them. Todd noted their delicate bone structure and how they stood with dancers' lissomeness. He had the feeling they had waited all evening for him to descend the stairs so they could strike a classic pose for his benefit.

"Uh-oh, you smiled a' them. Y'r in trouble now." Becca weaved and clutched his arm.

"Smiled? I?" Sure enough, Ping and Pong were approaching, their lips forming identical, pleased curves.

"You were gone a long time," said Ping.

"Sebby was sad," said Pong.

"Will you go upstairs with us?"

Todd tried to shake off Becca, then thought better of it because her presence on one arm prevented Ping and Pong from flanking him. "Where *is* Sebby?"

"Asleep." Outstretching his arm in a balletic move, Pong pointed, ending palm-up in invitation.

"Passed out, mean. You mean," Becca elaborated. Following Pong's gesture, Todd spied Sebby, stretched out on a sofa, his hands under his cheek in an attitude of prayer, his head in the lap of an older man with salt-and-pepper hair whom Todd did not remember meeting.

"Don't bother him now." Ping pressed himself against Todd's arm.

"He's with Leo," Pong said.

"Come upstairs and everything'll be okay," said Ping. Pong pressed up against Todd's back. Todd had not even realized that one of them had gotten behind him. Ping and Pong moved their bodies against his. Todd was not immune to such ministrations, though the presence of an inebriated Becca served as an offset to the eroticism of two pretty boys eager to get him between the sheets.

Exasperation made him blunt. "I am not going upstairs with you. I want Sebastián, and he is all that I want, and I would be appreciative if this subject were never brought up again."

"But he's asleep!" Ping remarked with great, wide eyes.

Todd sputtered. "I don't know what you mean to imply! I . . . How can I make you understand?" He threw his arms in the air, though neither arm moved, the one imprisoned in Becca's drunken clinch and the other pinioned to his side by Ping's body. Inspiration struck. "I'm from Minnesota."

"Ohhh." The sighing exclamation came dually from the rouged lips of Ping and Pong.

"It was lovely meeting you, ah, again. If you'll excuse me, Rosencrantz and gentle Guildenstern . . ." Todd made his feet move and was relieved when the two boys did not move with him. He walked Becca to a chair and eased her into it, leaving her with a bottle of Perrier before crossing the room to where Sebby lay. The man watched Todd approach, and Todd noted how the man's fingers stroked Sebby's hair. His own fingers remembered and longed for the feel of it.

"He's very drunk," the man said without preamble. His deep voice seemed to reverberate so that Todd felt its echo in his own chest.

"Oh." Feeling at a loss, Todd tilted his head to better view Sebby's face, slack in sleep, lips parted, long lashes dark against his cheeks.

"I'm Leo. Leo Holtz." He offered his hand, though the other hand continued its slow work through Sebby's hair.

"Todd, rhymes with God. I'm Sebby's boyfriend."

They shook hands. Leo showed no sign of moving.

"I think I ought to take him home?" Against his will, it came out as a question.

"That could be difficult. It would be better, I think, to let him sleep it off here."

Here? Does he mean here in his lap? Todd crouched and touched Sebby's face, feeling the heat rising from his skin, and Leo moved his own hand aside. Todd smoothed Sebby's hair as if to erase Leo's touch. "Erase erase erase," he said softly. "Sebby? Sweetheart?"

After a long moment, Sebby's eyes fluttered open and struggled to focus. His tongue came out and wet his lips, but still it took several tries before sound emerged. "Whaaat?"

"It's late, sweetheart. Do you want me to take you home?"

"Kayyy." The eyes closed. Deep and even breathing resumed.

"Let him sleep it off," Leo said.

"I must assume that you're his friend," Todd said, getting to his feet, "but I'm his . . . significant other, and I ask that you relinquish him to me. Sir," he added before he could stop himself.

Leo chuckled. "I'm not keeping him from you." He started to shift Sebby from his lap, then stopped and raised his eyes to Todd's. "You do realize he's too drunk for sex."

Todd's temper flared and loosed his tongue. "Jesus H. Christ, what sort of troglodytes did Sebby go with before me? And you think I'm one. You know what, fuck you, fuck all of you, I'm taking him home."

He sat Sebby up and drew Sebby's arm around his shoulders, talking to him the while, hoping he'd wake enough to walk to the car. Sebby murmured. His eyes opened, and he stared glassily before his eyeballs rolled up. It was apparent to Todd, who had grown up with an alcoholic mother, that this would be awkward at best, impossible at worst. Leo watched. Todd hesitated. He did not relish the idea of a fireman carry; Sebby didn't deserve to be so humiliated in front of his friends. He ground his teeth.

"You're right," he said. "It is better to let him sleep it off here." He met Leo's eyes. "Please move."

Leo got up at once, and Todd was surprised at how tall and well-built he was. "There's a guest room on this level. I'll see if it's free," Leo said. "If no one's taken it yet, I'll help you put him to bed. If you'll let me."

"Thank you, sir. I'd appreciate that."

Leo walked away, and Todd cradled the sleeping Sebby. Ping and Pong watched wide-eyed. Todd gave them a little wave, and they turned to whisper with each other. Becca appeared to have fallen asleep in the chair where Todd had left her. Few other guests remained, and Ethan moved about tidying up.

Leo returned. "Good news. It's unoccupied. Here, let me?"

Todd nodded, and Leo scooped Sebby up in his arms and carried him like Rhett carrying Scarlett. Envious of Leo's height and breadth, Todd followed behind. They went down a short hallway and through a door, into a cramped room that appeared to be stuffed with whatever furniture had been left over when two people moved in together and all belongings were merged. The bed, twin-sized, had been turned down, and here Leo placed Sebby—lovingly, Todd thought, as though Sebby were a cherished child.

"There. I'll let you take care of him, then." Leo rested his hand on Todd's head, a familiarity that Todd would have resented, but the hand was large and warm and reassuring, and sudden tears sprouted in Todd's eyes. Mortified, he knocked Leo's hand away and turned to remove Sebby's shoes.

"I'm sorry, Todd, for not trusting you. But Sebby has brought home some doozies in the past."

"'S all right. You don't know me."

Leo hesitated in the doorway. "You know why he got drunk."

"N-o." Todd resisted the temptation to look up at Leo. He started undoing Sebby's trousers, stopped, then went on. Fuck Leo if he suspected him of base intentions.

"He thought it might be easier for you to go with the boys if he was out of the picture for the night."

"God. Jesus God." Todd reached for Sebby's hair, brushed it away from his face, and stroked his thumb over Sebby's forehead. "I don't understand."

"I can't say that I do, either. But the two of you can figure it out. So . . . you need anything?" Todd shook his head. "Good night."

Hearing the door close behind him, Todd slumped to the floor, resting his head against the mattress beside him. "Sebby, what the fuck. Seriously, what the fuck. Your friends are a motley, motley crew." He heaved a sigh, found Sebby's hand, pulled it to his mouth, kissed it, and put it atop his own head.

Presently, he got up and finished removing Sebby's trousers, rolled him to his side away from the wall in case he vomited, and clambered over him to take the side nearest the wall in the narrow bed. Putting an arm over Sebby, he scooted close and pressed his face to the back of his neck.

"I love you," he said into Sebby's hair. If only he would wake. But Sebby remained limp as a drooping dandelion. "Sebastián, *je t'aime. Te adoro.*" He pressed his lips under Sebby's ear to make certain his pulse was still throbbing. Loneliness descended, so crushing that Todd nearly went looking for Leo or for Barry and Lawrence, anyone to keep him company. Perhaps he would have, had not despair weighted his limbs to the point where moving to pull the covers over Sebby and himself was almost more than he could do. "Wake up, please wake up," he whispered.

Eventually, pressed tightly against Sebby's back, he slept.

Chapter Sixteen

Mean Up

Todd awoke to the sound of retching, and lurched to the attached bathroom, where Sebby was clutching the porcelain. Todd put his hand to Sebby's hunched back. "Oh, Sebby, poor sweetheart, can I—"

"Go away!" Sebby's voice quavered. "Todd, get out!"

Chagrined, Todd backed up, shut the door, and left him to puke in private.

"Can I get you anything?" he asked through the door.

"Nooo."

Having slept in his clothes, Todd was stiff and rumpled and used up. He paced the room, which meant taking two steps to the huge dresser with a mirror, turning, and taking two steps back to the bed, all the while hearing retching noises followed by flushing and running water. Sebby emerged, pale and sweat-damp, his hair slicked back from his face. He brushed past Todd and, shivering, eased himself back into bed.

"Sweetheart, you'll be dehydrated. You need to drink something."

"I drank some water. Go away." Sebby's voice was wan as wax.

"Where am I to go? I am a stranger in a strange land."

"Go talk to Wayne or something."

Todd put his hand on Sebby's forehead. He stroked the damp hair. "You're shivering. I'll lie down with you?"

"If I have to puke again, it's easier if you're not in the way."

"Well, but, what if you need something?"

Sebby's croaking, muffled voice said, "*Dios mío*, I'm hungover, not dying of cancer! Leave me alone."

Todd shut his eyes. He ground his teeth. "Right, then. I'll check on you later." There was no answer, and Todd exited, leaving the door open a crack. He went down the hall and followed the scent of bacon into the kitchen, where Wayne and Ethan sat at the table, used dishes indicating they'd eaten. Ethan was reading the paper. Wayne was hunched over his laptop.

Todd stammered, "Ah . . . good morning, ah . . ." They looked up. "Sebby and I spent the night . . . You probably knew that . . . Ah . . . I'm afraid Sebby's not quite up to taking his leave just yet."

Ethan smiled. "Leo told us. Don't worry about it one bit. Sit yourself on down." He stood and began clearing the table. "I'll fix Sebby a hangover cure, huh? Becca can use one too, eh, honey?"

Becca's voice came from behind Todd. "I don't get hangovers. I'm too nasty." She dropped into a chair next to Todd. "Christ, Wayne, why don't you just hardwire yourself and you won't need one of those?"

"Someday we'll be able to do that," Wayne said in a reverent tone.

"I'm sorry to be a bother," Todd said, "but do you have any coffee?"

"We have an espresso machine. Will that do?"

"Me too, please," Becca said. "So. You didn't do the twinkies?"

Todd raised an eyebrow. "I did not. Nor do I plan to. Ethan, may I help? I can fry eggs."

"Sure, thank you, Todd. Help yourself. I was going to scramble one for Sebby."

Becca's nose wrinkled. "All Sebby's boyfriends do the twinkies. I think all. I dunno. I don't have a scorecard, but it's gotta be close to all."

Glad of an excuse to get away from Becca, Todd went to the stove and started cracking eggs into the hot skillet. "*All* is no longer an accurate quantification for this scenario, if, indeed, it ever was; if it was accurate, however, you may now say 'all but one.'"

"Bite me," Becca retorted.

Sometime later, fortified with bacon and eggs and conversation and several cups of espresso, Todd decided it was time to check on

Sebastián. He carried a tray and was once again waylaid by Becca, who followed and put a hand on his wrist before he reached the hallway.

"Yes?" he said, glaring at her, but unable to continue on his way without risking a spill.

"The way you're going, you won't make it with Sebby."

"It must be nice being prescient. I, myself, am not and must muddle through on instinct alone." Todd took a step, but Becca did not let go of his wrist.

"You seem like a nice guy. I just thought you should know . . . Sebby doesn't go for 'nice' guys. So if you want to, you know, stay with him, you need to mean up."

Todd's eyebrows leaped. "'*Mean up*'?"

"Get a little mean. Not abusive or anything." Becca poked at his shoulder with her other hand. "But if you're too attentive and sweet and shit, he's gonna decide you're a pussy and dump you. All on a subconscious level, of course."

Todd wondered whether it would be a breach of etiquette to tell her to go to hell. Perhaps she would take it as evidence that he was following her advice. "Thank you, Becca; I will give your words due consideration."

"Fuck you. God knows why, but Sebby likes you, and I'd like to see him have a decent relationship."

"If, as you say, Sebby likes me, then perhaps you should revise your estimation of what it is Sebby likes."

"Bite me," Becca said, showing no indication of letting go.

Gripping the tray with one hand, Todd dipped his fingers in the glass of tomato juice and flicked the droplets at her, quickly catching the tray again before it could unbalance.

Becca yelped and let go. "Asshole!" She mopped at her face.

"Napkin?" Todd inquired. He tossed one at her and walked off. Finding the door to the guest room slightly open, just as he'd left it, he peered in to see a Sebby-cocoon.

"Heyyy," he said softly. He tapped on the door. "Are you awake? You should try and eat something."

There was a groan, and a head emerged from the cocoon, squinting at Todd before falling back. "Tooodd?" he wailed, if such a limp and wan sound could be termed a wail. "Come heeere! I thought you left."

"You thought I left! What?" Todd hunted for a place to set the tray, but every surface in the room was lousy with clutter. He set it on the floor and perched on the edge of the bed.

"Someone said you left. I thought you got in your pickup and left." Sebby rolled over and pressed his face into Todd's side.

Todd twisted to stroke Sebby's hair and feel his forehead. Clammy. "*Who* said? Sweetheart, you must have dreamed it. My pickup isn't even here, remember? It's in your driveway."

"I thought you left." Face buried in Todd's side, he inhaled and exhaled noisily. "You slept with Barry and Lawrence, no?"

"No." There was silence. "Here, I made you breakfast."

Sebby pressed closer to Todd's side. "Augh, I can't eat, *chingados*, even the smell, take it away!"

Todd took Sebby by the shoulders and sat him up. "I've prepared for you a hangover cure breakfast, and you're at least going to sample it, or these scrambled eggs are going to have a seat in your pretty hair."

"Eggs are good for hair."

"Not once they've been cooked, you imp!" Todd leaned over and scooped up a bit of egg in his fingers.

Sebby's eyes widened. "Did you just call me an imp?" He rested against Todd. Todd sat him up again with one hand.

"Imp. A sort of little devil, demon thing." He brought the morsel closer. "Egg. Hair."

"Oh, um. Grrugh." He wrinkled his nose. "I can't, I can't, Todd." He gazed at Todd with big eyes. "Don't make me."

Todd's hand dropped. "I wasn't . . . I wouldn't . . . I highly recommend and humbly ask that you sample the repast that I, taking great trouble and forethought, created for you with my own two hands and help from no one unless one counts sarcastic commentary as help." He leaned over for a napkin and rolled it up around the bit of egg.

Sebby huffed. "*Ay caramba*, Todd, you're pitiful. Gimme the damn tray."

"I didn't know that people said, '*Ay caramba*' in real life." Todd fussed with the blankets and sheets, propped pillows behind Sebastián, and placed the tray, which had legs, over Sebby's lap.

Sebby picked up a fork, twirled it in his fingers, set it down. He picked up the glass of orange juice and stared into it.

"Hair of the dog. Bloody Mary or screwdriver. Being the thoughtful fellow I am and not knowing which you'd prefer, I brought them both."

Sebby bit his lip. He replaced the glass, and his eyes wandered over the tray. Spying the aspirin tablets, he reached for them, but Todd caught his hand.

"You can't have aspirin on an empty stomach. Try a bite of toast."

Sebby's hand was limp and clammy in Todd's, but then his fingers wrapped around Todd's and squeezed till it felt as if the knuckle bones might meet through the skin.

"Ow," Todd said.

Sebby let go, pressed his fingertips to his eyes, and took a great, gulping breath.

Todd had never seen Sebby cry, but Vivian had often been weepy during his spells, thus Todd was not as alarmed as he might have been. He perched again on the edge of the bed, carefully, so as not to upset the tray, and drew Sebby's head to his shoulder. "Shhh, imp. I get emotional about toast as well. It puts me in mind of God, for he must love us if he fills the world with toast."

"I d-don't believe in God."

"But, sweetheart," Todd began. Sebby burrowed into Todd, his body shaking with silent sobs. Todd steadied the tray and petted Sebby. Sebby smelled of unwashed sickly sweat, and Todd murmured into his hair, "*Cielito lindo*," which he had found when researching Spanish terms of endearment and which meant, *pretty little sky*. Sebby clutched at Todd's shirt. Still mindful of the tray, Todd rocked him and softly sang a verse of a song he had memorized: "*Ese lunar que tienes, cielito lindo, junto a la boca, No se lo des a nadie, cielito lindo, que a mí me toca.*" Gradually, Sebby's shaking subsided, and Todd picked up a triangular section of toast. "Won't you try and eat something? For me?" He waved the toast.

"Y-y-yes . . ." Sebby lifted his tearstained face, grabbed the toast, and crammed it entire into his mouth as though toast could stop tears. His head bobbed as he swallowed. He reached for the Bloody Mary.

"Oh, almost forgot . . . you may prefer the other . . . I dabbled my fingers in that."

"It'll taste extra . . . s-spicy, then . . ." He gulped at the drink. "W-why were you dabbling in my juice?"

"I flicked it at someone." He slipped his hand under Sebby's hair at the back of Sebby's neck and rubbed at the knotted muscles.

"Oh." Sebby's head lolled. He sighed, and Todd was so reminded of Vivian that he had to look away. Under pretense of rearranging breakfast items, he gave up the neck massage. Sebby's eyes opened. "Why? What'd Becca do?"

"How did you know it was Becca?"

"You mentioned sarcasm before." He took a long drink.

Todd was satisfied to note the glass was half gone. Sebby sipped again and swallowed the aspirin, and as he lowered the glass, Todd laughed.

"What?" His eyes were round and innocent and bloodshot.

"You, *cielito lindo*, have a Bloody Mary mustache." He reached out and traced the line of Sebby's upper lip, his finger coming away tomatoey. He licked his finger.

Sebby looked gravely into Todd's eyes. "I want you. Right now."

Touched, Todd stammered a bit before answering. "You aren't well, and . . . finish your breakfast."

"I feel fine, your hangover cure has cured me, and I want you." He touched Todd's shoulder, his neck, and stroked the lobe of his ear. "Don't say no."

"Sweetheart, oh. I can't here, there's a unicorn staring at me." Todd gestured at a nearby hutch, crowded with knickknacks.

Sebby ran his fingers through Todd's hair, his hand trembling so that it tangled and caught, and Todd winced. "Let it. I don't care. I don't care if the whole world stares."

Todd kissed his cheek, and that was his undoing. Sebby tasted of salty-sour sweat and salty-sweet tears, and Sebby's fingers worked their way through Todd's hair, and Todd kissed him again, and again. And again. Todd had been teased and then deprived the night before, and so he gave in to the inevitable and found that he could after all, even in the presence of a staring unicorn.

Chapter Seventeen

Love Is Selfish

Very late in the morning, they returned to Sebby's house.

"That was a good party, and everyone liked you." Sebby toed off his shoes, put his arms around Todd, and kissed his neck. "Mm, I'm going to take a bath. Do you want to take one with me?"

"Of course," Todd said absently, "but, first, could we discuss, ahhh, the party, and . . . I don't know . . . some things?"

"We can talk in the tub, yes?" Sebby walked backward, pulling on Todd's hand and towing him in the direction of the bathroom. "Your face is so serious. I know you're worrying. It's okay; nothing so bad happened, and even Becca likes you, I could tell."

"I fear they don't like me for myself. It's that, in comparison to your priors, I am apparently a saint."

"My . . . 'priors'?" He laughed and tugged on Todd's hand. "*Ven aquií.*" He leaned back and put all his weight into dragging Todd toward the bathroom.

Todd, shuffling along with Sebby, kept his eyes on the floor. "Do you think I . . . hurt Barry's and Lawrence's feelings? Erm, ah, or yours?"

Sebby stopped. "Is that what's bothering you?" Putting his hands on Todd's face, he tilted him into a kiss. "I'm sorry. I'm the worst boyfriend in the world!"

Drawn by sweet kisses, Todd followed Sebby to the bath.

Sebby's idea of *talking* involved more kissing than words, and it was the sort of assertion that brooked no argument. Sebby straddled Todd's lap and proceeded to loofah his chest.

Todd said, "I didn't mean to be prudish. I didn't mean to imply—"

This line of conversation was interrupted by more kissing. "I tried to push you into it. Because . . . they're my oldest friends, and it's kind of sad: they fell in love, and neither of them likes to fuck. I mean, they like to *be* fucked, so they find someone to do it." He dipped the loofah in the water and brought it, fragrant and dripping, to Todd's neck.

Todd stretched like a cat. "Can't they find someone more . . . permanent, then? Someone for their own?"

"They don't want one." Sebby kissed Todd as he rubbed the loofah over Todd's neck. "My boyfriends always like them. You don't like them?" He blew into Todd's ear.

"Sebby, ah, God! It's not a question of liking them! I want, nay, crave intimacy, and that is something one doesn't achieve on those terms."

"Can you be so sure?" He sucked Todd's earlobe into his mouth.

Todd hissed and pulled him closer. "You said yourself they want nothing permanent!"

"If something's permanent, does that mean for sure it's intimate? I don't think so. So how does the opposite for sure not mean it?" With a sound like an otter going down a mudslide, his lips moved down Todd's neck.

"What are you even talking about! Jesus God, this, *this* is intimacy!" He ran his hands down Sebby's slippery back, into the cleft of his buttocks. "One to one, knowing each other. L—ah . . ." He almost said *loving each other*.

Sebby went still, his face in Todd's neck. He murmured something, and Todd shifted in order to look him in the eye. Lips pursed, Sebby regarded him. "What about Vivian?"

Todd blinked. "What *about* Vivian?"

"If he showed up, you'd be interested in a three-way, I bet." Sebby smiled, but then he dropped his eyes and returned to exfoliating Todd's chest.

Todd's face flushed. A wave of hot blood crested from his heart to his head and on down again, leaving him cold. "What?"

"I'm wrong, aren't I? No, you'd just roll me out of the bed so you could have your *intimacy* with *him*." Concentrating on loofahing, Sebby sighed.

If he hadn't been naked and soaking wet with Sebby in his lap, he would have stormed off in a temper. And Sebby knew it, and that was probably why this conversation was taking place in the bathtub. "What is your point?"

"You don't deny it, though." Bringing the loofah to Todd's chin, Sebby kissed him, a long and gentle and lingering kiss, his tongue barely between Todd's lips, the loofah scraping his chin, and try though Todd might to refuse this kiss, he was unable. Sebby spoke against his mouth. "I'm not getting you to forget him. And I thought maybe you just needed a little meaningless sex, and ours isn't meaningless anymore, and Barry and Lawrence, they're sweet. I thought you'd like 'em, and they could help me."

He paused and bent his head, resting his forehead against Todd's chin. The loofah dropped into the water. He drew a deep breath. "And you didn't want to, and what's that mean?"

Todd's brain wound itself up in a turmoil. And he did not want to think about Vivian; he was fucking tired of thinking about Vivian; he longed for surcease of all Vivian-related thoughts. Deciding to ignore for now the mention of his ex, he said, "A three-way is something one does in college, not when one is a mature adult seeking to have a mature and loving and, yes, intimate relationship. I've done the casual, anonymous sex; I've—"

He realized that he was moralizing again, and he tore a hand through his wet hair. Who was he to judge? Plenty of people had long-standing, healthy, three-way relationships. But that wasn't what Sebby was suggesting. Was it?

"Aw shit. Sebby, I don't even know." He pushed Sebby away, stood up, and climbed out of the tub. "It's cold," he said, yanking a towel from a hook on the wall.

"It's a cold world," Sebby climbed out behind Todd. "Find heat where you can."

"How could you speak to me of monogamy and then wish me to sleep with Ping and Pong?"

Sebby rolled his eyes dramatically. "Don't call them that. I never said *you* had to be monogamous. I asked you if you cared if *I* fucked other boys."

Todd allowed this statement to ricochet around his brain before speaking. "What is that, some fucked-up double standard?"

"Well . . ." Sebby put his lips to Todd's collarbone and then laid his head on Todd's shoulder, his cold nose poking into Todd's neck. "If I've found a good thing, why should I be selfish?"

Todd fidgeted. "Because love is selfish! Shit." He had used the word *love*. Becca's statement came back to him, and his stomach started to hurt, despite the fact that he felt sure she was a deranged harpy. He clutched at Sebby's hands and peered into his face. "Aw, fuck. Am I treating you . . . the way you want to be treated?"

Sebby's eyebrows scrunched. "What d'you mean? I like how you treat me. More than anything." Drawing Todd's hand to his mouth, he kissed Todd's knuckles and whispered, "More than anything."

Todd's stomach settled like a turtle on a sunny rock. "Good. Um. Good. Ahhh . . . if it means that much to you, I suppose I could . . . manage . . . to sleep with Barry and Lawrence."

With a cry of delight, Sebby threw his arms around Todd and planted excited kisses over his face. "Oh, thank you, thank you! I'll call them right now. Maybe they don't have any plans tonight."

Todd balked. It was not what he was hoping to hear. *Todd, I appreciate your willingness to sacrifice yourself, but, no, I do want you all to myself.* "I must stop at home. Ah, rain check?"

Hands on Todd's shoulders, Sebby leaned away and narrowed his eyes. "You didn't mean what you said, Toddfox?"

"I mean it. But I ask for some time to prepare." *What the fuck did I get myself into?*

"You mean get used to the idea. *Querido*, let's just forget it, yes? Do you have to go home? Stay with me a while." Pressing his face into Todd's throat, he made a noise that Todd could only term a coo, and since Todd had apparently lost the ability to refuse Sebby anything, he stayed.

Chapter Eighteen

Olive Branch

*A*s Todd's truck pulled into the driveway, Ryan came sprinting out of the house, a small dog accompanying him and tangling itself in Ryan's feet. Ryan scooped up the dog and met Todd as he exited the vehicle. "Look, Uncle Todd, look, Mom and Dad got me a puppy!" He thrust the dog at Todd, who made a successful grab for the wriggling creature and regarded it nose to nose. It lapped at his face, and Todd laughed and held the roly-poly thing away at arm's length, turning it to and fro.

"Looks like a beagle?"

"It's part beagle. We don't know what the rest is. Help me think of a name for her!" Ryan gazed at the puppy with such love and happiness that his face glowed.

"What changed your mother's mind? I thought she didn't want animals in the house."

A semicrafty, semiguilty look came over Ryan's face, not completely replacing the love and happiness. "Mom felt bad because I was acting depressed about what happened the Fourth of July? So she said I could get a puppy. So we got one." He grinned, and the grin was so like Todd's own that it was a bit disturbing.

"Tugging on the mother's heartstrings to get your way, eh? Well done." He ruffled Ryan's hair, and they headed toward the house together.

"They feel bad for you too. Dad got you baseball tickets. I'm going to teach her to sit and beg and fetch and roll over, and I want to teach her some neat tricks that no other dogs know, like maybe you could think of some?"

"Baseball tickets?" He patted the wriggling mass of canine in Ryan's arms. It licked and then gnawed on Todd's fingers. They entered the house. "Hey, sis. What delectable repast have you prepared?"

"It's chili!" Ryan said. "Mom, can Puppy have chili?"

Donna threw a look of mixed affection and annoyance at Ryan. "Hi, Todd. Ryan, chili is bad for puppies. And put him in the crate while we eat."

"Her, she's a her, Mom! And she doesn't like it in there! She'll cry. Can't I just hold her in my lap while I eat? I promise not to feed her."

"No, Ryan, into the crate! The puppy has to be crate trained, or you can't keep it."

Ryan groaned and whined and put the puppy into the crate, where *it* groaned and whined but soon quieted. The family, minus Kenneth, who was out with his girlfriend, seated themselves around the table. Christopher and Ryan bantered name ideas back and forth.

"I think you should name it Fart," Christopher suggested.

Ryan giggled. "Chili Fart." He shoveled a giant spoonful into his mouth.

"Or Barfbag," Christopher said.

"Poopbutt!"

"Asswipe. 'Cause dogs wipe their ass on the carpet."

"That's enough," Lloyd interrupted. "Todd, I got three tickets for the Rockies game if you and Sebby want to take Ryan."

Todd blinked and somehow managed to keep his jaw from dropping open and displaying a mouthful of masticated cornbread. Ryan squealed.

"No fair!" Christopher protested. "Why should he get to go?"

"Did I say three? I meant four. Pass the honey." Lloyd helped himself to a large slice of cornbread.

It was typical of Lloyd to assume that any American male would enjoy baseball. Todd knew that Sebby did not follow sports, but attending a ballgame was not necessarily about the sport. It was about soaking up the sunshine, eating hot dogs, yelling at the ump, and singing during the seventh-inning stretch. It would be petty to knock aside the olive branch Lloyd was extending, and so Todd smiled. "Sebby and I would enjoy that. Thank you."

Chapter Nineteen

Bunny Eyes

"You're thinking about *him* again!" Sebby accused.

Todd started out of his reverie. "I don't— I, ah— No, I'm not. I'm sorry. Jesus. How did you know?"

Sebby rolled his eyes. "*Chingados.* You're so *obvious.* First you get this thoughtful look. Then you get this little smile. Then your eyes go all foggy, and then your face twists up like someone is pulling your guts out *Braveheart* style." He huffed and folded his arms.

Todd was taken aback, but concluded that Sebastián was probably just better at reading him than most people. "Sorry. I'm sorry. It's—it's your teakettle, it's the same as one Viv gave me, that's all. It reminded me, that's all, I'm sorry. I'll throw that one out and buy you a new one, shall I?"

Sebby huffed again. "*Everything* reminds you of him. I can't protect you from everything! Maybe you should go someplace where nothing will remind you of *him.* Dig yourself a hole in the ground, climb in, pull the dirt over you, and maybe then you won't see anything that reminds you of *him.*"

Wounded, Todd got to his feet and fumbled for his keys, but Sebby stopped him, appearing at his side so suddenly that Todd took a step back.

"No, don't go; I'm a bitch, don't go, I want you to stay." Sebby pressed himself all against Todd's side. "You can't help it. I thought I could make you forget him. It's just taking longer than I thought." He tugged at the sleeve of Todd's T-shirt, smoothed it up, and pressed his lips to Todd's shoulder. "It isn't your fault that he did this to you. Stay."

Todd groaned, dropped his keys, and pulled Sebastián close. He placed kisses over Sebby's face, and Sebby made wonderful gasping, bleating noises, and then Todd did forget Vivian, at least for a while.

The elevator shaft had been completed, and the crew no longer had to climb to the higher levels. Todd adjusted his hard hat and goggles, grinning at Gus as the two of them ascended. "Just think of all the exercise we're missing."

"You're banging Sebby," Gus said.

Todd stammered. "I would not name it so crudely." *As many times as I've imagined or dreaded this moment, you'd think I would have a response prepared.*

Gus's lip curled. "You're the worst kind of queer."

Todd had fielded many insults in his life, but this was a new one. "I beg your pardon?"

"You think if you bang a boy now and then it don't make you gay. Now, I've about had it with nancy bull queers taking advantage of Sebby's good looks and sweet nature. I've a mind to pitch you off this building." He pushed his face into Todd's, their hats knocked, and Todd stepped back.

"Sir, you have it all wrong. I fully admit that I am queer, gay, light in the loafers, on the sway side, or any other epithet you care to assign me."

"You two give each other bunny eyes and think you're invisible. And you strutting around like a rooster. You're horseshit."

Todd ground his teeth. "I've been posturing out of uneasiness as to how the crew would react to discovering a homo in their ranks. They don't seem to mind Sebby, but he has not invaded their territory, as I have"

"He ain't such a pissant, neither." The elevator stopped, and Gus shoved Todd through the opening hard enough that Todd had to run a few steps to catch his balance. "I got my eye on you." He made a V with his first and second fingers, pointed at his eyes, at Todd, at his eyes, at Todd, and stalked off.

"The fuck'd you do, Addison?" Dean stared after Gus.

Todd shook himself. "Eh, I nailed his momma."

Chapter Twenty

Be My Housewife

The yawping of the phone roused Sebastián from a deep sleep, and he reached in the dark for his phone and pressed it to his ear before he was even fully awake. "Hello."

"It's me. Can I come over?"

Sebby rubbed a hand over his eyes, peered at his phone, and pressed it back to his ear. "Todd? What's wrong?"

"Viv called. Can I come over?" The voice sounded strangled.

Sebby tried to wake up and think. He yawned. "It's late, *querido* . . . What did he say?"

"*Please* can I come in? My heart is breaking."

The plea tugged at Sebby's heartstrings, but something was wrong with the words. He yawned once more and started to ask again what Vivian had said when it dawned on him mid-yawn. His jaw snapped shut. "Todd. Where are you?"

"I'm in your driveway. I didn't want to frighten you, so I called."

"Oh, Todd, what?" It was like a splash of ice water. "I'll let you in." He slapped the bedside lamp on. There was something creepy about Todd phoning him from his driveway, but Sebby pushed the thought out of his mind.

"I don't mean to bother you. I . . . If you want me to leave, just say so."

Sebby let out a sigh. "You call me at two in the morning and tell me you're in my driveway and say you don't want to bother me? Todd, you're pitiful. Don't move."

He hung up, rolled out of bed, and thrust his arms through the sleeves of his robe. Knotting the belt, he trotted down the stairs and twitched aside the curtain that hung at the front door, flipped on the outside light and peered out. Todd was coming up the walk, and Sebby opened the door and stepped out to hold the screen door with his body. "Todd. *Mi casa es tu casa. Ven aquí.*"

Todd mounted the steps, and as the porch light reached him, Sebby saw that his eyes were puffy and his mouth was drawn in pain. Sebby closed the distance between them, enfolding Todd in his arms and allowing the screen door to bang shut. Todd clung, and his hands twisted in the material of Sebby's robe.

After a long moment, Sebby patted him. "Come in and sit. Do you want coffee?"

Todd shook his head ponderously against Sebby's shoulder as though the movement required massive hydraulics. "I want to sleep."

"You can sleep. Come in. Let's not stand out here." He backed away, fumbling for the door behind him. Todd plodded into the living room, sank to the sofa, and pulled Sebby to himself with the air of someone who would not take no for an answer.

Sebby recognized a man looking for forgetfulness in fucking, and this was not something Sebby minded. In fact, he had used sex to comfort Todd, offering his body as sort of a healing aid, so why should he be surprised now at the way Todd pushed him back into the sofa and slid his hands under Sebby's robe? It would be simple to allow his body to respond, and it wouldn't be the first time someone had fucked him on this sofa.

Something made him uneasy, though, and so he turned his face away from Todd's kisses. He stroked Todd's hair. "Wait, Todd. What did Vivian say?"

Todd sucked in his breath, and for a second, Sebby thought Todd might ignore him and continue on his merry way, but Todd, always the gentleman, did not. He sat up, once again as though it were a feat of engineering. "Forgive me, you are stunning—" there was a pause and visible swallow "—with your hair all tousled and smelling of bed. I'm afraid I nearly lost my self-control." Todd flashed him a grin, quickly gone, and his mouth fell back into a line of worry.

Sebby sat up, tucking his robe around himself. "So you had the postbreakup talk. Was it so terrible? What'd Vivian say? Does he want you back?" Though he spoke lightly, Sebby's rib cage tightened around his heart as it occurred to him that Todd might have come to say good-bye.

Todd's mouth twisted. "He begged me to come back."

Sebby's ribs collapsed like Lincoln logs, piercing his lungs and halting his breath.

"He begged me and said he didn't know what to do without me. He said he'd do anything I wished. He wanted to elope and be my *housewife*." He dropped his head in his hands and groaned.

Sebby somehow got some air into his lungs and blurted, "He wants you back? What are you doing here?"

"I'd be halfway there if I thought he meant it! Oh, God. Jesus God." Todd straightened and, taking a deep breath, met Sebby's eyes. "Sebby, there's something I neglected to tell you about him . . ." He hesitated.

"Yes?" Sebby's heart was jumping all over the place like a Mexican jumping bean, and, ha, that was funny.

"Viv has a chronic health condition. Much of the time he's fine, you wouldn't even know anything was wrong, but at times . . . he suffers episodes of dreadful pain." Todd squeezed his eyes shut as if he were feeling this terrible pain.

"And you took care of him," Sebby guessed. "Kept him company." Eyes closed, Todd nodded, and things clicked in Sebby's head. This explained so much—Todd's devotion and his anxiety. "No wonder you worry so. Is it . . . a fatal condition?"

Todd blinked and hesitated, and seemed to pick his words carefully. "Not precisely . . . It may shorten his life span, but no one is certain. The condition is so rare, its effects are virtually unknown."

Sebby drew Todd's hand into his lap. "And so he was having one of his bad times when he called you? He was hurting and you couldn't help him." Poor Todd. Sebby's heart went out to him while his stomach twisted in despair, for he knew he could offer nothing so romantically tragic. "Why don't you believe he wants you back?"

"Oh, I ache for him, it hurts." Todd's free hand settled over his stomach as if to hold his guts in. "And I knew— I think I knew he'd want me, and that's why I left, because I would go. If I was there in New York, I'd go to him, and I'd be with him, and then the next day I'd see the look in his eyes, of remorse, of—of . . ."

Todd hadn't answered his question, but the poor boy wasn't thinking straight, and Sebby didn't pursue it. "Remorse for what, that he broke up with you?"

"No! Remorse for asking me to come back, ruing that he called me. And all the recriminations and his family and, God, the horror. I don't want to put myself through that again!"

"But are you so sure?"

"Pretty goddamned sure. No, not sure at all. It's only . . . He's in pain, and he's vulnerable, and yes, he misses me, but does he in all veracity want me back? And if I did drive all the way to New York, by the time I arrived, the episode would be over, and he'd be in possession of himself again, and then he'd feel guilty for making me come back—God, the idiocy of it all." He tore his hand through his hair and looked plaintively at Sebby. "Why did he have to call me? Why now, just when I was starting to feel that I could live through this? When I was getting over him?"

Only the deepest feelings of sympathy kept Sebby from laughing out loud. Todd thought he'd been getting over Vivian? Not from anything Sebby had seen. "I don't know, *mi chico tierno*, but I know you need a drink."

He stood, but Todd, from his seat on the sofa, grasped him and buried his face in Sebby's middle, so Sebby put an arm around Todd's shoulders and with his other hand smoothed Todd's hair, and he let himself be cried on. "*Querido*, I hate to see you so sad."

Todd's arms tightened around him, and he leaned into Sebby, causing him to take a step backward.

Sebby could imagine what it would be like to have the force of this devotion turned on him. He could see how it could wear a person out, and maybe that was why this Vivian had broken up with Todd— he was just too young to stand up to the battering force of Todd's love. It would be daunting to one so young, frightening even.

Sebastián had no such misgivings. To be adored beyond reason, to be idolized, treasured, these were things Sebby would gladly endure. He knew that Todd loved him a little, because he'd slipped and almost said it a few times, but it wasn't the way he loved Vivian.

He kissed the top of Todd's head and gently removed Todd's arms from around his waist. "Stay," he said, holding his hand out in a cautionary motion. "I'll be right back."

Retying the belt of his robe, he hurried to the kitchen, where he pulled out the stepstool in order to reach the liquor cabinet. He poured a measure of Laphroaig into a tumbler and returned to find Todd with his head in his hands. "Here, drink this."

Todd accepted the glass and raised it to his lips as Sebby sat on the arm of the sofa and slid an arm around Todd's shoulders.

Todd's nose wrinkled, and his face twisted into an expression of revulsion as he turned accusing eyes on Sebby. "What is this!"

"It's fifteen-year-old Scotch. I know you don't drink, but it's just what you need right now. Try it. It's smooth as anything." He patted Todd.

The look that came over Todd's face was just short of panic. "I don't *need* a drink! That's self-medicating, and I cannot allow myself to fall into that trap." He pushed the glass violently at Sebby, who made a successful grab and prevented spillage of the expensive Scotch whiskey all over his nice couch. "My mother's an alcoholic; do you know how many times I saw her turn to the bottle seeking haven from her woes? If I can't get through my difficulties without a drink, I'm no better!"

"That's foolishness. You've gotten through all your difficulties all these months. I'm asking you to calm yourself down. Here, think of it as medicinal—"

"That's just what I said! Self-medicating! *I won't do it, do you hear me, I won't.*"

Sebby huffed. "*Coño*, Todd!" Sebby lifted the glass and tossed back the Laphroaig. It warmed the whole way down, and that was what Sebby had wished for Todd: the soothing heat. "All gone. See? I saved you from the evils of drink."

He set the empty glass aside. He flopped into Todd's lap and took Todd's face in both his hands. "I'm not the enemy!" Todd blinked, and Sebby was unsure if any words were sinking into that despair-soaked brain.

Todd's eyes watered. "No, not the enemy. I apologize. I'm not myself."

"I'll make you some warm milk, yes? Like my momma used to make for me. And you'll drink it, yes?"

Nodding vigorously within Sebby's grasp, Todd said, "Yes. A good idea. Warmed milk is a natural soporific."

Sebby didn't know what that meant, but Todd had agreed, and that was all he needed. "*Bueno*. I want you to go upstairs and get in bed and wait for me. You can warm up my bed while I warm your milk. Yes?"

Todd nodded again, and Sebby got up and pulled on Todd's shoulders until Todd was up. He nudged and shoved him to the stairwell and waited while Todd mounted the stairs.

"*Ay caramba,*" he said under his breath and continued talking to himself while pouring milk into a pan. The whiskey was coursing through his veins, and he was careful on the stepladder as he replaced the Laphroaig and rummaged for the Amaretto. Swirling the milk in the pan so as not to allow a skin to form, Sebby added sugar, cinnamon, nutmeg, and cardamom, waiting until the milk was warmed through before adding a shot of Amaretto. If Todd wasn't used to drinking, that should be plenty. He poured the concoction into a pretty Christmas mug and added a cinnamon stick. Sebby went up the stairs, carrying the mug on a large saucer. There was Todd, sitting upright under the sheets, *with his clothes on.*

"That smells good," Todd said, blinking, and Sebby took this as evidence of Todd's mental state, that he had lost his inner thesaurus, because, what, it only smelled *good*?

"Don't you know that to warm a bed you have to be naked? Off with those clothes." Todd just looked at him, and Sebby set the saucer and mug on the bedside table next to Todd, clambered over him, and began unbuttoning his shirt, but Todd took hold of his hands.

"Stop."

"I promise you're safe from me. Fiiine, do you want a nightshirt? I refuse to have people in my bed with their street clothes on. In fact, I think it's rude of you to get into my bed like that. I'm so insulted I might just go sleep on my couch."

Todd gave him the ghost of a smile before he took off his glasses, and then peeled his shirt over his head. He tossed it to the floor. His trousers followed.

Sebby repressed the urge to fetch the clothing and put it on wooden hangers. He sat above the covers, one leg tucked under, and handed Todd the mug of milk. "Stir it with the cinnamon stick," Sebby ordered, and Todd obeyed.

He sipped, and his puffy eyes widened. "It's good." He sipped again, and Sebby could see he was trying to figure out what was in it. "Almond flavoring? You didn't have to go to so much trouble." He took a longer drink and sighed. "It's good. It doesn't even remind me of anything."

Sebby supposed Todd meant that it didn't remind him of Vivian. Sebby bit down hard on his irritation. "Drink it all up, *mi chico*. Do you want a cookie? I should've brought a cookie."

"No." Todd put his hand on Sebby's knee as if to prevent his leaving, and Sebby put his hand over Todd's. He rubbed Todd's knuckles and smiled at him. Without his eyeglasses, Todd seemed so vulnerable. His pretty blue eyes were bloodshot, and Sebby remembered the first time he had looked into Todd's eyes. He'd been crying then too, and pretending about dust, and Sebby had touched him and touched his hair, and oh, he had wanted him so much. Todd's gaze traveled down to where Sebby's robe gapped open and up to Sebby's face, and Sebby's insides scrambled and melted and gelled and melted again. It was startling, the way Todd watched him sometimes, as though Sebby were the best thing Todd had ever seen. Sebby was used to being admired or lusted after, but this was different. It was like Todd meant it, and Sebby couldn't put it to himself any better than that.

He reached out and wiped the moisture from under Todd's eye with his thumb. Todd caught his hand and pressed a kiss to his palm, and Sebby was sure this must be a skill that Todd practiced, because it sent shivers clear up Sebby's arm and through all his limbs.

"Oh," he said, and there came a noise from Todd; maybe it was a sob, but it was hard to say. Todd's arms went around Sebby, he pulled Sebby to himself, and the mug tipped its contents on Sebby and on his nice robe and on his good sheets, and Sebby didn't care; it was warm and fragrant, and Todd was kissing him, and he tasted of almond milk and spices. Todd laid Sebby back and kissed him so gently, as if waiting for Sebby to stop him. Sebby drove his tongue deep into Todd's mouth, moaning just a little. He sneaked his hand between their two bodies to grasp Todd's cock, and it pulsed in his hand when he squeezed. Todd groaned, and some sort of acrobatic maneuver occurred, and Sebby was suddenly facedown and dizzy. He heard his pretty mug hit the floor, and maybe it broke.

There was a brief pause while the bed swayed, and then cold, lubed fingers went up his ass. He gasped at the chill of it and squirmed. The shock was exciting, maybe just because it was unusual—Todd always warmed the lube in his palm first, but this time Todd's cock followed his fingers without even giving Sebby time to adjust, and there was that moment of helpless pain, being pinned and impaled before he relaxed. Then Todd's arms went around him, and Todd kissed his hair and the back of his neck while he fucked him, and oh, Sebby's insides were molten pleasure and hot, sharp pain.

He must have made a noise because Todd stopped, and he was asking if Sebby was all right, and Sebby shouted, "Damn it, Todd, don't stop!"

It felt good to shout, so he shouted again, and he wasn't even sure that he was shouting in English, but Todd must have gotten the idea, because he lifted Sebby to penetrate him more deeply, and *oh just a little longer oh just like that yes Dios mío*—and then there were no more words or thoughts as Todd thrust even harder in the throes of orgasm, sending Sebby into a shuddering climax. The odor of semen mixed with the scents of the spilled milk as Todd discarded the condom, and Sebby collapsed with a drawn-out moan. Todd was touching him, asking if he was all right, and *Dios mío, will Todd* ever *stop worrying?* He managed to breathe one word, if it counted as a word: "'M'okay."

Too spent to move, he let Todd arrange the two of them as he would, and slept.

Chapter Twenty-One

The Way It Sounded

Sebby woke early. He always did; it was a curse. He had decided to spend the day wearing Todd out. Offering alcohol to Todd had been a mistake; he should've just gone with the sex in the first place. It was more effective, anyway.

Todd's face was slack with sleep as he snored. It was a cute snore, and Sebby listened for a few minutes before sliding out of bed.

When he returned, Todd was stirring. Sebby climbed on and straddled him over the covers and blew in his ear. Todd bolted upright and grabbed Sebby by the shoulders. Sebby yelped, and Todd's eyes went in and out of focus before asking, "What time is it?"

"A little before seven."

"Fuck. We're late." Dumping Sebby to one side, Todd leaped from the bed, jammed his eyeglasses on his face, and grabbed his trousers, cursing as his foot came in contact with the fallen mug and sent it skidding. Sebby was pleased to note that it wasn't broken. "Fuck! I'll have to go home for my work clothes! Unless... have I left any around here?"

Sebby watched with amusement as Todd got one leg in and hopped and almost fell. "Calm down, I called in sick for both of us. Come back to beeed." He reclined against a pillow, hoping Todd would look at him in That Way.

"*Both* of us?" Todd gaped. "But, ah. They'll, ah. They'll put one and one together and get *queer*."

"I don't give a shit. Do you give a shit?" He raised his eyebrows. "Come to bed."

"And besides." Todd thrust his other leg into his trousers and glowered. He was going to be difficult. "Who gave you leave to be calling in for me? I am perfectly capable of performing my duties."

"Oh, yes? Come here and *shooow* me how you *perfooorm* your *duuuties*."

"I don't call in sick unless I'm sick!"

Sebby huffed. "Toddfox, you're in no shape to be laboring ten stories above ground. You're emotionally exhausted. And physically too, I bet."

"What the hell do you think I've been doing for all these weeks? I'm emotionally exhausted every. Single. Fucking. Day."

Every day? It hurt Sebby's heart to think so. "I'm sorry." He bit his lip. "That was the reason why I—I could see . . . never mind. If you have to go, you have to go, but I'm worn out. I'm staying home." He pulled the covers over his head and buried his face in his nice soft pillow, with its nice one-thousand-thread-count Egyptian cotton pillowcase.

"Fine."

He heard Todd stomp down the stairs, and it suddenly seemed important that he change the sheets. They smelled of stale milk and stale sex and stale *Todd*. He tossed the covers in a heap and yanked the fitted sheet off. He had gathered them all up in his arms and was about to lug them to the washer when Todd came pounding up the stairs and threw his arms around Sebby, covers and all.

"Sebby!" he panted. "I didn't mean it the way it sounded. Forgive me, I beg you; I'm an ass."

Sebby clutched at his heap of covers, which made a convenient barrier between his naked self and Todd. "I know you're tired, and sometimes people say things they don't mean when they're tired. But sometimes they say what they really mean. It's not your fault. It's my own fault because I thought I could make you forget him. But you're still so attached to him, and it's hard on me, and it's time we broke up."

Todd stepped back. "Ah, God, no. Sebby, don't."

Had he looked that way when Vivian dumped him? Sebby averted his eyes. "I'm sorry. I want you to go. I know it hurts you, and I don't want to hurt you, but you're not even hurt because of me, it's because of when *he* broke up with you."

Todd gently took Sebby's hands in his, but there was a contrasting undercurrent of panic in his voice. "I swear that's untrue. Don't throw me out. Please, I don't want to stop seeing you. Please."

Had he begged Vivian in the same way? "You're not getting on with your life, and I almost feel like I'm part of it, like instead of helping, I'm enabling."

Todd's head snapped up. Sebby wasn't sure of what he'd said, he wasn't sure of anything, he wasn't even sure that he wanted Todd to go. *Couldn't you say you love me, or even just that you care for me?*

But Todd bolted. Down the stairs and out the front door. Sebby heard it slam, and he heard Todd's truck start, the engine rumbling to life and idling in a low grumble. Sebby's knees gave out, and he sat his bare butt down on his nice hardwood floor, his heap of blankets covering his bare legs. He laughed to himself. He'd fallen for a younger man, and the younger man was breaking his heart.

Chapter Twenty-Two

Love Is Not an Addiction

*T*odd threw himself into his truck, slammed the door, sending a shower of rust flakes into Sebby's driveway, and stuffed the key into the ignition. The truck's engine grumbled and roared. *Enabling!* What sort of Dr. Phil jargon was Sebby spouting? Implying that he, Todd, was addicted! To Vivian! Jesus, what a twisted notion.

Step one, consider: Am I powerless over Vivian? Has my life become unmanageable? Todd slammed his fist into the steering wheel and threw the gearshift, cautiously backed into the street, threw the gearshift again, and stomped on the accelerator, careering down the quiet street at twenty-five miles per hour. *God grant me the serenity . . . fuckfuckfuck.*

You haven't been to a Meeting in months, a reasonable inner voice reminded him. *And you do manifest some of the symptoms of addiction.*

That's preposterous! Love is not an addiction!

The inner voice sang a few bars of Robert Palmer.

Goddamn it. I'll go to work, I'll resign, I'll tell them to mail my last paycheck and . . . And what? Where could he run to next? "You great, loping coward," he said aloud.

Go back, the inner voice said. *Go back and be charming, and perhaps he doesn't have enough healthy self-interest to turn away someone who will ruin his life.*

When Vivian had broken up with him, Todd had run away because the rejection had stabbed so deep he was afraid that if he did not allow the wound time to knit, it could reopen and he would hemorrhage to death, but fuck all this, fuck this introspection; when you wanted something, you should fight for it and *step up*. He turned the truck around.

Be a man, he reminded himself as he stepped out of his truck and stumbled to Sebby's door. Nevertheless, he rang the bell instead of barging in. The curtain that hung at the door's window twitched, and Sebby peered out; Todd had the fleetest glimpse of brown eyes before the curtain fell back, there was a puzzling rattle and click, and then the door opened two inches, a chain lock having been placed.

One brown eye was visible through the gap, a lock of dark hair obscuring it. "What?"

Todd tried out a charming grin, though his lips trembled. "Pardon me, ah . . . you look like someone who would appreciate good coffee."

The eye blinked. "There's lots of things I appreciate."

Todd tried to see if a different angle would give him more of a view of Sebby's face. "I can't help being concerned for your coffee needs."

Sebby peered at Todd first with one eye, then the other. "Don't worry about me. Worry about yourself."

"I am, in fact, concerned for myself and, not having taken the time to obtain a morning cup of java—"

"I remember you prefer shit. Go back to it. There's a 7-Eleven down the street."

Todd shifted. Still, the door remained open, and was that not a good sign? "Having been introduced and become accustomed to the finer points of good coffee, I find myself unable to settle for a cheap substitute, even one gaudily arrayed with neon signs and fancy syrups."

One eye regarded him steadily. "Isn't that what you've been settling for? Me? A cheap and gaudy substitute?"

Todd inserted his fingers through the narrow opening in a gesture of appeal, though he touched woodwork and empty air. "No, never. You've never been a substitute for Vivian, and this I swear. I'm wretched that I've made you think so."

The eye dropped its gaze. "Not a substitute, then, a distraction. It's my own fault. I knew that's all I was to you, and I was happy to be that. But not anymore, and that's why I'm cutting it off. I'm not as generous as I thought. It's like sharing you with a ghost, and now it hurts to see how you're ready to run all the way across the country at the wave of his little finger."

"But I'm not! I didn't!"

"Yet. But you're gonna. I'm just something to kill the pain. An opiate."

It was uncharacteristic of Sebby to employ a metaphor, and Todd smiled despite himself: the idea of Sebby as an opiate was madly romantic. He imagined a soul-sick and world-weary version of himself descending into a dim, smoky den, passing through grimy bead curtains that fell back behind him with a sigh. He saw himself passing users who reclined alone or in groups, lost in stupor, and Sebastián, stepping forward through a haze of intoxicant, opening his arms to Todd, his lips curved in a smile, offering blissful, blessed oblivion.

The eye narrowed. "What're you thinking?"

Abandoning any effort at lightheartedness, Todd curled his fingers, still thrust through the door opening. "I must talk to you, and I cannot talk through a door. May I come in?"

"Aren't you late to work?" There was no sarcasm in the tone.

"For you, I am willing to blow off the entire construction industry." Sebby hesitated, and Todd reminded himself not to beg. It was unattractive, and it sure as hell hadn't worked with Viv. "I understand you're upset with me. If you wish me to go, I shall. But first promise me we'll talk later. It doesn't have to be today, if you need some time alone, but tomorrow? Don't say it's over without allowing me to . . ." *To what?* "I cannot bear to be parted like this!"

The eye closed. Sebby sighed and shook his head. "Todd, you are *pitiful.*" Todd held his breath. "Move your hand." Todd obeyed and the door shut; there was the clinking rattle of the chain unlatching, and then the door opened wide. Todd stepped inside. Sebby was wearing faded, ripped jeans and a frayed tee, and the effect was seductive, right down to his bare, brown feet, which Todd found himself wanting to kiss, fetishist or no.

"Thank you," he said gravely. Sebby huffed, shut the door behind Todd, and walked off. Todd trailed him down the hallway, his eyes straying to a horizontal tear in Sebby's jeans just under his left buttock. The tear widened and narrowed with his gait, alternately revealing and hiding his flesh, and Todd had to contain the urge to place his hand there, to thrust his fingers through the rent fabric.

In the kitchen, Sebby dropped into a chair and tucked his hands under his knees, one of which emerged from a wide hole. Todd could feel that knee against his mouth as if he were kissing it.

"You make it." Sebby nodded at the French press. Todd started. Feeling that this was some sort of test, he pulled a bag of Kona beans from the cabinet, hoping he could remember the procedure. He measured the beans, poured them into the grinder, and began turning the crank.

"I want to tell you a story," Sebby said.

"A story?"

"Don't stop in the middle of grinding. The grounds'll be uneven."

Todd obeyed, frowning.

"I once had a boyfriend who hit me."

Todd whipped around. The casual statement sounded like the opening of a bad limerick.

"The first time was right here." Sebby tapped his forefinger just under his eye. "Keep going."

Todd winced, but he scooped the grounds into the French press.

"It hurt, but I didn't make a sound; I was so shocked that it even happened. No one'd ever hit me before in my whole life, not like that, not with a fist. He knocked me down into a chair, and I stared up at him. I could see he wanted to hit me again, but then his face . . . crumpled . . . He was so sorry. He said he didn't know what happened, he kneeled on the floor and put his head in my lap. I was so relieved that of course I forgave him. I believed him that it wouldn't happen again."

Was there a moral to this story? Was Sebby going to compare Todd's angry words to being punched in the face?

"I had a royal bruise. He helped me think of a good lie: that a block of frozen cheese fell on me." He cocked his head. "Who wouldn't believe that? I'm little, and I keep weird shit in my freezer. The second time was here and here." He pointed to his left eye and the right corner of his mouth. Todd had to look away, with the excuse of filling the electric kettle. "I had a black eye and a split lip. Todd, no, use the spring water."

"Sorry." Todd poured out the kettle and fetched the spring water, adding enough to the teakettle for two cups. Waiting for the water to boil, he turned to face Sebby.

"He was just as sorry, and I sat there holding ice to my mouth and petting his head that was in my lap . . ." Gazing off at nothing, Sebby bit his lip.

Was Sebby saying forgiveness was a mistake?

"I was scared. We fucked." He shrugged. "Next day, I called in sick, because shit falling out of a freezer wasn't going to explain my face. But *he* went to work. I cleaned my whole house, cellar to attic, wondering what I should do. Finally, I called him at his job and told him it was over. I said I never wanted to see him again. He begged and even cried. I said I was changing the locks. Then he said I'd be sorry, that no one would ever love me . . ." He smiled at Todd. "But I was firm."

"Sebby—" Todd started, but the teakettle whistled. Todd poured the boiling water into the French press. He set the egg timer.

"The third time," Sebby went on, and Todd groaned, "he was waiting for me in my kitchen. It'd been weeks, and I'd heard nothing, and I'd thought he was out of my life. He still had a key. I'd never changed the locks. He grabbed me and . . ." Sebby stared off into space. "It was so familiar. He wanted sex, and the easiest thing would've been to let him, but instead I fought him. It was stupid. He's way bigger than me." He shook his head. "He could've just held me down and fucked me. He's that strong. But it was like he wanted to make me give in to him. Like it would be different then. Well, I wouldn't. We, um, scuffled, and he brought my arm down on the edge of the counter." Sebby waved his left arm. "I heard it snap. Or maybe I just felt it." He regarded Todd as he spoke musingly. "I blacked out. I woke up on the floor, and he was gone. It must've scared him."

Todd moved to Sebby's side and lifted the arm with which Sebby had gestured. He pressed it to his mouth, kissing the creamy skin on the inside of the forearm, feeling the sturdy bones. Sebby allowed it, but it was as if he was unaware of it.

"This time I knew I'd have to go to the hospital. I called Ethan. Wayne took me, and Ethan and Leo went and had a 'talk' with Collin."

It was the first time Sebby had mentioned the man's name. Cradling Sebby's arm to his chest, he stroked the soft skin. "You didn't go to the police?"

"What were they gonna do? It wasn't breaking and entering 'cause he had a key. They weren't gonna care for one queer beating on another. Anyway." He exhaled. "Leo and Ethan took care of it. I don't know what they did, and I don't want to know. They promised me they wouldn't put him in the hospital, and I suppose they kept their promise. You look like you want to rescue me. There's nothing to rescue me from. It was a long time ago."

"How long?"

"Last year. The timer went off."

"Oh." Not wanting to let go of Sebby's arm, Todd glanced from Sebby to the French press and back. Sebby raised his eyebrows and pulled, and Todd, who could not bring himself to use any force to retain the once-injured limb, let go. He turned and depressed the plunger of the French press and poured two mugs. Behind him, Sebby fetched cream from the refrigerator. Todd sank into a kitchen chair, and Sebby poured cream into Todd's mug as though he had forgotten Todd's coffee preferences.

Sebby was close, and Todd ventured to put a hand on Sebby's waist. "I'm sorry."

Sebby bowed his head. "Did I do the right thing?"

"About what? You mean fighting back? Not going to the police?" Todd pressed his hand against Sebby's waist, and Sebby poured more cream into Todd's mug.

"I'm talking about forgiving him. The first time. I mean, if I'd dumped him right then, the other shit, it wouldn't have gone that far, no? But still. I didn't know. And doesn't everyone deserve a second chance?" He turned a piercing glance upon Todd before again dropping his eyes.

Was he supposed to say that, yes, everyone deserved a second chance, so *give me one*? Pressing his hand yet more firmly to Sebby's waist, he spoke his mind. "You were innocent, Sebastián. It's not your fault that he hit you, that he broke your arm. Even if forgiving him was an error in judgment. I—I don't know. But I don't believe that anyone deserves a second chance to hurt you."

Sebby poured more cream. It sloshed over the rim. "Oh, Todd, I'm hardly innocent."

"I mean insofar as your contribution to or responsibility for the occurrence of abuse." Todd leaned forward and placed his other hand at Sebby's waist. "It was his choice to hit you, to break your arm, independent of anything that you did."

Sebby closed the cream carton, opened it, closed it. "He didn't break my arm on purpose. I'm not excusing it or anything. Just. He didn't mean to do that."

"He meant to hurt you, though. Agreed?"

Sebby exhaled sharply. "I don't know. I don't know if he knew what he was doing. Anyway, it doesn't matter."

Incredulous, Todd said, "Why doesn't it matter?"

"I had to protect myself, yes? So I couldn't take the trouble to find out what was his problem, no? I wasn't going to let him 'practice' a nonviolent relationship on me, tell him to get therapy and stay with him to see how it turned out, see if it would help, see if it would stop." He tried to move away, but Todd's hands seemed enough to stop him. Sebby set the cream down and pressed his fists to his temples.

"Sweetheart. Did you consider that?"

"What d'you *think*, Todd? What d'you think I was thinking about all day while I cleaned my house? Probably I even liked his roughness, so, you see, it was my fault, a little."

Todd nudged as if leading a dance partner. After a moment's resistance, Sebby allowed himself to be moved, and he eased into Todd's lap, putting one arm around Todd's shoulders and resting his forehead against the side of Todd's head, and it seemed to Todd that no one had ever fit so well in his lap. With one arm at Sebby's back and the other winding over his legs and around his hip, Todd tucked him closer. "I reject the notion that his treatment of you could be in any way your fault. Even if he thought you wanted to be hit, which I highly doubt, given your description of his remorse, then he certainly knew you did not want to be hit *again*."

"That's not what I mean. I mean that by choosing him— Oh, I'm worn out. I can't think. I give up." He slumped, and his face touched Todd's neck. "I give in."

"Give in to what?"

"This," Sebby said, without moving.

Troubled, Todd blurted out what had worried him since the party at Ethan's. "Do you *want* someone to be mean to you?"

"*No*," he said, voice muffled against Todd's neck.

"I ask because Becca said . . ." Todd hesitated and stroked Sebby's back. "Becca warned me that if I were too nice, you would dump me."

"Oh, Becca."

"And Leo said—" Todd hesitated again "—that you had brought home some 'doozies.' I am unsure as to the definition of that particular epithet, but the implication was men who did not treat you with respect." Sebby made an indecipherable noise. "Sebby . . ." Struggling for words to erase the hurt, words that were not mere excuses, Todd allowed his hand to stray up Sebby's back and under his hair. "I am a louse and I said something I didn't mean. Exaggeration. You may have noticed I have a tendency, nay, even a talent for that particular medium?"

"So you didn't mean *every* day?"

"No, no. Every day originally, but not now. Not for many days. I am desolate that I've hurt you, you who have been so kind to me, and more than patient. Anyone else would've thrown his arms up in disgust. And you've . . ." He choked and cleared his throat. "More than anything, you've brought me out and made me see, ah . . ." He choked again and reached for his coffee.

"What. What? See what?" Sebby tensed and raised his head.

That I can love again. "Many things," Todd said into his mug. "My point is— My point is . . ." What was his point? Todd remembered something. "Even Gus said something about it."

Sebby bolted upright and went stiff. "Gus? What'd he say?"

"'Nancy bull queers,' whatever the hell that is. I'm guilty by association. Everyone assumes because I am your boyfriend that I am a brute."

"*Ah, chingados*, I'm not a victim!" Sebby covered his face with his hands and reslumped.

"Are you a masochist?" Todd tightened his hold. "It's all right if you are."

"No." Sebby's cheek touched Todd's shoulder. One hand twisted in Todd's shirt.

"I, in point of fact, wasn't nice to you to begin with, and my behavior didn't deter you one iota."

Sebby scoffed. "Do you think you're scary, Todd?"

"Well . . . scary . . . no . . . but—"

"You're *cute*." Sebby slammed the palm of his hand against Todd's chest. "Swaggering around like a little boy in cowboy boots thinking you're fooling everyone that you're tough."

Todd flushed and pursed his lips. "Right, then. So we can rule out potential dominator as your reason for seducing me. Why, then? Sweetheart . . ." Shifting in his chair, he repositioned Sebby to look into his eyes. "Am I that different from your priors? Do you prefer someone who is more . . . tough? Ah, dominant? I can be more—"

"*No*, Todd. *Mierda*, is that what this is about? Why do I like you?" He grasped Todd's collar, held his gaze, and spoke in a hoarse, tight, and vibrating voice. "Because every day you looked at the mountains. And every day I could see your heart was broken. And every day you set your jaw and went to work, and first you really didn't notice me, but then you did. And, oh, I don't know, I'm not good with words like you; I can't say things like what you say. Don't ask me anything else; take me to bed."

Todd hesitated; he swallowed hard.

"Take me to bed!" The request tore at Todd's heart. "I hurt, Todd; take me to bed."

What could Todd do but take him to bed?

Chapter Twenty-Three

Manipulative Bitch

Sebby had not known that he could be such a manipulative bitch. He buried his shamed face in Todd's side. The Collin story had come out in orderly and sane words, but Sebby had slowly realized that he wasn't telling Todd something he ought to know about his boyfriend, he was telling Todd something to steer worrying away from his ex and toward Sebby. Then, to make it seem less awful, Sebby had lied and said it happened *last* year, when really his cast had been off only a short while when he'd met Todd. And Todd had made love to him with such tenderness that it had hurt more than when he'd been forceful.

And after the sex, instead of falling asleep, Todd had laid Sebby back and sung to him. It was the most beautiful thing ever. Sebby gazed into Todd's eyes, beyond the point where he could be embarrassed. They were so close that Sebby could feel Todd's stomach tighten with the effort of song. It was the most intimate moment of his life, and he knew it would all be downhill from here. Nothing could ever top this.

Now Todd slept, but Sebby lay awake under the jumbled sheets, with which he had hastily covered the bed when they had come back upstairs.

Things were out of control, and Sebby did not like out of control. How had the situation gotten to this point?

It had *never* taken him so long to get a man he wanted. A tilt of the chin, a touch, and a man would follow him anywhere. But Todd had been wary, it had taken *weeks*, and Sebby had been about wild with wanting. So the sex was probably not as great as he thought it was. Just because Sebby's insides melted like almond bark in a double boiler whenever he thought about it . . .

And then there was the sentimental stuff. To most men, in Sebby's experience, romance was a means to an end, and that end had better arrive quickly. A meaningful look, a run of the fingers through Sebby's hair: that was as romantic as things got. Todd was just so over the top that Sebby at first hadn't known what to make of it. It was cute, it was funny, but he hadn't taken it seriously until he figured out it was just Todd, as much a part of him as his smile or his nearsightedness. Then everything had changed, and it was out of control, and Sebby was thinking about forever, and he didn't even believe in monogamy, it was too much to expect of a person, and *qué mierda*, this was ridiculous. He sat up and poked Todd in the shoulder. "Todd."

Todd groaned and grumbled and woke up. "Yeah. What. Oh, morning. Again." He reached for Sebby, who drew back.

"I want to ask what you want for lunch, and also I want to tell you something."

"I will eat whatever your fair hands prepare. What do you have to tell me?" Todd fumbled for his glasses.

"You might decide to leave again." Sebby drew a deep breath. "I told you the story about Collin to make you feel sorry for me and make you want to stay with me. *Dios mío*, I'm terrible!" Sebby covered his face with his hands, and seconds passed before he dared to peek out.

Todd's face was scrunched up in consternation. "Are you saying you made that whole thing *up*?"

"No, no, no."

"W— But— Ah . . . I don't understand."

"I was . . . I was . . . You worry about Vivian so much, and I wanted you to worry about me. A little."

Todd's expression softened, and he got that look in his eyes, the one that made Sebby think that Todd must love him some, and he moved toward Sebby, who scooted away. "Sebastián, *ven aquí.*" The edge of the bed forced Sebby to stop or fall, and Todd took his hand. "You wanted to bond me to you."

"Um, bond?" Sebby twisted uncomfortably. "I don't know, I . . . I think I'm a manipulative bitch." He couldn't meet Todd's eyes. Todd pressed his forehead to the back of Sebby's hand. His shoulders shook, and Todd made a strangled noise that Sebby did not at first recognize as laughter. Indignant, he tipped his head to peer at Todd. "What? Are you laughing at me?"

Todd straightened and smoothed his expression, though his mouth twitched. "Imp. You think you might be manipulative? Or controlling?"

Cautiously, Sebby said, "Not usually . . . am I?"

"This is the second time you have falsely reported to my employer that I am ill. Don't do it again! It isn't that I don't appreciate an illicit day in bed with you, but—"

Sebby interrupted, "You were so tired and upset. I didn't want you slicing your arm open or *falling off a building*! Coffee or not."

"That's a controller's world view: that he acts in the best interest of the controllee, because the controllee cannot be trusted to act in his own best interest."

Sebby huffed and moved to get up, but Todd had hold of his hand and had somehow gotten an arm around his waist and was pulling Sebby to himself.

"Don't you need to call Vivian?" Sebby reminded, and he sucked his breath in, astounded at himself. What was *wrong* with him?

Todd tensed, his breath quickening, and it stirred Sebby's hair. "Yes. Ah, I should make sure he's all right."

He made no move.

Sebby's turned his head and rubbed the tip of his nose against Todd's cheek. "Would you rather have privacy or moral support?"

"Oh, moral support, to be sure." Sighing, Todd released him and rolled to the opposite side of the bed, leaning his torso over the edge and fishing his cell phone from where he had dropped his trousers. Todd sat up and gathered a blanket into his lap as he pressed his phone to his ear. He began finger-combing his hair. "Viv? How are you? Feeling better? Ah . . . any discomfiting memories returning to you?"

Sebby remained where he was and watched. *He* was on the other end of that signal, and a chill drained down Sebby's spine.

Shoulders hunched, Todd faced the wall. "It's good to hear your voice too. I was worried. Are you . . . more in possession of your faculties today?" Another pause. "That is what I meant, yes . . . I do, I . . ." Todd waved his hand in the air in a slicing motion. "Viv, it would be a dire and dreadful mistake for us to elope."

Sebby rolled his eyes.

"And what was all that nonsense about putting off college and being my 'housewife'? You *must* go to college. With apologies to housewives everywhere, a person with your gifts shouldn't be limited in that way."

So Todd thought *he* had *gifts*? Shocker.

"Wait. What . . ." Todd sputtered. "What happened to what *you* want?" There was a pause, and then Todd said, "Oh, Viv," and what had *he* said to bring that warmth into Todd's voice? Sebby fidgeted. "But, Viv, I had to. I couldn't have stayed; I would've been reduced to stalking. You would've seen me at the fringes of your graduation ceremony, a furtive figure in a trench coat." There was an awkward laugh, cut off. "I'm sorry, I was teasing. Of course I wouldn't have stalked you . . . I— Viv, help me to understand: why did we break up, then? . . . Oh, sweetheart, shhh, I'm sorry; I know you're sick."

Manipulative bitch. Sebby scowled. Horridly fascinated, he watched as Todd's free hand made a petting motion in the air. On impulse, he crept forward and ducked his head under Todd's hand. The hand settled on his head and stroked his hair, and a shiver went all through him. Todd wasn't even aware of Sebby, and the way his fingers moved through Sebby's hair was subtly different. In a perverse way, it was reassuring because it proved what Todd had said: that Sebby was not a substitute for *him*; Todd touched Sebby differently.

"I know, Vivid, forgive me." *Vivid?* Sebby cringed; the pet name was unbearably sweet, unbearably Todd. "I wish that too, I . . ." He glanced at Sebby. "You're still not yourself, I fear. I'll let you rest. I'll call you later . . . Yes, I promise. Love-you-bye." It hurt more than Sebby would've thought possible, hearing him declare aloud to Vivian what he had never said to Sebby. Todd ended the call, and his hand became familiar again at the back of Sebby's head.

"Jesus," Todd said meditatively.

That was it, then. Todd was leaving. Sebby flung his arms around Todd. He put everything into the kiss, all his longing, all his hopes. There was nothing to hold back. One hand tangled in Todd's hair, *Dios*, it was getting so long, and he hadn't noticed; his other hand clutched at Todd's back as if to sink his fingers through the skin. The kiss broke.

"Ow," Todd said.

Sebby tilted his head back and smiled, though his whole face felt tight, like the skin might just split right open. "He did mean what he said. He wants you back."

Todd blinked at Sebby. "Was that a congratulatory embrace? I suppose . . . Perhaps it would be a relief to you, to be well rid of me. But I'm not going."

The words were so unexpected that Sebby was sure he'd heard wrong. "Wait. What?"

"Sebastián. How can I leave you?" Todd's hand stroked the back of Sebby's neck in a hypnotic motion; it seemed to put Sebby's body to sleep, at any rate. He couldn't move, though his brain screamed at him to do so.

"*¡No chingues!* Don't, oh, don't fuck with me, I was right here, I heard you, you said you love him, and last night you said you'd be halfway there if you thought he meant it, and now you know he meant it. He means it." Some internal shutoff clicked, and Sebby stopped babbling.

Todd rubbed his forehead and sighed. "He wants me back *now*. But tomorrow? When he's no longer on painkillers? I couldn't bear the regret in his eyes. He has his family. He doesn't need me." Closing his eyes, he repeated, "He doesn't need me."

Sebby bit his lip. Todd was staying? He couldn't quite grasp it. "Need and love aren't the same thing. We like to think they are, but they're not. If you're staying because . . . of me, that's one thing, but . . ."

Todd's eyes opened and searched Sebby's face. "I am not the most prudent prune in the prune jar. Nor are my decisions often reasoned or well-thought-out. But I can't leave, not now. I don't promise anything; I can't. Shit. I don't even know what I'm saying."

Sebby drew a deep and shuddering breath, and some feeling returned to his limbs. "I don't expect promises. We've had a rough night; let's leave it, for now, Toddfox. What do you want for lunch?"

Chapter Twenty-Four

Apology

"I'm still in love with Vivian," Todd said. "I can't see myself ever not being so."

Holly groaned. "Todd-o. Are you thinking about going back to New York?"

"I miss him terribly. And I worry about him constantly." He paused. "But no."

"Well, okay, then. Give it time. Oh, guess what? I got a gig! At a dinner theater! *Sweeney Todd!*"

"Ha, really? Will they be serving meat pies?"

Sebby gave Todd his own key, and Todd came and went as he pleased. He hung his good clothes beside Sebby's, and his work clothes took up a dresser drawer. A razor and toothbrush found their way into the bath. His books were quietly filed away on Sebby's shelves. Long summer days shortened imperceptibly as fall approached.

To Todd, Sebby's home was a comfort, a refuge. He wasn't sure how Sebby felt about it. Todd didn't ask, and Sebby didn't say.

The day of the baseball game arrived. Ryan hopped as they emerged from the dark tunnel into the stadium proper, while Christopher feigned indifference, eyeing the crowd with a bored eye. They found their seats, Christopher and Ryan together between Sebby and Todd.

Ryan and Christopher pored over the program, and Todd's and Sebby's eyes met over their bent heads. Sebby gave a smile of rare sweetness, and Todd was filled with that warmth and belonging of having a family.

Lloyd had included spending money in his olive branch package, and they spent it: nachos, popcorn, hot dogs, coffee for Todd, beer for Sebby, and liters of pop for the two boys. The game progressed, and Christopher by impatient bits relayed the rules of baseball to Sebby, who did not even know what an *inning* was. Each time Christopher took it upon himself to explain some blow of the game, Ryan looked away or buried his nose in his program.

"Ryan, do you want one of those?" Sebby asked, noting his admiration of a giant foam finger. "I'll get you one."

Ryan glanced at him sidelong and leaned closer to Todd. "No, thank you."

Todd saw Sebby's smile falter and tried to communicate with his eyes that Sebby shouldn't take the snub to heart. He leaned over to breathe into Ryan's ear, "You don't have to hurt his feelings."

"What?" Ryan shouted, forehead wrinkled in puzzlement.

Sebby yelled at Todd, "I have to piss!" and with a jerk of his chin indicated that Todd was to accompany him.

"Yeah, okay, me too. Don't leave your brother!" he ordered, and both boys nodded. Out of the sunshine and into the cool, concrete darkness, Todd followed Sebby to the nearest restroom. Men jostled each other in line for the urinals and discussed the game.

"Ryan *hates* me!" Sebby wailed.

"He does not hate you. He'll get over it." Ahead of them a man about their own age lifted his young son to help him reach the urinal.

"Get over what? Why does he hate me?" Sebby's expression was so distressed, his lower lip caught between his teeth, his forehead creased between his eyebrows, that Todd couldn't help chuckling.

"You, *cielito lindo*, are not accustomed to people taking a dislike to you, are you?" Todd watched as the father lifted his son again to help him wash his hands.

"But whyyy? What'd I do?"

"You hit his favorite uncle. *C'est tout.*"

Sebby digested this in silence as they reached the front of the line and took care of business. They washed their hands, and Sebby glared at Todd in the mirror. "You deserved it."

"I told him that, or something to that effect." Todd ripped out a handful of towels and passed some to Sebby. Sebby accepted the towels and dried his hands, staring at them unblinking as he blotted between his fingers, patted his wrists, his palms, the backs of his hands.

"You think you deserved to be hit?"

"Weeell, you can't call that a hit. More of a love tap. Come on, let us away." Todd put his hand on Sebby's elbow.

"Ryan's right to hate me. ¡*Mierda*! Lovers shouldn't hit each other." Sebby blinked rapidly, and Todd moved closer, sliding his hand from Sebby's elbow to rub his back.

"You were overwrought. You slapped my face. It didn't even leave a mark. It's not as if you broke my arm or anything." As soon as the words slipped out, Todd regretted them. If severing his tongue would have taken the words back, he'd have bitten down and swallowed the blood.

Sebby didn't seem bothered by the reference. He tossed the towels in the wastebasket. "It's a matter of degrees, yes? I can hit you as long as I don't leave a mark." He hurried from the restroom, Todd trailing behind.

"I don't say that hitting . . . That wasn't even hitting. It was a slap, and, true, I would say that, in general, slapping one's lover is a bad idea. However, when said lover has frightened one nearly to death with—"

Sebby rounded on Todd, who came to an abrupt halt. "You can always justify it, you can justify anything. I need to apologize to Ryan." He turned again on his heel and marched off through the press of the crowd.

"Right, then." Todd hurried to catch up and once again took hold of Sebby's elbow. "Why don't you begin by apologizing to me, and I will speak to Ryan?"

Sebby stopped. His eyebrows arched. "So you do think you deserve an apology?"

"Love means never having to say you're sorry," Todd quipped.

Sebby rolled his eyes and shook off Todd's hold, continuing along the concrete walkway, Todd pursuing, till they reached the turn and began ascending the ramp into the daylight. It occurred to Todd that he had once again unwittingly used the word *love*, and his insides twisted.

"Sebby. Sebby!" Todd called, and Sebby stopped, turning to him with arms folded and a hostile expression on his face. "If an apology would make you feel better, have at it. I, myself, do not require one of you. I— You didn't *hurt* me. In point of fact, it was I who hurt you."

Sebby's expression did not change. "It didn't hurt you when I hit you?"

"Honestly, no. I would've forgotten it, had Ryan not returned my attention to it." Sebby's gaze intensified, and Todd realized that, somehow, he'd said the wrong thing. "It stung, it sobered me, rather. It made me realize how much I had worried you. I—" But Sebby had spun on his heel again and walked off, and Todd hurried to follow.

They reached their row and began to edge in past the other spectators. "I'm going to talk to Ryan," Sebby said over his shoulder.

"Sweetheart, don't do that. Let me talk to him."

"You don't even understand the situation. You'll just make him think it's okay to hit and be hit. And then someday if someone hits him, he'll think it's okay."

"Sebby, for God's sake, you're blowing this all out of proportion."

Sebby, who was smaller and nimbler, wove his way down the row more quickly than Todd, who excused himself as he stepped on toes or kicked shins.

"Stop!" he bellowed, and Sebby turned as he reached his seat and faced Todd, lips pressed in a thin, determined line. Christopher and Ryan looked up at the two of them as Todd grasped Sebby's arm. "No."

Sebby's eyebrows arched. "No?"

Todd was firm. "I said 'no.'" Their eyes locked. Todd's heart trembled with the effort, but it was Sebby who first lowered his gaze and dropped into his seat. Todd let go a sigh. "Move down," he said to Christopher, and the two boys obeyed so that Todd could take Christopher's seat next to Sebby.

Drawing Sebby's hand into his lap, Todd leaned to press his mouth to Sebby's ear while Sebby stared straight ahead, as if baseball were fascinating. "You'll make him more uncomfortable, don't you see? Sebby, sweetheart, darling of my eyes, he's eleven. The last thing he wants is a heart-to-heart from his uncle's boyfriend about lovers hitting one another. Jesus." Sebby's head bowed, his chin drooped. Todd squeezed the limp hand, massaged the fingers. "Let him warm up to you in his own way. I promise he will." Sebby nodded, his expression defeated. "Come to the house after the game. Make a fuss over Ryan's puppy. That's a sure way into his good graces."

Around them, the crowd rose to its feet, roaring, a giant, many-limbed thing intent on victory. Todd and Sebby were alone, and in that moment when all eyes were on the field, Todd briefly pressed his lips to Sebby's before springing up and pulling Sebby with him, throwing their joined hands in the air and shouting.

Sebby said something. Todd leaned close to hear, and Sebby repeated, "Double play. We're at bat again." And Todd laughed out loud that Sebby should have learned baseball so fast. "I was watching," said Sebby.

The Rockies proved victorious, and the jubilant crowd ebbed and flowed its way toward the exits. Todd led the way, and Sebby brought up the rear. "Do you want to sit up front, Ryan?" Sebby asked.

"Yeah! Shotgun!" Ryan leaped in an effort to slap a hanging sign as they passed under a low archway, missing it by at least a foot. Christopher jumped and brushed the sign with his fingertips.

"I should get shotgun. My legs are longer," Christopher grumbled.

"Yeah, but I wanted to ask you about batting averages." Sebby tapped his finger on the program. "What is it an average of? I mean, what numbers are they averaging?"

Christopher slowed his steps in order to peer at the tiny numbers. "It's, like, their at bats and their hits, like, divided or something. Like, 0.300 or higher is good."

"That doesn't sound like an average."

Todd could hear the frown in Sebby's voice, and he smiled to himself.

Christopher continued. "Yeah, no, it's not really. It's—we learned it in algebra—it's . . . what-do-you-call-it, when there's like two dots between the numbers, and you say 'to,' like 'two dot dot three,' but you say 'two to three,' and it's like really a fraction, like it would be two thirds, kind of."

"A ratio. Ohhh. That makes more sense." As they reached the parking area, Sebby went on explaining to Christopher what a ratio was meant to express, and Christopher explained to him how batting averages were important in baseball. Sebby had discovered the joys of sports statistics. Taking advantage of their preoccupation, Todd turned to take Ryan's arm and pulled him forward.

"Ryan, my lad." He wondered how to broach the subject.

"That was fun, Uncle Todd!" Ryan skip-hopped and, spotting the car, ran ahead.

"Watch the traffic!" Todd shouted, taking off after him through the parking lanes and catching up at the car's bumper. "Jesus. Don't do that. Another close call is all I need, nevvy, to be forever banned from your presence."

"That wasn't close."

"Ryan, ah. I want to talk to you about something . . ." Todd glanced behind them to make sure of Sebby and Christopher, but he couldn't spot them through the hordes of sports spectators.

"Okay."

"Sebby is, well, important to me, and I don't like seeing his feelings hurt."

Ryan gazed at him, jaw slack and eyes wide. "Who hurt his feelings?"

Todd lowered his eyeglasses in order to give Ryan an over-the-spectacles piercing stare. "You know very well who."

Ryan gulped. "You mean me?" Pleased at the success of his intimidation tactic, Todd frowned, folded his arms, and nodded. Ryan kicked at the car's tire. "Well, I don't like him."

Todd gaped and considered how to respond. "I don't require that you like him, Ryan. But I do require that you are cordial and respectful. Keep in mind that I care for him. If you care for me, you won't want to hurt his feelings." He thought that sounded awfully damned good.

"What about me?" Ryan burst out. "He hurt my feelings, and he hurt your feelings, and I don't like him!" He turned his back on Todd and stomped to the passenger door. "Unlock it!" Ryan jerked on the door handle.

"Why, Ryan!" Todd exclaimed. At that moment, Sebby and Christopher approached, deep in numeric discussion. Todd pressed the remote unlock and hissed, "Be nice." Ryan's eyebrows remained pulled down over his eyes. He yanked the door open and plopped into his seat, crossing his arms and glaring at the glove compartment, kicking his toe at the car's interior. Sebby and Christopher climbed in behind.

"Safety belts!" Todd announced. When Ryan didn't move to obey, Todd realized that this was a challenge to his authority. "Ryan, please. I cannot in good conscience operate this vehicle unless all passengers are secured."

"Put on your seat belt, dumbass." Christopher smacked the back of Ryan's head with the heel of his hand. Ryan's head flew forward, and he yelled.

"*Dios mío*, don't hit your brother!" Sebby said in tones that proclaimed he could not believe such things occurred, brothers hitting one another.

"Don't you talk about hitting!" Ryan said. "You . . . hitter!"

"Oh dear." It was Sebby's voice, and Todd cranked full around in his seat to see that Sebby sat still, regarding Ryan with big eyes. Slowly, those eyes turned to Todd, his mouth opened and closed, and he swallowed. Todd could see the words wanting to rush out, but Sebby was deferring to him. Todd was of half a mind to submit Ryan to Sebby's lecture; it was no more than he deserved.

"Shut up, retard!" Christopher hit Ryan again, on the side of his head this time, as Ryan had turned to glare at Sebby. With a cry of rage, Ryan launched himself at Christopher, and the two locked in one brotherly jumble of pummeling. Sebby and Todd both reached to intervene, Sebby wincing at the blows the boys landed on each other, and Todd grasping Ryan around the waist and pulling him back to his seat.

This is what it means to have a family, he thought sourly.

"Boys!" Sebby cried, but he stopped. Sebby had no brothers and thus had no concept, as Todd did, of the rough-and-tumble violence that is brotherhood. Both boys sat, breathing hard, Christopher's face flushed and angry, Ryan's twisted in a desperate effort to keep tears at bay.

"Right, then. Thank you for putting the perfect cap on this marvelous outing," said Todd.

"Retard," Christopher muttered under his breath.

Todd rested a restraining hand on Ryan's leg. "You can hardly claim surprise, Christopher, when your brother reacts to your name-calling and head-thumping." He drew a deep breath. "Safety belts on *now!*" he ordered, and was relieved to see the belts extending and hear the clicks as they locked. "As for the underlying reason for your upset, Ryan . . ." He paused. He chewed his tongue, feeling all eyes on him, though the weight of Sebby's was heaviest of all. "What, Ryan, would make you feel better about Sebastián's having slapped my face? A public apology? A stint in the stocks?"

"Hit him back," Ryan mumbled, shooting a glare at the backseat.

"*Sí*, Todd, hit me back," Sebastián murmured, and, in the rearview mirror Todd glimpsed Sebby's long-lashed lids falling and rising in coy invitation.

Todd slammed his fist on the steering wheel. "Ryan, I will never hit Sebby, never. Do you hear me? Never." He eyed Sebby in the mirror, turned to stare at Ryan and then at Christopher. "*Never.*"

Christopher's eyes rolled. "God, can we go home? Ryan's just a pissy little baby."

"I'm not a baby!" Ryan protested.

"If Uncle Todd doesn't care that he got his face smacked, why should you care? God!"

"Maybe Ryan wants to hit me." Sebby leaned forward, putting his face within Ryan's reach. "Do you, Ryan? Would you feel better then?"

"Yeah," Ryan said, a hard glitter in his eye as his safety belt went zinging into its retainer. The boy turned toward Sebby, raising his hand. A surprised laugh erupted from Christopher.

"Jesus. *Stop*," Todd caught Ryan's wrist and twisted in his seat so that he could regard them all. "This is ridiculous! No one is going to hit anyone. Sebby, what's gotten into you? What happened to violence solving nothing and not wanting Ryan to think that hitting is okay and—" He realized suddenly that Sebby had forced him into this position, the manipulative little wretch. "I give up. Have at it.

But I insist that, whatever takes place, safety belts remain fastened the while."

Ryan buckled his belt again, eyeing Sebby and his uncle by turns. Christopher made an exaggerated *aww* of disappointment.

"You're right to be mad at me, Ryan," Sebby said. "I shouldn't've hit Todd. I'm sorry that I did. You don't hit people that you care about, and that includes brothers."

"Who says I care about brothers?" Christopher kicked Ryan's seat. "Dumbass pissy baby started it."

"I don't forgive you!" Ryan shouted at Sebby, ignoring Christopher's baiting. Todd ground his teeth, making his way through the throngs of people as the endless line of vehicles crawled toward the parking area exits.

Sebby went on. "It's okay. I don't blame you. People that you care about shouldn't hit you, it makes you feel horrible, yes? Like it's your fault. But it isn't, it's their fault."

"It's your fault!" Ryan shouted.

"That's what I say: it's my fault."

Todd could keep quiet no longer. "I don't give a good fuck whose fault it is! Drop it!"

"I'm telling Mom you cussed," Ryan said.

"The truth is, the truth is . . ." and Todd paused to gather the truth to himself. "The truth is, that a friend of Sebastián's was once hurt—" he heard Sebby's indrawn breath and forged ahead "—by some men like the ones we encountered on the Fourth of July. And so he was frightened that the same thing might happen again. I was behaving irresponsibly, and he was afraid for me, and for you, Ryan, and for himself. It's understandable that, given the circumstances, he slap—" and Todd sliced his hand through the air "—not hit!—the person who had frightened him so. It rather sobered me, as was his intention. Nevertheless, he is sorry, and let's have an end of it!"

It was quiet in the car. Sebby would not meet his eyes in the rearview mirror. Ryan turned away, leaning his arm against the window and his head on his arm. Christopher, regarding Sebby curiously, asked, "What happened to your friend?"

There was more silence, and, in the mirror, Todd could see Sebby looking out the window, his face expressionless, his eyes darting as if following faces in the crowd. "I don't want to talk about it."

Chapter Twenty-Five

Every Man

Todd's twenty-fourth birthday came and went. "I'm catching you up," he said to Sebby. He tried not to think about how it widened the gap between himself and Vivian.

One evening, Todd sprawled on Sebby's sofa with a book of poetry and a large mug of coffee. He was alone in the house. Sebby had gone out to a horror flick with Barry and Lawrence. Right in the middle of a sonnet, the landline rang. Without taking his eyes from his poetry, Todd reached for the cordless extension, which was, after all, right next to him, and answered unthinkingly, "Todd here."

A noise answered him, something like, "Uhhhn," before the caller hung up. Todd realized that the caller might have thought he had a wrong number. He had no business answering Sebby's phone. When it rang again, he let it go to messaging.

At the sound of a key in the lock, Todd marked his place and, noting the late hour with surprise, rose to greet a flushed and sparkly-eyed Sebastián, a Sebastián whose hair was mussed, a Sebastián who threw his arms around Todd and pressed kisses to his neck. "Mmm. You smell good."

Todd could not say the same; Sebby smelled of booze and smoke, and Todd wrinkled his nose. Sebby leaned into him, forcing Todd to support him, and Todd realized that the flush and the sparkle were alcohol induced. He let go a sigh. "Did you drive home?"

"Nooo, Granny Todd, Barry was the whatzis driver tonight. Just a few drinks, anyway. After the movie. Um." Sebby teetered, and Todd walked backward, guiding him to the sofa where the two of them collapsed in a sort of heap, and Sebby apparently found this very funny. He looped his arms around Todd's neck and insinuated his leg in between Todd's, pressing his thigh against Todd's crotch.

The phone rang.

Todd said, "Oh . . . someone called earlier, twice. Maybe you want to answer that."

Sebby leaned over backward, wiggling his fingers in the general direction of the phone. Todd had to grab it for him and place it in his hand.

"Hellooo? Oh, you." Sebby sat up. "Fine. No, no, fine. Thank you. Wellll . . . no. I'm with someone now. In fact he lives with me, so, no. But thanks for calling. But don't call back. Nope, really. *Really.* Whattaya mean? He's right here." Eyes shut, Sebby collapsed backward, lying down on the sofa, legs in Todd's lap, and holding the phone away from himself. After a moment, Todd took it and put it to his ear.

"Hello? Hello . . . They've hung up." Todd replaced the phone in its dock.

"I lied a little," Sebby murmured. His eyes moved beneath his lids like a dreamer's, and Todd, watching, placed his hand on Sebby's head and smoothed back his damp hair.

"Former boyfriend?" Todd guessed, and Sebby nodded.

"I don't want him to call anymore. I don't want any old boyfriends to call. Except Ethan. He can call." His eyes flew open. "Todd. I want to fuck."

"You dated Ethan? You never told me that!"

"I did tell you." He stretched, raising his arms over his head and arching his back. "He's one of the older men whose heart I broke, that I told you."

"Ethan isn't old."

"Not old. Olderrr. He's thirty-four. I was twenty." Before Todd could determine whether Sebby meant that Ethan was thirty-four now or then and calculate what age difference this constituted, Sebby reached for Todd, curling a hand behind his neck, and pulled him down.

Todd resisted. "You are drunk."

"Sooo whaaat. Not too drunk to consent, and anyway, I'm yours, so consent is stupid."

Frowning, Todd removed Sebby's hand from around his neck. "I cannot agree. Consent is at the heart of any healthy sexual relationship."

Closing his eyes, Sebby pressed himself against Todd. "*Oh, tengo ganas. Ahora.*"

Todd gave him a brief kiss. Sebby tasted of ashes and whiskey, and Todd recoiled. "Have you been smoking?"

"Maybe one." Sebby's hand reached to smooth Todd's hair and then fell back as if his arm were just too heavy. "Every man there wanted me, but I came home to you, and now you don't want me." His tone was pure bewilderment.

"*Every* man?" Todd traced one finger over Sebby's lower lip, pulling it down to reveal the tender pink inside. "Drinking, smoking. What else?"

"Nothing else." Sebby squirmed and nearly fell off the sofa in an effort to maneuver himself into a more aggressive position. Todd fended off his advances and clamped his hands on Sebby's upper arms. Sebby gasped and shivered, and his head lolled back, exposing his sleek throat. Todd found himself pressing his mouth to that throat, kissing and then biting. Sebby cried out and struggled before going boneless in Todd's arms. He let out a long moan as Todd's lips wandered down to the V-shaped indent where the collar bones met breastbone, and then farther down to where Sebby's shirt hung open. Todd paused to ease Sebby down on the sofa and unbutton Sebby's shirt. He mouthed his nipples, and relished the sound of sharply indrawn breath. Hands plucked at Todd's shirt as Todd backed up and kissed his way down, laving Sebby's stomach with his tongue, feeling the muscles quiver beneath his mouth. Todd inched the low-slung jeans lower till Sebby's erection sprang free, and pressed his face there, nuzzling. Resting his cheek against Sebastián's thigh, he curled his fingers around Sebby's cock, swirling his thumb in the moisture on the mushroom-shaped head.

Sebby twitched and clutched at Todd's hair. All in a rush, as if he hadn't breath to get the words out, Sebby cried, "Please, oh, *por favor, querido*, oh, don't make me beg, please!" Todd refrained from pointing out that he *was* begging, and—feeling grateful that Sebby was there with him instead of out with God-knew-whom—he had only to roll his head to reach Sebby's cock with his tongue. Sebby gasped, he writhed, he cried out in Spanish. Encouraged, Todd took Sebby's cock into his mouth. The taste of pre-ejaculate was sweet. Fitting his lips just around the glans, he thought how perfectly formed it was, as if designed for just this purpose. The tip of his tongue poked into the tiny cleft—rather like his habitual treatment of Sebby's dimple, he realized.

Sebby's breath came in bursts: a long pause of held breath followed by an exhalation and gasp, followed by another long pause and another exhalation. He held still, the trembling stillness of someone who feared that movement would bring an end to pleasure. Todd shifted and, positioning his tongue at the base of the glans where the sensitive bundle of nerves lived, began to hum.

He had never tried the humming with Sebby, and the effect was immediate: Sebby arched and cried out, "Todd! Oh! Ah! Ah!"

Todd was pleased to hear his name at this most delicate of junctures, and he continued his serenade a few more seconds until Sebby's orgasm stopped him. Grimacing, he swallowed and sat up.

Sebby's hands slipped from Todd's hair; his eyelids fluttered without opening, and he sighed, his body seeming to sink into the sofa cushions as the breath left him. Todd sipped his lukewarm coffee and watched Sebby's face relax into sleep, saw how his lips parted and curved as if to smile, how his tangled hair lay against his forehead. It seemed nigh onto sacrilege to disturb such angelic repose, and after a minute, he stood, fetched a throw, tucked it around Sebby, and settled himself into the corner of the sofa with his book.

Chapter Twenty-Six

I'm Not Vivian

*E*arly light sent knives through Sebby's eyelids. His foot had fallen asleep, and he soon realized that this was due to Todd's form slumped over Sebby's legs. He needed to piss, but the pain in his head beat time to "My Sharona," and he was afraid that if he moved, he'd puke. He shifted under the cover, pausing upon the realization that his jeans were sort of only halfway on. He remembered coming home last night, but trying to remember anything else made his head pound, and so he stopped. He could remember things later. He wiggled his legs out from under Todd, who muttered something and slumped further. Sebby eased himself into a sitting position and was able, with feeble kicks, to wake his foot up and also rid himself of his jeans. He rested, before standing and hobbling to the bathroom.

After freshening up, he braced himself to face Todd, equipped with a towel full of ice. "Todd," he croaked, and again, a bit more loudly, "Todd." Wincing at the sound, he pressed the ice to his head. Todd stirred, groaned, sat up, and peered around as he adjusted his skewed eyeglasses. He stretched and flinched, probably cramped from his hunched sleeping position, but Sebby was preoccupied with his own aches and was unsympathetic.

"Good morning!" Todd said with a glowing smile as his eyes traveled up and down, taking in Sebby's attire, which, Sebby remembered, was an unbuttoned shirt and nothing else, and, *mierda*, Todd had better not be wanting to fuck, because no fucking way.

Sebby could only nod, and it wasn't even a nod—he just moved his chin a little.

Todd's face fell into lines of concern as he rose and oh-so-gently put his arms around him. "Poor sweetheart. How do you feel?"

Terrible, Sebby wanted to say, but that was too many syllables. "Sick." He rested his head on Todd's shoulder for a moment, but Todd's fingers in his hair irritated him. "Go home." He squeezed his eyes shut.

"I'll help you to bed," Todd said, and Sebby, baffled, allowed Todd to draw him to the stairs, where he balked and hung back. All those steps. Todd might as well just knock him in the head and get it over with.

"I don't need to go upstairs. I wanna lay on the couch." Oh, it was too many words. Why couldn't Todd leave him alone?

"We slept there all night, *cielito lindo*. You'll rest better in your bed."

He turned and glared at Todd with dark suspicion. "You mean *you'll* rest better."

One eyebrow arched. "Who needs a bed? I could fuck you on the couch. You're not so particular."

Sebby's mouth fell open. A screech would have emerged if he wasn't afraid of giving himself a brain hemorrhage.

"I'll help you to bed, and then I'll leave, if that's what you want."

"*Coño*," Sebby whispered. "You're mean. I can get up the stairs myself, if I want to, and I don't. I wanna lay on the couch." The towel slipped, spilling ice cubes. Sebby sniffled and blinked. *Chingados*, why did he always cry when he was hungover?

Arms went around him, gentle but firm, and pulled him inexorably up the stairs, more under Todd's power than his own. Todd talked quietly the while. "If you remain downstairs, you will sleep fitfully, you will awaken rumpled and unrefreshed, and I refuse to allow your binge to ruin our entire Saturday."

They reached the bedroom. Sebby shed his shirt and couldn't help moaning as he crawled naked between the cold sheets, burying his face in his pillow and covering his head with the damp towel. He was conscious of Todd drawing the covers over him. "Fuck off. I don't need you."

The covers froze in their movement and were dropped, covering Sebby only halfway, and he wriggled, annoyed. Todd's footsteps receded and stopped, and Sebby peeked out, but his pained eyeballs couldn't focus.

"I need someone to need me," Todd said, so quietly that the words were almost lost in the pounding of Sebby's own head.

Sebby growled. Dragging the towel aside to make sure that his words were clear, he said, "I'm not Vivian."

Then Todd was gone, closing the door behind him so carefully that Sebby couldn't discern even the click of the mechanism.

When Sebby awoke for the second time that day, it was to the uneasy feeling that he'd done something terrible. There was a sodden towel dampening his pillow. Pushing it away, he rolled over and frowned at the Todd-free space next to him. Unwelcome memories came slinking back through the hangover fog. *¡Puta!* Pressing fingertips to his aching eyeballs, Sebby winced. *"I'm not Vivian."* Oh, *Dios mío*, had he said that? He fished for his cell and then remembered it was downstairs and grabbed the cordless extension instead. Todd answered on the first ring.

"Are you mad? Can you come over?" Sebby winced at the whine in his own voice.

"Of course I'm not mad. I'll be there directly." In the next second there was a knock on his bedroom door, and Sebby started, his throat clamping shut, until he realized who it must be.

"Oh, Todd. Come in?"

The door opened. Phone to his ear, Todd stepped in, crisp and fresh in pressed khakis and a pale oxford shirt. "Good morning."

"Morning." Sebby dropped the phone and pressed his fingers to his eyes, this time to push the tears back in. Todd must have stayed downstairs or in the spare room, just waiting.

"Sweetheart, aren't you feeling any better? You should drink this."

Sebby looked up, and Todd had produced from somewhere a tall glass of ice water, the sight of it so good and cold that Sebby's tongue swelled.

"You should eat something. Do you think you could eat?"

Sebby spoke humbly. "Whatever you think best, Todd. But what I want is, I wish you would come over here and just hold me a little."

It must have been the right thing to say, because Todd's expression warmed, and he glided across the room. Todd insisted that Sebby drink the water, and Sebby guzzled half the glass. Then Todd perched on the edge of the bed and gathered him up, so tenderly, as if Sebby were one of those eggshells without the egg inside. He pressed his face into Todd's shoulder.

"Lay down with me?" he begged. Todd hesitated but removed his glasses and crept carefully over the covers to lie down facing Sebby. *He's trying not to jostle me too much*, Sebby realized, and felt even worse. He scooted close to Todd and hid his face in Todd's chest so he wouldn't have to look at him. "Todd, you are *pitiful*." His voice broke. Todd's arm went around him, he stroked Sebby's bare back, and Sebby pressed closer yet.

"I know," Todd answered. He took a deep breath; Sebby felt Todd's rib cage expand against his face. "I've done a lot of thinking this morning, and I vow to change. I won't—"

"No!" Sebby interrupted. He pulled at Todd's collar, rolling it around his finger. "No, stay the same, stay pitiful; I'm a bitch." He raised his head enough to press his mouth to Todd's throat. He circled the Adam's apple with his tongue.

"Shhh. Don't." Todd didn't move, but the gentle remonstrance was enough to stop Sebby. Todd wouldn't want a guilt fuck, oh no, not he.

"I know it's not fair, I know it was wrong, but I thought you'd want to fuck, and I was so sick!"

"You thought *what*?"

"Did Vivian— Was *he* a bitch to you when he was sick?" Sebby held his breath. He knew what the answer had to be.

Todd turned away. The lines of his throat flexed as he swallowed. "No. But you aren't he."

Sebby bit his lip. He fingered Todd's collar, trying to press it flat again and pushed his nose into the hollow of Todd's throat, breathing the scent of soapy clean skin.

"The first time ever I stayed with Viv when he was ill, he thought the same thing: that I was there to get laid. So . . . evidently, there is something about me that leads others to such a conclusion."

Sebby huffed against Todd's skin. "Yeah. Because you're such a pushy man-whore," he said sarcastically.

"You said that I would not let anyone take care of me, but it's you who won't allow me to care for you and who informs me that you can take care of yourself, that you don't need me."

Tears gathered again. Sebby squeezed words past the lump in his throat. "You take care of me lots." He stretched to press his cheek against Todd's. "It's just, when I'm sick, I can't have someone hovering. I can't stand it."

"I know. It's all right."

"I don't know about *need*. You said, 'I need someone to need me,' not, 'I need *you* to need me,' like it doesn't matter who, just anyone. And *need* is like you don't have any choice about it, but I *want* you, I choose to be with you. Isn't that better?"

"No. I don't know." Todd pulled away, rolled to his back, cast his arm over his eyes. "I told you once before that I am too needy."

Sebby drew a breath. "*Querido*, I can't talk about all this now. My head hurts." He didn't care if this was blatant manipulation; it was no lie: the ache in his head was surging, his eyes pulsed with unshed tears, and his throat swelled with thirst and anxiety. He whimpered. Surely, Vivian had never been so pathetic.

Todd shifted; his broad, warm hand smoothed Sebby's hair back. "Poor sweetheart." Lips touched Sebby's forehead, pressed silken kisses all along his hairline, making Sebby shiver, and Todd paused to pull the covers up over Sebby's shoulders.

"More?"

Todd complied. His fingers worked through Sebby's hair and massaged his scalp. The pain eased. He moaned; he couldn't help it.

Todd stopped. "Too much? Did that hurt?"

"Nooo, don't stop, no." Sebby reached both arms around Todd's neck, pulled him down, and kissed him.

"Cease and desist, imp," Todd chided. Taking hold of Sebby's wrists, he drew them from around his neck and crossed them over Sebby's own chest. He pulled the covers to Sebby's chin, sat up, and resumed the scalp massage. Sebby went limp. He resolved to be fake-sick once in a while and let Todd take care of him. It was such a simple thing, and it made Todd happy. Maybe he should be afraid of spiders, if that would make Todd feel strong, to be the brave spider killer. He could pretend things were too heavy for him and let Todd do the carrying. He could—

He could just tell him, he could say the words *I need you*, and that would be simple too.

Todd made him drink the rest of the water and then went on to massage his neck and back. Sebby's headache evaporated. He felt loose as a jellyfish, and still Todd kept kneading his flesh, and Sebby ached for a more intimate touch. But Todd was standing on pride now, and if Sebby was going to seduce him, he was going to have to be subtle about it.

"Can we fuck now?" he said, because, subtlety, ack. Overrated.

Todd froze. "End of massage."

He moved away, and it was all Sebby could do just to rotate his head on its limp neck in order to give Todd the eye. Todd lay back, lacing his hands behind his head and training his eyes on the ceiling.

Sebby wiggled closer. "I know what you're thinking. That if we fuck now, it'll just prove me right, what I thought before about you wanting to, but that's not true. 'Cause now I want to."

"Of course, that was my intent all along," Todd said, staring at the ceiling. "Erotic massage to weaken your resistance followed by fucking." He didn't move as Sebby's hand snaked over his abdomen, until his fingers began working at a button, and then Todd took hold of those fingers, wrapping his own around them.

Sebby pouted. "I don't care, I want you." Todd lay atop the covers, while Sebby was under them, but he managed to throw a blanketed leg over Todd's legs, ignoring Todd's rolled eyes and noise of exasperation. He pressed himself against Todd's hip. Todd turned his head away, but that exposed his neck for Sebby's convenience, and Sebby put his mouth there, finding Todd's sweet spot.

"Stop," Todd said, and Sebby hesitated. He put his lips to Todd's ear.

"I'll do anything you want," he murmured, and he held his breath, letting the promise hang in the air.

Todd repeated, "Anything I want."

Sebby pressed his thigh to Todd's thighs, wriggled his fingers within Todd's tight grasp, licked his earlobe.

"Anything," he breathed. And, oh, it felt reckless to lay himself open in this way.

"Very well." Todd cleared his throat and pulled Sebby's hand to his chest, and Sebby's heart leaped and galloped off. "I'd like you to tell me about your friend, about what happened to him."

Sebby's brain, steeped in desire, did not understand. "What?"

"Your friend, Sebby. The one who was hurt by homophobes."

Sebby was silent and motionless for long moments while Todd stroked his fingers. "Todd, sometimes you're such a prick."

"You said 'anything,'" Todd said mildly.

"Pretend you didn't know I meant sex. *¡No chingues!*"

"I'm sorry. You said 'anything,' and I admit I took advantage of the situation."

Irritation made him want to order Todd out of his bed. He rolled over, facing away.

"You won't share that with me? I feel that you hold things back, that you're not honest with me."

Sebby bit his lip. He had no commitment to Todd. Todd had no commitment to him. How far did you let someone in who might leave you any day? The further in you let them get, the more you got ripped open when they left.

"It might help to talk it over," Todd said. "Shared burdens are halved, *n'est-ce pas?*"

"It won't help. And I'll be sad the rest of the day, and you'll have to put up with sad me. Also, you can forget about getting laid, *puto.*"

"Forgotten," Todd agreed.

Sebby squirmed out of bed, stopping to toss Todd his eyeglasses. He waited until Todd had adjusted them on his face, and then pivoted in place, giving Todd the three-hundred-and-sixty-degree view. "I can't talk on an empty stomach. Cook me breakfast while I shower." Leaning backward, he touched his abdomen and let his fingers trail an indecent line from the apex of his rib cage to his navel and on down. "I'm hungry."

He had the satisfaction of seeing Todd go wide-eyed and slack-jawed, and Sebby ambled from the room.

The smells of food and coffee reached Sebby all the way upstairs, making his mouth hurt. He hurried. He had organized his thoughts into sane and orderly words, and he was in no mood to procrastinate.

Todd's expression was stressed as he greeted Sebby. "Er, ah, it's edible. At any rate, I believe it to be edible, though its appearance is hardly appetizing." Sebby seated himself and was presented with a plate of black-speckled yellow lumps sprinkled with red and green chunks. Sebby blinked at it.

"Coffee," Todd continued, placing a steaming mug at the corner of the placemat. "I remembered to use the spring water."

Sebby touched his fork to the mess. "What is it?"

"In its former life, it was an omelet. It died and was reincarnated as this." Todd waved his arm.

Sebby inhaled, and his stomach growled. "Smells good." Todd beamed, the corners of his eyes crinkling, and Sebby forgave him for being a prick. Lifting a forkful, he examined it and found the red and green chunks to be chopped bell peppers. He smiled, his heart lightening. Todd was so cute, after all, trying to make him an omelet. "Aren't you eating?"

"Having arisen with the sun, and my appetite with it, I ate many hours ago."

"But 's lunchtime."

Todd settled in the chair opposite Sebby. "I'm too much in suspense."

The eggs turned to ashes in Sebby's mouth. He swallowed hard and looked down at his plate, surprised to see that the mess was half gone. "Now it's had this huge buildup. It's gonna be—what do you call it when the ending is a letdown?"

"Anticlimactic? I hope it is."

Sebby tapped his toe, realized he was tapping it, and stopped with an effort. *Get it over with.* "He got beat up, like I said. Kind of bad. I wasn't there when it happened. So. But. And then he …" Unexpectedly, his throat closed up, cutting off his nice, orderly explanation. He grabbed his coffee, feigning a dramatic pause and hoping Todd didn't notice how difficult he found it to swallow.

"He was more than a friend, wasn't he?"

"No." Sebby met Todd's eyes. "Just friends."

Todd's forehead creased. He adjusted his glasses and leaned forward, peering at Sebby, who held his gaze. In the most astonished tone imaginable, Todd said, "You're lying to me, aren't you?"

Sebby squirmed. Dropping his eyes, he scraped his remaining eggs into nice, neat sections on his plate. "Fine." Things were getting too serious when someone could tell he was lying. "It makes me so sad," he whispered. "We were lovers. And the first I heard was his sister calling me from the hospital. She knew about us; his parents didn't. Anyway. So I went over there, and it was bad. He looked bad. Um." Sebby paused. He was getting into more detail than he had intended. "So, we were friends is what they, his parents, thought, yes? You know. Finally, we got a minute alone. I came close to him, well, he—he told me then that he couldn't see me anymore. I—" Sebby again paused to stop himself from revealing distressing details. "He said that he couldn't be gay anymore."

"What!"

Sebby nodded. "I— He— I thought it was just stress, well, understandable, identity crisis or whatever, and he was hurt. I told him to not worry, we would talk about it later. But, what ended up was, he went to Jesus camp. He got married. To a woman. Now he has a kid. He says he's happy, and I don't know, maybe he is."

There was a longish pause. Now it was grinding at him, the old frustration, the helplessness, the utter wrongness and inability to convince others of the wrongness. "So you see what could happen if they think they can beat it out of us?"

"Sebby! Jesus." Todd's eyes were wide behind his glasses, his hands clenched around his mug as if to squeeze it to smithereens.

"Come here?" Sebby asked, and Todd set his coffee aside. Sebby shoved his chair back, and Todd regarded him confusedly for a moment before sliding into his lap and allowing Sebby to wrap his arms around him. "I had to let him go," Sebby murmured, his face buried in Todd's chest. "He wanted to go, and I let him."

Todd pressed his cheek to Sebby's hair. "I'm so sorry."

"It happens. It's . . . It happens. Anyway—" he sighed "—that's what happened, and are you satisfied now?"

"I'm sorry."

"Do you think he's happy?"

"How can I know? Do I think homos can be happy living the straight life? No. If he was bi, then that would be different, though the circumstances would still be worrisome."

Todd shifted, and Sebby felt that he was uncomfortable sitting in Sebby's lap instead of the other way around, but Sebby wasn't ready to let him go yet and locked his arms around Todd's waist. "He wasn't bi. He's not bi. "

"It's been done, whatever the reasons, fear not the least of them. But, in all likelihood, he's deceiving himself and his family, and it will result in more hurt." He cleared his throat. "That is something you need never fear that *I* would do—recant my sexuality."

After a long pause made up of shallow breathing, Sebby said, "Maybe."

"Oh, Sebby, never! They could beat me within an inch of my life, or an inch outside of it, and I would cry out, 'Still it moves!'" When Sebby said nothing, Todd continued, "That's what Galileo allegedly said after being forced to recant: 'Still it moves.'" Sebby remained silent, and Todd put his finger under Sebby's chin to tilt his face to him. "I assure you I'm secure in who I am."

Sebby sighed. "No, Todd, you aren't."

"W— But— Ah . . . Sebastián, how can you say this?" Todd put his hands on Sebby's shoulders; he shook him a little. "What do you mean?"

Sebby reached to touch Todd's cheek. "I can't touch you at work, can't kiss you good morning. We can't arrive or leave together. You pretend to have girlfriends. You talk to me, but it's wearing a mask. It's all a lie, and I'm yanked right into the lie with you."

"But that's only at work! I'm out everywhere else, everywhere that matters: at home, with your friends, and everywhere we go. Work doesn't matter."

This was very Todd: acting like, since Gimondi Brothers was unimportant to him, it was unimportant altogether. Sebby brushed his fingers over Todd's lips and across his cheek, trying to soothe. "It matters to me."

Todd fidgeted, but Sebby pulled Todd as tight against himself as he could, wanting to feel Todd's bones crush against his bones, and he didn't let up, even when Todd made an *oof* noise.

"I didn't realize it bothered you," Todd said.

"It's my fault, because I said it was okay, and I went along with it. I know. But I'm telling you now: it makes me unhappy."

"I'll come out tomorrow," Todd said, the words running and bumping into one another. "I mean Monday. I'll make an announcement. I'll take out a full-page newspaper ad. Hire a fucking billboard."

Sebby smiled against Todd's chest. "It doesn't have to be so dramatic. It doesn't have to be anything. Just stop lying." He drew back to smile at Todd, and Todd's face was pale and strained, Todd stared off into space, and his mouth worked. "It's not as big a thing as you think. Gus already guessed, and I don't think most of the boys will be that surprised." He spoke gently, knowing that Todd considered himself good at his het act, but, really, you would have to be blind, deaf, and stupid to be around Todd all day and not suspect he was gay.

"I should tender my resignation," Todd said, as if speaking to himself. "It'd be easier, and what am I doing there anyway?"

Sebby rubbed Todd's back. "If you're more comfortable with that. But can I talk about you at work, then? Can I have your picture on my desk and on my screen saver?"

Todd did not answer.

Chapter Twenty-Seven

Kaput

Todd didn't tender his resignation, and he didn't hire a billboard, and this didn't surprise Sebby, but Todd growing distant, this surprised him. Todd acting more formal toward Sebby at work, Todd spending more time with his family, all this surprised him. Days passed, and Sebby wondered if Todd was seeing someone else. At least that was something Sebby could understand and deal with. Monogamy, even to someone who said he was a monogamist, must get old.

After days of being ignored and put off, Sebby, at quitting time, trailed Todd to his pickup.

"Come for dinner?" he asked, and oh, he was ashamed of how his voice quavered.

"Not tonight." Todd adjusted his rearview mirror. "I made plans with Ryan."

"Oh." Sebby froze. There was nothing to say to that, though he wanted to protest, *Who spends Friday night with their nephew?* "Well. I can make plans too."

He risked a glance at Todd, Todd was nodding and looking away. *Preoccupied*, that was how he seemed, and what was he preoccupied *with*? Vivian, the horrid bitch—maybe he'd called again. But Todd didn't really have the Vivian look on his face.

Sebby walked off, feeling for the first time in their acquaintance that Todd was not watching him walk away.

If only people could make as much sense as spreadsheets.

Four hours later, Todd's plans for the evening were kaput, Ryan having received an invitation to spend the night at a friend's—friend trumping uncle in any eleven-year-old's world. Todd thought of calling Sebby, but he didn't feel that he could see him without first doing as Sebby wished, and this simple task had proved more formidable than Todd had imagined. The entire week had passed without his accomplishing it.

No matter how often he rehearsed, each time he opened his mouth to speak, the words tripped him up, leaving him sweating and stammering. Two simple words! Well, one contraction and one simple word—*I'm gay*—and, in trying to say them, it was as if he were Mr. Banks endeavoring to pronounce *supercalifragilisticexpialidocious*. Sebby had accused him of pretending about girlfriends, and this had wounded Todd, for he'd never mentioned girls. He had allowed his coworkers to make their assumptions. *Just stop lying*, Sebby had said, but Todd had never outright lied.

His evenings were occupied with the job search and retooling his résumé. He swallowed his pride and put in a call to Rita, his boss when he'd been an intern in Minneapolis. Months ago, when Todd had quit his New York job and fled to Denver, Rita had phoned him and reamed him out for giving up the job she had placed him in.

"Goddamned irresponsible, Addison," she had said. "I gave them a glowing review, got you your job, and this is how you repay me! And it's not just me you've screwed, but my future interns. How can I ever place an intern in New York again?" Then she had tried to convince him to return to Minnesota and, upon his refusal, had offered him freelance work, which he had promised to consider, but on which he had never followed up, till now.

Rita was glad to hear from him and promised to send him an assignment, but was leery about being his reference. "Goddamn it, kid; I don't trust you. You're unreliable. Some new boy'll ditch you, and you'll quit and run off again. Denver'll be shut to me too. Or," she went on, knowingly, "that boy'll want you back, and you'll run off to New York. Ha. They'll blackball you there."

"Rita, I *quit a job*. It's been done before. They don't hold it against me."

"No, they hold it against *me*. Fine, you're looking for a new job? Tell 'em to call me. I'll tell 'em you're unpredictable, but crazy talented."

"Thank you, Rita. I'm in your debt."

Todd had telephoned all of the contacts on the list Wayne had emailed him, and polite interest had been expressed. He arranged for meetings with two of them. The email from Rita arrived, and he began work on her assignment. The week passed, he hadn't come out, and he didn't know what to say to Sebby, any more than he knew what to say to his coworkers.

And now it was Friday night, and he was alone.

Todd loitered in the front yard. *Once a coward, always a coward. Why can't you be a man?* He pulled out his phone, hesitated, and dialed Holly.

He was dismayed to learn that Holly had lost her gig at the dinner theater due to a heavy sunburn. After commiserating with her over this turn of fate, Todd broached the subject that was at the top of his brain.

"Sebby wants me to come out."

"I thought you *were* out. I mean, except for your mom."

Todd began pacing the yard. "Not at work. I told him I'd do it. And I tried, and I . . . seem unable to do it. And now we are not speaking to one another, Sebby and I."

"So he gave you an ultimatum?"

"Er, not exactly."

"Um. What exactly did he say?"

"He said . . . Well, first I said that I was out everywhere except work, and work didn't matter, and he said that it mattered to him and that he was unhappy."

"But he won't talk to you until you do it?"

"He is not denying me the pleasure of his company, if that is what you are asking . . ."

"Ohhh. You mean *you* won't talk to *him* until you do it."

"Well . . ."

"You're, like, punishing him for the fact that he's making you do something you don't want."

"But . . . but . . ." Todd stammered in his eagerness to communicate his frustration. "How can I face him until I fulfill my promise? I vowed to do it on Monday, and the entire work week has passed!"

"Well, you already broke your promise, and not talking to him doesn't fix it."

Todd was silent. It hurt to think that there was no retrieving the broken promise.

"So I think you should talk to him, say you're sorry. Don't you think he probably understands that it's hard? Are you really scared, like *scared*? Or just nervous?"

"Stage fright has never been one of my weaknesses."

"Todd-o." And Holly paused for thought, and when she spoke, her voice was grave. "On stage, everything is pretend, and clever lines are written out for you, and punches don't connect with your jaw. Don't act like this is some big drama. This is your life, you know? If it's really not safe for you, then Sebby should understand that."

Todd mulled this over, not liking the implications. "I'm a coward. I *am*." He smoothed his hair. "The problem is, I am perfectly happy with the status quo. Therefore, I have no motivation to change anything."

"But *Sebby's* not happy. Doesn't that motivate you?"

"Apparently not enough. You're right, though: I should call him." *There's no guarantee he'll answer. Even if he is there.* "Or text him. Thanks, hon; I'll call you later."

Todd began to compose a text.

Chapter Twenty-Eight

Setup

Sebby worked late, trying to bury himself in paperwork, but even his orderly columns of numbers could not ease his anxiety. Finally he gave up. After all, he had said he could make plans, so why didn't he? He texted Barry and Lawrence and convinced them that a movie night at his house would be more fun than clubbing.

They were several screams and clutches into the movie *The Descent* when the landline rang.

"It's Todd!" Lawrence said, upon viewing the caller ID. He was nearest the phone, and Barry was on the other end of the sofa, the two of them flanking Sebby.

Why was he calling on the landline? Sebby raised his head from Barry's shoulder. "Should I answer?"

"Yes!" Barry and Lawrence declared in unison, and Lawrence grabbed the cordless phone from its dock and shoved it into Sebby's hands. Barry paused the movie, and both regarded Sebby expectantly.

"Whatever," Sebby huffed, and pushed the Talk button. "Hello?"

"Sebastián. It is I, Todd. You didn't answer my texts. Are you mad? Can I come over?" Sebby recognized that Todd was echoing his own words back at him, and it made him smile, but before he could answer, Todd went on, "I miss you."

"Oh, Todd. I miss you too." Relief made him go limp and lean back into the cushions. Barry and Lawrence high-fived over his head. Sebby elbowed them. "But maybe not tonight." Barry and Lawrence shook their heads frantically. Lawrence leaned over the edge of the sofa, and a second later Todd's voice came over the speaker as Lawrence sat back with a smug look.

"I understand. I don't expect you to break plans for me. I've been miserable this week, and I unreasoningly felt"—Sebby wrestled his way across Lawrence and turned off the speaker, remaining there, draped across Lawrence's lap—"that you wouldn't want anything to do with me." Playfully, Lawrence tapped the speaker on again. "I'm an ass, and a coward, and—" Sebby slammed his hand down on the speaker button, glaring at Lawrence. Lawrence and Barry raised their eyebrows at each other and giggled behind their hands. "Is someone there?" Todd asked.

"I have friends over, but I'm not kicking them out just because you don't want to be alone on a Friday." Barry and Lawrence's eyes went wide. They mouthed silent *oohs*. "I want to see you, but, you might as well know, I'm pissed off. What the fuck was up with you all week? But I don't want to talk about it on the phone, so are you coming over or what?"

"I'll be there directly," Todd said humbly.

Sebby's voice softened. "Good. Um. Okay. I'll watch for you." He hung up, sighing.

"Byeee." Lawrence hopped up.

"Sebby said he's not kicking us out," Barry reminded him.

"That was just for show. C'mon."

"No, I meant it," Sebby said. An idea bloomed like a crocus through the snow. It was time to shake things up. Show Todd what he was missing.

Make him want to stay.

"This might be your chance," Sebby said.

"Ohhh. Our chance." Lawrence sank back down.

Barry scooted forward to perch on the edge of the sofa. "This could work! This could work. Okay, he likes musicals, you said. So, do you have any of those around?"

"I don't have any makeup on!" Lawrence screeched, his hands flying to his face.

"Todd doesn't care for makeup all that much," Sebby said, and to Barry, "I don't know, check the shelf."

"That's fine for you and Barry! But I need it." Lawrence's fingers walked from his cheeks to his eyes to his hair, to his chin, to his clothes.

"Oh, Lolly, that's ridic! You're as cute as either of us." Barry put a hand on Lawrence's shoulder and kissed his cheek. "Anyway, I bet Sebby has makeup somewhere, don't you?"

"I don't know. Probably. Check the bathroom." Sebby couldn't focus, couldn't think. This had to work. He drew his knees to his chest, curled his arms around his legs, and rested his forehead on his knees.

Lawrence fled, and Barry pounced on the DVDs. A moment passed before he cried out, "This one!"

Sebby peeked out to see a red and black case, *West Side Story*. The dance-fight movie, Sebby remembered. He'd never gotten around to watching it with Todd.

Barry ripped open the case. "We'll pretend we've been watching it, we'll skip to one of the dance numbers, and press play when he gets here like we've just been watching the whole thing." Turning away, he opened the DVD player, replaced *The Descent*, and waited for the menu to load.

Sebby jittered, too nervous to give Barry's plan due consideration. Barry flicked through the scene selection. Lawrence, having prettied himself up, came bounding into the room. "Ooh, Jets and Sharks!"

"Can't do the Jets song, it's at the beginning. It has to seem like we've been watching it all along." Barry shook his head and went ahead a few scenes.

"Ooh, we're setting a trap!" Clutching Barry's arm, Lawrence bounced, leaning toward the television.

"This one," Barry declared, stopping the movie at a number called "Cool." He punched the volume and stepped back, concentrating on the gang's dance moves, fingers snapping and feet shuffling. Lawrence giggled and bounced and sang, bumping into Barry and getting in his way.

Within minutes, the first viewing was over and Barry had reset it to the beginning of the number. Lawrence got down to business, imitating Barry, the two of them nearly identical in their moves, as they were in most things. Sebby watched. For sure Todd wouldn't be able to resist them this time.

"Watch for him!" Barry ordered, and Sebby went to stand by the door, pulling back the curtain and gazing out into the dark, waiting for the lights of Todd's truck to cut their way into the driveway. Behind him, the "Cool" song repeated again and again, and Sebby began to think *West Side Story* must be the worst movie ever made.

"He's here!" he yelled, so loud that the pane of glass in front of his face vibrated. Barry and Lawrence shrieked and fell over themselves as they took their places and reset the song to the beginning. Sebby opened the door and stepped out to greet Todd, who got out of his vehicle and stood, holding on to his truck door, shifting from one foot to another. Sebby beckoned.

Todd approached, breaking into a run and leaping up the steps to catch Sebby in his arms. "I'm sorry, sweetheart, oh! I've missed you . . ." And Sebby was melting into a million pieces, but no, when you melted, you weren't in pieces—the pieces melted together. Sebby pressed his face to Todd's neck. Todd froze. "Are you watching *West Side Story*?" He pulled back and blinked, looking past Sebby through the open doorway, toward the sounds of that song that Sebby never wanted to hear again as long as he lived.

"We are, yeah. Come on." Sebby tugged on Todd's hand.

"You were watching it without me?"

Sebby almost confessed all on the spot, Todd sounded so hurt. "Oh . . . Barry found it on the shelf. And I was mad. Come on. Watch it with me." He towed Todd through the doorway, and Todd blinked again at the spectacle of Barry and Lawrence, hunched over into their dance routine, snapping their fingers and doing kick ball changes or whatever. Sebby watched Todd's face closely, watched his eyes dart from the dancing boys to the television screen, to Sebby, and back to the boys.

"Are you hungry?" Sebby asked.

"W— No. No, I ate." Todd rubbed the bridge of his nose and pushed at his glasses. His face changed slowly, almost comically, from hurt and confusion to curiosity and approval. Barry and Lawrence, conscious of their audience but keeping their eyes locked on each other, moved in an almost mirror image dance, though Barry's movements were more controlled, more contained, like the characters on screen, while Lawrence's were broad and easy, as if at any moment he might lapse into the hokey pokey. The number ended, and Todd applauded, grinning. The boys collapsed against each other, panting and chuckling.

"I'm sorry to arrive late for this viewing. I can see that I've missed a great deal."

"With us it's interactive," said Lawrence.

"We can back up," Barry offered. Sebby caught the double meaning, and he doubted that it got past Todd.

"If you want to do it with us," Lawrence added.

"The Jets song? You can be Riff," Barry said.

The movie was set back. Assuming the roles of gang members, Barry and Lawrence flanked Todd, and the game was on. Sebby faded back into the upholstery, watching the three of them. Todd hammed it up, at one point leaping onto the ottoman. The two boys cheered, and Todd dismounted, though thankfully he didn't try to do a flip in the air like Riff in the movie did.

They moved with greater and greater abandon, with air punches and flying kicks that made Sebby fear for his bric-a-brac. The number ended, and Barry opted to skip the boring parts and go right for the action. As they moved on to "Mambo," which involved couples dancing, Todd partnered them, taking first one, then the other into his arms. Sebby remained quiet, noting how Todd's attention turned to him less, and how Barry and Lawrence moved closer and touched him more often. The room was filled with their merriment and shouts. The next song they selected was so silly that they couldn't sing for laughing, and it brought the house down. The three of them collapsed to the floor, puffing and wiping sweat from their faces. Lawrence clung to Todd's arm, and Todd's free arm was draped over Barry's shoulders, while Barry's hand rested on Todd's knee. Sebby averted his eyes and took advantage of the moment to slip away to the kitchen.

He set about grinding beans and hunting through his cupboards for something to eat. His hope was that Barry and Lawrence would now invite Todd home and he'd go, without Sebby having to be involved at all. He would fix himself a snack, curl up, watch the rest of *The Descent*, and go to bed and have crazy nightmares.

From behind him came Todd's familiar tread, and Sebby turned to see him in the doorway, eyes bright, face flushed, hair damp. Had he come to ask permission? To say good night? Todd's eyes followed the motion of Sebby's fingers. "Are you making coffee?"

He wanted coffee now? "You don't want any, do you?"

"I always want coffee. But, at the moment, I long for water." From the refrigerator, Todd fetched three bottles of water, unscrewed the cap from one, and drank it half down. "You're quiet tonight," he said, gasping a little, before gulping the rest of the bottle.

"Been a quiet week, no?" Sebby softened his words with a smile. "It's fun watching you with them."

"Barry and Lawrence are quite fun when they aren't attempting to get into my pants."

Sebby had to turn away to hide his smirk.

"About the quiet week . . ." Todd had set aside the bottles of water and come up behind Sebby, and his arms snaked around Sebby's waist. There was a not unpleasant smell of dance sweat. "You did ask what was up with me all week."

"Are you seeing someone?" Sebby kept his tone casual. "It's okay if you are, but I'd like it if you'd tell me."

Todd pulled him even closer against himself. "No. I'm seeing you and you alone."

Arching backward, Sebby reached up and behind to tangle his fingers in Todd's hair, and Todd's hand slid up Sebby's rib cage.

"It's harder than I thought," he whispered.

"Is it?" Sebby laughed and pressed his rear back into Todd's front. "I can't tell."

But Todd didn't laugh. "It's harder than I thought . . . coming out."

"I knew that was it!" Sebby exclaimed, and he wiggled in Todd's grasp, turning around to stroke his cheeks and tuck loose strands of hair behind Todd's ears. He pressed a kiss to the corner of Todd's mouth; the taste was salty. "Todd, I don't care. I'm sorry I nagged you. When you're ready, it'll be okay."

"I can hardly call that nagging." Todd looked so worried. Oh, he was the worryingest boy. Sebby told himself that he should be more careful what he said to Todd. "You told me how it bothered you, you recommended I stop lying, and I promised I'd tell them. I promised!"

"Shh. I didn't ask you to promise." Sebby put a finger over Todd's lips and then kissed him in earnest, and Todd's hands roamed over Sebby's back and then his front, and Sebby squeaked in surprise when Todd's hands gripped hard under Sebby's armpits, hefting him and plonking him down on the counter. He wrapped his legs around Todd, and Todd leaned in, pressing Sebby backward, one hand cradling his head. Sebby forgot for a moment that he was supposed to be sending Todd off with Barry and Lawrence.

Over Todd's shoulder, Sebby spied Lawrence jitterbugging in the kitchen entrance, smiling, his lower lip caught between his teeth. Lawrence waved. *Byeee*, he mouthed.

The plan. There might never be another chance like this. Todd needed to realize what a good thing he had here. The three of them combined had to be better than Vivian. *No*, Sebby mouthed back, and beckoned with one finger as he tightened his legs around Todd. Lawrence glided forward to lean against Todd and slip his arms around the two of them.

Todd tensed, his head jerking up. "Hey!"

He tried to pull away, but Sebby wouldn't let go, and Lawrence pressed close against Todd's back. Taller than either of them, Lawrence rested his cheek against Todd's hair, and he swayed from side to side. Sebby did the same, the two of them rocking Todd. Smiling reassuringly, Sebby let go with his legs to allow Lawrence to press closer, and Todd shivered; his face contorted, his eyes squeezed shut. Trembling, he hid his face in Sebby's neck.

Lawrence leaned forward as well, his body following Todd's, as if they were molded together. Over his bent shoulder and Todd's bent head, Sebby spotted Barry where Lawrence had stood earlier, his expression anxious, his eyebrows raised. Sebby gestured him away; *Wait*, Sebby thought at him, and Barry swayed in sympathy where he stood.

Lawrence shifted, and Sebby couldn't tell what Lawrence was doing, but Todd's reaction was to tighten his arms around Sebby so violently that the air was forced from Sebby's lungs in a grunt.

"Don't you like me?" Lawrence's voice was small and wistful.

"It is not a question of liking you, Lawrence, but of liking Sebby more."

His lips near Todd's ear, Sebby whispered, "Liking me doesn't preclude you from liking other people." *Preclude*, that was a word Todd liked to use. "I want you to go with them." He nuzzled Todd's ear, his hair, his face.

In turn, Todd pressed his lips to Sebby's ear. "I want you. You," he insisted.

"We just want to be good to you," murmured Lawrence. "For two things. 'Cause Sebby asked us to, and 'cause we like you."

"A lot," Barry remarked from the doorway, and Todd twisted to see.

"I am assaulted on all fronts," Todd said soberly.

"You have more than one front?" Lawrence said.

"Just what we need," said Barry.

Feeling Todd tensing again, Sebby spoke. "Guys, can you give us a minute?"

Barry nodded, and Lawrence moved away, his arm lingering as it slid from around Todd's body. Taking Barry's hand, he towed him into the hallway.

The moment they were out of sight, Todd dropped into a kitchen chair and wilted, laying his head down on his folded arms. "This whole thing was a setup."

"Only kind of." Sebby hopped down from the counter. Drawing a chair close to Todd's, Sebby sat and put his hand on the back of Todd's neck. "Toddfox, I want you to go with them. It'll be good for you, yes?"

"No. Why?"

Sebby hesitated. "How many boys have you been with since Vivian?" That brought Todd's head up, but he just stared. "You don't want to tell me. And it's not because there's been so many."

The lines of Todd's throat flexed as he swallowed. "Am I less of a man for having had less men?"

Smiling, Sebby smoothed Todd's worried brow. "*Why* so few? What I think is, deep down, you believe he'll ask you back, and when you go back, you'll feel proud that you've only had X-many boys between Vivians."

Todd shook his head and dislodged Sebby's hand.

"And you could feel righteous if your number is lower than *his*." Sebby sat back and ducked his head. "Every boy you're with separates you a little more from Vivian, no? And I'm for anything that does. I try and try, but I can't make you forget him."

"A thousand boys could not make me forget him. Any more than they could make me forget you."

Todd was probably sincere, but it still made Sebby feel like second-best, that Todd would add it as an afterthought. Sebby could've screamed his lungs out. "You need some fun. Loosen up. Just go fuck them and come back and tell me how much you hated it and I'll never mention it again."

Todd peered at Sebby. "You're hiding something from me. What do you think our relationship will gain if I sleep with them?"

Sebby raised his eyes to Todd's and realized that there were many things he kept from his lover, and that it all stemmed from keeping one thing from him, the most important thing, a secret that shouldn't be kept, not from the one person who should know. Todd must have seen something in Sebby's eyes; he leaned forward, and Sebby, before things could get dangerous, planted a kiss on his cheek and continued briskly. "Me and Barry and Lawrence have always shared. When we were just kids, safety in numbers, yes?" Sebby laughed as he realized the double meaning to himself: he loved numbers, they were his refuge. "Later, it wasn't so much about that, but if one of us found someone nice, we'd share a good thing. It's hard for me, Todd, to have someone and not share. It's like all the time I'm thinking how much they'd like you, and I feel guilty."

"So, now," Todd said, regarding Sebby with a penetrating stare, "it's about you and your guilt, not about me and my memory retention."

"It's both. It's everything. And one other thing: sometimes it's good to get a second opinion. Someone who's not involved can see, can tell me, 'Yes, he's great, keep him,' or, 'Hey, you know, he's not so great.'"

"And what of the bone breaker?" Todd said. "Did he sleep with them?"

"Yeah."

"Did he hit them?"

Sebby winced and bit his lip, hard. "No. Just me."

"But he was a good thing you had found and were willing to share."

"Not . . . not . . . not after he hit me." His breath quickened. "Barry and Lawrence tried to tell me. They did tell me, I mean. But I couldn't see it, wouldn't listen. I just thought they didn't know him like I did."

"And so this line of reasoning fails as well. You do not value their opinion."

Sebby stared at the bottles of water still sitting on the table. How tiring it would be, how humiliating, to tell Barry and Lawrence that Todd wouldn't go with them after all, how exhausting to go upstairs with Todd, who didn't respect Sebby even a tiny bit, who thought Sebby was a whore, a wreck who'd never had a decent relationship. No wonder he thought about Vivian all the time.

"You are concealing from me the true reason for wanting me to go with them," Todd mused aloud. "And from yourself as well, it seems." He stood and stretched. "No matter. I've grieved you, it's plain to see, and, not wanting to break another promise so soon, willingly I go, if for no other reason than to see a smile return to your face." The swift turnabout had Sebby blinking and gaping before Todd's arms went tight around him, pulling him to his feet. "If to love you I must love them, so be it."

Sebby's heart threatened to gallop off, as it did whenever Todd spoke heedlessly of love, but he reined it in and tried to breathe. Todd meant lovemaking, not love—two different things, things that often had nothing to do with each other. "It's not a 'must,' Todd."

"You want me to go, I go. I begin to feel I can refuse you nothing."

Sebby's heart was really not behaving itself, and then Todd was kissing under Sebby's jaw and down his throat, taking his time about it, as if he didn't have two pretty boys waiting for him in the other room. It was so difficult to breathe, and Todd stopped at Sebby's collar bone, taking it between his teeth and then soothing the tooth marks with his tongue. "You're quite certain you want me to go?"

Sebby had been alone all week, and Todd's breath on his skin was a torment. "Oh! You don't fight fair. Yes, go, you can come back to me later, or stay all night with them, I know you'll probably want to, but stop that, stop!" Arching against Todd and closing his eyes, he hoped Todd would take him seriously. Sebby didn't have the will to stop him, and his friends were going to give up and leave, if they hadn't already.

Thinking this, Sebby's eyes flew open, and he wriggled from Todd's grasp, nearly fell, twisted away, and leaned back against the counter, breathing hard. "If you don't go now, you never will. It's not going to work, trying to kiss me till I change your mind . . . *my* mind."

Todd was grinning, the irksome boy. "It was worth a try. Right, then." Todd drew a deep breath, and his face fell into tragic lines.

"Smile! Don't look like a martyr, you'll hurt their feelings!"

"I rather thought my smile was making you angry, *cielito lindo*." His grin returned, and he approached Sebby, holding out his arms. "Good-bye kiss?"

Sebby glared. "No!"

"And off I go." Todd clicked his heels together and bowed like a butler, the strange boy. He turned and went off down the hall. Sebby followed. Barry and Lawrence were curled up together in a corner of the sofa. They had turned *The Descent* back on.

"Hmm," Todd *hmm*ed, taking in the content on the screen. The two turned to look over their shoulders. "Sebby, you do guarantee they're not dragging me back to their lair to make quick work of me?"

"Oh, we'd never make it quick." Lawrence bounced up.

"And you don't, either," said Barry. "We've been waiting forever!"

"We almost left." Lawrence took Todd's arm.

"But we were patient." Barry took his other arm. "You can follow us in your truck."

Sebby intervened. "Barry, you go with Todd in his truck, so he won't get lost. Lawrence, come here and I'll give you some coffee. Todd has to have coffee."

"What Sebby means," said Todd, "is that he fears I'll make a getaway, if left to my own devices."

"No. I fear you can't fuck without coffee," Sebby said, and Barry and Lawrence tittered.

"I really cannot argue with that," Todd said gravely.

Sebby had to push them out the door and drag Lawrence to the kitchen.

"'Sup?" Lawrence demanded, hopping up on the counter and swinging his legs.

With an effort, Sebby ignored the heels kicking his cabinets. "He likes to cuddle after, so make sure you don't ignore him."

"Kay. What else?"

"Don't ever act like anything hurts, 'cause he freaks."

"Kayyy . . ." This with a puzzled look.

"Um. If he gives you any trouble, just start kissing his neck. Hard, like to leave bite marks. It drives him wild; he can't resist that."

Lawrence cocked his head. "Whattaya mean, 'trouble'?"

"He's nervous about it. So if he seems like he's changing his mind, just get busy on his neck."

Lawrence appeared to think this over. "*You* seem nervous."

Sebby shoved beans into the grinder. "Yeah. That he'll ruin things, that's all."

"Doesn't he really want? Or don't you want him to? I've never seen you act like this before."

"I think I might love him." Sebby began to grind the beans, but the noise of it did not quite drown out Lawrence's squeal. Lawrence dropped to the floor and threw his arms around Sebby.

"Sebbyyy! Are you in love? Does he love you back?"

Sebby kept turning the grinder crank. "He does, at least a little, but I know he's not ready to say it, because . . . he still loves his ex." Sebby scowled. "I thought I could make him forget him." He shook his head and bit his lip; the grinder blurred in front of his eyes. "Make him want to stay, Lawrence. Make him forget."

"We'll brainwash him," Lawrence promised fiercely as he kissed the top of Sebby's head. "The three of us'll keep him so busy, he won't know day from night. That motherfucking motherboard'll be *wiped*."

Sebby laughed, and the sound of it was like a sob.

"Sebby, Sebby, don't cry," Lawrence said, fluttering.

"'M not. 'M just glad." Turning, Sebby reassured his friend, bagged the ground coffee, and sent Lawrence on his way.

Chapter Twenty-Nine

Stop Being So Mean

Sebby curled up on the couch with an afghan and some soy crackers and hummus dip. Having turned out all the lights and set *The Descent* back to where he'd left off, he settled in to be scared, and was only a few minutes into his viewing when the landline rang. He glanced at the caller ID, and it wasn't a number he recognized, so he let it go to messaging. Scarcely had the phone stopped ringing when it sounded again. Again, he let it go to messaging, but the same thing happened: it stopped ringing and began again. Someone was determined to talk to a human being. Sighing, Sebby paused the movie and picked up. "Hello?"

"Hi, there. It's me."

Collin. Icy-footed ants raced up and down Sebby's back. "Oh, you."

"How are you?"

"Fine. It's very late."

"You're up, though." It was not a question. "I want to talk to you."

If Sebby hung up, he would just call again. Maybe if he agreed to talk, Collin would say whatever he had to say and that would be the end of it. "So talk."

"I want to know how you're doing."

"Fine."

There was a pause, a noise of the phone being shuffled from one ear to the other, and then he spoke. "I want to tell you how sorry I am. I know it was wrong and terrible, and I want to apologize. I didn't mean to hurt you. I've never been so scared in all my life, and then I made it even worse by running away instead of staying to face what I did, to make sure you were okay."

The temperature in the room seemed to drop twenty degrees. Sinking, he pulled the afghan tighter around himself. "I know it wasn't on purpose."

Collin's voice warmed. "I'm in counseling. And I'm in a program. And we're supposed to make amends to people we harmed. And that's why I'm calling."

"Okay. Well . . . you can cross me off your list, now."

"I want to see you."

Sebby felt strangled. He put his hand to his throat. "Collin, no. I'm glad you're dealing with your . . . issues . . . and I'm glad you called to apologize. But all that's over with now. You need to move on. And I'm with someone now."

"Not tonight, you're not."

The strength drained right out of him. He could hardly believe his arm was still holding the phone to his ear.

"You sent him off with the twinkies. And you lied about him living with you too."

The affront jolted Sebby. He sat up straight. "Are you watching my house?" There was no answer, not even the sound of breath, and Sebby fell back against the sofa cushions. "Collin, this is so wrong. What would your counselor say? Listen to me. They have an after-hours number, yes? I'm going to hang up, and you call them." There was more silence, and a pleading note crept into Sebby's voice. "You've been working so hard, no? In your program, the steps, and whatever they have you doing—"

"You're acting like I'm a stalker or something," Collin interrupted. "I want to see you, and I had to see this guy that you were supposedly living with. I just want to hang out. Can't you even let me in to talk?"

"I'm hanging up now. Do what I said. Don't call back." Sebby hit the End button on the cordless and pressed Call, listening to the dial tone, not wanting to hang up and hear it ring again. He leaned over, unplugged the phone, and switched on the lamp.

He couldn't call Todd or Barry and Lawrence, not after making such a big thing about them going home together. Ethan, maybe Ethan. He and Wayne went to bed early, but it was worth a try. He texted Ethan's cell phone first, then Wayne's, and finally called their landline, where he left a message. "It's me. If you get this, call me right away, even if it's late. Um, everything's fine, just call."

Who else could he try? Leo! He was an insomniac, he might answer. He texted, *Are you up?*

Sebby held his breath, but the response came almost immediately. *Yes. Everything all right?*

Yea. No. Collin called here and creeped me out. Do u think u could maybe come over?

What about your boyfriend? Call him.

Sebby paused for thought, sucking at his lower lip. *No Todd's not available right now. I tried Ethan but it's so late. Please?*

All right. I can't sleep anyway.

K call me when u get here so I know it's u!

He had just set his cell phone down when it went off, and he nearly jumped out of his skin. It was Leo calling, telling Sebby to call the police. Sebby argued. Leo told him to say he'd seen a prowler, no need to say anything about an ex-boyfriend. Sebby agreed in order to get Leo off the phone, but he didn't call the police, only shrank and tried to disappear under his afghan. Could Collin see into the house? His eyes darted around the room: all the shades and curtains were drawn. Collin couldn't see through them, could he? The doors were locked; Sebby always locked them.

This was ridiculous. If Collin *was* still watching, Sebby didn't want him to see that he was frightened. He hurled the afghan away from himself, knocking the box of crackers to the floor. The hummus container toppled, splattering the couch, the floor, and the afghan. Sebby pressed his lips together and growled as he gathered up the mess and the afghan. Intending to toss the afghan down the basement stairs to the laundry, he took three steps and froze, certain that Collin was waiting in the kitchen. It was the place Sebby had last seen him. A twinge in his arm made him wince.

"There's no one in the kitchen," he said aloud. He marched through the house, switching on lights as he went. He dropped the hummus into the garbage, and continued to the basement door, where he froze again, hand on the doorknob, his eyes locked on the back door, which led out to the deck. The dead bolt was disengaged, the mechanism pointed right instead of left: unlocked. How could it be unlocked? He remembered locking it! Could Collin have gotten in the house—in the basement? Was he right there on the other end of the doorknob? Sebby thought he felt the knob turning within his grip; the door was going to fly open and Sebby would be knocked to the floor. *Move!* He backed up a step, eyes darting from one door to the other, when an immense bang sounded, the noise of it smacking his eardrums like a sudden increase in air pressure. Sebby cried out and skittered backward till his hip clipped the kitchen table, and he realized that it was the screen door banging in the wind. But he knew he'd latched that door, and it couldn't have come unlatched unless someone had unlatched it.

And then he remembered. Earlier, Barry had left the room to smoke, and he must have gone out on the deck, must have neglected to lock the door when he'd come in. Sebby's breath was swept from his lungs as he wilted and clutched the afghan to his face. Oh, what a picture he was making for Collin, if Collin *was* watching.

The screen door banged again, and Sebby jumped despite himself. Catching his lower lip between his teeth, he lunged at the door, dropped the afghan, and flipped the dead bolt. The screen door could bang until Leo got there. Sebby didn't know how much time had passed; it seemed like days.

What if Collin *was* in the house? In the basement . . . or upstairs, or in the bathroom, past which Sebby had walked on his way to the kitchen. Even now, Collin might be lurching down the hallway . . . Sebby whipped around, so certain of seeing Collin's hulking form, that for an instant he did see it, black against the hallway light. In the space of time it took for him to draw breath to yell, the apparition vanished, and the air drained from his lungs in a deflated sigh. "*Ay, Dios*, get a grip. Collin does not want to hurt you, he said so . . ." His voice trailed off, and he jittered from one foot to the other until his cell sounded, and he was relieved almost to tears to see Leo's name on the screen. "Leo?"

"I've pulled in your driveway. Nothing looks suspicious."

"Oh, Leo, I'm so glad you're here. *Carajo*, he was watching my house, he said he knew I was alone. Leo, he was *watching my house*!" Sebby flew to the door, tossed the lock, and threw the door wide. There was Leo coming up the walk in slacks and a button-down shirt, holding his phone and giving Sebby a little wave. "*Mi casa es tu casa. Gracias*, thank you for coming." The words tripped over each other, filling the quiet night with babble till Leo reached the door.

"Are the police on their way?" Leo took Sebby's elbow and steered him away from the door, closing and locking it behind them.

"I don't need them; you're here now." Leo clucked but said nothing, and Sebby threw shaking arms around him, pressing his face into Leo's shirt that smelled of fabric softener and cherry cigar smoke. "He was watching my house!" he repeated, the fear giving way to outrage. Leftover adrenaline ebbed and flowed, seeking an outlet.

"There, there." Leo put his arms around Sebby. "You're safe." He patted Sebby's trembling form.

"I'm safe," Sebby agreed, pulling away with reluctance, letting his arms slide from around Leo and linger at his buttons. He smiled up into Leo's face.

"You're going to have to get a restraining order."

Sebby grimaced. "Are you hungry? Want something to eat? Or some coffee?" His fingers stroked Leo's buttons.

"I could use a drink," Leo allowed, and Sebby flew to his nice, bright kitchen. Leo followed and reached the Laphroaig down for Sebby, and he latched the screen door so it wouldn't bang anymore.

They went back into the living room with their tumblers of Laphroaig on ice. Sebby frowned when Leo seated himself in an easy chair rather than on the couch where they could cuddle, but then he simply sat in Leo's lap. Leo shifted and patted Sebby's back as he sipped his drink. Sebby took a long swallow.

Leo cleared his throat. "Did you and your young man, Todd, break up?"

"No," Sebby said in surprise. He took another swallow, and the smooth, golden warmth began to leak through all his limbs. He slumped until he could rest his head on Leo's shoulder.

"Is he out of town?"

"No." It occurred to him that Leo must wonder why Todd wasn't available on a Friday night. "He's with Barry and Lawrence tonight."

"Ah." Leo nodded and sipped, breathing into the tumbler.

Sebby snuggled closer and smoothed his free hand over Leo's chest and down his abdomen. "I like this shirt." Leo was endearingly soft around the middle, after the manner of an older man who eats what he likes and exercises just enough to keep from getting fat.

"You're putting my leg to sleep," Leo complained, his deep voice reverberating inside the tumbler of whiskey.

"Sorry." Sebby shifted his weight, wriggling indecently. "Better?" he murmured into Leo's neck.

"Not really."

Sebby shifted and wriggled more. He pressed a quick kiss just under Leo's ear. "Better? Don't want your legs to quit working. You might need them."

Leo stomped the offending foot, bouncing Sebby, who laughed and clutched Leo, spilling a small amount of whiskey down Leo's front.

"¡Mierda! All over your nice shirt. Ay, let me get it in the washer before it stains."

"Very funny." Leo plucked at the wet spot on his shirt, holding it away from his skin.

"No? I feel responsible." Sebby leaned down and put his lips to Leo's shirt, sucking the fabric into his mouth.

Leo sighed and tugged till his shirt came free of Sebby's mouth, and then he pulled Sebby close, laying his cheek against Sebby's hair. "You had a bad fright."

Sebby ignored this piece of irrelevance and nuzzled Leo's neck. He nudged Leo's collar with his nose. "I just want to know if your belly button is still as cute. You had the sweetest belly button." His hand crept down to pull Leo's shirt free of its tuck. He remembered how it felt to smoosh his face into Leo's soft flesh and kiss his navel.

Leo did nothing to interfere with the shirt untucking. "What do you plan to do about this Collin situation?"

"There's no situation!" Sebby protested. "It was just a phone call. Won't you kiss me? Even if you don't want to do anything else, just kiss me?"

Smoothing back Sebby's hair, Leo kissed his forehead with a loud, condescending smack. "What'd Collin say?"

"Nooo, I don't want to think about it." Sebby squirmed, out of discomfort and out of the hope that this action would make Leo stop being so mean.

"You're going to have to."

Sebby could've shouted with exasperation. "Fiiine." First gulping the remainder of his whiskey, he stared down into his glass, swirling it so the half-melted ice cubes slid around and around. "He said he was in a program, he said he wanted to see me, he said he had to make amends, and he said he knew I lied about Todd living with me, and he knew I was alone because Todd was with Barry and Lawrence. I told him I didn't want to see him and to not call me back and to call his therapist."

Twisting at the waist, Sebby turned, leaned, and stretched, reaching to set his glass on the end table, testing Leo's arm to see if he would let him fall. Leo steadied him, and Sebby sat upright again. "Now, kiss me, you mean man, yes?" His hand resumed tugging at Leo's shirt, and his fingers found bare flesh and walked their way to his navel. "Mm, there it is."

Leo's hand sought Sebby's and pressed it, and he tilted his head and laid his mouth against Sebby's, but Sebby's elation was short-lived, as the kiss was so passionless as to be insulting. He opened his eyes to find Leo regarding him. His brow was furrowed, and Sebby traced the lines on Leo's forehead. "What are you thinking, *cariño*?"

"I thought I heard something. A car in the driveway, maybe?"

Sebby levitated straight into the air and dove for the door, and he leaned out into the night. In the driveway, only Leo's black Nissan was visible.

"You're hearing things," he said, returning and plopping into Leo's lap. Sebby wrapped an arm around his neck. "Clean out your ears." And he poked his tongue into Leo's ear.

"Whoa!" Leo jerked away and swiped at his ear. "I could've sworn I heard a car." He smiled, and it was such a kind smile that Sebby couldn't be angry at having been tricked. "I've never seen you move that fast. Hoping it was Todd, or afraid it was Todd?"

"Both, I guess," Sebby mumbled. He dropped his eyes. Slipping his hand down over Leo's chest, he began maneuvering the first button from its buttonhole. "I know what you're saying. Yeah, Todd wouldn't like it if, you know, he found me kissing you." He took a deep breath, his fingers making their way to the second button. "But he's not here, and you are, and I need someone."

At that, Leo's eyes softened, and he smoothed Sebby's hair with both hands. "I'm sorry he's not here for you." Leo took Sebby's chin between his thumb and forefinger. "I just met him the one time, but he seemed like a decent young man. I hoped you'd outgrown your victim phase at last."

Guilt nibbled at the edges of Sebby's conscience with nasty, sharp teeth, because Todd *was* a decent young man, and *victim phase*, what the fuck was that, but Leo had taken hold of Sebby's wrists and pulled his arms wide, leaning in to kiss Sebby hard, his lips warm and tasting of good Scotch, and *I don't care, I don't care, I don't care*, Sebby told himself. He arched and moaned. Leo pushed him to his feet, ducked and, butting his shoulder into Sebby's middle, hoisted him over his shoulder and carried him out of the room and up the stairs. From Sebby's vantage point, the floor undulated as if it were alive, but Sebby was safe from it and from everything.

Chapter Thirty

Mirror

*W*hen they left the house, Barry slid into Todd's truck and began fiddling with the radio. *If I can just get through this night,* Todd thought. Why was Sebby so insistent on this encounter? What gap in their relationship did he believe existed that could be filled in this manner? Sebby had often said that monogamy was unnatural; perhaps he feared Todd would stray, and this was his way of steering the straying. Well, if it made Sebby feel better, he would go along with it. He had resolved to cease his judgmental ways. Relationships were all about compromise.

Barry directed Todd through the turns required to get on the interstate. His fingers moved in a hypnotic motion up and down the length of Todd's thigh. Todd chewed his tongue and searched his brain, which was rapidly being deprived of its fair share of blood, for a topic of conversation. "Sebby says you're his oldest friends." *That's appropriate. Talk about the boyfriend on whom you are ostensibly cheating.*

"We knew each other in church, and pretty fast we knew we had something in common." There was an awkward pause during which Todd waited for Lawrence to comment—Lawrence who was not there because he was driving his own vehicle—until Barry, glancing around, supplied the rest of the thought: "We were both going to hell."

Todd laughed and touched his fingers to Barry's. "The road to hell is paved with pretty boys, so I am told."

"It doesn't seem so bad now, but it was scary then. The Lake of Fire."

Todd blinked. "The what? What are you, a Baptist?"

"Sebby didn't tell you? The Church of Jesus Christ of Latter-day Saints."

Todd gaped at Barry before remembering where he was and returning his eyes to the road. "Sebby's a *Mormon*?"

"Ex-Mormon. Sometimes I wonder, though, if you're ever really an ex." There was another pause, and Todd could almost hear Lawrence's voice chiming in before Barry continued. "Once a Mormon, always a Mormon."

"But. He's an atheist."

"That's what he says."

"Perhaps," Todd said dryly, "this explains his predilection for sharing his significant other with the two of you."

Nodding, Barry giggled. Eschewing the safety belt, he scooted all the way across the bench seat of the old truck to cuddle next to Todd and cup his crotch. "Be our hubby, Todd, and we'll be your wives. Your own little harem." Again there was that odd, Lawrence-shaped pause before Barry finished. "Like King Solomon in the Bible."

The reference made Todd uneasy. "Safety belt," Todd insisted, and Barry, laughing, obeyed and slid back to his place. Todd shifted in a useless effort to ease the pressure at his groin. "So . . . what was it like growing up Mormon?"

"Lots of friends and family. Stuff to do. Lots of church. On my knees a lot." Todd caught the coquettish look but was spared the discomfort of thinking up a clever rejoinder, as Barry continued. "Sometimes I miss it. Miss all my family."

"You don't see your family?"

"You can't be a fag Saint."

Todd's hands clenched on the steering wheel. "Fuck." *Another gay estranged from his family.* "I'm sorry."

"You can swear. *Ex*-Mormon, remember?"

"That wasn't what I meant. Ah . . . but Sebby sees his father."

"Sebby's dad's a convert." It was said with offhand contempt that Todd found both heartbreaking and amusing. "My family's been Saints for generations, and none of their kids can be fags." His heart twisting in sympathy, Todd reached for Barry's hand and laced their fingers together, and Barry returned the squeeze of his hand.

"And Lawrence . . . he was Mormon too?"

A smile spread over Barry's face. "Nooo. Lawrence moved to our school, and he was so . . . different. Happy. He was so . . . out, and he didn't care who knew it. He's a year older. We started hanging with him. I wanted to be like him. Then Sebby's mom died." Barry grimaced. "She had cancer. We all prayed, but it didn't help; she died anyway. That's when Sebby quit believing in God. He went kind of wild, and I went with him, and Lawrence knew all these places and all these people . . ." He turned to look out the window. "Who wants to go to Heaven, anyway? I don't want to go anywhere that Lawrence won't be."

Greater love hath no man, than to give up all hope of Heaven for his friend. "Does Lawrence, then, refuse redemption?"

"Lawrence says when he gets to the pearly gates, he'll kiss Saint Peter's beard and tickle his ears until he lets him in."

Todd could well imagine the look of astonishment upon the face of the stalwart saint, and he laughed.

"Right? I told him that there's no such thing as the pearly gates, but he doesn't listen."

"But, surely, you don't continue to suffer under the misapprehension that you will be condemned to hell for faggotry?"

"Sodomy," Barry said. "The Bible's pretty clear on it."

"In point of fact, it's not," Todd said. "The tale of Sodom and Gomorrah, if read in a spirit of scholarly impartiality and placing the text in context with its time and culture, is viewed as a cautionary tale of disobedience to God as well as maltreatment of guests. The sacred duty of hospitality was one of the highest—" He cut himself off, for Barry's brow was furrowed in confusion, and Todd reminded himself that Barry had had a conservative upbringing with traditional interpretations of Biblical texts, and one freeway lecture would not be adequate to enlighten him. "Besides. I could never respect a God who did not want you around."

There was a soft *aww* and a whispered, "I can't wait to tell Lawrence what you said!" Barry scooted across the seat again. He pressed a kiss to Todd's jaw and laid his cheek on Todd's shoulder. "Sebby got a good one this time."

This time. Todd nuzzled Barry's hair, inhaling the lingering tang of dance sweat before saying in a soft voice, "Safety belt."

Safety-minded as he was, Todd always kept to the speed limit, so Lawrence, who had no such compunctions, had arrived at the apartment before them. Todd was barely inside the door before he was sandwiched between the two boys: Barry against his back and Lawrence against his front. The two of them kissed one another over Todd's shoulder with little exclamatory moans, as if the excitement of being reunited after a twenty-minute separation was almost too much to bear. "Todd said he could never respect a God who didn't want me around!" Barry announced.

Lawrence appeared puzzled, but his brow smoothed upon determining that it was a compliment, and he turned beaming eyes on Todd. "Ohhh! That was a sweet thing to say!"

"Say something sweet to Lawrence, now," Barry commanded.

"Er," Todd said, trying to catch his breath, and feeling put-upon or like a performing monkey. "First, might I trouble you for a cup of coffee?"

"Sure!" Stepping back, Lawrence took Todd by the hand and towed him into the living room. "Sebby ground me some coffee, but we don't have his fancy-dancy gay coffee maker."

"You're a fancy-dancy gay coffee maker," said Barry.

"Just what do the two of you do?" Todd wondered how they could ever manage to be apart for an entire work day.

"Tend bar," Barry said.

"And pick up boys. Have a seat, Todd. Barry, help me." The boys disappeared into the adjoining kitchen, and Todd could hear a whispered conference and the clink of dishware as the coffee brewed. He chose a corner of the sofa but, reconsidering, moved to the middle and sat on his hands, taking in the room around him. Inexpensive mismatched furniture hugged the walls.

On the scuffed coffee table stood a framed portrait of Barry and Lawrence. The photo struck Todd the moment his eyes fell upon it, arousing in him the tenderest feelings of affection; it was a studio portrait of the two boys in profile, their heads inclined toward one another, foreheads touching, eyes downcast, lips curved in identical gentle smiles. Todd picked it up; the photographer had captured a moment's expression that said a thousand words on the subject of Barry and Lawrence.

"You like that picture?"

Todd lifted his head to see Lawrence offering a mug of fragrant coffee. "Very much." He replaced the photo.

"I can get you one of those to keep!" Lawrence said, and bounced out of the room.

"One of what?"

"He means the picture." Barry settled himself next to Todd.

"Oh. Ah . . ." Something seemed inappropriate about accepting a photo, but Todd wasn't sure how to refuse. Returning, Lawrence landed on Todd's other side, wallet-sized snapshot in hand.

"Thank you." A glow of pleasure filled him to be holding the pretty thing. After all, what could be wrong with carrying a picture of one's friends?

"Put it in your wallet," Lawrence ordered. Todd set his coffee aside and shifted in order to fetch out his billfold, but Lawrence helpfully removed it for him, his hand sliding everywhere around the area before finding what it sought. Todd froze in place until the wallet was handed to him. Relaxing backward, he found Barry's hand waiting, and Lawrence's fingers wormed their way back to where his wallet had been. The ensuing exploration of his anatomy caused Todd to inhale and bite his lip. It was a replay of the party, weeks earlier, but there was no nearby press of people and no inhibiting presence of boyfriend.

As Todd tucked the photo away, he realized that the reason it had seemed wrong to accept the gift was that he had no picture of Sebastián in his wallet, and the portrait of Barry and Lawrence was joining the picture of Vivian that still resided there. He tossed the wallet onto the table, retrieved his mug, blew on his coffee, and took a long swallow. He needed the fortifying beverage, the essence of the beans that Sebby's hands had purchased for him, had ground for him.

"Is it good?" Lawrence asked. "The coffee?" Two hands slid up Todd's thighs, reaching inward and upward at the exact same moment, meeting in the middle, and the skillful choreography of the two young men drove all thoughts of former and current loves, if not completely from Todd's mind, at least into its depths where they would be silent for a time. Todd whispered that it was very good, and he gave in to their ministrations, his muscles tensing and relaxing by turns.

Two mouths found his neck, bestowing wet kisses and lapping tongues and then sucking at the tender flesh, drawing involuntary cries from him. He writhed and found himself pinned, Lawrence's knee on his leg, Barry's arms restraining Todd's arm. Lips, tongues, teeth caressed and tortured his neck, his throat, until in a spasm of combined fury and passion, Todd freed one arm and threw off Barry, who laughed and shoved Todd into Lawrence's arms. Clothes were shed on the way to the bedroom. Lawrence, ivory of skin and slender of waist, walked backward, beckoning like a siren, and Barry followed behind Todd, his hands on Todd's shoulders.

"You're beautiful," Todd whispered, eyes riveted. "Beautiful."

Lawrence smiled and continued to beckon, each arm in turn reaching and curving back on itself, until Todd was stopped cold by the reflection of three naked young men in the floor-to-ceiling mirror that covered one bedroom wall.

"Do you like the mirror?" Barry nuzzled Todd's ear.

"Some boys don't." Lawrence glanced over his shoulder at his reflection and preened.

"It has a curtain if you don't." Barry's mirror-eyes met Todd's real ones.

"No. No curtain." Todd reached for Lawrence. His hands marveled at Lawrence's satin-smooth chest, stroking his shoulders and passing down his back to the taut buttocks. Barry moved closer and put his arms around Todd to touch Lawrence. The taller boys kissed each other over Todd's shoulder; Todd tilted his head to see, and it was all becoming too, too much.

They turned their attentions to him, kissing him by turns, until Lawrence whispered, "Barry first," and as one many-legged being, they approached the four-poster bed. The room was bright; of what use was a mirror in a dark room? Unlike the cheap furniture in the living room, the bedroom set was of the highest quality, and the mattress was spread with a down comforter and mounded with pillows, pillows that Lawrence swept to the floor before reclining there. The sight of Lawrence as he stretched out full length, pale against the midnight-blue comforter, made Todd groan with need. Lawrence passed a condom to Barry, who knelt and pressed kisses to Todd's flank and stomach as he rolled it on for him. Todd wound his fingers in Barry's thick hair, and Barry mouthed Todd's cock before taking Todd's two hands in his and pulling himself upright. He turned away, and there was the sound of something being poured, and he turned back, his hands dripping, taking first one of Todd's hands and then the other, anointing Todd's palms and the length of each finger in slippery stuff.

Barry kissed him and passed his slick hands over Todd's chest and stomach, and then encircled Todd in his arms to slather his back, pressing their oiled bodies together, his cock hard against Todd's belly. Turning away, he leaned over the bed, legs spread, draping his upper body over Lawrence and rubbing against him.

Todd spent all of half a second admiring Barry's shapely ass and the lyrical bumps of his arched spine before sliding lubed fingers inside him. There was a whimper and shivering, and wordless noises of comfort from Lawrence, and Todd guided his cock inside and then held himself still, eyes closed, feeling the tension in Barry's body and waiting for him to relax. Barry whimpered again and moved. Todd moved with him, massaging Barry's oiled back. His hands encountered other hands, and opening his eyes, he saw that the boys' arms were wrapped around one another. Barry's face was hidden in Lawrence's neck, and Lawrence crooned to him, "Shh, Barry, it's all right, it's all right, Barry. It's good," and so on in a continuous murmur.

"Is . . . something the matter?" Worried, Todd almost backed up, but Barry was clenched so tightly around him that it would likely hurt Barry if he pulled out.

"No, it's good, Todd. I talk to him like this." Lawrence went on encouraging Barry and rubbing his back.

Feeling ridiculous, Todd joined in after a moment, telling Barry that he was beautiful, that he was sweet, and he smoothed his hand up and down Barry's spine and over the curves of hip and buttock and thigh till he felt Barry relax. Todd began to move, and his words lost sense until he was repeating over and over, "Oh, sweet, oh, sweet." He began to thrust harder, and there was a strangled sort of noise from Barry, a muffled cry, which caused Todd to pause. "Have I hurt you?"

"Those are just his sounds, Todd, don't worry."

There was another cry, and Barry raised his head, the better to be heard. "Go, Todd!"

Lifting his eyes to his reflection, he found that he hardly recognized himself. Who was that buff, oiled young man with the long, tangled hair who appeared to be fucking two boys at once? He stared uneasily.

"Harder!" Barry begged, and Todd complied. Lawrence went on talking to Barry in an undertone. Todd caught the words *I love you* and heard them returned, and moments later Barry whimpered and shuddered in climax. Todd forgot that he had ought to save something for Lawrence, and he came in the next moment and stood, shivering and clutching at Barry. At last, Barry moved and rolled away, and Lawrence coaxed Todd onto the bed, and the three of them collapsed in a sweating, panting heap. It reminded Todd of how they'd dropped, laughing, to the floor during *West Side Story*, and it made him smile. Barry's eyes were shut, and Lawrence smoothed Barry's hair and kissed his forehead. Their devotion to one another was touching; it made Todd's heart lurch. He pressed his free hand to his aching ribs and squeezed his eyes shut.

Lawrence was having none of that, however, and with complete confidence, he turned his attention to Todd and worked his wily ways to bring Todd up again. Minutes later, Todd found himself flat on his back, Lawrence straddling him and lowering himself onto Todd's cock. He wiggled until he was comfortable, while Todd clenched his teeth with the effort of keeping still, and then Lawrence leaned back against Todd's bent knees, spreading out his own legs on either side of Todd. Todd smoothed his hands up and down them, tickling Lawrence's knees to make him squirm. Barry shifted to press his mouth to Todd's neck, and kissed his way down chest and stomach to where he could take Lawrence's cock into his mouth.

No one could expect this to last long, and it didn't, and then Todd fell into an exhausted sleep, a pretty head nestled in the crook of each shoulder.

Todd awoke in the middle of the night to find that he was sleeping alone. Barry and Lawrence had curled up together like puppies, limbs entangled to the point where it was difficult to tell which belonged to whom. No one had bothered to get up and shut off the lights, and Todd crawled out of bed and trudged to the doorway, where he paused, hand on the switch, gazing at the tangle that was BarrynLawrence. The head of one rested under the chin of the other, and their faces appeared similar even in sleep, lips parted, eyebrows arched in the same expression of innocence. *They're like a* duprass, Todd thought, remembering the Vonnegut-invented religion of Bokononism, *a* karass *consisting of two people, their spirits and their destinies interwoven so tightly that there is no room for anyone else's*. Todd felt privileged to have basked in the reflection of such an enduring love. After a last wistful glance, he switched off the light, pulled the door to, and ambled down the hallway, gathering up his clothes as he went, easily plucking his more sober colors from among Barry's and Lawrence's bright clothing.

"Are you leaving?"

Todd straightened and turned around. A tousled Lawrence stood in the hallway, hugging himself and eyeing Todd.

"That would hardly be honorable." Draping his clothes over one arm, Todd came back to place a hand on Lawrence's shoulder and peck his cheek. "No, I wouldn't leave without saying good-bye."

"Come back to bed," Lawrence cooed. "Aren't you cold?" He shivered, as if to demonstrate that he, Lawrence, was cold and it would be most unchivalrous of Todd not to warm him.

"In point of fact, I woke up chilled," Todd said, and regretted the words as a look of guilty alarm crept over Lawrence's face, his eyes shifting. Wanting to reassure him, Todd put his clothing-draped arm around Lawrence's waist and brushed the fingers of his free hand over Lawrence's cheek. "Thank you for . . . allowing me to stay the night, Lawrence. It isn't something I'll soon forget."

"You didn't stay the night," Lawrence protested, leaning into Todd with a sigh, and tucking his head into the curve of Todd's neck and shoulder. "Not until it's morning. Come back to bed."

Todd hesitated. The boys were sweet, but he missed Sebby. After all, he'd barely seen him all week. "Thank you, but I'm afraid I'm done in. Without an infusion of coffee and a breakfast of champions, I'll be of no use to anyone."

"That's what you think," Lawrence said, and Todd, feeling a playful hand creep near his privates, backed away. Lawrence regarded him, hurt and worry playing over his features, and Todd relented.

"I'll come back to bed. To *sleep*," he emphasized.

Satisfied, Lawrence led him off to bed, where two young men warmed Todd up in more ways than one, and it was some time before any more sleep occurred.

Chapter Thirty-One

Migas

A batch of *migas* steamed in the frying pan, and Sebby's teeth worried at his lower lip as he stirred with a wooden spoon. He hoped Todd would sleep late. He wasn't an early riser like Sebby. He'd sleep late and then Barry and Lawrence would keep him busy for the morning, wouldn't they? And Leo would be up soon, and Sebby would feed him *migas*, and he'd leave.

But wishes were like fishes—sometimes you caught them, sometimes they got away, and Sebby heard the front door slam. He jumped; his wooden spoon dropped to the floor. He ran to greet Todd and caught him in the living room. Could he somehow send him home? "You're early. How'd it go?"

"Fine. Whose car is that in the driveway?" Todd's smile was genuine, but there was a tightness about his eyes, not the way Sebby's boys usually looked when they returned from B&L.

Everything faded into the background as Todd's arms slid around him, and Sebby dropped his chin and pushed his nose into Todd's throat. Todd smelled of Barry and Lawrence. To Sebby, it was a comforting smell, but he tensed and wondered if Todd could smell Leo on *him*.

"Mm, I missed you," Todd said into Sebby's hair.

"'Fine,' what's 'fine'?" No one had ever said *fine* after a night with them. "Did you like them? Did they like you?" He opened his eyes and noticed for the first time the mottled flesh of Todd's neck, bruised up and down—on both sides, he saw as he tipped his head. *He must have had a good time!* Sebby pressed his finger to a bright mark, and Todd shivered. He nuzzled Sebby's hair, not in a seductive manner, but like a cat seeking comfort.

"I can't speak for them, but I think I carried myself well enough." He sighed. "To me, it was rather a lonely thing. Once they had me primed, their attentions were all for each other."

Lonely! A rope of good curse words uncoiled in Sebby's head. "Did you come straight here? Do you need to go home?"

"I'm yours for the day."

Sebby fidgeted.

Todd sniffed. "Do I smell *migas*? It's ambrosial. Jesus, I'm ravenous. Whose car is in the drive?"

"Yes, *migas*. I need to go stir it." He pulled away, glancing at the stairs as he passed them. No sign of Leo yet. Todd followed him into the kitchen. "Do you need to go home and check in?" That was how Todd always put it: *check in*. "Do you need to go home and shower and change?" The *migas* had scorched, and Sebby *tsk*ed, pushing the skillet away from the burner.

"I wasn't going to stop at home. I thought I might soak in the tub." He paused in the act of opening a cupboard. "Is that all right?" There was another pause as he placed two plates on the kitchen table. "Are you trying to get rid of me?"

Sebby, his back to Todd, pushed the knuckles of one hand into his teeth. With an effort, he put a teasing note into his voice. "You caught me, Toddfox. I got used to being alone all week. It's hard to adjust." He turned and flashed him a smile. "Let's eat out on the deck." He could sit Todd down with the *migas* and then go shoo Leo out of his house.

But Todd wasn't moving. He stared at Sebby. "What is going on?" And then, sharply, "Sebastián. Whose car is in the drive?"

Sebby snatched a tortilla and began shredding it, letting the pieces drop to the floor. Todd gaped. Drawing a deep breath, Sebby lifted his eyes to meet Todd's. "It's Leo's. I got scared last night, and I called him to come over."

"Leo was here? He's still here?" Todd shook his head. "If you were scared, why didn't you call me?"

"How could I?" Sebby flung the rest of the tortilla into the sink and turned back to seize the skillet. He scooped a large measure onto each plate. "After making such a big thing about you going with them, how could I call and make you come back? You would've thought I was crazy."

"I'd have thought you were scared! I'd have thought you . . ." Todd's throat worked as he swallowed ". . . wanted me." His eyes fell to regard the *migas* on his plate. Footsteps sounded in the hallway, and they both turned to see Leo entering the kitchen. Washed and dressed, every hair in place, he could have stepped from the pages of *Esquire*, if not for the whiskey stain down his shirtfront. He eyed Todd with clear disapproval, and Todd's eyes went from Leo to Sebby and back.

"You're not hungry, are you Leo? You're never hungry in the morning." Sebby could've bitten his tongue for this slip-up. *Never in the morning*, chingados!

"Starved." Leo dropped an arm around Sebby's shoulders and kissed the top of his head. Sebby stepped away.

Todd opened his mouth to speak, then his jaw snapped shut. Sebby thought he heard the clack of his teeth. Todd strode from the room, and Sebby glared at Leo. "*¡Siéntate, chingados!*" He pointed at a chair, and Leo sat down and helped himself to *migas*. Sebby hurried after Todd, calling his name, and came to an abrupt stop in the living room. Todd stood in the middle of the room, looking around as if bewildered.

"Tell me you didn't sleep with him."

He couldn't lie, not about this, not to Todd. "I slept with him."

Todd's chin hit his chest, but then he lifted it hopefully. "You mean long ago?"

Sebby's insides were dying. "I mean last night."

"Jesus, Sebby!" Todd collapsed onto the sofa and dropped his head into his hands.

"I'm sorry. I didn't mean for you to be hurt. I . . . It doesn't mean anything." Sebby reached to touch Todd's shoulder, and at least Todd didn't pull away.

"If that's what you wanted, why didn't you say so? You didn't need this subterfuge; you didn't have to farm me off to *them*. I would've stayed away, I—" His voice cut off.

It was Sebby's turn to gape. "No! That didn't have anything to do with it, I didn't plan for it, didn't mean for it to happen. I just got scared, so scared that I couldn't be alone, and I called Leo for company. That's all."

Todd raised his head. "I don't understand. The movie frightened you? You watch those things all the time, you told me they're fun."

Sebby hesitated. "A . . . a girl in the movie fell and broke her leg, and it reminded me of when I broke my arm." This was such a terrible lie that he squeezed his eyes shut. It was a lie in which the truth was hidden, for the memory of his broken arm *had* frightened him; oh, why couldn't Todd just drop it! "It's just that I needed someone, and you weren't here."

"I wasn't *here* because you pimped me out to *them*!" His voice rose, he pushed Sebby away, and he stood and headed for the door. With his hand on the knob, he turned back as if he had more to say, though he just stared.

"I know it's my fault; I didn't mean that it was your fault that you weren't here, that you were gone." Sebby was babbling, and now Leo's footsteps were approaching from behind.

"Everything all right?" Leo said, and Sebby could imagine him giving Todd a warning look, but Sebby didn't dare take his eyes from Todd, who was now staring at Leo with an indescribable expression on his face. It wasn't anger, it wasn't jealousy—Sebby didn't know what it was.

"Leo, go away!" Sebby begged.

"Your boy had a bad fright last night. You—"

Sebby cut him off with a warning shout: "Leo!"

"He told me," Todd said.

Leo's voice was calm, steady. "He needed you, and you weren't here."

Todd flushed a dark red. "I find it quite fascinating to hear that from you, as it wasn't long ago that Sebastián told me, in no uncertain terms, that he did *not* need me."

Sebby buried his face in his hands and groaned.

"There's no reason to be angry," Leo said in a reasonable tone. "He wasn't doing anything you weren't doing."

The flush drained from Todd's face. His mouth opened. Sebby could hear his indrawn breath, but whatever he intended to say, no words came out. His mouth closed. He scrubbed his hand over his forehead, through his mussed hair, and across his lips. "Right, then."

He turned to go, feeling his pocket for his keys.

This was out of control. And Sebby did not like out of control. And it was silly, and Todd was overreacting, and Leo was overprotective. "Todd, sit! Leo, I'm walking you to your car."

Todd, looking lost, obeyed, and Leo followed Sebby outside. Sebby marched out to Leo's Nissan, which seemed even sleeker and blacker next to Todd's ugly, rusted truck. The remote entry chirped as Leo pressed it, and Sebby opened the door and held it for Leo. "I misled you."

"Oh?"

"Last night. I wanted you to sleep with me, and I let you think Todd was . . . a lowlife. I think. So you'd feel sorry for me. And he isn't. I know you're old-fashioned and you don't like when my boyfriends go with Barry and Lawrence, but Todd didn't even want to go! I nagged him till he went, because he won't forget his ex, and I'm so tired of fighting his ex all the *time*, Leo, so tired."

Leo's eyes rolled heavenward, and he heaved a sigh. "Making your boyfriend sleep with your friends won't bring him any closer to you."

Sebby grimaced. Leo didn't understand the situation, the whole Vivian thing. He didn't know what Sebby was going through.

Todd hadn't really liked it, though. He'd called it *lonely*. What if . . .

"I should apologize to Todd." Leo turned back toward the house, but Sebby hastily blocked his path.

"No, Leo. I'll tell him for you. It was all my fault anyway, not yours."

Leo frowned, but he climbed into his car and pulled the door shut. The engine came alive, and the window slid down. "If you care for this one, you shouldn't treat him like he's disposable."

Sebby's mouth fell open. "I didn't! It just—"

"I'll leave the two of you to figure out what to do with each other," Leo said. "And leave me out of it."

The window went up, and the car glided out of the driveway. Sebby bent his head, set his jaw, and marched back into the house.

On the sofa, Todd slumped, head in hands. He lifted his head as Sebby entered, and Leo's apology died in Sebby's throat. Todd's face was contorted; it was an expression Sebby had come to think of as "the Vivian look," the look of a man being ripped inside out.

Sebby was the cause of it, and euphoria made the blood rush to his head.

If Todd could look like that because of Sebby, it could only mean one thing. Todd loved him. Not a little, a lot. Real love. *You jump, I jump. You had me at hello.*

"Todd," he said, and he had to clear his throat and say it again. "Todd."

"I can't do this." Todd's eyes glimmered.

Oh, he couldn't bear it if Todd cried because of him. He nearly leaped to get close to him, to sit down and wind his arms around Todd's arm, half expecting him to try an escape. But Todd sat there like his life was over and nothing that ever happened to him again could matter.

"Can't do what?" Sebby asked gently.

"I can't—" Todd hesitated before continuing "—do this kind of relationship."

"What kind, sweetheart? What do you mean?" Sebby had never called Todd *sweetheart*; it was Todd's word, and it was an odd enough thing that Todd's eyes met Sebby's briefly before averting.

"An 'open' relationship. Whatever you want to call it. Both of us fucking whomever we want. I can't do it."

That was a gross overstatement of revenue. But Sebby let it go. "I know." He raised one hand in order to smooth Todd's rough, tangled hair.

"It's not in my nature."

"I know." Sebby kissed Todd's temple, and Todd's eyes squeezed shut, too late to stop the tear slipping out. Sebby's heart contracted around a core of broken glass.

"I'll say good-bye, then." He tensed as if to rise, but Sebby tightened his hold and kissed away the tear.

"No. Stay," he murmured against Todd's cheek as he pressed closer. "I shouldn't've made you go with them. I was stupid. And I—I didn't mean to sleep with Leo. I just wasn't thinking, I was so scared. I just . . . *Mierda*, I wish I could take it back. More than anything." Todd turned away, and Sebby bit his lip. "I don't want to fight. I think we both want the same thing, if we would just say it, and so I'll say it." He took a deep breath and closed his eyes. "I want you to live here. Move in with me. Stay with me every night." He held his breath and waited on what seemed like the edge of everything for Todd to answer.

Todd sat very still, and neither one of them breathed for minutes and minutes. "What sort of invitation is that? An insurance against further incidents of infidelity?"

"It's not like that. It wasn't like that." Sebby pulled Todd's arm more tightly to his own chest, digging his fingers into the flesh.

Todd shifted. "I feel that I don't even know you. You hold things back, you manipulate me, and now this. This is not what I want from a relationship. I want—" Todd scooted forward, and he swiped at his tears; his eyes sparked. "Someone who is everything to me and to whom I am everything."

If they could just get through this, it would be all right. "I'm sorry, Todd, I'm so sorry. But 'everything'? You expect too much from a relationship." Sebby squeezed and kneaded Todd's arm. "I'm human, you're human, things happen."

Todd shook his head sharply. "It *isn't* too much. It's everything. I want what I had with Vivian. Someone who completes me: my other half, my split-apart. My soul mate."

And Sebby went dead inside. He was sure he was dead, except death couldn't hurt this much. All that broken glass in his heart was working its way out through muscle and bone. The tortured look on Todd's face had had nothing to do with Sebby; it had been the Vivian look after all. A vicious desire to hurt Todd pierced him, and so he spoke the truth out loud, because nothing hurt like the truth, and Todd was so blind. So blind. "Todd. You didn't have that with Vivian. You only thought you did."

Todd sprang to his feet, wrenching himself from Sebby's grasp. "Oh, fuck you. Fuck you. Fuck."

And he stormed out.

Chapter Thirty-Two

Big Lie

Sebby wasn't sure how long he'd sat, staring straight ahead at nothing, before the phone rang. He didn't make a conscious decision to answer it, but somehow the phone was at his ear. "Hello."

"Hello. It's Wayne. I just got your message. Is everything okay?"

Sebby had to think. His brain moved like sludge. He had forgotten that he had told Wayne and Ethan to call him. "Fine."

"Oh. Okay." There was a pause. "Do you need to talk to Ethan?"

"No."

"Oh. Okay."

Sebby knew he should say something, but it was too much work to fish anything out of the sludge.

Wayne said carefully, "Well, okay. Good-bye."

"Wait. Wayne?"

A silence. "Yes?"

"Is Ethan your soul mate?"

More silence, and then a guarded, "Y-y-yes."

"Is he . . . everything to you?"

"Everything? Nothing's everything, what do you mean? I have my work, and that's something; I have family, and that's something; and my home; and hobbies. Books."

Sebby leaned his head against the sofa back and stared at the ceiling, pressing the phone hard against his ear. It hurt. "Do you feel like you need him?"

A note of panic sounded like a doorbell in Wayne's voice. "Of course I need him. What the hell are you talking about? Why are you asking?"

"*Dios mío*," Sebby cursed under his breath. "*Ay*, Wayne, I'm sorry. I don't mean to worry you. Todd, he— We had a fight."

"Oh." Another pause. "Again?"

"I asked him to move in with me, and he said no, because he wants a soul mate!" That summed it up pretty well, as far as Sebby was concerned. "What do I do, Wayne? I don't know about soul mates!"

After several beats of silence, Wayne said, "Here. Talk to Ethan." There was the noise of the phone being shuffled and Wayne saying, *It's Sebby*, and then Ethan's voice.

"Sebby?"

"Ethan, I asked Todd to move in with me, and he said no, and he said he wants what he had with Vivian, and I said he didn't have that with Vivian, and he said fuck you and left, and—" Sebby gasped and grabbed a tissue "—he said he wants a soul mate, someone who's everything, and I don't even believe in souls, and what should I do?"

"Oh, Sebby. Honey, I'm sorry. He really said no?"

"I can't be a soul mate! He just wants too much."

"Well, he was on the rebound, wasn't he? That's never a good thing."

"I knew that he was, though. But I thought I could make him forget." Sebby gave in and wailed the pain of unrequited love. "I don't care! I love him, and he doesn't love me!"

"Aw, honey. Look, you want me to talk to him? Maybe it's a misunderstanding, or maybe it's just too soon. You've known him, what, six months?"

"Four," Sebby admitted.

"Uh-huh. What'd he say, exactly?"

Sebby tried to calm down enough to relate what had passed.

"What a mess," Ethan said. "I don't know, Seb. Not every guy likes your cheating-with-approval thing. He probably feels rejected. It sounds to me like he thinks *you* don't love *him*."

"I asked him to move in, didn't I? *¡Mierda!*"

"Did you tell him you love him?"

Sebby breathed noisily into the phone. "Not in those exact words. He should say it first."

"Why? Because he's 'the man'? I thought you didn't approve of stereotypical gender roles in homosexual relationships."

"That isn't why! It's because he'll say it when he's ready, when he's over *him*."

"If you love someone, you should tell him, and fuck the consequences. Otherwise, every moment you spend with him is a big lie."

And Todd had accused him of being dishonest. "But he said he wants a soul mate!"

"It's just a word. It means the one you love, doesn't it? The one who's a match for you, who you take care of and who takes care of you."

That was poignant, coming from Ethan. There had been times when Wayne had needed a lot of care. *Soul mate. Everything.* Was that kind of love too much for Sebby—to be adored beyond reason, to be idolized, treasured—as he assumed it had been too much for Vivian?

But Todd never said he loved me. All he said was that he wanted what he had with Vivian. He didn't even say he wanted it with . . . me.

"Anyway, he's so mad this time, he might never speak to me again."

"Tell him," Ethan said. "Tell him, and figure it out."

They said good-bye. Sebby cradled the phone, but the thought of calling Todd made him jitter. Procrastinating, he called Barry and Lawrence, who yawned and stretched and blinked. Sebby could see it all in his mind's eye as their sleepy voices ambled over the signal. They put the call on speaker, as they always did, so they could both talk. "Sebbyyy, it's so earlyyy," they complained.

The clock showed 10:36, and Sebby had no sympathy. "Well? How was it? What'd you do to him?"

There was a pause, and Sebby imagined Barry and Lawrence mouthing at each other. Finally, Lawrence spoke. "He's gentle, isn't he?"

"Yes. Yeah, he is. So?"

"He's just not that into us," Barry said.

"Figuratively. 'Cause, literally, he was," Lawrence said.

"Several times," Barry agreed.

Sebby rolled his eyes. "He said he was lonely. I told you not to ignore him!"

"We didn't!" Lawrence protested in a hurt voice.

"Lawrence got up out of a nice warm bed to go fetch him."

"Barry tried real hard not to sound like anything was hurting."

"Like I said, he's just not that into us."

"Figuratively."

"Literally too, at the moment." There was giggling.

Sebby was too irritated to laugh. "Well, did anything happen that I should know?"

"He was a gentleman," Barry said.

"He likes us," Lawrence said.

"But I don't know if he'd come back."

"Are you..." Sebby hesitated, for he'd never pried much into Barry and Lawrence's personal relationship. He took them for granted, a constant, BarrynLawrence, they just *were*. "Are you each other's soul mate?"

"'Soul mate'?" Barry repeated, and laughed.

"You mean, like, do our souls fuck?" Lawrence said.

"I've heard of mind fuck, but—"

"Maybe he meant 'sole,' like, you know, feet."

"Foot-fuck?"

"That was *your* thing, Sebby."

"Never miiind." Sebby sighed in exasperation. It was all delaying tactics. Time to face the music. He said good-bye and dialed Todd.

Chapter Thirty-Three

Why You Can't Forget

"I'm Todd, and my mother is an alcoholic."

"Hi, Todd," polite voices chorused.

Todd drew a deep breath and knuckled his eyes. "Yesterday, I realized that I expect too much from a relationship." He sighed. "I realized this because my boyfriend told me that I expect too much from a relationship." There were some appreciative chuckles. "Naturally, I screamed at him and stormed out." Rueful smiles. *Been there, done that.* "But I thought it over for a day and a night. And I've not been to a meeting for . . . months, so I hunted up Denver-area meetings, and here I am." He paused and scrubbed his hands against his thighs. "Because I'm fucked up and can't make it without the program. My childhood was fucked up, my adolescence was fucked up, and I couldn't wait to get out of there, because *they* were fucked up, not I. Once I was away, I knew my life would be . . . happy. Normal. Perfect. I want it so desperately I place far too much pressure on my loved one. And on myself." He tilted his head back and regarded the ceiling, an effort to keep tears back. "He made a mistake. He is not perfect. Nor am I. And . . . that's all. I pass."

"Thanks, Todd," came the chorus. The woman next to him patted his knee. Relaxing back in the folding chair, he prepared to hear the rest of the confessions, epiphanies, and sob stories.

Todd had turned his phone off upon exiting Sebby's house and left it off. After the meeting, there were numerous texts, seven missed calls, and one voice mail. He scrolled through them: Sebastián,

Sebastián, Sebastián, Sebastián, Vivid—his eyeballs froze to the word on the screen like a tongue to a winter lamppost. He had heard nothing from Vivian since the gut-wrenching call when Viv had been ill. Todd's heart knocked about in his chest. Was Viv all right? Did Viv need him? As he stood there, staring, the phone went off in his hand. He started, nerves singing, but it was Sebby. He hesitated before answering. "Todd here?"

"Oh, you. I've been calling and calling. Todd, will you please come over here so we can talk?"

Todd's stomach tightened. "I— You— I should. I should." He couldn't think. Viv had called. Viv had left a message . . . or had Sebby left it? "Did you leave me a voice mail?"

"No, I didn't leave a message. I just kept calling. Toddfox, I'm sorry about everything. Can we talk about it? Please, I . . . care about you, and I know you do too? And I had no business saying that about Vivian. Will you please come home?"

"I—I— Let me call you back." He pressed End without waiting for a response and accessed voice mail. Viv's voice chimed in his ear. There was a chair, he sank into it.

Vivian's voice was sober, rational, neither weepy nor spacey. Vivian missed him, Vivian wanted him to call. Todd played the message again and once more, *Vivian wanted him*. He sat paralyzed for several seconds that stretched like spandex, till they snapped back on him and he called.

Vivian wanted to see him. Vivian offered to meet him halfway, somewhere in flyover country, if that would work. Vivian had had a lot of time to think things over and felt he had made a terrible mistake. Vivian was lost without him. Vivian had never expected that Todd would move across the country. Vivian had thought Todd would be there when he needed him.

Vivian wanted to maybe get back together. With split infinitives and everything.

The sun was setting behind the mountains. Nervous energy sent Sebby zooming around the place, combing his hair, changing his clothes, tidying up his already tidy home. Todd's voice had sounded grim; after hanging up on Sebby, he had called back and said he was coming over, that he had something to tell him. *Breakup* buzzed unsaid in his tones. If Sebby could speak before Todd did, he could head it off.

There was a knock on the door; Todd wouldn't use his key? Sebby flew to the door, tripping over the vacuum cord and banging his shin on the coffee table. He threw the door open and flung his arms around Todd. Sebby pressed his face to Todd's neck and kissed him. "*Querido, do you forgive me?*"

Todd's muscles tensed under his lips. "Yes . . . it's fine. I—"

"Come in here, *mi casa es tu casa.*" Todd was already in, but he was standing there, and Sebby tugged until he moved and allowed Sebby to tow him to the sofa to sit. Todd's eyes were glued to his shoes. "I don't want to fight anymore." Sebby smiled, but his dimple was wasted. "You're no good at it, Toddfox; it's no fun."

Todd shook his head, looking dazed. "I'm leaving."

Ack, no, he said it. "Oh." He sat back. "Oh no. Because of Leo? I'm sorry! I fucked up but don't leave!"

Todd's eyes met Sebby's, in complete surprise. "What? No. I don't care about that. Well—" And he laughed once, like the bark of a seal. "That's untruthful. I suppose it was rather obvious that I cared. But it's not . . ."

His voice trailed off; his eyes roamed the floor. Sebby took Todd's limp hand in both of his.

Todd drew a deep breath. "Viv called. He wants me back."

Sebby's heart dropped like a swatted fly; it twitched and buzzed somewhere on the floor of his bowels. His eyes snapped to Todd's face. *"I'd be halfway there if I thought he meant it!"* Todd had said, and so he must be convinced that Vivian wanted him back this time, and Sebby couldn't even muster any anger at Vivian. He could feel nothing but sorry for himself, and aggravation that he'd fallen in love with a hopeless cause. He had fucked it up—fucked it all up.

Could it have been any different? If he hadn't made Todd go with Barry and Lawrence, if he hadn't slept with Leo . . . Or would it have ended up this way anyhow? And Todd was squeezing Sebby's hand in both of his. "What can I do? It's Vivian!"

He spoke as if Vivian were a force of nature. As if Vivian were an act of God, a thing that would be listed in an exclusion clause of an insurance policy, and when you filed a claim, your insurance adjuster would say, *Sorry, that's a Vivian, it's not covered.*

"I understand," Sebby mumbled. "It's . . . *him.*" Sebby's eyes locked on his bare toes. He wiggled them to prove he was awake. To prove he was alive.

"I'm sorry!" Todd cried, and Sebby winced.

"Liar," he breathed. *¡Ay, Dios!* Wrenching his hand from Todd's, he pressed his fingertips to his eyes. He swallowed. A gluey lump like refried beans had lodged in his throat. Moments passed before he could force the lump down. Todd got up. Sebby raised his head to see Todd standing in the middle of the room, wringing his hands.

"I have to go to New York."

"I know." Sebby managed a smile, though it felt ghastly.

"I have to see him," Todd said, as though Sebby were arguing, as though he'd said that Todd must not go, as though he'd begged him to stay. "We parted badly. There was never closure."

"Liar." And he said the word louder this time, and Todd blinked. "You're not going for closure. You're going for reopener. And . . ." Sebby took a deep breath ". . . it's good that you're going. Because . . . if he is your soul mate . . . then there's no room for me."

"I'm leaving tonight. Get as far as I can. I'll be gone about a week, I should think. If I do decide to relocate back to New York, all my things are here, in Denver. Sebby. Sebastián . . ." Todd's face crumpled; he was going to cry, *Dios!* If Todd cried, Sebby would cry, and that was not how he wanted to say good-bye.

Wanting Todd to remember him as pretty and desirable and what-fucking-ever, Sebby rose, smiling, and glided into Todd's arms. Todd's entire body was tense as a coiled spring, and Sebby guessed that as soon as the good-byeing was over with, Todd would be gone like a shot.

"If I could wear you like a tattoo under my sleeve . . ." That got Todd's attention. His gaze sharpened, curious. ". . . Maybe then you'd finally believe . . . I can't remember why you can't forget . . ." And Sebby brushed his fingers over Todd's forehead, trying to erase erase erase, make him forget. Todd drew Sebby's hand to his mouth and laid a kiss in his palm. *Sebastián Jonathan Nye, be strong. Nothing lasts forever. Be glad for what you had.*

"I believe." Todd's lips moved against Sebby's palm. "I cannot forget."

Apparently, he didn't recognize the song, and that made Sebby smile. Maybe someday Todd would hear it on the radio and think of him. He stroked Todd's cheek. "I have to tell you one thing before you go. I hope it works out for you. I do, because, when I met you, you were so pitiful, and all I wanted was to see you smile a real smile, and I've seen it. Probably, it *will* work out for you. But—" Feeling Todd shift restlessly, Sebby took a firm grip on Todd's shirt and spoke to head off an interruption "—if it doesn't . . . *come back to me*. I know you won't want to. You'll feel guilty. But *don't*. I'd want you to come back, I'd throw my arms around you and kiss you helpless, I'd—" Feeling his throat begin to close, he stopped.

"I promise. Sebby, if things could have been different..."

"But they can't. And . . . I always knew it would end this way, didn't I?"

Todd kissed him. It was a good-bye kiss, a kiss that could lead to nothing. Todd pulled away, and Sebby followed him out into the evening twilight. On the front walk, Todd stopped and fumbled for his keys.

"Oh," Todd said, and Sebby saw that he was jimmying the catch and working Sebby's key from the fob. Todd held out his hand, offering the key, and Sebby took it. His arms went around Todd and locked, and he did not imagine how he could let go. It was going to be embarrassing. Todd was going to have to pry Sebby's hands loose, and there would be a struggle, and Sebby would be left gasping and sobbing on his front walk. They stood there, Sebby's face pressed to Todd's throat, Todd's cheek pressed to Sebby's hair, and then he was gone—Sebby had let go—and that old, ugly truck started. It backed out of the driveway, the headlights came on, and Todd left.

Chapter Thirty-Four

Magnetic North

*A*t last, Todd could point himself toward his soul's magnetic north. Vivian loved him, and the swelling of Todd's heart threatened to impede his breath. *Vivian*, against whom Todd could never win an argument. *Vivian*, who was so vulnerable and yet had an innate strength with which Todd could never quite come to grips. *Vivian*, who always, always, tasted of tea. Longings on which Todd had kept a firm lid sprang free and careened about inside his head, knocking him dizzy. Every capillary swelled with memories: Vivian's pale, blue-white skin, marred by scars. Viv's alarmingly countable ribs. The long, lean muscles of his legs. Viv's lip ring cold against Todd's mouth. Vivian's voice sighing his name or crying it aloud in passion.

A car horn's blast jerked Todd out of his reverie, and he realized he'd been drifting into the next lane. The gods would have their laugh, would they not, were Todd to be killed or maimed now, just when his life was about to resume? Taking hold of the steering wheel in a white-knuckled grip, he fixed his mind on the immediate tasks ahead. He had to go home. Tell Lloyd he was leaving. Say good-bye to his nephews. Throw some things in a pack. Gas up the truck.

Sebby had been a sport about the whole thing, but was he really all right? Todd shook himself. Sebby would be fine. And Todd never should have left New York, never should have met Sebby in the first place. It had never been meant to be. Vivian needed him. Sebastián did not.

Sebby hugged himself and watched until the truck was out of sight before going in and leaning back against his closed, locked door. Turning, he pushed the curtain aside and rested his forehead against the cool glass, looking out at nothing, just looking, but not really looking at all. He wandered into the kitchen. Cooking was not worth the effort, but he was hungry, so he pulled a flour tortilla from the refrigerator and stood over the sink, tearing it, stuffing the bits into his mouth, and chewing mechanically. It was half gone when he shoved the rest down the garbage disposal. The liquor cabinet called to him, but, no, tomorrow was the fourteenth, paychecks had to go out on the fifteenth, and he couldn't be sick tomorrow. He made coffee instead. While it steeped, he grabbed a grocery sack out of a drawer, went into the bath, and plucked all of Todd's things from the sink, from the shelves, and dropped them into the sack, tied the handles into a granny knot, and hid the sack under the sink.

Sitting cross-legged on the sofa, he turned on the television. Sipped coffee. Turned the television off. Lay down. The song he'd quoted to Todd ribboned through his mind: *"I miss your laughing looks, I miss your playful way, I miss each magical brilliant word you say. And I know how . . . I know how . . ."*

"Damn it, Todd," he mumbled, and pulled out his phone.

He texted Lawrence. *Todd left. He went back to HIM.*

Nooooo, came the response, and then they called. With a sigh, he answered.

"Nooo," Lawrence cried. "Oh, Sebby."

"And we were so good to him!" Barry said.

Pushing breath through his lungs to speak seemed almost more than Sebby could manage. "It's not your fault."

"Shitty, shitty, shit, Sebby. Come over. We'll ditch our date," Lawrence offered.

Sebby considered, and sighed. "I don't want to fuck up your evening. And. I don't know. I'm so tired."

"That's not tired; that's depression," Barry said.

"You shouldn't be alone. We'll come over there," Lawrence said.

"We just have to ditch our date," Barry repeated.

"Or . . . we could bring him," Lawrence said thoughtfully.

Why not? At least . . . it'd be something to take my mind off . . . "Kay. Why not."

There were squeals and a longish pause, and then Barry's breathless voice saying that their date had agreed.

"It'll be just like old times!" Lawrence said.

"We'll cheer you right up," Barry promised.

"You'll like this ma-han! We call him 'Hugh.'"

"For Hugh Jackman," Barry whispered.

"He sort of looks like him. If you squint."

Sebby, who had been feeling like he might never smile again, laughed. "*Ay caramba.* You'd better not be squibbing or I'll drop you on your pointy ass, yes?"

"I have a pointy ass?" Lawrence cried in horror.

Barry laughed.

There was a knock on the door—a sort of timid knock, like the person outside wasn't completely sure he wanted anyone to answer. Sebby froze. "*Dios mío,* Todd's back!" Exclamations of wonder, of disbelief emitted from the dropped phone as Sebby sprinted for the door. Maybe he had only come back because he forgot something, but maybe . . . He threw the locks and yanked open the door, but where he had expected to see Todd's sheepish expression was instead a broad chest clad in a tight, black T-shirt. Sebby's neck cranked upwards as his eyes moved up to light on Collin's face—that smooth baby face that had so taken Sebby in. Sebby stepped back, swinging the door shut, but Collin had already shouldered his way in; before Sebby could turn to flee, Collin's fist closed over his forearm. His arm spasmed with remembered pain. Sebby wished he believed in God so that he could pray for help, but God had never helped when he *had* believed. Sebby stared up into Collin's anguished eyes, and his mind raced. He could talk himself out of this.

Chapter Thirty-Five

Coffered Me

"What the hell? This kid calls you, and you take off, just like that?" Lloyd's arms were folded, his face stretched in annoyance.

Donna spoke reproachfully. "How can you abandon that darling boy?"

Todd endeavored to sound rational, like a man who had made a reasoned decision. "Vivian is a darling boy too. You never had the chance to meet him, but if you had, you would understand."

"I understand you have something good and you're giving up on it."

Todd fidgeted. His foot itched to be tromping down on the gas pedal, but duty demanded that he sit in this kitchen while his brother and sister-in-law gave him the third degree. "Some things are not meant to be."

Lloyd snorted. "Bullshit. This kid messed you up, and you're going back for more; it's masochism." He held up his hands. "Look. I'm not gonna tell you how to live your life. You wanna go back to New York, go. All I'm saying is, sleep on it."

"It's dangerous to drive through the night," Donna said. "Imagine if you got in an accident! What if you were in the hospital for weeks, or paralyzed, or killed?"

She had a point, Todd had to concede. He was rather giddy. A night's sleep might help sober him. Not that he expected to be able to sleep a wink.

"You know," Lloyd said, "you could fly. There's direct flights from Denver to New York. You could leave later and be there sooner. You've got some money socked away, don't you?"

Out came the laptop. Todd was persuaded, and a seat on an 11 a.m. flight was purchased online; Donna agreed to drive him to the airport. "I still don't see how you can abandon Sebby like this."

"I'm not 'abandoning' him," Todd said, hooking quote marks in the air. "It's called *breaking up*. Sebby understands. He knew all along that this might happen, that I was still in love with Vivian. He even said, and I quote, 'If it doesn't work out, come back to me. I would welcome you back. I—'" The look on Donna's face stopped him cold.

"Find your own ride to the airport. Maybe you can get Sebby to drive you." She slammed the laptop shut and flounced from the room. Lloyd and Todd looked at each other.

"Nice bit of insurance, there." Lloyd leaned back in his chair and folded his arms again.

"Meaning?"

"Do what you want."

Todd flushed. "This is quite unfair to Vivian. Naturally, you're all in Sebby's corner."

"Look. I don't care. Do what you want."

"Will you cease giving me the evil eye, then?"

Lloyd rolled his eyes, evil and all. "I'm not giving you any damn evil eye. You're imagining it."

"You mean to say that my guilty conscience is causing me to imagine the condemnations of others."

"I mean to say that you're so full of shit you better make a trip to the shithouse pronto, before you unload in your boxers." Lloyd stood and stretched, rolling his shoulders. "But I can't drive you tomorrow. Take a cab or drive and park." He left the room.

"At the age of twenty-three, I am capable of getting myself to the airport," Todd called after Lloyd. He sighed, rubbed his forehead, and wandered from the kitchen into Ryan's bedroom.

"You're leaving," Ryan said.

"I'll be back," Todd promised in his best Arnold Schwarzenegger voice.

"You're going to see that Vivian?"

The dubious tone was more than Todd could take. "Are you against me too?"

"No. I'm for you. But I thought . . ."

"What. *What*?" With an effort, Todd gentled his voice as he tumbled, fully dressed, into bed. "What did you think?" Ryan was silent, and Todd, rather put out, said, "You don't even like Sebby!"

There was a long enough silence that Todd thought Ryan had given up and gone to sleep, but at last the boy's voice came out of the dark. "Did Sebby break your heart?"

"Oh." Todd's impatience evaporated. "Oh, Ryan. No. Some things, Ryan my lad, are simply not meant to be."

"Uh-huh." The bed creaked as Ryan rolled over. "But some things are?"

"Indeed."

"How do you know which is which?"

"You feel it in your heart. You know it in your soul." Todd pressed his hand to his chest.

"Uh-huh. Like I know in my soul that I'm never gonna be in love."

"Exactly," Todd agreed, keeping his voice solemn even as he grinned.

"Uh-huh. But, Uncle Todd?"

"Right here."

"Sebby, um, does he care? That you're going?"

Biting his lip, Todd considered. "I can't say that he doesn't care."

"I hope it broke his heart."

"Ryan!" Todd sat bolt upright, nearly whacking his head. "What a cruel thing to say!"

"He deserves it, and I'm glad you dumped him."

"It—" *It wasn't a dump*, Todd wanted to say, but of course it had been. *Was* Sebby all right? It had been an easy breakup: no tears, no hysterics. Clearly, their relationship had been on the wane. They'd squabbled and gotten on one another's nerves. They hadn't even been true to one another. Still, perhaps he should call . . . His arm reached toward Ryan's dresser where his cell phone lay, but his hand closed into a fist. What could he say? *I just wanted to see if you're okay since I dumped you.* He brought his fist to his mouth and chewed on a knuckle. *Let it be a clean break. It's self-serving to call him now.* "Ryan, I hope his heart is well. Having suffered a broken heart myself, I wouldn't wish it on anyone, least of all on someone about whom I care deeply."

"'Deeply'?" Ryan made gagging noises.

"Yes, deeply." There was no reply, and the even sounds of breathing soon indicated that his nephew slept.

Though Todd expected to lie wakeful, he dropped off and fell into a nightmare in which he arrived at the airport and was pulled aside by an oily-haired security official who had found a gun in Todd's carry-on.

"That's not mine! I've no idea how that got there!" Todd protested.

"How can you abandon that darling boy?" the security official demanded, with disgusted looks at the gun and at Todd.

"It's Vivian!" Todd explained. "My soul mate!"

The official took hold of Todd's wrist, his grip making Todd's bones grind, and propelled him away. "Wait in this line." And he left Todd at the end of a queue of exhausted people and luggage, a line that stretched endlessly down the dim terminal.

"I'll miss my flight!" Todd shouted, but the official strode away.

An overwhelming sense of relief woke Todd. His arm was bent beneath him, senseless as a block of wood. He sat up, his limb hanging like a dead thing. A burning anxiety began to chew through his gut.

Dreams are bullshit, Todd told himself, *full of sound and fury, signifying nothing.* Kneading his dead arm with his other hand, he considered. It was merely the subconscious expressing anxiety over getting to the airport on time. There was no relief like waking from a nightmare to find it was only a dream.

But I was relieved in the dream, not when I awoke! His arm prickled. The discomfort was enough to make him squirm. He rolled out of the bunk and pumped his arm in the air, grimacing. *I was relieved to miss my flight? What the fuck? Fucking hell, I don't want to go. I don't want to leave. Oh, fucking fuck.*

Todd shuffled out of Ryan's room, through the silent house, and into the front yard. The grass was thick, soft, and cold under his bare feet. The night sky arched over him, and the late-summer breeze soothed his overheated body, lifted his hair. With no idea of where to go, he climbed into his truck and started it, and the voice of some pop vocalist floated into the air—Barry had turned it to a "lite" station the other night.

If I could plant you in my garden like a tree

Maybe then you'd have to stay with me

Was he afraid to see Vivian again, afraid that things between them could never be as they had been? He knew he feared that very thing, but that was not why his guts were clenching and burning. Leaning against the headrest, he turned his eyes to look out at the night through the truck's open window. Ryan's words, spoken with such relish, came back to him: *"I hope it broke his heart."* The thought of Sebby curled up in a trembling, weeping ball of woe made him cringe. True, Sebby had cheated on him, but hadn't Todd implied it was acceptable by agreeing to sleep with Sebby's friends? Sebby had literally raised Todd up from the dirt, brushed him off, offered him coffee (*coffered me,* Todd thought), brought him back to life.

"I don't want to leave," he said aloud, "but it's Vivian!" Vivian needed him, and Sebby had said that Todd could come back, and he *would*, when it was over, he would come back.

"Ah, God." Todd's heart fell dead. If he had a heart. If the thing in his breast deserved to be termed one. *"Nice bit of insurance, there,"* Lloyd had said, and Todd saw now what he meant.

Deep down, Todd expected no lasting relationship with Vivian: a few months of rapture, after which he would again be a broken man, but he could haul his wounded carcass back to Sebastián, who would once more pick him up and set him right. "What a fool I've been."

And the radio answered him in a seductive tenor.

If I could wear you like a tattoo under my sleeve,
maybe then you'd finally believe
That I know how. I know how.
I can't remember why you can't forget,
But, baby, don't run out on me yet.

The voice was so intimate that the singer could have been right in the cab of the truck. "He was quoting me a song!" Todd murmured in wonder, and he listened till the voice ran out:

Steal me a moment,
sing me a rhyme,
live with me, laugh with me,
partner in crime.
Steal me a moment,
sing me a rhyme,

live with me, laugh with me,
partner in crime.
I miss your laughing looks, I miss your playful way,
I miss each magical brilliant word you say.
And I know how,
I know how.
Remember me, forget me, it's all the same.
Maybe in your dreams you'll hear my name.
And I know how.
I know how.
I can't remember why you can't forget,
but baby, don't run out on me yet.
Steal me a moment,
sing me a rhyme,
live with me, laugh with me,
partner in crime.

The words struck him so, Todd gripped the steering wheel as if to bend it in half. Wonder and excitement filled him with the forgotten realization that life was, above all, a grand adventure, and that one never knew what may come barreling at one from around the next corner—a grand adventure, but how infinitely better an undertaking if one's hand were clasped the while by someone whom one loved and who loved one back.

Chapter Thirty-Six

Wail at the Heavens

*T*odd's hand went to his pocket, but his cell phone was resting on Ryan's dresser. He could just drive to Sebby's house, but . . . no, he'd given Sebby back his key; Todd would have to pound on the door to awaken him, and that would frighten the bejeezus out of him.

He trotted back into the house and used the kitchen phone, hoping against hope that Sebby might be awake, might answer, but was unsurprised to receive his voice mail.

"Sebby, I'm not going to New York. I'm staying. Please, please call me the instant you hear this." He left much the same message on Sebby's landline, and then fidgeted and paced the kitchen for a bit.

On his way back to bed, he paused, filled with chilly misgivings. Oh, God, what could he say to Vivian? Vivian, he knew, was likely to be awake, even at this hour. Oh, how he wanted to procrastinate. Maybe Viv wouldn't answer, and he could just leave a voice mail, dump-by-phone. God, he was a coward. He decided to wait. Part of him was relieved to put it off, but mostly he felt that it was kinder to let Viv down by the light of day than in the cold predawn hours.

After checking his phone to be certain the ringer was on, he texted Sebby for good measure and then crawled back into bed, not bothering to undress. He dropped into a deep and dreamless sleep until the morning alarm sounded. Almost before he was awake, he reached for his phone. No texts, no missed calls. *Please call me*, he texted. He began to worry; Sebby was always up by this time. Was he angry?

Donna was delighted at the news, hugged him, and volunteered to get his ticket refunded. Lloyd rolled his eyes and left for work. Todd texted Sebby's cell and called his landline several more times, concluding that he must have spent the night at someone's house, perhaps Leo's. A pang struck him at the thought. At any rate, he'd see him at work. It was almost payday, and nothing short of a nuclear blast would keep Sebby from making payroll on time.

Todd was on his way to the construction site before remembering that he had not yet phoned Vivian, and he pulled over to do so. It would not be fair to delay the call any longer; it was two hours later in New York, and Viv would be planning his day around meeting Todd at the airport.

He had a speech all prepared: *My vivid one, I will always love you, but love, I've found, to my sorrow, does not conquer all . . .* But the sound of Vivian's voice chirping hello made the words seem pretentious. He hardened his resolve. It hurt, oh, how it hurt, to hear the suppressed tears as Viv assured him that he understood, that he didn't expect him to drop everything on his account . . .

Todd's view of the highway blurred like a third grader's watercolor. Head bowed over the steering wheel, he waited for several minutes before trusting himself to drive. He was exhausted, and his day had not even begun.

Some of the men were milling around the site when Todd arrived. Heads turned as he pulled up. Todd jumped from his truck before the dust of his passing had settled, intending to go directly to the mobile office, but Gus separated from the group and marched straight at Todd, head lowered like a bull.

"Hey," Todd said as Gus approached, "is something up?"

One fist smashed into Todd's stomach, nearly lifting Todd off his feet. He dropped to the ground, to hand and knees, his back arched, one arm clutching his abdomen. Unable to make a sound, his mouth pulsed like a fish's; he could neither gasp nor groan, his diaphragm spasming, preventing his lungs from drawing air. An iron medicine ball burned white-hot just under Todd's ribs, blocking his respiration. Spots skipped in front of his eyes; he was conscious of people around him, someone shouting, someone's hand on his shoulder. Seconds ticked off while Gus bellowed at him, and the shouts resolved into words.

"Take off your glasses! Stand up and take off your glasses, you son of a bitch!"

Someone grasped Todd's arm and pulled; Todd groaned and jerked away from the helping hand. He drew a careful breath. The ball of iron was dissolving into acid. Settling to the ground, one leg folded under himself, he panted shallowly, waiting to see if he would vomit.

"Damn coward, after what you did to Sebby, what're you about, showing your face here!"

So Sebby had confided in Gus? That was strange, but Todd never claimed to have understood their relationship.

"You okay, man?" someone asked him.

"Sorry," Todd said. The word came out watery. "I didn't know what I was doing." Talking hurt so much that he stopped.

"I oughta call the cops. Somebody call the cops!"

A voice spoke in disbelief, "Addison did that to office boy?" A jumble of voices responded.

"Goddamn pissant! Get up and I'll knock you on your ass!"

Todd lifted his head; blurred images solidified into acquaintances. Members of the crew were standing in a semicircle, a couple of them grinning and enjoying the conflict. Dean's gaze shifted between Todd and Gus, whose face shone red as a farmers'-market tomato, shaggy eyebrows meeting over his eyes in a fierce scowl. His hand was fisted, his arm cocked to throw the instant Todd moved. Rob, the young man who had bled all over Todd some months ago, was crouching by Todd's side, one arm under Todd's, ready to help him up. Todd had no intention of moving until Gus calmed down.

"Sorry," he repeated. "Gus, it was all a misunderstanding. I'm here to make it right."

"Make it right! I'll make it right. On your feet and take off those glasses! Fight like a man."

"It couldn't've been Todd," Rob said. "Just back off."

Something did not make sense. "What couldn't've been me?" A terrible suspicion rippled over him like a chill. "What's happened? Where's Sebastián? Where is he?"

Todd lurched to his feet but doubled over, groaning. Gus, whose eyes had burned as Todd got to his feet, stepped back.

"Where do you think, pissant? Doing payroll, when by rights he should be in the hospital."

"The hell you say! What's happened?" Todd straightened slowly and, in desperation, turned to Rob, who still held him by the elbow. "Rob, for the love of Christ, what's happened?"

"Somebody beat him up," Rob said. "It's like he got jumped or something: his face is messed up, and he was holding his arm funny. But I don't think it's—"

"Jesus God!" Not waiting to hear the rest, Todd broke and ran in a stooped-over, shambling gait, aware and not caring that Gus was close behind. He slammed into the mobile office. The door hit the wall and rebounded. Two men at the table started and stared, and Sebby, bent over his desk, lifted his head. The sight registered with Todd as an impossibility; he'd left Sebby mere hours ago, a perfect and beautiful Sebby. He could not connect the dots to this swollen apparition: two black eyes—how could he SEE?—the nose puffed to twice its size, the right side of his mouth fat. What was he doing *at work*?

Sebby's expression was unreadable through the bruising, but his hands fluttered to his face. He hunched as if to hide in the papers strewn about his desktop. His eyes darted about the office. Finally, he lifted his chin to gaze at Todd. Rooted to the spot, Todd barely noticed when Gus shoved past him. He was convinced it was a nightmare, his brain having made heartbreak appear as a physical manifestation. Todd's lips moved; he thought he said, *What the fuck?*

Sebby, his battered mouth making an odd mumble of the words, had to repeat himself, his voice so calm, unreal: "Todd, I'm okay."

Todd's ears rang. His mouth worked soundlessly before he could force words out. "What happened?"

Sebby drew a breath, noticeably hesitating. "What are you doing here? You left last night, I thought." His voice changed, and a narrowing of the eyes was audible, if not visible. "Did someone call you? Did Ethan?"

"No one called, no. *Why* did no one call me? What happened?" Todd started forward. Sebby slumped, his body language so dejected that Todd paused, glancing at the men, before saying under his breath, "Screw this," and rushing across the room and around the desk to Sebby's side. There was a loud protest behind him—Gus, prepared to defend his office boy—and Sebby raised his head long enough to wave dismissively at the man.

"What are you doing here?" Sebby asked again, not meeting Todd's eyes.

"I decided to fly instead of drive, but I'm not going now. Sebby, what happened?" Todd, afraid to hold him, afraid of what injuries might be hidden by clothing, reached to touch the back of Sebby's neck.

Sebby flinched. "No," he breathed, and louder, "No. I won't have you stay . . . because of *this*." His hands clenched into fists, crumpling his paperwork.

"My poor darling!" Todd moved closer, peering into the ruin of Sebby's face, though Sebby turned his head away. "Not because of this." He placed his other hand over Sebby's clenched fist, noting as he did so the bruised and skinned knuckles. "Whatever happened, you must have been unable to check your messages. I think I left you a dozen. I decided to stay."

"Liar," Sebby whispered. The papers in his clenched fists crackled.

Todd glanced back towards the door. They had an audience, and most of the men weren't making any pretense of disinterest. "On my honor! I decided to stay before I knew anything was amiss. Had I known you were in distress, I would've come for you." Todd moved closer, itching to get his arms around Sebby, but fearing that if he tried, Sebby would bolt. "What happened." It came out as a command. *Tell me.*

Sebby shook his head, not raising his eyes. Todd waited, and tense seconds ticked by before Sebby drew breath, hesitated, and murmured, "Cheese fell out of my freezer."

Of course, that was it, and Todd had known that was it, but hearing it was like taking another punch to the gut. For moments he was unable to breathe. "Sebby. Jesus. Why didn't you *call* me?"

There was a one-shouldered shrug and the briefest eye contact. "You left me," he said simply.

Todd thought he would weep; he was going to wail at the heavens if he did not get out of here. "I'm taking you home." Standing, he announced to the room, "I'm taking him home."

The men shifted, muttering. "What about paychecks?" someone asked.

"Fuck your paychecks!" Todd shouted.

Sebby's fist moved under his hand and pressed his fingers. He spoke in such a low voice that Todd had to bend to hear it. "Todd. Don't make a scene. I wasn't going to stay all day. Wayne's waiting for me down at Java Hut. He drove me, and he was going to drive me back. I'll be finished in an hour and a half." He turned to frown at his computer. "Unless Checkwriter goes down, or I can't reset the batch, or—"

"Fuck Checkwriter, fuck the goddamn batch, fuck Wayne, fuck Java Hut. You can't tell me that there's no one to back you up and do the goddamn payroll!"

Sebby glanced up at him then, with a ghost of a smile. "My backup is on maternity leave, and her backup is struggling to do *her* payroll. In fact, I'd be helping her, but I told her to call support. If I don't do our payroll, it'll be late."

"So it's late! I don't give a shit; why do you give a shit!"

"Because," Sebby went on, with implacable logic, "if payroll is late, federal regulations require that the employer pay interest, which isn't good for the company and is just more headache for me later. But, more important, these boys have mortgages and bills and groceries to buy, and some of them live paycheck to paycheck; they don't all live with their brother rent-free."

Todd made an exasperated noise.

"The more you argue with me, the longer it'll be till I'm done."

Todd ground his teeth. This was intolerable. "Right, then. Clear the room!" he hollered. "If you must have your wages, give the man peace and quiet in which to operate!" With many a backward glance and much jaw flapping, the men filed out.

"You too," Sebby said as Todd prepared to pull up a chair next to him. "I can't concentrate with you looking over my shoulder. Anyway, your shift started."

Todd grabbed a blank sheet of paper and pen and scrawled: *I quit. Signed, Todd Addison.* He dated it and slapped it into Sebby's in basket. "There. Official written fucking resignation."

Shaking his head and *tsk*ing, Sebby got slowly to his feet. He slid his arms around Todd's waist, meeting his eyes before ducking his head, and Todd winced, as much from the sight of Sebby's bruised face so close to his own as from Sebby's body pressed against Todd's sore middle. "I promise I'm all right, and I promise not to take any longer than I have to. If you really quit, then go wait with Wayne at Java Hut. I'll call when I'm done."

Todd fumed. "You are impossibly stubborn!" He put one arm carefully around Sebby.

Sebby laid his cheek on Todd's shoulder. "I know."

Todd petted Sebby's hair. "Are you quite certain you're all right?"

"My head is pounding. My heart feels like it's palpitating. I can barely stay awake. All I want to do is take some aspirin and lay down, but I have to finish this, and will you please not make it harder for me? Please, either go to work or wait with Wayne."

"Oh, sweetheart." Todd combed his fingers through Sebby's tresses. "This is ridiculous, but, as you wish." Sebby gave him a crooked smile, and Todd's fingers found the bandage on Sebby's temple, hidden by his hair. "What the fuck?"

Sebby wilted. "It's nothing. A few stitches. Please, Todd, please. Please?"

Chapter Thirty-Seven

The Loudest Rendition of Happy Birthday

Todd purchased a large coffee at the counter and spotted Wayne in the farthest corner of Java Hut, hunched over his laptop, elbows tucked in, knees locked together, ankles curled around the legs of his chair. Todd had an urge to sneak up and shout *Boo*. Instead, he approached Wayne, jangling his change in his pocket to give him fair warning. "Good morning, Wayne; it is I."

Wayne hunched even further before moving only his eyes to peer up at Todd. "Oh, hi." He relaxed. "I thought it might be that coffee girl again. It's, like, I bought a coffee, leave me alone!"

Todd slid into the seat opposite Wayne, then removed the lid from his cup and blew on it. "Wayne, what the fuck happened?"

"Oh, you're not supposed to be here!" Wayne exclaimed, looking at Todd over his laptop. "Didn't you go to New York?"

"I changed my mind. Or, rather, I came to my senses."

"Oh shit." Wayne paled. "So you know what happened."

"I don't know what happened, which is why I'm asking you!"

Wayne peeked back down at his laptop. His fingers tappety-tapped, and Todd waited for several seconds. "Will you stop blogging and answer me!"

"Blogging!" Wayne said in an injured tone. "I'm trying to work! Of course, I'm the one who has to ferry Sebby to work and wait for him. Ethan has a real job, Leo has a real job, but Wayne? No, Wayne doesn't have a real job. All he does is *blog*."

"You are being taken unfair advantage of," Todd agreed, tamping down his impatience. "I apologize for the blog remark. You know I respect your work, Wayne."

"Yeah. You and no one else." Wayne appeared to be wrapping himself in self-pity.

"That's not true. Ethan is always bragging you up. If you knew how often I tell him to *shut the hell up about Wayne*."

Wayne smiled one of those quick smiles, gone so fast that Todd wondered if he'd imagined it. It was more like a facial twitch. "Yeah."

Todd reached across the table to catch Wayne's hand, drawing it away from the keyboard. "Wayne, I'm begging you. Tell me what happened. I've seen Sebby. He told me it was the ex, but that's all he told me. Well, that and to wait here with you." He paused. "You know, there's no reason for both of us to wait. If you tell me what happened, you can go. I'll ferry him back."

Wayne's eyes lit up, but his expression went wary. "I should let Sebby tell you, though."

"Wayne, if you don't start talking in the next five seconds, this coffee shop shall be treated to the loudest rendition of 'Happy Birthday' that, I venture to say, any of its denizens have heard in their lifetimes. I'll throw in the monkey verse, as well. The coffee girl will shower you with free donuts."

Wayne's eyes widened. "You'd do it, too."

Todd started to get to his feet. "Five . . . four . . ."

"Okay, okay!" Wayne tugged on Todd's hand, and Todd relaxed. "Just let me . . ." Tappety-tap went his fingers.

"Three! Two!" Todd lunged to his feet and took a deep breath.

"No, no! Wait! Okay." Wayne nudged his laptop an inch to the right, and his eyes left it just briefly as he talked to Todd, who resumed his seat. "I don't know a lot. Sebby won't talk about it. Barry and Lawrence won't stop talking about it." He tapped the keyboard but withdrew his hands as Todd cleared his throat. "So, you know about the ex."

Todd nodded, his stomach clenching. "Collin, the one who broke his arm last year."

"That wasn't last year. It was this year. Like, right before you showed up, I think." Wayne pursed his lips in thought, staring at his laptop. "Yeah, it was, 'cause I remember I was just finishing up the Claremont project. That was a long-term deal! They had all these embedded menus—"

"What do you mean? Sebby told me it was last year." Hadn't he?

"No, it was this year. I do know what year is what. I own calendars. It was this year, and he's been bothering Sebby and calling him and stuff ever since, but Sebby never told anyone. So, last night when you left, Sebby was on the phone with Barry and Lawrence, and he said *you* came back. But he didn't hang up the phone. So Barry and Lawrence heard everything, and it wasn't you, it was *him*."

Todd's arms rippled in gooseflesh. He clutched his coffee, pulling it close. "*What* did they hear?"

"Who knows? You can't get a straight story out of those two."

In any other situation, Todd might have laughed at the use of the word *straight* in conjunction with Barry and Lawrence.

"But they called nine-one-one and then Hugh drove them over there. They got there before the police did, and Hugh beat the guy down, is what Barry and Lawrence say. The police show up, arrest them both."

"Hugh? Who is Hugh? Arrest who both?" If Sebby had told no one that Collin had been harassing him, how did Wayne know? And, Jesus, what had Collin done? Was Sebby hurt more than he'd let on? Had Collin— Had he— Todd couldn't bear to think it.

"Hugh got released. Sebby stayed at our house. Nobody got any sleep! Sebby had to give a statement, Ethan stayed with him, took him to the hospital."

"What did they say at the hospital? Is Sebastián all right? Why didn't anyone call me?"

"I dunno." Wayne's eyes were glued to his screen. His lips moved as he read silently before his eyes refocused on Todd. "Except, every time one of us was going to call you, Sebby went apocalyptic. He said you broke up with him and went back to New York."

Todd bit his lip. "Wayne, who was arrested? You said 'both' were."

"Hugh and Collin. They were fighting, so they got cuffed and hauled downtown to get sorted out." Wayne rolled his eyes, and his forehead wrinkled halfway up his bald scalp. "Man, my head hurts just imagining the screaming from Barry and Lawrence."

Todd's head was beginning to hurt as well. "Who is Hugh, again? I don't believe I know a Hugh."

"Well, that's not his real name." Wayne's eyes wandered back to the laptop's screen. His fingers trembled on the table, air-typing.

Todd stared. "What is his real name, then?"

Wayne shrugged. "Collin's still in jail, unless he made bail, I suppose. Sebby didn't want to press charges, but they convinced him to. I don't know what his problem is." He made an aggravated noise in his throat. His hand wandered to tap surreptitiously on the laptop's touch pad.

"He said he was all right, but is he?"

"No!" Wayne shouted, his face washing a pasty gray. Todd started, but it was apparent that something on the computer screen had agitated Wayne. "Oh, *hell* no, this'll set me back *weeks*." Settling back in his chair, Todd took a fortifying gulp of coffee, and his mind wandered as Wayne went into an impassioned diatribe regarding JavaScript and Internet Explorer and Chrome, voice winding down to a mutter punctuated with occasional expletives as he typed.

Time crawled. Todd drank coffee. Wayne worked. Sending a silent prayer to the payroll gods, Todd drummed his fingers and stared into space.

When Wayne's cell went off, he pressed it to his ear without taking his eyes off the laptop's screen. "Yeah, he's here." Wayne's face puckered as though around a mouthful of lemon. "Well, that's just great! Call him on his own phone, damn it!" He slapped his phone off, and Todd's phone rang. Wayne glared. "He doesn't need me! You drive him back!" And, with that, Wayne began packing his belongings.

"Wayne, I did tell you you could go," Todd reminded as he dug his phone out. "But thank you for keeping me company. Otherwise, I'd've gone mad."

Sebby's wan voice, welcome as Christmas, sounded in Todd's ear. "I'm done. Will you come get me?"

"On my way." Taking Wayne's elbow, Todd guided him through the assortment of customers, relief carrying him along like a surfboard. He saw him to his car, thanked him, and headed back to the construction site.

The site was clear of workers, all the crew being high up in the structure, and the mobile office was empty but for Sebby, who was wearily sorting papers on his desktop. It hurt Todd's throat to look at him. "Ready?"

"Yeah. Just trying to organize some, but it can wait." Sebby got to his feet, fished a key out of his pocket, and dropped it on his desk. "Payroll's all done," he murmured, in evident satisfaction, and he gave Todd a smile halved by bruises.

"Oh, Sebby." Todd waited until Sebby reached him before tenderly taking him in his arms. Sebby settled against him with a sigh. "I hope they appreciate it," Todd grumbled.

"I'm not that bad off," Sebby said, his voice muffled. "I'm perfectly capable of performing my duties." And Todd recognized his own words being used back at him.

"Well, I should've listened to you." Taking Sebby's hand in his, Todd led him across the room and opened the door to find Gus mounting the steps. Gus's shaggy eyebrows slashed a single, threatening line low across his brow, and Todd raised his arm in a defensive gesture.

"Gus, I left a key on my desk so you or whoever can lock up," Sebby said. "Payroll's done. I got confirmation on the direct deposits, and the paper checks are there. The check stubs are in the other stack." He indicated piles of envelopes on the table and hesitated, his face lifted to Todd's. "I don't think I'll be in tomorrow?"

"He won't," Todd said. Still, Gus stood in the doorway, blocking their exit. "Excuse us."

"It's okay, Gus; Todd's taking me home. He won't let anything happen to me."

"Horseshit. He let this happen."

It was a low blow, and Todd almost felt it was deserved. "I'm sorry," he said miserably.

"Todd, it wasn't your fault. Gus, move." Taking firm hold of Todd's hand, Sebby started forward.

Gus backed down the steps and let them pass, but his stare made it obvious that he held Todd responsible for anything that happened to Sebby.

"The light's so bright," Sebby murmured, holding his hand to his eyes, and Todd slid a supportive arm around his waist.

"Close your eyes. I'll guide you." Others had apparently noted Todd's arrival and decided to check up on office boy. A few hard-hatted men loitered outside the office. Rob gave them a nod. Two guys, unloading a truck, elbowed each other. Dean stood, his jaw slack, a cigarette dangling from his lip.

"Guess I'm out," Todd said from the corner of his mouth.

"And it wasn't so bad, was it?" Sebby leaned his head on Todd's shoulder as they made their way across the dusty expanse that served as a parking lot.

What the hell. I may as well be all *the way out.* As they reached the truck and Todd glanced back, he could see that most of their audience had dispersed. He traced his fingers along Sebby's jaw, brushed his thumb over Sebby's lips, and closing his eyes, pressed his lips to the uninjured side of Sebby's mouth. Sebby made a small noise and touched Todd's hand where it rested against Sebby's neck. Straightening, Todd opened the truck door and helped Sebby inside. "Let's go home."

"Not home. Ethan's."

"Why Ethan's?" Todd shut the door and sprinted around to the other side, waving jauntily at the few remaining observers before hopping in and starting the vehicle. "You'll rest better in your own bed. And I'll be with you," he added, thinking that Sebby feared Collin might pay another visit.

"I can't. I don't want to. It's a mess. I can't face it." Without opening his eyes, Sebby fastened his seat belt and leaned back.

"Your house is a mess? Shit." What had happened? It would hardly be chivalrous to press Sebby for details at the moment. Changing the subject, he said, "I do have some job nibbles, so quitting my job was perhaps not entirely irresponsible."

"Oh . . . that."

"What?" Todd's suspicions boiled. "Sebastián. What?"

"Well. Who do you think processes those things?"

"Shit." Though exasperated, Todd couldn't get angry with Sebby, under the circumstances.

"You wanted me to hurry and finish, yes?"

Todd ground his teeth and said nothing.

"It's still there, if you still want to quit. Otherwise, you took a sick day. Or two."

Chapter Thirty-Eight

Four-Car Pileup

Sebby led the way into Ethan and Wayne's house. There was no sign of Wayne, and Ethan was still at work. The late-morning sunlight streamed in through the high windows, lighting the spacious entryway and great room. "Wayne's annoyed with me 'cause I slept with Ethan last night. Just slept," he added, glancing at Todd.

"Wayne will get over it," Todd assured him.

"I wouldn't be annoyed if you slept with Wayne, if he needed you."

"Wayne's is not a generous soul, as yours is. He is rather insecure." It was not a fair comparison, since Ethan and Sebby were former lovers, and Todd and Wayne were not, but Todd chose not to remind Sebby of the fact.

"I should've slept alone," Sebby fretted, crossing the great room. Todd followed him to the kitchen, where Sebby opened a prescription bottle and tapped a pill into his palm. "It's for pain. They gave me something to calm me down too, but I'm fine without it, no?" He ran water into a glass and swallowed the pill. "I didn't *ask* Ethan! He wanted me to sleep with both of them, but Wayne wouldn't. He told Ethan to take me into the other room, and I could see that he wanted Ethan to say no, to not leave him. I tried to tell Ethan. He wouldn't listen. So he slept with me. Just slept."

"Sweetheart." Todd pulled Sebby close and pillowed his cheek on Sebby's hair. "I'm so sorry I wasn't there. I'm sorry I left you. Had I stayed, none of this would've happened."

"It would've happened," Sebby mumbled. "Eventually." He pushed his forehead into Todd's throat. "Why are you here?"

Because I love you. The words tumbled into Todd's mouth, collided with his teeth, and rear-ended each other, a four-car pileup.

Todd's tongue swept his mouth, clearing the collision away before he spoke. "I do love Vivian." Sebby fidgeted, and Todd held him close, stroking his hair. "But what I saw last night was that I've no real hope in my heart for any lasting relationship with him. He was made to break my heart, and he would do so again. And then I would come back to you, because you so generously said that I could, and because I would want to." Pulling away, he placed his hands on either side of Sebastián's head, hoping that Sebby would read the sincerity in his eyes, but Sebby's eyes were closed. "I am at my destination, why insert a detour loop?"

"There's lots of reasons for loops. Like a century day." Sebby opened his eyes. Todd was on the point of asking what a *century day* was when Sebby went on. "That's good enough . . . for now." Sebby pressed his fingertips to Todd's lips. "I want you for my own. I don't care about Vivian. I'm selfish, and I don't care if he's sick. I don't care if he *needs* you." Sebby's eyes remained focused on the motion of his own fingers, brushing over and over Todd's lips. "Last night, after everything happened, I felt so sorry for myself. Ethan's arms were tight around me, trying to comfort me"—Todd tightened his own arms—"but he doesn't love me. He loves Wayne. Are you still mad at me? About Leo?"

"No, Sebby." It all seemed so long ago. "It was . . . an odd situation. We'll talk about it. Later. When you're feeling better."

"I think I want to lay down now. Will you lay down with me?"

"Willingly."

A cold pack was obtained, and together they went down the hallway to the small, cluttered guest room. The porcelain unicorn, with its spiraled horn of delicate rainbow hues, still reigned among the objets d'art. Sebby tossed aside the cold pack and put his arms around Todd to tug Todd's shirt free of its tuck.

Todd tried with utter futility to catch Sebby's nimble hands. "Oh, sweetheart," he protested in anguish as those hands lifted his shirt, and Sebby bent to kiss Todd's chest. "Sweetheart, don't . . ."

There was a cry from Sebby, who went rigid. "What happened to you?" Sebby looked up, his swollen face betraying little, but his voice washed in distress, and Todd returned his gaze with confusion. "Did you go after Collin? You couldn't've! You said you didn't know anything was wrong!" In one swift motion, Sebby swept Todd's tee over his head and dropped it on the floor.

"I—" Todd tucked his chin as Sebby's fingers fluttered over his abdomen, and saw that a magnificent bruise had come into flower under the arch of his rib cage: deep purple and feathering to red at its edges. "I forgot about that," he said, with some embarrassment.

"Forgot!" Trembling, Sebby's fingers outlined the damage.

"Er. Gus thought I was responsible for your injuries and took swift and terrible retribution."

"Gus did this to you?" A string of Spanish expletives unrolled.

Worried that Sebby was getting himself worked up when he should be resting, Todd ran his fingers through Sebby's hair. "It was one punch. Don't be too hard on him. He thought he was protecting you, and, surely, the perpetrator deserves this and worse."

"Gus needs to mind his own fucking business!" Placing a hand on either shoulder, Sebby shoved Todd against the bed. Todd sat. Sebby gripped Todd's shoulders and threw a leg over Todd's legs, collapsing with him, burying his face in Todd's chest while avoiding his sore middle. "I'm going to get him fired," Sebby mumbled. "See if I don't."

"Imp. Don't do that, I beg you. He was defending your honor. Quite chivalrous of him, you must admit." He slid his hands up and down Sebby's back.

"He can't hit another employee whenever he feels like it!"

"Evidently, he can. Hush, please? Leave us discuss the matter another time. Rest now, please?"

"I can't. I close my eyes and see . . ." Sebby shuddered, and then he shifted, lifting his head to regard Todd. "I want you."

"I'm here," Todd said, pretending obtuseness. "You need to rest. As do I."

But Sebby shut his swollen eyes and laid a kiss on Todd's mouth, and Todd winced at the pain he imagined blossoming in Sebby's bruised lips. "Kiss it away, Todd," Sebby whispered.

Tenderly, Todd moved his lips to the uninjured side of Sebby's mouth, and Sebby's tongue darted out. Sebby moaned, and that was unfair of him, Todd thought, as guilty desire stirred.

"Where's that cold pack?" He turned his head and reached with one arm, his hand closing on empty air, and Sebby took advantage of Todd's loose hold to peel his own shirt away, revealing the marks of abuse that had been hidden—contusions over his ribs, grip marks around his arm. His skin was feverish against Todd's.

"Kiss it away," Sebby murmured. Urgent hands swept down Todd's rib cage and insinuated between his flesh and the waistband of his jeans. "Don't say no. I need you."

Todd's breath caught. Holding Sebby tightly and ignoring the pain that flared across his abdomen, he rolled them both over, ending with Sebby's shoulder and part of his back pinned to the wall. He covered Sebby's face with flower petal kisses, and Sebby clutched him.

"Harder, kiss me harder. Please!" His fingers plowed furrows in Todd's back, his hip. "Kiss it away!"

Todd hesitantly laid his mouth full on Sebby's. The injured flesh tasted of old blood, and Sebby grasped the back of Todd's head, tangling both hands in Todd's hair and pulling him hard to his mouth. They both cried out, Todd in fear, Sebby in what could have been either pain or release.

Sebby arched and hooked one leg around Todd's hips. "Do it hard, oh, do it hard." It was the quietest murmur.

Trembling, Todd hesitated for long moments while Sebby writhed ineffectually. Of a sudden, Sebby went limp. He dropped his hands and turned his face away, lifting his chin and exposing his slender neck as if for the kill, and that simple gesture seemed the single most erotic thing Todd had ever seen. He closed his fingers over Sebby's throat and felt him swallow; he laced his other hand into Sebby's hair, compelling Sebby's head down and back into the corner formed by bed and wall. He pressed his lips to the place where neck joined shoulder, drawing the flesh into his mouth to create a new bruise, at the same time bearing Sebby with more force against the wall. Sebby's moan was like a low siren heard off in the distance, and as Sebby wrapped both legs around him to bring their groins tightly together, control slipped away.

Chapter Thirty-Nine

A Secret

Silent sobs shook Sebby's frame, and he was thankful that Todd was a heavy sleeper. He hadn't cried when Collin had hit him, or when one of the policemen had given him a look of mingled lust and contempt, or when Wayne had snubbed him. Not even when Ethan had tried to comfort him, or when Todd had kissed him outside the mobile office. But now he could not stop crying.

Even though the medication made him drowsy, he couldn't sleep, and his throat ached with the effort of swallowing his tears. It wasn't on purpose that he dated assholes. It was just that . . . he loved the feeling that the hand stroking his hair had the strength to crush his skull. And that had led him wrong a few times. And Todd . . . Todd hadn't yelled at Sebby or blamed him. He hadn't thrown a tantrum—well, he had shouted a little. He hadn't vowed to murder Collin. He was being so patient, and he hadn't once pestered Sebby about the events of last night, even though he must be dying to. Sebby dreaded relating the story to Todd. If only everyone would just forget about it, pretend it hadn't happened. He didn't want this to be the pivotal event of his life.

But Todd said he'd decided to stay *without knowing about any of it*. Todd had chosen Sebby over Vivian. Did Todd love him? He hadn't said so; in fact, he had said, *I love Vivian*. As the words resounded in his head, his chest heaved in ever greater sobs; his ribs were trying to crush his heart. A noise escaped him, and Todd stirred. Sebby held his breath until the danger passed, but it was the middle of the day, and Todd wouldn't sleep much longer. Covering his own face with the cold pack, Sebby tried to compose himself. Ethan was right—he had to tell Todd that he loved him. He'd do it today. In sane and orderly words.

Todd yawned, and Sebby froze. Todd muttered, "Sebby . . . are you all right?"

"*Sí, bien.*" His voice was tight, and somehow all the nice, planned words evaporated from his head.

Todd's hand moved over Sebby's chest. "Have I . . . Did I . . . hurt you?"

Had Todd heard him crying? *Dios*, did he think Sebby was crying because of him? Sebby peeked out from under the cold pack. "No."

"Was I too rough?"

"No. Oh, *mi chico tierno*, you worry so." He moved to catch Todd's hand, brought it to his mouth, and kissed it, letting the chilly plastic slide away from his face. Todd's eyes were naked and anxious, the skin puckered between his light eyebrows. Sebby hesitated. "I don't know how you'll take it if I explain."

Todd closed his eyes. "This is a good time to tell me something I might not like."

"Because you can't get mad at me." Sebby gave Todd a smug smile. He sat up and folded his legs under himself. Todd followed, reaching for his eyeglasses, and Sebby waited till he had them adjusted and then took Todd's hands in both of his. "Todd. *Querido*. You aren't rough." Todd blinked. "You aren't rough," Sebby repeated, pressing Todd's fingers. "Hurt me? You never would. You're the most gentle lover I've known. Even when you were trying to be rough, just now, you didn't grab my hair and yank my head back, you wove your fingers into my hair and eased me back . . ." Sebby had to close his eyes and catch his breath. Todd made no sound, and when Sebby opened his eyes, Todd still looked unconvinced.

"Right, then. But you're telling me that didn't hurt, my kissing . . ." And Todd laid a finger against the fat side of Sebby's mouth.

"A little," Sebby admitted. "But that wasn't your hurt. Or, it was, but . . . it was your hurt covering up his hurt. Canceling it out. You see, Toddfox, it all comes down to debiting one side and crediting the other, so that, in the end, everything is zero."

"That analogy makes no sense at all." But Todd smiled, and it warmed Sebby like whiskey. Tears sprang to his eyes again. He threw his arms around Todd's neck.

"I have a secret to tell you," Sebby mumbled, barely able to get the words past the lump in his throat.

"A secret?" The smile was audible in Todd's voice. "A good secret?"

"I've been keeping it kind of long, and I shouldn't keep it secret from the one person who should know. The person who . . . should know." He drew a painful breath. "It's nothing earth-shattering. Just that I love you. That's all. I love you, Todd."

He could feel that Todd had stopped breathing, stopped moving. Todd's arms hardened into marble statues. Anxiously, Sebby petted Todd's hair, pulled at it a little to wake him up. "Breathe. It's not such a surprise, is it?"

Todd heaved a shuddering breath and wilted, burying his face in Sebby's neck. "The earth is shattering. It's raining down around me in brilliant blue shards."

That was a pretty thought. Sebby rubbed Todd's back briskly, hugged him as tightly as his arms could manage. "Do you know what *querido* means?" Todd shook his head. "It means *beloved.*" Sebby paused to swallow and to breathe. "I love you. *Querido, te amo.*" His ribs were crushing his heart again, but this time it was because Todd was squeezing him so hard. He waited, and still Todd was silent, and Sebby could wait no longer. "You love me too, yes?"

Todd nodded against Sebby's neck, nodded and made no sound. At least, Sebby hoped it was a nod, but then Todd moved and breathed a word. "Yes."

"Can you say it?" It was scary how much he wanted to hear it.

Lifting his head and looking Sebby straight in the eye, he enunciated the words. "I love you."

Sebby's swollen face prevented him from smiling as broadly as he wanted to. Todd loved him. Maybe not the way he loved Vivian, and maybe it never could be that way, but he loved him.

Chapter Forty

Impossibly Stubborn

E vening arrived. Ethan got home from work, and upon sighting Todd, a grin spread across his face. "Todd! You're here!" Wayne emerged from his office and heated a pan of frozen lasagna. The four of them eschewed the formal dining room and sat at the kitchen table. Wayne chatted equably enough with Sebby.

As they were eating, the doorbell sounded. Ethan went to answer and returned with Barry, Lawrence, and a huge man who was a stranger to Todd. The man's face was rather homely, with a large, hooked nose, ears that stuck out at near right angles to his head, and a mass of uncontrolled hair of nondescript color growing back from a receding hairline. He dropped his eyes as Ethan introduced him as Hugh.

"Tooodd!" Lawrence exclaimed. "Sebby didn't tell us you were back!"

"Hugh saved Sebby's life," Barry declared, beaming at the homely man, who colored. Barry's arms were wrapped around Hugh's right arm, and Lawrence had the left. Rising and offering his hand, Todd regarded the man with interest. His biceps strained at his shirtsleeves; his chest seemed in danger of tearing through his T-shirt. One hairy forearm sported a tattoo of a trident-carrying merman, the tail of which braceleted his wrist.

"Todd, rhymes with God," said Todd, as his hand was all but swallowed in the man's enormous mitt. "I am in your debt, then, sir."

"Oh. Naw. Just glad I was there." The man shrugged his substantial shoulders. "Name's not Hugh, uh, they just like to call me that."

"'Cause he looks like Hugh Jackman!" Lawrence exclaimed, resting his chin on Hugh's shoulder with greedy glee.

"If Hugh Jackman were handsomer," Barry added, likewise resting his chin on Hugh's other shoulder. The man looked from one to the other with a shy smile that gentled his entire visage. Todd couldn't detect even a slight resemblance to Hugh Jackman.

Ethan grinned. "Let's have drinks in the living room! The dishes can wait."

Wayne installed himself on the corner of one sofa with his laptop, though this didn't stop Ethan from somehow lying down with his head in Wayne's lap, his fingers making idle circles over Wayne's left knee. Hugh settled into an overstuffed easy chair, and Barry and Lawrence perched on the chair's arms, leaning against him. Todd and Sebby took the love seat, Sebby reclining in Todd's arms, his head on Todd's chest.

Todd kissed the top of Sebby's head and then just rested there, inhaling the fragrance of Sebby's hair. "Did he save your life?" he whispered.

Sebby moved his shoulders in a minimal shrug. "Who can say?"

Todd pressed his face to Sebby's neck, to feel his pulse jump, to feel the live warmth of him. "Tell me what happened."

Sebby gave his head a quick shake.

"I want to hear this tale of heroism," Todd declared.

Sebby shrank. Hugh reddened. Barry and Lawrence preened as one. "You tell it, Hugh," Lawrence prompted, and then immediately went on. "After you dumped him, Sebby called us."

"Then he said, 'Todd's back!'" Barry's lined eyes were wide.

Wayne groaned. "Not this again."

"Don't tell this right now," Sebby pleaded.

Todd sat up straight. "Someone saved the life of my love, I believe I'm entitled to hear the details."

"He set the phone down!" Barry went on.

"But he didn't hang up," Lawrence said.

"We didn't hang up, either," Barry said.

"We thought we might hear some sloppy makeup sex!" They both giggled.

"But it wasn't Todd," Barry said solemnly.

"It was Collin!"

There was a dramatic pause. Sebby rose so gracefully that Todd did not realize he was doing it until it was done.

"Shit," Todd said under his breath as Sebby left the room.

"He doesn't like hearing it," Barry said.

Hugh pursed his lips. "Maybe you shouldn't tell it, then."

"So modest!" Lawrence smoothed his hand up and down the broad chest.

"Especially for a hero." Barry's hand mirrored Lawrence's. They beamed at each other and at Hugh, who appeared positively twitterpated.

Sebby slipped away to the kitchen. His hands were shaking, so he had trouble removing the lid from the anxiety medication. There was no reason to be upset, he told himself. Barry and Lawrence enjoyed telling the story. It was an exciting one: Hugh breaking down Sebby's door and peeling Collin off Sebby as if Collin were a paper doll. It was the sort of thing Sebby would've leaned forward to hear. He would've peppered them with questions. He would've praised Hugh's heroism—if the story had been about someone else. From the corner of his eye, as he drew water from the sink, he saw Todd enter the kitchen and hover.

"I'm sorry," Todd said.

Sebby gulped his pill and turned. "'S okay." He pulled a smile from somewhere. "I should let them tell you, 'cause then I won't have to." He waved his hand, shooing Todd away. "Go back in there. Think I'll go to bed." In the next moment, Sebby threw himself at Todd. "Oh, *querido*, I love you. But I can't talk about *that* right now, and I can't hear about it. You understand? I understand you want to know about it, but do you understand I can't?"

"Sweetheart. *Te amo. Comprendo.*" Todd bent his head to kiss Sebby's upturned face, to brush his lips over Sebby's eyes. "But Wayne said Collin has been harassing you for quite some time. Is this true?"

Pressing his face into Todd's neck, Sebby sighed, unsurprised that Todd wouldn't drop the subject. "Harassing? He called me a few times, that's all. Not harassing."

"Calling is not necessarily harassing," Todd agreed.

Sebby was grateful that Todd didn't argue or lecture. "But then," Sebby said, biting his lip. "But then he, the night with, you know, Leo, Collin called and said he knew I was alone, he knew you went with Barry and Lawrence. He was watching my house!" Sebby clutched the front of Todd's T-shirt. "That's why I called Leo, because I got so, so scared. I told you it was because of the movie, but that was a lie."

"So many lies," Todd murmured, as if to himself.

"You said I held things back from you, and I did. But it all came from one big lie, from never telling you I love you. If I couldn't be honest about that, how could I be honest about anything?"

"*Comprendo*," Todd repeated.

"*Lo comprendo*," Sebby corrected. "Or, it would make more sense to say, *lo entiendo*. Leo told me to get a restraining order, and I should've."

"*Lo entiendo*. Yes . . . but don't blame yourself. Restraining orders are notoriously ineffective, and had you gotten one, it might have served to provoke him further." He shifted his arms; Sebby was resting most of his weight on Todd. "Do you want to go to bed?"

"I want to go for a walk," Sebby decided.

"But the medication . . . does it make you sleepy?"

"It takes a while to hit me. And there's a nice walking path. And maybe I'll talk a little, yes?"

The two of them slipped out the back door. It was one of those nights of late summer when the breezes whispered of autumn, and Sebby was glad for his sweater. He breathed the sweet air. A quarter moon had risen, orange on the horizon and looking larger than was natural. The paved path was dotted with security lights. It meandered through grassy areas and on into a rocky area, the stretching tendrils of the Rocky Mountains.

Todd said, "I still don't understand why you chose to call Leo that night and not me." He slowed his pace. "Was it because you believed he would be better able to protect you? You once called me Don Quixote and said that you would not even bet on me against one man."

"No, Todd," Sebby declared, even though it made his heart contract in fear to imagine Todd going up against Collin. Look what Gus had done to Todd, and Gus was an old man! "It was just because

Leo knew all about it. I didn't want to tell you!" A woman passed them, walking her poofy little dog, which yapped at them.

Todd *tsk*ed. "But why didn't you want me to know? You had already related to me the story of your broken arm."

"I hadn't told you the whole story! Oh, *Dios*, I still haven't."

"But why? *Cielito lindo*, why?"

"Because I thought you wouldn't want me!"

Todd made a noise that sounded sad and pitying to Sebby, and Sebby sped away, avoiding Todd's arms. They stopped at the crest of a hill, Sebby panting, Todd groaning and clutching his middle. Playground equipment stood nearby, empty swings moving in the wind. Sebby paced. "I felt pathetic. It starts to define me, no? Like 'victim' is tattooed on my forehead. And that isn't me. Some things happened, that's all, bad luck and bad choices. But when I think about it too much, I *feel* like a victim. Like nothing's ever happened to me but this. Like *I've* never done anything in my life. Things were done *to* me." He folded his arms and glared at Todd. "*You* got hit. No one thinks *you're* a victim."

"Well. They might if I wore a cropped tee." Todd rolled his shirt up, displaying his purpled midriff.

"And don't say it's different. It's no different."

"It is, in point of fact, quite different."

"Why, because I'm small? You're not so big."

"Bigger than you." Todd came close and leaned toward Sebby, looming over him, if two inches could be called looming.

"Your ego's bigger." But he allowed Todd to take hold of his elbows and pull Sebby's arms around him.

"It's very different when one who is supposed to love and care for you instead causes you harm."

"Gus is a foreman," Sebby retorted. "He's supposed to care for his crew members."

Todd inclined his head. "In a sense. I concede the point. But Gus is not my lover, nor my ex-lover, and— Oh, fucking fucking fucking hell. Oh, *no*, Sebby."

"What?"

"Jesus God, tell me I'm wrong."

"You're wrong. What, Todd, what?"

"You. Gus. Ex-lovers."

Sebby's jaw dropped; he busted out laughing. "Oh," he said, and found that he couldn't speak—the priceless expression on Todd's face hurled him into a new fit of hilarity, and he'd have doubled over but for Todd's support. He buried his face in Todd's shirt; tears of merriment dampened the fabric. Just when he had begun to regain control, Todd grumbled under his breath, and that set him off again. At length he wiped his streaming eyes and raised his head. "Oh. It hurts to laugh." He laid the back of his hand against his flushed cheek.

"You'll recall that you told me you had broken the hearts of many older men."

The idea of him breaking Gus's heart made him lose it again. He laughed so hard that he thought he might piss himself, and each time he tried to calm down in order to say something, he squeaked and pitched a new fit. Finally, exhausted, leaning on Todd, he drew deep breaths and sighed. "Toddfox, you're mean to make me laugh so. Oh, my face hurts."

"I humbly apologize," Todd said loftily.

"*Querido*, you're so sweet. You think every man is dying of love for me?"

"Gus is exceedingly protective of you."

Sebby considered this. Lots of people were protective of him. He took it as a matter of course. "I don't know why he is. But it's not because we were lovers." He grinned again at the thought of it, and, oh, his face did hurt. "*Lo prometo*. But, anyway, you changed the subject, which was that Gus hitting you is as bad as Collin hitting me."

"Gus did not harass me, nor stake out my home, nor force his way into said home, nor hit me in the face, nor did he follow up his one punch with any others. Besides which, I remind you, he thought I'd hurt you. What excuse did Collin offer?"

"Plenty." Sebby turned away and wandered in the direction of the empty playground. Todd followed, and their feet crunched in the pea gravel. Sebby sat down in a swing, wrapping his arms around the chains and letting his legs dangle. The sling seat pressed snugly at his hips.

Todd seated himself in the next swing, facing the opposite direction. He reached to close his hand over Sebby's. "What did he say?"

With his toes, Sebby idly pushed himself back and forth. "He said I looked so sad that he couldn't stand it. Last night, he was watching my house—" Sebby ground his teeth and squeezed Todd's fingers "—and he saw us on the front walk, saw you give me my key, saw me standing there, and he figured we broke up. He wanted to comfort me." It was a little funny, now that he thought about it. Some comfort.

Todd looked stricken. "It *was* my fault, then."

"It would've happened. There would've been another time that you weren't there, and he would've convinced himself . . . whatever he needed to convince himself." Todd's face crumpled, and Sebby knew he should feel sympathetic, but he couldn't feel anything much. Probably, this meant that the medication was working. "Not your fault, Toddfox, so don't look like that." Sebby leaned back, faced the sky, and spoke quickly, getting the words out: "He didn't rape me."

Todd's hands tightened on Sebby's. "Good! Not being . . . er, *that*. Is good."

"He wanted me to consent," Sebby went on. *Just the facts*, he reminded himself. *State the bare facts.* "I wouldn't." He smiled at Todd, trying to reassure him. "We talked some, and at first I thought it would be all right. But he heard the phone . . ." Sebby shuddered violently. He cleared his throat. "BarrynLawrence, their voices, and he said, 'Who's that on the phone?' because I hadn't hung up. And he was suspicious, and he grabbed the phone and threw it at the wall. It smashed, and I was so, so scared. I told him he needed help. It was stupid of me to say that, and he slapped me. I tried to—to get away. I threw my coffee in his face, but it wasn't very hot anymore, and he grabbed the mug and hit me with it. The mug broke, that's the stitches, the bandage." Sebby paused to catch his breath. His heart was beating painfully fast, and he pulled one hand from Todd's grip to press it to his chest. "He said that since you left me, I had no excuse not to get back with him, but I wouldn't, oh *Dios mío*, I wouldn't. He said I was a whore and no one would ever love me, everyone would leave me but him, and he hit me, *hijo de puta*, he hit me and said, 'You want me now?' And I said no, every time I said no. I was so angry, it was like white lights in my head. I would've said no until he killed me."

Gasping for breath, he stopped. Todd had thrown his arms around Sebby and the swing, and their two swings lurched crazily.

"He wanted to break your spirit." Todd's voice shook, and Sebby couldn't tell if it was rage or sadness that moved him.

"But I'm impossibly stubborn, no?" Sebby muffled the words against Todd's throat. He rested his nose at the collar of Todd's tee and inhaled the unwashed smell, the faint scent of sex, the smell of himself on Todd's skin. Todd held him, and he was safe.

They walked back more slowly, Sebby immersed in a deep, peaceful weariness and leaning on Todd more than he needed to. He reached to twirl his fingers in Todd's longish locks. "What are we going to do with this hair? You look like Tarzan." He yawned.

Todd threw back his head and let out a bellow, alarming Sebby mid-yawn so that his jaw snapped shut. Todd pounded his chest. "Me Tarzan. You gay."

Sebby laughed until he squeaked. "I love how you can make me laugh. And I'd love to see you in a loincloth."

Todd's face went solemn. "Sebby love Tarzan. Tarzan love Sebby." He grinned and waggled his eyebrows. "Tarzan drag Sebby to cave."

Todd talking in jungle-speak was so absurd, Sebby tittered helplessly as he backed away. "Nooo."

Advancing, Todd extended his arms in invitation. Sebby continued to back away, shaking his head, until Todd darted at him, ignoring Sebby's shriek. Todd wrapped an arm around Sebby's back and bent as if to lift him.

"Todd, stop!" Sebby tried to look forbidding, but he wasn't sure how much his face responded. He put sternness into his voice. "You'll hurt yourself. Or me."

Todd straightened. His look of disappointment was almost comical.

"Some other time, Tarzan," Sebby promised. He kissed Todd's cheek.

Todd's good humor apparently rebounded. "Just as well. Sebby corpulent."

"'Corpulent'?" Sebby protested. "That means fat, no?"

"Tarzan not know. Tarzan have limited vocabulary."

"Stooop! Oh, I can't laugh anymore."

They returned to the house, and Todd left Sebby at the love seat. "I'll get you some ice." He went to the kitchen and fetched ice in a baggie and hurried to return, nearly running into Ethan.

"I didn't want to tell Sebby yet," Ethan said without preamble, "but I called the station, and Collin's out on bail."

"Fuck."

"Yeah. You're staying with him, right? I mean . . ." Ethan gestured broadly. "Right?"

"Yes."

"I don't think Collin'll try anything as long as someone's with Sebby. He wants to catch him alone."

"I won't leave him alone. Not for a second."

"Yeah." Ethan rubbed his forehead with the heel of his palm. "He won't get any prison time. Unless he has a record, I suppose. But I don't think he does. He'll plead guilty to some lesser offense and get probation."

Todd had no firsthand experience with the justice system, so he nodded.

"It's ridiculous. The guy's a menace. He'll do the same thing again, to someone else, down the road. A bag of pot'll put a guy away for years, but beat up your boyfriend? Nada." He opened a cabinet and stared into it.

"You're worried for him."

"Old habit." He shut the cabinet and grinned at Todd. "Don't mind me, I'm settled. But, God. Don't run out on him, hey?" He turned and reopened the cabinet. "Shit, I forgot what I came in here for."

"More drinks?" Todd suggested.

Ethan snapped his fingers. "That was it. Hugh wanted a beer." Closing the cabinet, he crossed to the refrigerator. "Barry and Lawrence, aw. I think they're in love!" Head in the refrigerator, he laughed. "Or they're in heat, but that's nothing new."

"Yes. Ah, I mean, no." Todd juggled the bag of ice to his other hand and blew on his chilled fingers. "Did you sleep with them, Ethan? Er, when you were with Sebby?"

Ethan straightened, a bottle of Heineken in his hand, and he looked at Todd. Todd wondered if he had overstepped his bounds and was on the point of apologizing, when Ethan said, "No."

"Ah." There was an awkward silence as Ethan continued to regard Todd. Todd could feel a flush creeping up his neck.

"Sebby's a sweet kid, but he's got his, you know, his things. Hang-ups." Ethan paused and drew a labored breath through his teeth as he pried the lid from the Heineken. "God, he'd kill me for saying this, but . . . you have to be the man. Don't take his shit? He'll run all over you if you let him. And not respect you."

That sounded remarkably like Becca's advice to "mean up," but coming from Ethan, the sentiment took on a new significance. Todd pondered. "I appreciate the advice. But we, Sebby and I, are both men."

"You're not getting what I'm saying." Ethan came closer and, evidently forgetting that the beer was for Hugh, sipped from the open bottle before taking Todd's elbow. "You'll want to indulge him. Trust me, I know. He looks at you with those big eyes, and it's sayonara, samurai. But don't let him have his own way all the time."

"I don't." Todd's brow furrowed. "I don't think?"

"And he likes, uh . . . he likes, uh . . ." Ethan leaned away, peering out into the other room before steering the bemused Todd into the far corner of the kitchen. "God, he'll kill me. Can I tell you without you telling him I told you?"

"Of course," Todd said, his curiosity piqued.

"It was a fucking mystery, and he won't tell you. You're supposed to figure it out, uh . . . what he likes."

The flush, which had abated, began creeping its way up Todd's neck once more. Was Ethan about to reveal intimacies of a sexual nature? "Go on."

"He's not into pain, okay? But . . . he, uh—" Ethan glanced around again and lowered his voice. "And he's not a sub. He doesn't like someone having control over him, like."

"I understand that. I'd never hurt him. I don't see . . ." His voice trailed off, remembering the times he'd been rough and Sebby had seemed to enjoy it. Why, even earlier . . . but then Sebby had assured him that he was not rough at all.

"You still don't get me." Ethan put a hand on Todd's shoulder and brought his face close to Todd's, wafting a cloud of beer breath. Pulling Todd almost into an embrace, one hand on his shoulder, one arm about his waist, Ethan placed his mouth in Todd's ear. "He likes to be scared," Ethan whispered, and drew back, smiling.

"Scared," Todd repeated, shrugging his shoulders against the uncomfortable closeness with Wayne's husband.

"Haven't you ever taken him to a horror movie? And he's all over you?"

"It's fun being scared when you know you're safe." Thoughts, feelings, memories fell into place. It even explained Sebby's lapse in judgment over Leo. *"Your boy had a bad fright,"* Leo had said.

"Try sneaking up behind him sometime and yelling." Ethan laughed, hiccupped, and planted a kiss on Todd's flinching cheek. "I'm glad he has you. You're a sweet kid, honey. Sebby deserves the best."

"Er, ah. Thank you?" Todd inched away, turning in a sort of pirouette to unwind himself from Ethan's arm. "For implying that I am the best. And for the sage words. Rest assured they'll be held in confidence."

Ethan waggled his fingers at Todd, following him out of the kitchen, still sipping from Hugh's beer. Sebby stood looking out the window into the dark, the fingers of one hand stroking his temple. Barry and Lawrence had curled up together on Hugh's lap, the three of them the picture of contentment—Barry's fingers laced with Lawrence's, their heads on Hugh's chest, their foreheads pressed together as in the photo Todd carried in his wallet. Hugh's arms encircled them both.

Todd smoothed his hand down Sebby's back. *"Cielito lindo.* Let's go home where we're comfortable."

Sebby paused in thought and then said, "Take me home." He paused. "Please, Tarzan? Drag me to our cave?"

Chapter Forty-One

Foot Down

There was no police tape over his doorway, nothing to indicate that the place was a crime scene, and that was a relief. Maybe they just used that yellow tape for murders. Sebby shivered, even though he didn't believe that Collin would ever have killed him. It was too dramatic to think so, too . . . egotistical. To still the trembling of his hands, Sebby twisted his fingers in the tail of Todd's shirt. He hadn't wanted to come home yet—the mess, the reminders.

"Key?" Todd said.

"Lock's broken." Sebby stepped past Todd and gave the door a shove. It swung open, and Sebby heard Todd's intake of breath as the chaos inside became visible. "*Hay mucha mierda,*" Sebby swore. He had to clean all that up before going to bed, and he was so tired, and he hurt.

Todd crouched to inspect the door. "You should buy a new door soon, a strong one."

"Whatever you think best. It'll be your door too."

Todd straightened, wiping his hands on his thighs. Pushing the doorframe flat, he managed to close the door by leaning on it, twisting the knob, and pushing with his knee. He engaged the chain, wiped his hands again, and glanced at Sebby. "You . . . want me to move in?"

"I did when I asked you, and I still do. So will you?" The corner of Todd's mouth quirked, and Sebby's heart cricketed. Todd had said he loved him. Was there a *but*?

"If we are to cohabit, Sebastián, we must first have a serious discussion."

"*Sí.* For one thing, if you want to live in my house, you have to start tying that hair back."

Todd fingered the ends of his hair, his forehead crinkling.

"Toddfox, I'm too tired to be serious. So, okay. Don't answer me if you can't. Tomorrow, yes?" He turned to the debris-covered living room and slumped. "Will you get me a trash bag? They're under the kitchen sink."

"What for? Oh, no. Sweetheart, that can wait."

"It can wait, but I can't. I'll never get to sleep knowing this mess is here."

"It can wait, you can wait. Upstairs."

"What? Just— No. It won't take long." Sebby bent and righted an overturned floor lamp.

"It'll take half the night! I'm putting my foot down." Todd's arm went around Sebby's waist, and Sebby found himself propelled from the room and at the foot of the stairs before he could speak.

"You're putting your foot down? Has it been up somewhere?"

"It's going up your posterior if you don't get up these stairs."

Early in the morning, Sebby arose without waking Todd and went downstairs to set things to rights. When he had fallen, he had taken a floor lamp with him, and its light bulbs had burst, and he had bled on the rug and sofa. There were cleaning solutions he thought would get the blood out, but first he had to clear away the debris.

Most of the damage had occurred after Hugh had arrived. In shoving Collin away from Sebby, Hugh's arm had taken out a Tiffany-style table lamp. Collin had stumbled backward, overturned an end table, grabbed an antique Fenton vase, and hurled it at Hugh, who had ducked, allowing it to shatter against the wall. Several more items had followed before Hugh had reached him and put a stop to the destruction—to that particular destruction, anyway. The two of them had gone on blundering about the room, Collin mostly trying to get away and Hugh not letting him. Sebby had collapsed in the arms of Barry and Lawrence, whose screams Sebby had barely heard over the ringing in his own head.

Sebby plucked the larger pieces of broken lamp, porcelain niceties, and Depression glass from the floor. He sighed over this and that item and deposited them in an old plastic ice cream bucket.

He was facedown on the floor, and he lay there for some seconds before finding reason to wonder what he was doing there. He turned his head, and there was the bucket, on its side, some of the glass spilling out. *I fainted*, he realized, astounded. He pushed himself slowly into a sitting position and scooted sideways until he could lean against the couch. His face stung, and his fingers came away bloody when he touched it. Oh, Todd was going to freak.

No, he should go clean up. He didn't want Todd to know.

No, he needed to tell Todd. He needed Todd, and he needed to tell Todd. The big lie had died, and all the little ones had to follow. He pulled air deep into his lungs and shouted. "Todd! Todd, Todd!"

There was a noise above him like someone's feet hitting the floor, or maybe someone falling out of bed.

"Todd," he shouted again, "everything is okay, but can you come here, please?"

There was an unintelligible answering shout and then the sound of feet pounding down the staircase. Todd appeared in his boxers, hair about his face in a wild tangle, eyes heavy with sleep behind glasses that sat crookedly on his nose. "Wha—"

"Not quite a loincloth, but it'll do." Sebby eyed Todd, whose blotchy bruise had faded from eggplant to lavender. Sebby tried to smile. "I think I fainted."

Todd insisted that Sebby go to the emergency room, and Sebby counter-insisted, since it was during business hours, that he go to his regular physician instead. When Sebby had fallen, some of the glass fragments had embedded themselves in the skin of his face and forearm, not badly, but the fragments were too small to be easily removed, and dabbing at the blood would send the glass deeper. In the kitchen, Sebby drew Todd to the sink. There, Sebby had Todd spray him with the sink sprayer, which sluiced away the bits of glass. Pink with red threads, the water swirled around the white ceramic surface and down the drain, and when it was over and Sebby was toweling himself and the counter off, Todd sank into the nearest chair, lowering his head between his knees.

Sebby regarded his face in the rearview mirror for most of the drive. He kept forgetting how ugly he was, and it was even worse now, his face speckled with red spots like acne. No wonder Todd didn't want to move in with him.

The doctor's office was crowded, and Sebby was a walk-in; they would have a wait. A television mounted on the wall was broadcasting a game show. A harried-looking mother grabbed *Green Eggs and Ham* and sat down with her toddler. Sebby squeezed Todd's hand and turned his face away.

"They won't draw blood, will they?" Todd said under his breath.

"Why? You going back with me?" Sebby said, surprised. "I needed you to drive me, but I don't expect you to go in with me."

Now Todd was surprised. "You would prefer to be unaccompanied?"

"No," Sebby said. "No, but I understand. I don't expect you to . . . blood, doctors . . ."

Todd's arm slid around Sebby, pulling him close, though Sebby resisted. Todd's breath ruffled his hair. "It'll be all right. Everything will be fine."

"Of course." Sebby kept his spine rigid and refused to lean back against his boyfriend.

Patients came and went. A soap followed the game show. Several different parents read *Green Eggs and Ham* aloud. "*Ay*," Sebby said, "I hate waiting."

"I do not like to sit and wait. In fact, it is a thing I hate."

The Seuss talk was catching. "Would you like it in a box? Would you, could you, with Toddfox?"

Todd laughed out loud, the sound falling on Sebby's ears like firecrackers. The ache in his face as he smiled reminded him again of how ugly he was, and he scowled. Which also hurt. Fucking depressing. Sebby stood and stretched, and caught Todd watching him with that intent look, like Sebby was a rare penny on the sidewalk and Todd was a coin collector.

"What?" he demanded, hands on hips.

"I was just thinking . . ." And Todd blushed.

"Well, don't hurt yourself." *Dios*, he was bitchy today.

Todd smirked as if he found Sebby's bitchiness charming, and maybe he did. "Doctors. Blood." He blushed more deeply, and Sebby was mystified.

"Yes? Doctors? Blood? This gets you hot?"

Todd stammered. "It's about time that I, myself, had a checkup." There was more stammering before he went on. "We could get checked up together."

Sebby blinked, sinking down next to Todd. "Oh. I see. You mean . . ."

"Er."

"That still doesn't explain the look on your face. Going to the doctor is romantic, Zorro?"

Todd shifted. "I— We'll talk later. As you said."

"Todd, I will squirm like an itchy armadillo! What?"

"Very well. Come here, then." He pulled Sebby close against himself and pressed his mouth to Sebby's hair.

Sebby tensed. How Todd could be so worried about being outed at work and so oblivious out in public exasperated Sebby, especially now when his nerves were bristling.

"I was thinking," Todd went on, his fingers stroking Sebby's abdomen, his voice a breath caressing Sebby's ear, "that if we both were tested . . ."

"It wouldn't hurt, I guess. Much."

". . . and, assuming we both are free of contagions . . ." Todd nuzzled.

"Uh-huh."

". . . and we both agree to mutual exclusivity, then . . ."

"Then?" Sebby breathed.

"We could . . . dispense with prophylactics."

"Dispense?" Sebby repeated stupidly.

"As in . . . not use them."

It had been years since Sebby had had unprotected sex. He never even considered it anymore, and the idea was shocking. A thrill went through him. It was dangerous, it was bad, the opposite of everything he thought he associated with monogamy—safety, stability, sameness. "Um, not right away," he cautioned. "If we are clean, then, still—"

"Six months," Todd interrupted. "Tested again, and then."

"*Then* . . . think you'll still be around *then*?"

"Sebastian Nye?" called a nurse from the doorway, mispronouncing his name.

Sebby got to his feet, and Todd followed, holding on to his elbow. "That's the plan."

There's a plan? Sebby blinked rapidly, and even that hurt.

The nurse took Sebby's vitals, cleaned the scratches, entered information into the touch screen on the wall, and left them with the assurance that the doctor would be in soon. Sebby perched on the examining table, hands tucked under his thighs, and swung his legs.

"Are we clear now, at least on that one point?" Todd asked.

"Which one point?"

Todd hesitated, then drew close to Sebby and slipped his arms around Sebby's waist, resting his chin on Sebby's shoulder. "On the point of exclusivity, *cielito lindo*. I tried to tell you: I can't do that kind of relationship. I need to know that you understand."

"You do not like it, Sam-I-am. Yes, we are clear. I promise not to pimp you out to any more of my friends."

"And you . . ." Todd's hair was tied back as Sebby had requested, and had anyone ever looked more earnest than Todd did at this moment? His light eyebrows arched in anxiety over his clear blue eyes. "And you . . ." he repeated, "what do you want?"

"I'm sorry about Leo," Sebby whispered. Todd pressed his fingers. "I want you. Just you. You and me. No one else."

"I can't tell you how relieved and happy that makes me," Todd said.

"It's strange to me," Sebby admitted. "A little scary."

"It's fun being scared when you know you're safe," Todd reminded him, grinning. His eyes behind their lenses sparkled.

"Monogamy fun because it's scary . . . Didn't think of that."

"*Cielito lindo*. And I promise—"

There was a knock at the door, and Todd jumped away to sit in one of the chairs. Sebby threw mental daggers at his doctor, who stepped through the door at such an inopportune moment, stethoscope around her neck, platinum-blonde hair twisted at her crown. "Hi, Sebby, how are you? What are you here for today?" Her Ukrainian accent always made her seem kind of mysterious to Sebby. She seated herself and began reading his chart on the touch screen.

Sebby opened his mouth to answer, but Todd butted in. "He was assaulted night before last. He has bruises and contusions and blunt trauma to the head, and this morning he briefly lost consciousness."

"Todd," Sebby warned through clenched teeth. It was fucking annoying that Todd should speak for him like that.

The doctor raised her head and peered at Todd over her green spectacles. There were deep frown lines around her mouth. "And you are?"

"Todd, rhymes with God. I'm his boyfriend."

Sebby ground his teeth on Todd's air of possessive pride.

"Todd, I am Dr. Roodnitsky." Unsmiling, the woman drew near and put a hand beneath Sebby's chin, peering into his face. "Describe what happened when you fainted."

While she shone her penlight into each of his eyes in turn and examined his face, Sebby explained how he had found himself facedown on the floor. She assessed his mental status with a few questions "You have taken medication?" She stepped back and referred to the touch screen. "Emergency room report is here. They prescribed you two medications."

Todd was on his feet, handing her two prescription bottles. "I brought them," he said proudly. Sebby blinked. He hadn't thought of bringing them along; when had Todd grabbed them?

She peered at the bottles and back at the touch screen. "You take these this morning?"

"This morning? Just the one for pain. About six thirty. I took the other last night, but not since then."

She nodded. "You take with food?"

"No. I didn't have breakfast. Just coffee."

"X-rays?"

"Yes. They took one of my face, my head, my arm . . . They said everything was fine."

She nodded. "Radiology report is not here. We will check with hospital." With that, she was gone.

"Todd. What were you going to promise me?"

Todd blinked and shook his head.

"Right before she came in," Sebby urged. "You said, 'And I promise—' Tell me. Please? Don't be mean. It'll distract me while we're waiting."

"I was…" Todd hesitated. "I promise not to pressure you. I promise to be less intense. And not to expect so much from our relationship. In short, I promise to be reasonable." He grinned crookedly.

It wasn't the promise he wanted to hear. Sebby dropped his eyes, biting his lip until he felt Todd's restraining finger across his mouth. "I did say that you expect too much. But I don't want you to change. Besides, I think I expect too little."

"What do you mean, my love?"

"Todd, I didn't expect you to come back with me for the exam. I didn't expect you to mow my lawn, or take care of me when I'm hungover, or be so fucking nice to me. I didn't expect you to care so much how I feel or to want only me, or a thousand other things. You said I hold back, and that's true too, and I don't want to anymore, I don't want to hold back from you."

"Sweetheart, then don't! Hold my hand, jump with me!" Todd seized Sebby's hand in his.

"Jump?"

"Plunge! Hurtle! Abandon caution!"

This is less intense? But he didn't say it. After all, he had just said he didn't want Todd to change. "Yes." Sebby squeezed Todd's fingers. Closing his eyes, his fingertip-hold on his reserve slipped, slipped, and he mentally uncurled his fingers and let go. "Geronimo."

There was a knock, and they both turned; Todd stayed near this time, Sebby's right hand gripped in his own right hand, his left arm at Sebby's back.

"Radiology report is here. No fractures." The doctor picked up Sebby's prescriptions and rapped them on the counter. "Medication is working for your pain?"

"Yes. It works good."

"The medication is mislabeled." She shook the bottles at them.

"They gave me the wrong meds?" Sebby squeaked. Todd made a noise of outrage.

"Meds are right. But the label's missing. Take with food. Avoid caffeine. This is probably why you fainted." She sat down at the computer.

Sebby wilted, feeling foolish, like he couldn't even take his medicine the right way.

"Your scratches are not bad. Keep them clean; apply antibacterial ointment. You have this?" Sebby nodded. "They won't scar. And keep cold on your face fifteen minutes of every hour. It is more swollen than it should be." She went on with her instructions as Sebby's insides curled up in misery. "If you take medication, take with food. No coffee. You will not clean the house. You will let him, your boyfriend, do this. You will lie down the rest of today and all day tomorrow. Okay?" Sebby nodded. "I will write an excuse for your employer." She turned away and scribbled on a pad of paper, ripped off the top sheet, and handed it to Todd. The lines around her mouth melted away in a broad smile. "Such a nice boy you have. You are lucky."

"Thanks, doc." Todd looked surprised.

"Thanks," Sebby echoed faintly. Dr. Roodnitsky squeezed his shoulder and exited the room.

"Jesus!" Todd collapsed into one of the flimsy plastic chairs with such force that Sebby winced. "Best fucking medical care in the world nearly gets one killed!"

"Was she talking to you or me?" Sebby hopped down.

"You or me what? They couldn't take thirty seconds to caution you about your prescription?"

"Maybe they did caution me, maybe I forgot. Maybe they did make a mistake; mistakes happen. Was she saying you or me is lucky, having a nice boy?"

"Oh. I thought she was talking to me." Todd's face reddened, and he raked his fingers through his hair, surprise blooming on his face as he encountered the unfamiliar tie at the back of his neck.

"We're both lucky. *Vamos, querido.*"

Sebby had sat and fidgeted as he watched Todd pick up the broken glass and set the room to rights. Even though he was so tired, it had been hard to sit still, and hard to keep from bossing Todd too much. Later they cuddled on the sofa under an afghan, making plans for Todd to move in.

"Ryan will be so sad," Sebby said. "He loses his roomie, and to me, who he doesn't like."

"I'll remind him of the alternative—that I could be moving all the way back to New York."

Sebby groaned at the thought and snuggled closer, insinuating his knee between Todd's legs, pressing his thigh to Todd's groin and wiggling about as if he were trying to get comfortable.

"Stop, love," Todd said firmly. "The doctor ordered rest."

"I want you. I had plenty of rest today, yes? And we haven't . . ." He hesitated. "We haven't made love since we said we love each other. And I think it'll be different, no?"

Todd's eyes softened, but still he shook his head no.

Sebby pouted. "Who put you in charge of my sex life, you dictator?"

"You did," Todd replied, and his expression went solemn. "When you said you loved me and asked me to be with you. We are now, each of us, in charge of the other's sex life. It is a grave responsibility." He untangled Sebby from himself, stood, and drew Sebby to his feet. "You're more weary than you realize. Don't you imagine that I can see you are not quite yourself?"

"I—I—" He gave up, shrugging. Maybe he was too ugly for Todd to want him. "Okayyy. I'm not going to beg you. You just let me know when you think I'm myself again. It's your *grave responsibility*. Don't expect me to ask you again, 'cause I won't." He huffed, but Todd pulled him close against himself, and maybe Sebby *was* tireder than he'd thought, because Todd's arms had never felt so unyielding. "Ohhh!" he wailed, giving up and burying his face in Todd's shirt. "I can't make you do anything!"

"Didn't I say you were not yourself?" Todd's voice was full of amusement.

Chapter Forty-Two

Monkey Flinging Feces

"So do you quit, Todd? Or are you coming to work tomorrow?" Sebby asked.

A pretty head of coffee-scented hair was pillowed in the crook of Todd's shoulder, and Todd felt that he would comply with any request issuing from that head. They had come to an agreement that Sebby had had enough rest to allow sex, and now they were cuddling contentedly on the last morning of Sebby's leave.

"Since that dilettante of an accountant they employ has not yet processed my resignation, I feel I must put in an appearance. Besides, I need to protect my investment, lest the others attempt to go where Todd has gone before."

Sebby laughed. "Oh, you think you've put ideas into their heads? All those construction workers will be lining up outside my office?"

"They already do that, *cielito lindo.*"

Never before had Todd and Sebby arrived at work at the same time, in the same vehicle, Todd's truck no less. Numb fingertips could not feel the press of Sebby's fingers, numb lips barely felt the morning peck as they parted, and his breakfast roiled in his belly as he donned his hard hat and joined the crew.

"Clean out the trucks," was the closest thing to an apology Gus uttered.

Morning break arrived, bringing Sebby with his thermos of pressed coffee, no different than any other morning, except that Sebby's free hand slid all along the inside of Todd's arm before lacing their fingers together, and he leaned on Todd as Todd, trying not to look furtive, drank his coffee. Gus's expression stopped short of a scowl. There were some unfriendly stares as the crew headed back to work, and from somewhere behind him he heard the comment, "Get a room." He ignored it, but it got him to thinking. On the occasion that a wife or girlfriend showed up at the site, there might be a hug or a peck. But the beaming, the hand-holding, the leaning . . .

The trucks were as clean as they were going to get, and as he joined the others, Rob posed the question: "So what happened?"

Silence fell. Todd hesitated; it was, after all, Sebby's business. But Sebby was now in the role of Todd's significant other, and it was natural for coworkers to ask Todd about him, as they asked each other how a sick child was faring, how a divorce was unfolding. "Violent, obsessed ex-boyfriend," he said.

Rob pursed his lips and nodded. "What're you gonna do about it?"

"He was arrested. Charges will be pressed. A restraining order will be filed."

Rob's question haunted Todd the rest of the morning. *"What're you gonna do about it?"* He had not been planning to do anything about it, other than keep Sebastián safe and support him in his pursuit of justice.

Lunchtime arrived, and Todd went to the mobile office to fetch Sebby.

"Just a sec, just a sec," Sebby mumbled as he finished something up on his computer.

Todd nodded. "I'll meet you at the truck." As he made his way across the dusty expanse where the crew parked, he was brought up short by an eye-searing hue of pink splotched all over the side of his pickup. It began with a drippy *F* on the driver's door, and oozed across the cab and down the side of the truck bed. *Faggots burn in hell* was the inscription, surmounted by a pink triangle and underscored by a row of what appeared to be wilted pizza slices—flames, Todd conjectured. He stared numbly, waiting for someone to comment, someone to be outraged, before a thing resembling sense stirred and said, *Don't let*

Sebastián see this. Todd bit his tongue at the thought. *The truck's not working; it's the transmission, must get it towed.* He pivoted, his lips rehearsing the lie, and there was Sebby, rooted.

Large, wounded-deer eyes wandered back and forth, back and forth along the side of the truck, as Sebby's lips rounded to shape the question that would not quite emerge, but that Todd heard anyway: *Who would do such a thing?* Dismay crept over Sebby's visage, and Todd knew that Sebby did not want to believe that any of the men whose paychecks Sebby so lovingly cut would commit such an affront. "It wasn't directed at you, *cielito lindo.*"

"Todd, don't even! If it's at you, it's at me. You think if we'd driven my car they would have left it alone?"

"Yes," Todd replied honestly. He reached for Sebby, who drew back, folding his arms.

"There's an *s* on 'faggots.' That means more than just you, and that means me."

"I believe it to be a generalized plural rather than specific. There is no comma after 'faggots,' therefore it is not meant as a directive."

"If it's generalized to say all faggots burn in hell, that includes me too."

"It does not say *all* faggots. I don't believe it to be a prediction, merely an observation. Faggots do burn in hell, some of them. I offer up a fervent prayer that Collin will."

Sebby huffed, swiped his hand across the bright letter *F,* and rubbed his dry fingertips together. Belatedly, Todd craned his neck. If only he had thought to look around when he'd first seen the graffiti! He might have spotted the perpetrator attending the reaction to his handiwork.

"You have to fill out an incident report."

"Later. Lunch." Todd unlocked the door.

"What! In that? You're just gonna cruise through the McDonald's drive-through?"

"No. I intend to park in the Star of India lot. We've spent enough time there together; I doubt they'll be surprised."

"You have to fill out an incident report!"

"Not on an empty stomach, I don't." Todd opened the truck door and climbed in. "Coming?"

For answer, Sebby glared and hollered, "Gus! Get over here!"

"Sebby, leave it."

But Sebby planted his feet, and Gus made his way over. Resignedly, Todd dismounted and slammed the door, that Gus might view the thing complete.

"Son of a bitch," Gus said. "When did this happen?"

Sebby said, "This morning. Here. Someone here did it."

"You gotta fill out an incident report," said Gus.

Sebby smiled triumphantly. "*Sí.* I know."

"And you gotta call the site manager. Gimondi Brothers'll reimburse you. For removing the paint. Or repainting."

Sebby tilted his head to one side. "Gus, what're you doing for lunch? Can we tag along?"

That afternoon, an inspection was called. Nothing incriminating was found. No one confessed or informed. They were all sentenced to attend diversity training. Gus pulled out a random orbital sander and exfoliated the graffiti from the truck, down to the gray primer.

At home, an incensed Sebastián stabbed with a wooden spoon at frying chorizo and vegetables. "Diversity training! *¡Qué mierda!*" Bits of hot food flew from the pan, and Sebby ignored the mess.

"There may be more value to diversity training than you think." Todd winced at the flying food. "I'm sorry you were hurt."

"I'm not hurt, I'm pissed off!" Sebby shoveled the food onto plates. They clunked as he dropped them on the table.

Over his protests, Todd gathered Sebby into his arms. "Imp, you excel at making me see my own frailties, but you hide from your own."

"Don't psychoanalyze me!" But he laid his head on Todd's shoulder and sighed.

"Wouldn't dream of it." Todd laughed at his own joke, but it either went over Sebby's head, or he didn't find it funny. "I imagine you feel betrayed. Disillusioned."

"I insisted you come out, and I told you everyone would be nice. How could I be so wrong?"

"You were right, for the most part. It may have been only one individual proclaiming his displeasure."

"*Dios mío*, Todd! All these years, at Gimondi's, no one's ever, ever been anything but nice to me."

"It's the classic don't-ask-don't-tell mindset. As long as it stays underground, they can pretend to themselves that it doesn't exist. But if it gets in their faces, they become upset."

"You're telling me I should back off."

"I didn't say that."

"You're thinking it, though!" Sebby slumped. "If I do, it's showing them that their little terrorism is successful. They're upset because they think it's shameful and *belongs* underground. But if we don't hide, we're saying that it's good and right, and that's what they can't handle. That someone thinks it's good and right."

"I'm not asking you to change your behavior. Er, our behavior. Er."

"You wish I would, though!"

"No. I don't know. Perhaps we were a tad inappropriate. You don't see the others with their significant others leaning on them during break."

"Damn it, Todd!" Sebby lurched upright, his face inches from Todd's. The swelling had gone down considerably, but the flesh surrounding his eyes was still the deep purple of a late-summer evening. "You don't even understand the issue! You would have fought those men downtown on July Fourth, but where it matters, where you go to work every day—" Sebby paused to smack the flat of his hand against Todd's chest "—you will roll over and take it in the ass."

Todd bit back a venomous reply, reminding himself that Sebby had been hurt and deserved a turn at drama queen. He forced mildness into his tone. "Interesting choice of words, considering."

"You act like it doesn't matter! Aren't you even angry? It's like you expected it, like this is how the world works."

"Do I appear so jaded? I assure you, I am not."

"You appear jaded, yeah."

"What would have me do?"

"Stand up for yourself! Stand up for *me*!"

It was wounding, bewildering. Rob's words from that morning echoed in his head: *"What're you gonna do about it?"* And his own, implied response: *Nothing*. Well, he could change that. The next person who looked at him or at Sebby cross-eyed would receive a good clip to the jaw.

Sebby drooped, and his next words came out muffled against Todd's neck. "It's like monkeys flinging feces on your prom outfit. You feel beautiful and special, and then . . . shit!"

Todd's mouth quirked. "While I cannot speak from personal experience, I would venture to say that one ought not to wear one's prom ensemble to the zoo."

There was silence, and Todd realized that, while he had been flip, Sebby was finding significance in his words. "That is deep, I . . . But, no, it is not like prom at all. Shit washes off, but . . . *Carajo*. I . . . I'll stop leaning on you. At work."

"I love when you lean on me," Todd murmured, rubbing his cheek against Sebby's hair.

Sebby squirmed and placed his hands around Todd's neck as if to strangle him. "Well, which is it? You want me to back off or no?"

"No."

But there was no recovering the blissful hours of that first morning back at work. Self-consciousness made them wary, as encountering a worm in an apple will make the eater watchful while consuming the remainder, unable, with mincing little bites, to enjoy the fruit, no matter how sweet.

Chapter Forty-Three
Mausoleum

"*Y*our dimple is back!"

Up early as usual, Sebby had been startled at Todd's sudden appearance in the bathroom. He had jumped and yelped before breaking into peals of laughter that brought out his dimple.

In Todd's eyes was such tenderness as he cupped the side of Sebby's face, that Sebby felt the frozen ball in his chest soften. He could breathe again, breaths that quickened as Todd pressed a kiss there, poked his tongue into the little depression that had, till this morning, been buried under swelling and bruises.

"I missed you," Todd murmured to the dimple, his lips warm against Sebby's face, and the icy chunk, made of fear and anger and helplessness, melted and dribbled away.

Warmed through and through, Sebby sighed in contentment. "Oh, I want you here. When are you moving in, already?"

Todd clucked. "Not much to move in, *cielito lindo*. Your home is suitably furnished without crowding my things into it."

"But you have to have things here. You have to make it your home."

"I've the things I want and need most: my books, my music, some clothing, and you."

"If you don't move things in, it feels temporary. Please, Todd." Todd stirred restlessly, and Sebby was afraid, afraid that temporary was how Todd wanted it. Sebby drew back. "If you're not ready, then you're not. I love you either way, here or there. But be honest."

Todd fidgeted, and his mouth worked. The corners of his eyes crinkled into worry lines. "I'm damaged goods, and you've already said I expect too much, and I've things in my life, things I need to work on, and so I attend, I need to attend, Al-Anon meetings. In fact I'd pledged to attend regularly, and by regularly I mean twice weekly, but with everything that's been happening..." His voice trailed off.

"*Querido*, we're all damaged goods. Are you an alcoholic, a reformed one, I mean? You said your mother is. You didn't say you were."

Todd's eyes turned to the ceiling. "You're thinking of Alcoholics Anonymous. Al-Anon is a sort of adjunct group, a support group for friends and families of alcoholics. Many of the unhealthy behaviors of an alcoholic are adopted by those around him. Thus, we all have recovery to recover."

Sebby nodded, though he felt confused and impatient. "So you don't want to move your things in because—what?"

"Because ... er ... I wasn't sure you would want me. If you knew everything."

¡Dios! Did Todd think it was so shocking or shameful? Grasping Todd's shoulders, he locked eyes with him. "I want you. With all your dark corners and things I might not know." He felt Todd relax a little and gave him a quick kiss. "You never know everything about someone else. A relationship means always finding new things." He frowned. "Should I come with you to these meetings?"

There was a stunned silence. "No one has ever asked me that before."

There was a flurry of snow, the day they drove to the block of garages where Todd's things were stored, though it was too warm in mid-October for anything to stick. Down one long row and up another, they meandered till they reached the correct number, parked, and hopped out. With a rattle and bang, the garage door went up. Sebby grabbed Todd in mock horror. "Do you have someone's head in here?"

"Yes, and now I've brought another to keep it company." He put his finger to Sebby's neck in imitation of a knife, flicked on the light, and pushed him through to the dim interior. The garage was Lloyd's and was half full of castoffs. Todd's items occupied the front half. Box springs and mattress were upended against the wall near a bookcase, sofa, desk, and standing lamp. Boxes were piled haphazardly, many of them having been opened and ransacked. "I never had the money to spend on, well, decorating," Todd explained. "When I was just an intern, I barely made enough money to live, and for months I saved to move to New York. Even when I had a real job, I was, ah, saving to buy, ah, Viv's ring." He cleared his throat.

"It's all right. What about your boxes, though? There must be things you want."

"Indeed, there are, though not many. I have linens, but none so nice as yours. They can stay. Dishes, well, same scenario. Some framed photos. More books, if you can spare the space."

Sebby helped Todd go through the boxes methodically, repacking their contents and stacking them. They removed their jackets as the work warmed them. Some boxes made the cut and were placed in the truck, while others were doomed to remain, for now, in dusty darkness. Two lonely cartons had been pushed beneath the desk, and Sebby squatted to drag them out, noting that they were still taped shut.

"No, no, love, leave those," Todd admonished, taking Sebby into his arms and drawing him away.

"Whyyy, what's in them? Chopped-off heads?" Sebby teased, but Todd just kissed him. *Vivian souvenirs*, Sebby assumed, and he was glad not to have to sort through it.

"*Fini.*" Todd took a last look around. "Oh . . . I left my keys there. Grab them?" He gestured at a stack of boxes and turned away.

Sebby moved to get the keys, *tsk*ing at Todd's absentmindedness. The light went out. The garage door banged down behind him, and Sebby made a jump-turn in the sudden darkness.

"Shit," Todd said. The gray shape of him outlined itself as Sebby's eyes began to adjust.

"Shit what? What shit?" Sebby squeaked.

"The door . . . Ah . . . I think we might be locked in." The gray shape ducked, and there was a disturbingly loud clanking as the door was rattled.

Sebby put his hands over his ears until it stopped.

"*Nada*," Todd said, and he stood, a silhouette against glowing cracks of daylight. The shape moved toward Sebby. "You've arrived at your mausoleum, *mon cher*. You've had that feeling . . . that chill . . . when someone has walked across your grave? That was I, pacing amongst these relics." He advanced a step.

"You're teasing. I know you're teasing. The door isn't really locked. Is it?" Sebby's voice was an octave too high. Despite himself, he scurried backward, using little mouse steps to avoid tripping in the darkish, confined place. He yanked his cell phone out of his pocket. Reassuring light spilled out as he tapped it.

"That will not help you," Todd purred as he crept forward. "There is no signal, nor no hope, here in the sepulcher."

The phone showed one bar, but before Sebby could unlock it, Todd's hand closed over Sebby's wrist; the other hand plucked the phone from his grip. Sebby squawked. Todd shoved. Over they went, and Sebby landed on the sofa. Blood pounded in his ears, and with Todd atop him, he couldn't catch his breath. "Todd! W-w-wait. Wait!" He squirmed, but Todd was a dead weight, pinning him. The sofa smelled like old corn chips.

"Death waits for no man." Todd nipped gently under Sebby's jaw.

Sebby struggled, and his ass sank down between the sofa cushions. He cried out. Todd's hand clamped over Sebby's mouth, either because he feared they would be heard, or as part of the game. If it was a game.

"Such a lovely head. I'll cherish it. Shhh." Todd let go of Sebby's mouth and began fingering Sebby's shirt buttons. *He'll take my shirt in his hands and just tear it right off my body, pop the buttons.* In his head, Sebby could hear the *pops* as the buttons flew, the *pings* as they landed on the concrete floor; they would roll away, and mice would carry them off. But, because he was Todd, he carefully undid each button, nibbling his way down the exposed flesh of Sebby's chest. "You wonder what is in the sealed boxes, do you not?" Todd's voice went on, melodic against Sebby's navel. "Soon enough, you'll see. Curiosity killed *le chat*."

Sebby pummeled Todd's back. He screamed a little; he couldn't help it. He wrapped his legs around Todd to pull him closer; he couldn't help that either. "Please . . . please?"

"There's no one to hear you." His hands worked at Sebby's jeans, undoing them, inching them down.

How long could Todd keep this up? "Let me go. I'll, I'll—" Thoughts evaporated as Todd's mouth found his cock. "¡Dios! No! Oh!" He hardly knew what he said, if he said anything.

But Todd was cruel. He was going to torture Sebby for real, and he lifted his head too soon, sitting up and pulling Sebby roughly into his lap, back-to-front, calloused hands coarse against Sebby's waist. There was the sound of Todd's zipper. Sebby moaned; Todd's erection prodded at his ass. Sebby swallowed and his voice quavered. "Wait, wait, Todd, really, wait. Do you have a— Do you have a . . ."

"Absurd boy." Todd nestled Sebby in his lap and nibbled at the nape of his neck. "In an hour, this exquisite head"—and he ran his hands down the sides of Sebby's head, smoothing his hair flat to his scalp—"will join the others. You are freed from worry over such mundane things as disease." He yanked at one sleeve of Sebby's shirt and then the other, and the shirt was tossed aside; the air stirred as his shirt floated away, and he shivered at the chill on his skin, at Todd's buttons digging into his back. There was a slight sound, like the unwrapping of a condom, and Sebby relaxed slightly.

It was cold—Todd's fingers so slick and so cold pressing inside as if to find his vitals—that Sebby gasped and shuddered, and Todd didn't wait as he usually did. He pushed in immediately, and it was like that other time, that time that Sebby would remember if he could think, when Todd had been so insistent, so unyielding. But, no, it wasn't like that other time—then, Todd had been desperate, hurting, and this time he was cold, distant, and completely in control, which only made Sebby feel more out of control. It hurt some, but it was good, the tightness, the fullness, and drawing deep breaths, he pushed back as Todd pushed in.

Todd wrapped him up, pinning Sebby's arms to his sides. The coldness gave way to slippery heat. They rocked, the metal teeth of Todd's fly scraping Sebby's flesh, and Sebby ached, oh, how he ached. He went limp, letting his head loll back against Todd's shoulder. Todd's hand swept upward to stroke Sebby's exposed throat, up one side, over his face and lips, down the other side, across his Adam's apple to cup his jaw. His thumb pressed into the jump of his pulse, pushing his head back to where he could lay his mouth to Sebby's neck. Sebby's words came thinly from his stretched throat: "*Dios,* Todd, I'm so close, please? So close . . ."

He arched against Todd's restraining arm. Had he spoken in Spanish or English? Could Todd understand? He must have gotten the general idea, because his hand on Sebby's waist moved, the fingers fluttering over Sebby's aching cock, and even that light touch made him lurch and cry out.

Todd chuckled in his ear. "Do you wish it over so soon? With it ends your life. I had thought to prolong it as well as I could."

"No! Oh, Todd, now, oh now, I can't. Please?" He moved encouragingly, but Todd clamped down, and Sebby whimpered in frustration. "Please!" he repeated, and then, playing along with Todd's game, because maybe that would make him hurry the fuck up—"I don't want to die!" It was a pitiful, whimpering cry. He didn't care if Todd *did* kill him, as long as he could come first.

"It will be worth it." Todd reached then to take Sebby in hand and—first with long, slow strokes that made Sebby feel as if his cock were lengthening impossibly, and then with short, quick strokes that nearly hummed, and finally with a murmur in his ear: "Die now"—brought him off, and it *was* like dying, a sliding, sliding away, blossoming and wilting, the Little Death.

As awareness seeped back in, he realized Todd was penetrating him again—again, how could that be? When had Todd pulled out? Breaking character at last, Todd was saying his name, telling him how he loved him, how he could never hurt him. Brainless and boneless, Sebby tried to reciprocate, to move with Todd's thrusts, to be anything other than a jellyfish, but it hardly mattered. Todd came quickly and loudly, and then held Sebby hard against himself as shudders shook him. Moments went by, and then, pulling Sebby with him, he collapsed to lie down on the sofa. The two of them released joint sighs as they settled. Todd's hands moved lazily over Sebby's stomach. Sebby pillowed his head on Todd's chest, willing to pass the afternoon in sleep.

"I could stay here forever," he whispered.

"And so you shall, for this is your final resting place."

In the darkness, Sebby did not have to hide his smile. Todd was so funny, scaring him in his strange way. "Todd, that was so good. It was . . ." He shivered, and Todd shifted, moved; Sebby thought with disappointment that he was getting up, but in the next moment there was a draft, and then a blanket settled over the both of them. Sebby, lying naked atop a clothed Todd, was grateful for the warmth. Todd must have left the blanket handy when they had gone through the boxes of linens. Todd was so thoughtful!

Sebby almost felt guilty; he was sure that he himself was not so thoughtful, ever. Even in sex, and he went over it again in his mind as he snuggled, as Todd began to snore, reliving the sensation of sliding away. He understood suddenly how Todd had penetrated him again after Sebby had come; it was because he had withdrawn during Sebby's climax. Sebby was familiar with the technique—had used it himself on lovers when fingering them—how a slow pulling out during your partner's ejaculation could intensify an orgasm, but he had never known anyone who had the control to do it *during sex*. Or, he thought as sleep crept in, maybe it was just that no one had ever cared enough.

Chapter Forty-Four

Like It Rough

The prosecutor's office took Sebby's deposition. Sebby's lawyer filed a restraining order against Collin. As Ethan had predicted, Collin pleaded to a lesser offense and was given probation.

Todd had two interviews, and one of them resulted in a second interview to follow.

He awoke one night with severe pain radiating all the way from his ear to the middle of his back. He tried to ignore it, but Sebby insisted that he see Dr. Roodnitsky. She determined that he was suffering a muscle spasm, probably due to overexertion. The treatment called for ice and heat alternating, and pain medication with muscle relaxant.

Todd balked at the drugs. He mistrusted anything that affected his mind's operation.

"You need them," Sebby said, his eyes narrowing. "How are you going to get better if you don't take them?"

"But they make me stupid!" Todd said. "I can't think!"

"You don't have to think all the time," Sebby said. Todd continued to protest, and Sebby put his hands on his hips and stared Todd down. "Take them or I'll never watch another musical with you again."

Todd took them.

After a few days, Todd had recovered enough to forgo the medication. Though he was not cleared to return to work, he was able to sit at a table in Java Hut and hammer at his borrowed laptop, pausing every hour to perform the prescribed exercises for his neck, shoulder, and back.

The current assignment from Rita was to come up with a theme for a series of ads for a Minnesota casino, and Todd was feeling stumped. Personally, he didn't care to gamble and was at a loss to understand the motivations of those who did, but an ad man couldn't allow his feelings to interfere with his job of convincing others that they needed and/or wanted a particular product or service.

He stared at his blank screen and rubbed his upper lip, humming to himself, and became aware of someone's eyes on him. He glanced up and, not recognizing the young man who sat at his ease on a sofa—one ankle crossed over the other knee, his arm thrown across the sofa's back—Todd returned to his work.

Lucky. Good luck. Bad luck. Blind luck. She's lucky, you're lucky, we're all *lucky!* He chuckled to himself. A reminder popped up on his screen telling him to exercise. Obediently, he stood and raised his right arm straight in the air and caught the person still staring. The guy was attractive in an all-American sort of way. His skin glowed, his lips were full and pink. His hair, the color of wet sand, had careful highlights and was combed back from his forehead in a soft wave. Eyes sparkled with a lively curiosity as he looked Todd over. Frowning, Todd reseated himself and hunched over his laptop, doing his best to send the message that he was unavailable. However, the young man picked up his beverage and stood, revealing himself to be tall and to possess a gym-sculpted body. He wore a loose shirt unbuttoned over a wifebeater, and Todd could imagine his six-pack rippling as he approached. He came close and stood over Todd, smiling and shaking his finger at him.

"You're . . ." his eyes narrowed in thought, "Sebby's boyfriend. Aren't you?"

Todd brightened at once and sat up straight. "I am. Todd, rhymes with God. I'm sorry, have we met?"

"Yeah. At the thing. Okay if I join you?" Without waiting for an answer, he folded himself into the chair opposite Todd. He took a sip of his tall coffee and licked the foam from his lips. "What's Sebby up to these days?"

Todd wasn't sure to what "thing" the man might be referring, but he had met many of Sebby's acquaintances, and it was possible he'd forgotten this handsome young man among the many that Sebby seemed to know. "Still working at Gimondi's. Toying with the idea of getting his CPA. Sorry, I didn't catch your name?"

The man hesitated, his smile fading. He wet his lips. "I'm Collin."

Todd's mouth fell open and then snapped closed. He inhaled sharply. "How you've the gall to approach me . . ."

"I just want to know how he's doing." Collin's eyes dropped. "I'm not supposed to call him or anything, and I just want to know he's okay."

Todd stared. "How can you possibly expect I would find it credible that you are even remotely concerned for Sebastián's well-being?"

"I know what you think." Collin swirled his cup and staring into the foamy depths. "But . . . I never meant to hurt him."

"You broke a fucking coffee mug over his head!" Todd's voice cracked with outrage, and a few patrons glanced in their direction.

"I never! God, is that what he said? Yeah, I broke the thing, threw it at the wall. I lost my temper a little."

"You lying, seeping, septic tank."

"Ask him! Look him in the eye, make him look you in the eye, ask him what happened to the mug!"

"Fuck off and die." Not a classy response, but always appropriate.

Hazel eyes begged Todd to understand. "You haven't figured out yet what a little liar he is. He's a manipulative pretty boy. And he does like it rough. You can't have been with him this long and not know that. That night, it just got out of hand. He was so sad . . . he was *crying* . . . because *you* left. He needed someone. He wanted . . . to blot everything out."

Against his will, memories surfaced in Todd's mind, memories of Sebby crying out in delight when Todd pushed him roughly to the bed, Sebby moaning as Todd pinned his arms to his sides.

Collin nodded and leaned forward. "You've hurt him, haven't you? Without meaning to. You know what I mean."

Todd shut his laptop and slid it into its case. "This conversation is over."

Collin pressed on. "He's so little. It's hard not to hurt him."

"I get the idea that it is hard *when* you hurt him."

Collin's face darkened. "It's not what I get off on. It's what *he* gets off on. You don't care about him. You left him. You'll do it again. You only came back because of what happened. He ought to thank me."

Rattlesnake-like, Todd's hand darted out and seized Collin's forearm where it rested on the table. A part of Todd's brain registered the softness of Collin's skin under his calloused palm. He clamped down, wanting to feel the bones grind, wanting to see him flinch, wanting to hear an exclamation of pain.

"Stay away from him," he said, pitching his voice dangerously low. "You can manage that, can't you? If you ever come near him again, I cannot promise I won't kill you." Never had he uttered such a threat. He stared at Collin over the rims of his eyeglasses, and Collin shifted uneasily in his seat.

"Whatever. I could pound you with one hand tied behind my back."

"I am amenable to that suggestion." Todd smiled. "Do you carry twine or duct tape upon your person?"

He let go of Collin's arm, and the latter dropped his hands beneath the table—rubbing away the feel of his grip, Todd guessed— but then Collin stood. He towered over Todd, and Todd, not to be at a disadvantage, sprang to his feet. He had concluded that Collin was soft. He was a gym lizard, not a fighter—an abuser of those smaller than himself. Todd was smaller than Collin, but Collin wouldn't find it so easy to break a mug over Todd's head.

Collin looked Todd up and down, shaking his head. "You're not worth it. I wouldn't even be able to reach you. I'd have to get on my knees to make it an even match."

Todd threw back his head and laughed. "Did you seriously just offer to go on your knees to me?"

Collin flushed. "Stupid cunt." Laying a hand on Todd's shoulder, he shoved him. Todd lurched, bounced back, and in his turn, shoved Collin with both hands.

"Okay, okay." Collin held up his hands in a gesture of surrender and glanced over his shoulder. "I didn't come here to fight."

"For what did you come here, troglodyte?"

"Coffee. I didn't know you'd be here."

"You're lying, aren't you? What is this, a stakeout?"

Collin's eyes dropped. "I just wanted to know if he's okay," he muttered.

Todd glared, his temper rising. *No, he's not. He has nightmares. He's terrified of being alone.* "His 'okayness' is my responsibility and none of your business."

"You think you're so superior. Sebby was better off with me. How much do you pull down a year, laying bricks?"

Todd laughed, amused. "I'm not a bricklayer. In fact bricklaying is a skilled calling far beyond my humble aspirations."

"God, the words! Do you hear yourself? Can't you talk like a normal person?"

"Your mama. There. I'm done trading insults." He grabbed the laptop and tried to thrust his way past Collin. The man refused to move. Todd's hold on his temper began to slip. "Excuse me," he said through clenched teeth.

Collin placed one hand against Todd's forehead and pushed him backward, holding him at arm's length. The condescending gesture made him snap. Dropping his laptop, he ducked and punched Collin squarely in the stomach, first a jab with the weaker left hand and followed up with the stronger right: the good ol' one-two.

He danced backward, grimacing at the sudden pain in his shoulder, and had the satisfaction of seeing Collin drop like an anvil, much as Todd had dropped when Gus had hit him. How his mouth opened and shut like a fish's, how the line of his back swayed like a warped bench, how his whole form trembled like to disintegrate!

Thus, in his heady moment of triumph, Todd didn't notice the stranger approaching, and failed to see the fist coming at him like a Clydesdale. At the last split second, he sensed a moving shadow and turned toward it. Instead of landing on the side of the head, the punch hit his eye, and his head seemed to split open from the impact. Blinding pain made him stagger. He had the vaguest impression of an unfamiliar face above a musclebound neck before the attacker's follow-up roundhouse connected with his jaw. *I never counted on Collin having a friend. The guy is just so damned unlikeable,* Todd mused as he, in his turn, dropped to the floor.

Later he would remember that he had characterized the pain as "blinding" and laugh, for while some men like Gus the foreman were raised never to hit a woman and never to hit a man in the face who wore glasses, that was old school. Younger generations knew nothing of such sportsmanlike niceties. Nor of the inadvisability of hitting someone while wearing large, bejeweled rings.

Chapter Forty-Five

Blur

*I*n the half-awake state prior to opening his eyes, Todd knew he was in a hospital and that someone was in the room with him. It was imperative that he think of something clever to say upon awakening. He was loath to utter a cliché such as *Where am I?* or *What happened?* If it was Sebby keeping him company, he could say, *I told you if I stepped foot in a coffeehouse I'd need hospitalization.* Or, perhaps, *That coffee really packs a punch!* No, too cheesy. He opened his eyes.

Only one eye opened. Todd reached to rub his eyes, but his arm was weighted down. He tried the other arm, and his searching fingers encountered bandages over the right side of his face. *Right, then. That explains it.* Todd blinked at the dim surroundings. A solution-filled bag hung next to his bed, trailing plastic tubing. A wall-mounted television soundlessly broadcasted something too blurry for Todd to discern without his glasses. An angular figure sat on the nearby sofa, gray head bent over a paperback, eyes riveted to the printed word. Todd's astonishment was such that he forgot his resolve that his first utterance should be something witty, and he blurted, "What are you doing here?"

The head lifted, and blue eyes like Todd's own looked back at him. She replied with something equally unoriginal. "You're awake."

The fact that his mother was here alarmed Todd more than if he'd awoken to find himself missing a limb. How serious was his condition that his mother had traveled all the way to Denver? Or had he been flown to Minneapolis? How long had he been out, for either journey to have taken place?

"Where am I?"

"You're in the hospital." She leaned forward to place her icy hand over his forearm, which was strapped to the bedrail.

"Obviously. But in Denver, or . . .?"

"Denver."

Todd couldn't imagine his mother negotiating a road trip of several days' length. "Is Pop here too?"

"He's working. I flew out." Her chilly fingers patted his arm.

They had spent money on airfare? "Jesus. Am I dying?"

"You think I wouldn't come unless you were dying?" Her tone was indignant. The cold hand withdrew.

"I think it's a fair assumption, yes." He cleared his throat again. "Water?"

"I'll get you some ice chips. Maybe a doctor should look at you."

"Man wakes up from a coma, and not a doctor in sight. It was never like this on *Scrubs*." His last sentence dissolved in coughing as his irritated throat rebelled.

"You weren't in a coma, Todd. You've been awake, you just don't remember. I'll be back in a minute." With a labored sigh, she rose and left the room. Todd groped for his eyeglasses, but the nightstand was on the side opposite his free arm, and he couldn't grope there without sitting up, which he tried to do, but fell back, woozy.

A woman in pink scrubs entered. "How are you feeling this evening?"

"Parched."

"There's a pitcher of water here. Don't sit up, young man," she warned, lifting a hand as Todd attempted to raise himself. "Here." She handed him a remote control. "You can raise your bed. A little, mind you."

"How many days?" Todd demanded. He pressed the Up button, and the bed hummed and moved. It *was* dizzying. Todd let go of the button and the motion stopped.

"You were admitted six days ago. You've been heavily medicated. How is your pain level, on a scale from one to ten?"

Six days? Damn! He had missed his job interview. "I don't feel any pain, other than being painfully parched."

"All right. That's good. The doctor discontinued your morphine drip, but you can have Naproxen. But if that doesn't do it for you, we'll get you something stronger." She poured him a glass and held it for him, positioning the straw. He drank the entire cup. "I'll check on you again later."

"May my arm be released, ma'am?" Todd asked.

"Oh, I think so." She reached, and the velcro protested as it was ripped away. Todd chafed his freed arm with his other hand.

The nurse left just as his mother came back, ice chips and spoon in hand. She sat down and silently offered him a spoonful.

"I can do that myself. Just give me the cup."

His mother exhaled through pursed lips and handed it over. She put the spoonful of ice in her own mouth and spoke around it. "I had to go all the way down the hall to the other kitchen. They were out of spoons. Now you don't even want the spoon."

"Sorry. Thank you." He tilted the cup to his mouth, and drops of melted ice trickled over his tongue. He tapped the cup and was rewarded with a small shower of ice chips, not all of which made it into his mouth. He downed several mouthfuls before speaking again. "So. I'm not dying."

"No. You've just lost an eye. That's all."

Several ice chips found their way down Todd's windpipe. He coughed, and his unbandaged eye watered. "God. What? Did it roll down a manhole or something? Can no one climb down and fetch it?"

"Don't pretend you didn't know. What did you think the bandage was for?"

"Genital herpes. Jesus, Mom. Why the . . ." His voice trailed off. He tipped more ice chips into his mouth. He tried to wrap his brain around the news. His eye was gone? "Will it grow back?"

His mother apparently thought he was serious. "No, Todd. There's nothing to be done. I'd give you my own eye, if I could. I even asked them about it."

"At least it would match." He was a Cyclops. He could never again roll his eyes. Fuck it, why had he resorted to violence? Then again, perhaps they would have waylaid him in any case. And, anyway, it had become imperative that Collin knew that Todd was willing and able to protect Sebastián.

Sebby! Where was he? Where had he been the past week, and was anyone keeping him safe? "Where's Sebby?" he demanded, forgetting that his mother had never been introduced.

"He'll be back. He visits you every day. That boy is so worried about you."

Todd ground his teeth on that bit of news, and on the disturbing idea of Sebby and his mother sitting around discussing Todd's health. "He's my . . . close friend and . . . please be nice to him."

His mother drew herself up. "I'm nice to him! I'm a nice person. Janet was just saying the other day, right before I left to fly down here, that I'm one of the nicest persons she knows." She shifted in her seat and smoothed her hair. "Sebby said how nice it was of me to sit with you in the hospital when you don't even know if anyone's here."

Todd winced.

"I should ask them for some Naproxen for my back." She leaned forward in order to press her hand to the small of her back. "Sleeping on this couch hasn't been good for it. Just because it folds out into sort of a bed doesn't make it comfortable. I haven't seen any other parents sleeping here at night. Probably because the couch is so hard. Not everyone will put up with that."

"What time is it?"

"There's a clock on the wall." His mother nodded in the direction of the clock that was supposedly there.

"Where are my glasses?" Afraid of dislodging the IV, he pushed the button to raise his bed, stopping when vertigo threatened. Turning his head, he could view the nightstand, which held the pitcher of water, a telephone, a couple of paperback books, some greeting cards, and a box of tissues.

"Broken."

"Both of them? I mean, both lenses?"

"Uh-huh."

"Fucking hell." How many pairs of his glasses had been broken in fist fights over the years? Fights he maybe could've avoided but chose not to, chose instead to *be a man*, to demonstrate that *yes, he could defend himself*, despite the fact that he knew which Broadway productions had won Tony awards and who Jerome Robbins had been and which Richard was a hunchback. Win or lose, it mattered not; it was the demonstration that mattered.

And look where the demonstration got you. You showed everyone you could be a man, all right.

Tears gathered in his eye. *Stop it. Be strong. Be a . . .*

What a load of horseshit.

Chapter Forty-Six

Empty Socket

*T*odd had no way of knowing what time it was when he was awakened by a feeling of unease, unease that deepened into dread. *Empty socket.* The words thrummed in his head. *Empty socket*—a gaping hole where for his entire life his eye had resided. *Empty socket.* And was it, in fact, empty? Was it packed with wads of cotton, was it oozing pus and caked with dried blood and remains of eye jelly? Beads of sweat broke out on Todd's forehead as it occurred to him that at some point the bandages would come off and they would be cleaning his *empty socket*, rinsing it or anointing it.

"Oh shit, oh God," he muttered, squeezing his remaining eye shut. "Mom. Mom?" There was no answer. "Mom!" Forgetting that he wasn't supposed to, Todd sat up, and in the dim light was able to make out the couch across the room, empty. Vertigo rocked him, and he clutched at the bed's guardrail.

Todd suddenly wanted something so badly that it hurt, hurt like a motherfucker—like a fist prying his ribs apart and squeezing his heart. The something that he wanted was Sebastián, and the way that he wanted the something was miles and eons away from the way he had wanted it before—not to comfort but to be comforted, not to protect but to be shielded from horror. It was a need like drowning in deep water, knowing air was above but out of reach—to hear Sebby's voice telling him that losing an eye was not so bad, that Todd could be brave, that Sebby would still love him even though he was maimed.

Ignoring the wave of dizziness, Todd grabbed the telephone and dialed Sebby. After several rings, he was rewarded with a worried, thick-voiced "Hello?"

"Sebby!" he exclaimed in relief. "Oh, Sebby love, your voice is a panacea."

"A what? Todd, is everything okay?"

"Yes. No. I just had a, hum, well . . . a sort of panic attack."

"*Dios mío*, Todd. You panicked about something? Was it blood? Needles?"

"No, it was . . ." Todd shuddered as the words *empty socket* slithered through his mind once more. "I don't want to think about it. I'm . . . I can't think, and I'm afraid, and I need to hear your voice!"

"Shh, *querido*, everything will be all right. The worst is over. You're going to be fine. You should be resting, slee—" a yawn interrupted "—ping."

"Talk to me, Sebastián. I promise I'll sleep if you talk to me."

Sebby hesitated. "Is your mother there?"

Todd shook his head, forgetting that Sebby couldn't see him. "She has absconded from the premises."

"Okay. Everything will be okay. You're safe now. And I love you."

Todd settled back into his pillows with a sigh. "Talk to me in Spanish, Sebby."

The soothing cadence of Spanish lulled him. His eyelid drooped. He slept and did not wake when the CNA slipped in and replaced the phone in its cradle. In the morning, he remembered only that he had dreamed in Spanish.

Chapter Forty-Seven

Posse

*T*odd's mother still had not reappeared when the breakfast tray was delivered. The scrambled eggs were passable. Todd's spirits lifted as the calories made their way to his vitals. He was polishing off the fruit cup when a doctor entered, his posse trailing behind.

"Hello-hello-hello!" the doctor exclaimed, coming near enough that Todd could make out his long nose and narrow black eyes. "Do you know where you are?"

"I've been hoping for the set of *Punk'd* or *Scare Tactics*."

Someone in the posse laughed, but the doctor said, "Sorry, no. I'm here to assess your mental status, Todd. Do you know where you are?"

Todd pushed the tray aside. "I am aware that I am in hospital."

The doctor nodded, and so did several members of his posse. "Do you know which hospital?"

"No one's told me."

There was a significant nod from the doctor, and murmurs from the posse, which made Todd uneasy. "Denver North Medical Center," the doctor supplied. "Do you know your name?"

"You mentioned it mere moments ago. Todd, rhymes with God. And, unless someone has changed it while I slept, the rest of it is Marvin Addison."

"Good. Can you tell me what year it is?"

"Of course. It's—" The year. He knew the year, knew that he knew it, yet he drew a blank. The doctor and posse watched expectantly. "Er . . ." He stalled. "I haven't slept through New Year's and into the next, have I?" As one, they shook their heads. Still, he couldn't summon the correct year, nor any year at all. He thought of his tax return, which he could remember completing before leaving New York. What year had been printed at the top of those forms? It was like trying to bring to mind a particular word, a word that one knew existed, that held the exact shade of meaning one meant to convey. Normally, Todd would fall back on a thesaurus: *year, month, day, century, eon, era, date, calendar* ... Calendar! He glanced at the near wall, where a large whiteboard dominated. Squinting, he was able to make out the date, written in large black strokes, and with great relief, proclaimed the correct year aloud.

"Nothing wrong with looking at a calendar," the doctor commented to his posse. "That's what you or I would do if we didn't know the date, and that's what SLP will train patients with memory problems to do."

Memory problems? And what was *SLP*? "There's nothing the matter with my memory."

"That's what we're assessing," the doctor said. "Can you tell me what you did yesterday?"

"I just woke up yesterday evening. My mother was here. I spoke with her. Went back to sleep. *C'est tout.* Er, that's all."

There was another significant look from the doctor to the members of his posse. Heads nodded. Notes were taken. "What?" Todd demanded, annoyed.

"Do you remember what you had for lunch yesterday?"

"Is that a trick question? Nothing! I wasn't awake yet!"

"No tricks," the doctor said. "But you were awake yesterday, and have been for several days. You're having short-term memory issues."

Todd started to protest. Disoriented, he rubbed at his good eye until sparks popped behind his eyelid.

"Do you know why you're here, Todd?"

"My mother informed me that I've lost an eye." He reached to touch the bandage. "You're not here to tell me you've found it?"

Someone in the posse laughed again, but the doctor seemed to feel the need to explain. "*Lost* in the sense that it was too badly damaged to save." The posse members nudged one another. "The remainder of the eye was removed."

Todd stared. Did they think he was so out of it, or was the doctor completely lacking a sense of humor? "What kind of doctor are you?"

More significant looks. "Dr. Kampf, neurosurgeon. We've met, but I'm not surprised you don't remember."

"And your posse?" Todd gestured at the group.

"My . . .? This is a teaching hospital, and I agreed to take these students on my rounds today. If it bothers you, I'll ask them to step out."

Impatient for details, Todd waved his hand. "It's fine. Please go on. You operated on my eye, then?"

"No, that was the ophthalmologist." He turned to his posse and explained, "The brain often reacts to surgery as to an injury, and his memory has been disturbed. Painkillers and sedatives don't help, of course."

"So my brain has had a reaction to the—" Todd had to swallow before he could go on "—the removal of my eye?"

"No, to the removal of the tumor."

Todd was too stunned to gasp. His mother had said nothing about a tumor. "My eye had a tumor?"

"No, you had a brain tumor. Let me explain—"

"Are you saying I've had *brain surgery*?"

The surgeon folded his arms and leaned forward, smiling and nodding the while. "An X-ray was taken to assess the damage to your orbital bones." A long finger made a circling motion around one eye. "There wasn't any, but a mass was found in your frontal lobe." He tapped his forehead, between his eyebrows. "CT scan and MRI followed. It was determined to be a meningioma, a tumor of the lining of your brain. It had to come out. It was close to your optic nerve and would've grown around it, threatening the sight in your remaining eye."

"Jesus." Todd felt his head. His hair had a lank, unwashed feel, but it was still there, all of it, as far as he could tell.

As if divining what Todd was looking for, the surgeon continued. "A craniotomy was not required. The placement and size of the tumor allowed an endonasal approach." He went on explaining the surgical procedure, but Todd's concentration was wrecked, and it all sounded like gibberish, so he blurted the question uppermost in his mind.

"Cancer?"

"No," the surgeon said. "Nonmalignant. It was a slow-growing tumor that wouldn't have made its presence known for years, and then the size of it would've required a craniotomy. It was a lucky chance that an X-ray found it early."

"I should thank him," Todd muttered, rubbing his forehead.

"In the ICU, after the surgery, you suffered an episode, a—"

A disturbance moved through the posse, like to that seen in water agitated by a passing speedboat, and Sebby appeared in the wake. Recognizable to Todd even with uncorrected eyesight, the small figure emerged from the midst of the students.

"Excuse me," Sebby said, glancing neither right nor left. "Better this morning, Todd? Coffee?" He came close, sliding in front of the surgeon, who was forced to step back. He carried a familiar thermos in his brown hands.

"French Press!" Todd exclaimed. "Oh, hell yes!"

Looking over the breakfast tray, a tiny frown knitted between Sebby's eyebrows. "You ate their breakfast? Oh, Todd. I brought you *migas*." He produced a plastic container and set it next to the tray.

The surgeon held up a hand, as if to seize the contraband. "He needs to limit his caffeine intake."

"It's decaf." Sebby unscrewed the thermos. "But good decaf," he assured Todd. The aroma wafted from the poured cup and filled the room, nudging out the clinical smells. Several posse members craned their necks and sniffed. Todd grinned. *Eat your hearts out!* Sebby pressed the cup into Todd's ready hand. "Here y'go, buddy."

Todd blinked. Sebby smiled blandly and retreated, seating himself in the far corner. "I'm not interrupting." He nodded at the surgeon.

The surgeon cleared his throat. "Ahhh, yes. You suffered an episode—"

Sebby interrupted. "Are you explaining this to him again?"

"Excuse me, an 'episode'?" Todd urged.

"A seizure," the surgeon elaborated. "They occur in about—"

Once again, Sebby interrupted. "What's the point of upsetting him every time? Wait till he can remember, then tell him!"

The surgeon turned to Sebby. "He's demonstrating improvement in that area."

"A seizure?" Todd repeated.

"Drink your coffee while it's hot, Todd," Sebby encouraged.

"By what or whom was I seized? Were my Fourth Amendment rights violated?"

"Convulsion," the surgeon explained, turning back to Todd. "They occur in about three percent of brain surgery patients."

"Jesus. But . . . but . . ." Todd could not think of the first thing to ask.

"It's all right, Todd," Sebby said. "Please don't upset yourself."

Looking at his watch, the surgeon cleared his throat and went on, as if reciting. "Dilantin was administered and breathing tube reinserted. A subsequent CT scan showed intracranial bleeding at the surgical site. Whether the bleeding caused the seizure or the seizure the bleeding is anybody's guess." The surgeon grinned, as if brain bleeding were the coolest thing ever. "Brain swelling and a little bleeding after surgery is expected, of course, but you've had more than we like to see. We're giving you Decadron for the swelling. It's a steroid." In an aside, he spoke to his posse, using clinical terms in the same way a computer technician would talk about SQL servers or a partitioned DOS.

"Will there be permanent damage?" Todd interrupted.

The surgeon blinked as if distracted. "Shouldn't be. I'm pleased with your progress. I expect your memory problems to clear up as the brain heals itself and the swelling goes down, though it might take weeks. The location of the swelling, here in the frontal lobe"—and he tapped his forehead again—"can affect memory and decision making."

It was a frightening thought. What might he have done in the last few days that he'd forgotten?

Sebby piped up. "Don't worry, Todd. You haven't embarrassed yourself. Much."

The smile in Sebby's voice was audible, but his visage was too blurry to allow for dimple viewing. Todd twisted his hands in the blanket.

"Any questions?" As Dr. Kampf glanced at his watch and stepped back, his smile became a pasted-on expression.

"I don't know. I'm . . . overwhelmed." Todd groped for something to ask as the surgeon paused in the doorway.

"Understandable. Well, unless there are more complications, which I don't expect, your doctor will be taking over your care." Off he went, and the posse followed.

Sebby remained where he was, and silence fell. From the hallway came the sounds of bleeping nurse calls and Dr. Kampf briefing his students on the next patient.

"Sebastián," Todd implored, "does my condition necessitate that you keep your distance?"

"I'm keeping my distance out of respect to your momma," Sebby said softly. "And you, I suppose."

"You don't have to do that." Todd could not make out Sebby's expression, but he could see him shake his head and look away. "Did something happen? Did I do or say something I don't remember?"

"No." Sebby stared at the thermos, which was tucked between his knees. He twisted the lid back and forth. "You're fine. Everything's fine, and you're going to get better. Please don't worry." Sebby's voice puckered with anxiety, and Todd's heart went out to him. As though Sebby had not been through enough, Todd had to go and add unnecessary complications. He cleared his throat.

"I owe you an apology. I shouldn't have gone all vigilante the other day. I never intended to get into a fight."

Sebby's head came up. "You remember that now?"

"Of course I do!" Todd cried. "I remember everything up until the moment I was knocked down."

"Well, yesterday you didn't." His voice became thoughtful. "He must be right. You are getting better."

The idea was too disconcerting to be encouraging. "I'm not too fragile for an embrace, am I?" And he held out his arms.

Sebby rose but, head lowered, made a beeline for the door. "I have to get to work. I just stopped by to press some coffee for you. I'll bring you lunch, kay? *Nos vemos.*"

Todd concluded that Sebby was irritated with him. He hated for Sebby to go to additional trouble for his sake. "French Press, wait! There's no need. I'm certain my board here includes meals. You needn't go to any—"

Sebby stopped dead. "I'm not letting you eat hospital food! You need to eat organic, and also foods that promote healing, and—and brain food! I'll bring you something good. And more coffee. Bye, Todd."

He was gone as quickly as the surgeon before him, as if not hearing Todd's appeal and not seeing Todd's reaching arms. The weight of all he'd learned in the last fifteen minutes settled on him. And, damn! He hadn't even asked about his eye!

Chapter Forty-Eight

Buddy

Todd napped and was woken by a woman in bright-green spectacles.

"Much more alert today," she noted. Her mouth quirked between the parentheses of etched smile lines.

Todd eyed her, from her french-braided platinum hair to her sensible shoes. "You're Sebby's doctor. Doctor . . . Doctor . . ."

"Roodnitsky," she supplied. "Your doctor, also." She straightened.

"Oh. Of course. You treated my shoulder."

She was from Ukraine, Todd remembered. Seating herself at the wall computer, she scrolled through screens that Todd assumed made up his chart.

"Things look well." She turned away from the computer and gave her attention to Todd. "Tell me, who is president of the United States?"

"I am," Todd said. "I'm also Napoleon. And on weekends I'm Kim Kardashian."

Dr. Roodnitsky clucked. "You use humor to cover uncertainty. Still memory issues."

"I use humor to cover irritation," Todd retorted, scooting backward to sit up straight. He folded his arms. "Very well, ask me your questions. I'll put a cap in it."

She proceeded to prod at his memory, but was both more thorough and more patient than the surgeon had been. "Much more alert," she said again. "Rehab will evaluate you so you can transfer to acute rehab as soon as possible."

Todd absorbed that for several seconds. "I'm no addict, so what in hell is 'acute rehab'?"

"You will receive intensive therapy. Loss of an eye means loss of depth perception. You would need therapy for this alone, though it could be outpatient. Add to this: insult to brain, which affects balance, memory, thought—brain is confused and angry, and must be coaxed to heal and relearn. One to two weeks."

"One to two *additional* weeks in the hospital?"

"Acute rehab is a separate wing of the hospital, yes."

"The surgeon said nothing about rehab."

Dr. Roodnitsky waved one hand. "Surgeons. They care only to operate. It is fun for them. Recovery, it is dull. Takes too long." She went on to discuss his eye in a businesslike manner, her words clicking along like abacus beads and adding up to no big deal. "Ophthalmologist will explain more, but I will give you the basics. The eye was too damaged to save. Pieces of eyeglass lens and also pieces of frame were driven deep into the eye. Eye was removed. Enucleation, it's called. Implant was put in place—"

"Already?" Both Todd's hands flew to his damaged eye. "How could they? Doesn't one have to be ordered and matched and fitted? If I even want one. I don't want one, I—" He cut off. Perhaps he had approved it and forgotten.

"An implant is not prosthesis. You are thinking a false eye is round like a marble. It isn't. You can't pop it out and have an empty socket like in movies."

The words *empty socket* sent a shudder through Todd, and gooseflesh rose on his bare arms. "Explain."

"Implant takes place of eyeball in socket to hold shape of eyelid, so eyelid does not become sunken. It's sewn in and membrane sewn over it. If you look in mirror, you will see pink membrane, like inner eyelid. Not so bad. If you choose to get prosthesis, false eye, it is thin and curved to fit over membrane and under eyelid. Like large contact lens."

"I don't want it!" The exclamation came out more harshly than Todd intended, and he moderated his voice. "I prefer an eye patch."

Dr. Roodnitsky nodded. "The ophthalmologist will discuss options with you."

Todd resisted the impulse to curl up and pull the blankets over his head. "How many times have you explained this to me already?"

"Hm." She pursed her lips and referred to the chart. "Upon admission, ophthalmologist explained the procedure. After surgeries, you slept several days. Seizure makes sleepiness. After that, we talked, but you were too groggy to understand. Then each day you ask and we talk." She smiled at Todd's expression. "Normal for this kind of surgery, not remembering."

"What if tomorrow I don't recall this conversation?"

"Then I will explain again." She regarded him sternly. "I worried for you, young man. But, yes, you are tough. So maybe one week."

"You might mention to Sebby how tough I am."

She lifted an eyebrow. "He does not agree."

When his lunch tray arrived, Todd hesitated, mindful of Sebby's admonition against the hospital fare, but a nurse entered with medications and instructed that they be taken with food, and so Todd dug into the chicken a la king.

"Todd!"

Startled, he looked up from his half-demolished meal. In the doorway stood Sebby, bearing the thermos and a foil-covered plate. "Don't eat that! Did you forget I was bringing you lunch? Oh, Todd, it's okay. I should've called to remind you." He stepped forward and nudged Todd's tray aside with the plate.

"I didn't forget. But the flesh is weak." He reached for Sebby's hand, but Sebby drew back and pushed the wheeled dining stand closer to Todd.

"It's cold salmon. I'll bring you something hot for dinner, though." He paused. "You like fish, no? Fish is brain food."

"What, with all that mercury?" Todd quipped, covering his hurt with cynicism.

Sebby frowned. "It's wild Yukon Coho salmon. I order it online directly from a fisherman in Alaska. No mercury." He folded his arms.

"Pardon me for insinuating that Sebastián would ever serve me anything unhealthful." Todd ripped off a section of the foil and regarded the salmon fillet, which was a lovely shade of coral and sprinkled with herbs. "Sebby you don't have to go to so much trouble. I'm sure the hospital food is fine. After all, they feed ailing invalids."

Sebby huffed. "The food is cooked in humongous quantities! It's cafeteria food, highly processed, no fresh ingredients."

"Even the salad?"

"Do you know what they spray on the lettuce to keep it from wilting? You might as well eat Windex. Anyway, I brought you green beans from the garden." Sebby retreated to the corner chair. Todd forked a bit of salmon. He twirled the fork, and the bit fell back to the plate.

"Won't you eat it, Todd?" Sebby's voice was anxious. "Not hungry anymore?"

Todd squinted at Sebby, his memory supplying the wounded puppy eyes that his myopia made impossible to discern. "I will eat," he said humbly, and began to do so, hardly tasting the seasoned fish.

"Stop sighing," Sebby ordered.

Between bites, Todd asked, "How long can you stay?"

"I just want to make sure you eat. Then I'll go." Sebby turned his head to see the clock.

"I'll eat slowly, then." Intending to chew each bite fifty times, Todd counted to twenty before swallowing, watching Sebby shift impatiently. "I can't see you, you know." He felt a change in the air, like a dart of electricity, and he noted how Sebby ceased his fidgeting, how his chin jerked up.

"Yes. Your glasses are broken."

"If you moved closer, I could make out your face."

"My face is the same as always."

"Unlike mine." As Todd tapped at his bandage, a thought occurred to him, and he stared down at his food, appetite having fled. Perhaps Sebby no longer found him attractive. Todd rubbed his jaw, feeling the soft bristles signifying neglect. He smoothed back his unwashed hair.

"Todd, eat! I have to get back to Gimondi's."

Todd shoveled the remainder of the fish into his mouth and then, using his fingers, fed himself the beans one by one. Glancing down, he realized he'd dribbled chicken a la king down the front of his hospital gown. The gown itself bore flowers sprinkled over a field of sky blue, just the shade to bring out the color of his eyes.

Of his *eye*, damn it.

"Todd, I gotta go." Sebby had risen and stood twisting his hands. "I can't use sick leave, 'cause we're not family. They're understanding, but to a point."

"Of course. I regret being a . . . an inconvenience."

"You aren't. I'll bring dinner, and we'll have a nice long talk, yes? It's just, now, I have to get back."

Once again, Todd held out his arms, thinking that if Sebby didn't hug him this time, he would cry himself to sleep. But Sebby hurried out, stopping at the last moment to warn, "If you remember I'm bringing you food, don't eat the dinner they bring you."

With a little wave, he was gone, and Todd stifled the urge to call out again. There must have been something he'd done to offend, something he'd forgotten.

The afternoon passed quickly, as Todd was visited by three therapists in succession. "Speak, spirit," Todd said wearily in way of greeting, when the third, a speech therapist, arrived. "You are the spirit of therapy yet to come?"

The therapist laughed. "They warned me you were a feisty one."

The physical therapist labeled Todd a fall risk. To Todd, it was something of a humiliation, since it meant he wasn't allowed to dress himself or visit the restroom without supervision. Todd was ready to complain bitterly when Sebby arrived. As Sebby peeled back the foil, though, the mouthwatering aroma of freshly sizzled fajitas drove all thoughts but appetite from his mind.

"Ye gods!" Todd exclaimed, eyeing the peppers, onions, steak, and tortillas. "However did you manage it?"

"Rehab is just down the hall and to the right and down another hall, and they have a kitchen—for patients to practice in? They let me use it." Sebby was smiling, but his eyes had a tightness about them that Todd attributed to worry and lack of sleep. "You're dressed," Sebby noted. To Todd's frustration, he again retreated and slid into the faraway chair.

"Thanks to the capable hands of an insistent occupational therapist, I am in a state of clothedness." He was also clean and clean-shaven, due to the same therapist, though he had been unable to wash his hair because of the bandage. "Does it make me more attractive? Or do you enjoy seeing me with my bum hanging out?" He waggled his eyebrows, and began folding steak and peppers into a tortilla.

"It doesn't hang out," Sebby said, in a tone that suggested eye rolling. "Not when you're bedridden."

"Aren't you going to eat?"

"Don't talk with your mouth full. And I will later."

"Have some of this. I can't eat it all. Here, I'll make you one." Todd began scooping food into another tortilla.

"I know how much you eat, Todd, and, yes, you can."

"Ah, but the capacity of my stomach has shrunk due to recent bedriddenness. Come hither, *cielito lindo*." He waved the filled tortilla in the air. Sebby uncurled, but Todd sensed hesitation and adopted a wheedling tone. "I'll get indigestion of loneliness."

Slowly, Sebby got to his feet and came several steps closer, close enough that Todd could see he was biting his lip white. Todd kept his own expression neutral, offering the folded fajita.

Todd's mother spoke from the doorway. "Something smells good! Oooh!"

Sebby turned so fast that Todd was unsure he had really seen Sebby's face twitch in panic before smoothing out into a welcoming smile. "Hello, Lois." To Todd's astonishment, Sebby, on tiptoes, hugged his mother.

"Is there enough for me?" Todd's mother grabbed the tortilla from his hand, and Todd was too stunned to prevent it. She took a huge bite and *mmm*ed in pleasure.

"Sure," said Sebby. "Todd can't eat much."

"There's something wrong with you if you can't eat much of this, Toddy," she mumbled, and Todd noticed that Sebby said nothing about *her* talking with her mouth full. Sebby only stepped away and switched on the television. Todd's mother swallowed and *mmm*ed again, closing her eyes.

"Oh. I brought your glasses." Holding the tortilla in one hand, she twisted in order to rummage through her purse with the other, cursing under her breath and finally producing an eyeglass case. "I ordered them before I left Minnesota, and it took this long for them to get here." She placed the case in Todd's hand, which was still outstretched, and seated herself on the sofa.

"Oh. God. Thanks." The glasses settled firmly enough over the bandage. "I can see!" he cried, making a show of gaping wide-eyed and turning his head to gaze about. "It's a miracle!"

Everything seemed to jump out at him with laser-edged clarity, and he marveled in the novelty: the sight of Sebby's neat form; his fetchingly curved ass under the pressed trousers; his shoulder blades standing out against the fabric of his polo shirt stretched tight due to Sebby standing with arms folded; his head tilted back to view a football game on the wall-mounted television.

Football?

Todd's mother snorted. "If it was a miracle, you'd see out of both eyes."

"I have a lovely view of the inside of a bandage. Sebby, turn it to TCM."

"It's the Vikings." Sebby did not take his eyes from the screen. "And they're playing Green Bay."

"I can *see* that," Todd said. "And a more venomous rivalry doth not exist. But since when do you—"

"I got money on this game," Sebby interrupted.

"My land," his mother said, around another mouthful. "You boys and your sports."

"I've fallen into an alternate universe. Any second now, Spock-with-a-beard will enter." Todd rubbed his forehead. Gambling was an activity that Sebby abhorred, calling it the nonplanner's retirement plan.

"Eat, dumbass!" Sebby commanded, glaring.

Todd goggled. "W— But— Ah . . ." He looked down at the half-eaten fajita on his plate, up again at Sebby's tight lips, and again at the television screen. He grinned suddenly, and Sebby's eyes narrowed. "Touchdown!" Todd cried, throwing his hands in the air, just to see what Sebby would do. Sebby stared at Todd uncomprehendingly.

"Who?" His mother finished her tortilla and licked her fingers. "Minnesota or Green Bay?"

Turning belatedly to the television, Sebby shook his head. "Todd's being a dumbass. No one scored." Quite ungracefully, he plopped his butt down on the corner of Todd's bed and continued to watch the game as though football were his life.

"What down is it?" Todd asked, moving so he could prod Sebby with his toes. Catching Sebby out ought to be easy.

"Third, Green Bay," Sebby responded promptly. "They're on their twenty-six yard line."

He was doing better than expected. "What's the point spread?" Surely Sebby wouldn't know what that meant.

Sebby turned to punch Todd's foot with his fist. "Five."

"Ow." Either Sebby had pulled a number out of his ass or he knew what he was talking about. Probably the latter, Todd realized; he had gotten a taste of sports statistics from Christopher, and the accountant in him must know all about things like wagering and odds. He finished his fajitas, watching Sebby watch the game and listening to him chat with his mother. Sebby's attention rarely wavered from the screen, but he showed no reaction to fumbles or penalties or touchdowns. The sky outside darkened to dusk, and Todd found himself nodding off.

"Todd's tired. I can watch the rest at home," Sebby said. Todd jerked awake to see Sebby standing and holding his hand up for a high five. "Vikings lead, fourteen–six, buddy!"

There was that word again! Todd allowed Sebby to slap his hand. *What the fuck is going on?* he wanted to shout.

Lois stood to hug Sebby good-bye, and Todd, watching them, felt his insides tighten in wistfulness. "I want cookies," he declared. They blinked at him, moving slightly out of their clinch, Sebby's hands on her shoulders, hers on his elbows. "I want cookies! By God, can't a man in the hospital get cookies?"

"I have Fig Newtons in my purse." His mother sidled over to grab her purse.

"Fig Newtons aren't cookies!" Todd asserted. "I want a proper cookie."

"What kind? I can make you some and bring them tomorrow." Sebby stepped back as Lois dropped her purse with a thump.

"I said a proper cookie! Not some organic, carob-chipped, fat-free wafer. I want a cookie made with real butter and so drenched in sugar that it sparkles like Disney on Ice."

"I have real butter and sugar. *Organic* real butter and raw sugar," Sebby said.

Having fished her billfold from her purse, Todd's mother straightened with a groan. "I suppose I have to head down to the snack shop. They're open till ten, and they have fresh-baked cookies."

"Oh, no, no, Todd can't have those," Sebby insisted, laying a restraining hand on her arm. "They probably use commercial premade dough, and it's full of preservatives and artificial ingredients."

"What the fuck, Sebastián, let me have a cookie!"

"Lois, don't get him one. They're bad for him."

"I want a cookie! Motherfuck!"

Both Sebby and his mother regarded him with alarm. "Did his brain get that thing where you swear all the time and you can't help it?" his mother asked.

With a censorious glance at Todd, Sebby said, "Remember, they said he'd have some irritatedness, that's normal with brain surgery."

"It's been about a week. Seems like he should be over his irritatingness by now." His mother shook her head. She bent to replace her billfold in her purse, and Todd realized he wasn't going to get his cookie.

"Irritability! English, people, it is a language! One might also say tetchiness or petulance, did this category apply to me, which it does not. I just want a motherfucking cookie, goddamn it!" He flushed. He was at their mercy; they could thwart his desires in any way they wanted. "I don't have to eat your food," he growled at Sebby.

"You'll eat what I bring you, and you'll say thanks. I know what's good for you."

"The hospital menu has cookies. You can't stop me from getting one."

"Your tumor. It could grow back, you know," Sebby said.

"From a cookie?" Todd asked, now thoroughly confused. Was this conversation about what he thought it was?

"Oh, they said the chance of that's so small," his mother put in.

"So was the chance of a seizure."

Spoken so quietly, Sebby's words seemed to weigh pounds apiece, and Todd felt at a loss. Were they keeping something from him? Perhaps his situation was more serious than anyone had let on.

He tried for flippancy. "Should I die, I want the autopsy to show that I died a happy, cookie-filled man."

His mother rolled her eyes. "Don't be so dramatic. You're not dying, I told you that already."

"He probably forgot," Sebby said. "Lois, are you staying here tonight?"

"I don't know. My back has been bothering me."

Though he never thought of his mother as good company, the picture of himself alone in a darkened hospital made Todd's heart jitter. "*You* stay with me," he said to Sebby. "Ensure I do not sneak illicit cookies."

"I'm not family. Bye, Todd. See you in the morning." With this abrupt good-bye, Sebby exited, leaving Todd perplexed and grieving. Sebby must know, he reasoned, that with a kiss or a touch he could get Todd to agree to anything, including cookie abstinence, yet his manner was just short of cold.

"Mom."

Looking up from handbag rummaging, his mother regarded him with pursed lips. "You're not going to bug me for a cookie."

"Fuck the cookies. Is Sebby mad at me? Did I, er, do something, say something I don't remember, something that pissed him off?"

His mother shook her head and went back to her purse. "He doesn't seem mad to me." She came up with a flask in her hand. "Are you going to give me a hard time about this? If you are, tell me now, and I'll leave."

"No, ma'am," said Todd, making a snap decision that a drunken mother was better than no companion at all. "Ah, he's . . . not quite acting like himself, and . . . he's always in a hurry to leave."

Twisting the cap from her flask, his mother glared at him. "You're the most ungrateful person, Todd. You should thank your lucky stars for a friend like him. If you knew how he's fussed and worried over you. Almost as much as me." She paused and tossed back two quick swallows, then bared her teeth and exhaled. "If he's not himself, it's 'cause he's worn out with worrying and trying to have a job and spending all his free time here. Bringing you meals, and then you whining for cookies. It's a wonder he's *not* mad at you."

Todd lay back against his pillows, trying to absorb his mother's words. "I'm sick; you're supposed to be indulgent," he muttered. "Jesus, I feel as though I've a memory of my life, of the world, and reality is playing me false. I've only one eye, and it is forced to see the truth, whereas those with two eyes can choose what they see."

"You can still choose what to see with one eye." She took another swallow and paused, running her tongue around the mouth of the flask. "I don't know about seeing truth. You probably see less of it now. If you don't want to see something, you can turn a blind eye." She laughed, and the sound reverberated in the flask before she tipped her head to drink.

Todd snorted. "I'll try to be less ungrateful, ma'am."

"You never appreciate *me*, either." She screwed the cap back on the flask. "You act like you had the worst childhood, like you were abused or I don't know what, with your Al-Anon and your *meetings*, and I'm not even that bad of an alcoholic." As if to prove her point, she removed the cap for one more swig before closing it up and putting it away.

"No, ma'am. Not that bad."

Chapter Forty-Nine

Blind

A container landed on Todd's tray, and Sebby ripped back the lid to reveal a pile of golden-brown cookies. Todd, who'd been assisted to a chair by a CNA, lifted a cookie reverently, turning it this way and that, disregarding the crumbs and grains of sugar that fell to his lap. The cookie glittered in the early sunlight as though encrusted with gems.

"*Ave*," Todd breathed.

"Ave?" Sebby repeated. "Is that 'thank you'? 'Cause it better be."

"It's Latin for 'hail.' But I do thank thee, yea, verily, Sebastián." Marveling, he picked up another. Sebby was smiling at him, Todd had cookies in hand, and all was right with the world.

"My land," Todd's mother remarked, sitting up and yawning with an operatic howl. "You must have been up half the night, Sebby."

"No. Todd, cookies can be your breakfast. And here's coffee." He poured a cup for Lois as well.

Todd dunked his cookie in the fragrant beverage and sank his teeth into the dripping confection. The cookie was crisp on the outside, buttery and chewy within, and Todd closed his eye in bliss. "Heaven." Opening his eye, he smiled at Sebby. "Thank you for temporarily giving up the organic obsession."

Sebby smiled tolerantly in return. "Didn't. They're organic, dude. Close your mouth."

Todd did so, wondering anew at Sebby's attitude, dunking the cookie and finishing it in a subdued manner. "I am humbled."

There was a burst of laughter from his mother. "That'll be the day!" Laughing, she rolled out of bed and shuffled to the bathroom, taking her purse with her.

Todd felt the need to explain. "She never has breakfast."

"I know," said Sebby.

"Unless a little nip counts."

"It doesn't."

Todd nibbled at another cookie and watched Sebby stare out the window. "Nice day," Todd commented.

"Yes."

"Not that I'd know firsthand."

"No."

"*Gracias* for the cookies."

"*De nada.*"

When Lois emerged from the bathroom, Sebby turned, but she proceeded out into the corridor without a word, and Sebby went back to staring.

In the silence, Todd nibbled at another cookie. The food felt to be congealing into a flabby lump in his stomach. He took a long swallow of coffee. "I don't wish to seem unappreciative, but I feel . . . uncomfortable that you are going to such lengths to ensure that nothing of which you do not approve passes these lips." He dabbed at his mouth with a napkin.

"No lengths," Sebby said, evidently either fascinated by the view or bored with Todd's conversation.

"Please, I'm concerned about you." Though he was not supposed to without assistance, Todd shoved the wheeled tray aside and pushed himself up from the chair. His legs felt weak, but they held.

"I'm fine, Todd."

Gripping the chair's arms, Todd took a careful step, testing his balance. "You're not 'fine.' You seem distracted, perhaps because you are exhausting yourself, and I don't wish to be the cause of . . . of . . ." Feeling a trifle unsteady and finding nothing to cling to, Todd let go of the chair, leaned forward, and stumbled to the window, trusting in momentum to avert a fall. He ended with his palms out, *slap*, against the glass.

Sebby whirled. His eyes raked Todd's form, his expression betraying something like panic. "What are you doing!"

"Please don't continue to bring me meals. Hospital food won't harm me. You're being overly cautious—"

"I have to be! Because you're reckless!" Grasping Todd's arm so tightly that it hurt, Sebby steered him across the room.

"Ow!" Todd protested.

"Set your ass down!"

Todd did so.

"Eat your cookie!"

"You're not going to slap me, are you?" The last time he'd seen Sebby this worked up had been the Fourth of July.

The question triggered an avalanche of Spanish, and Todd thought he was doing well not to cower. Sebby paced across the room and back, breathing stentoriously before stopping to face Todd once more. "Processed food is full of chemicals, and lots of chemicals are carcinogens. So you won't eat their food, and you *will* eat my food."

Todd blinked up at Sebby, digesting the words. *Jesus God, I am obtuse.* The hospitalization, the tests, the bad news, and the surgeries must have dredged up Sebby's memories of his mother's illness and death, when he had been able to do nothing but pray, when he had believed that prayer was all that was needed. That belief had been crushed to the point where he was not able even to do that for Todd. Sebby couldn't control events, but he could control what Todd put into his body. "Sebby, it was nonmalignant. I do not have cancer."

Sebby's expression was stony. "A nonmalignancy can be just as dangerous. And things like growth hormones in livestock make tumors grow more."

"That's just a theory. But," he added hastily as Sebby's eyes narrowed, "I'll comply with your wishes and consume nothing that is not stamped Sebby-approved. This I swear." Todd could at least give Sebby this assurance, if he could guarantee nothing else.

The words needed time to soak in, and the little Latino stood still for long moments before his face relaxed into a smile. "Good. Todd, it won't be bad food, *te lo prometo*. Everything will taste good."

"I'm counting on it."

"And when you come home, I already went through the cupboards and threw out everything you shouldn't eat."

Todd groaned inwardly, but thanked Sebby, who brushed his thanks aside and declared that he was late for work. He reminded Todd to wait for lunch, and vanished.

"Stitches coming out today."

The words brought Todd up short, and he stammered before he could reply. "What st-st— What?"

"In the eye." Dr. Roodnitsky tapped Todd's forehead above his ruined eye, ignoring his flinch. "Bandage comes off, stitches come out, area is cleansed, and they teach you to care for it as it heals."

"But—but . . . no one said . . . st-st-stitches."

Dr. Roodnitsky had assessed his mental status before springing this news on him and pronounced his brain well on the mend, while admonishing him to expect setbacks. Now she was peering at him over the rims of her glasses.

"You are not afraid of this, a big boy like you?" Seeing his shudder, she pursed her lips. "It's all right. I will order sedative."

"No, no," Todd protested. "I'll be . . . fine. It's fine. No sedative. Thank you."

She raised her eyebrows at him and waited, but Todd held on to his resolve. After a moment, she pushed away from the computer. "It's your choice. It will be this morning, but exact time—who will know? Depends when he can get to you."

As soon as she was out of the room, Todd seized the phone and called Sebastián at Gimondi Brothers. "It is I, your wounded one."

"My . . .? Doesn't sound nice."

"Listen, ah . . . they will be, ah, removing my, ah . . ." Todd paused and gathered his courage before spitting out the word. "*Stitches.*" He let out a breath. "This morning. And cleansing my, ah, wound."

"Good. I'm tired of looking at that bandage."

"Yes, ah. I, also. So . . . I thought you'd like to know." His voice trailed off. There was no good way to ask that Sebastián be present at said event and hold Todd's hand throughout.

There was a pause. "What time?"

"Dr. Roodnitsky said, 'Who will know?'" He imitated the good doctor's accent and was rewarded with a laugh.

"Kay. You want me to be there?"

Dr. Borne was an immense black man with a deep, resonant voice. It was difficult to imagine that such a man had not left an impression deep enough to withstand a little brain surgery, yet the ophthalmologist seemed unfamiliar. The nurse raised his bed. The doctor's fingers, encased in surgical gloves, were deft and gentle as he removed the bandage and palpated the tender flesh.

"Looks good, overall." The doctor nodded and turned to his nurse, who put an instrument tray on the wheeled stand.

As Dr. Borne moved out of their respective lines of sight, both Sebby and Todd's mother made noises of distress—Sebby's a gasp followed by murmured Spanish, and his mother's a loud "Jesus God, oh, where's my camera." At least she wasn't ducking into the bathroom for a quick nip, Todd thought to himself as he posed for the camera, and so his eye (or the place where it had until recently resided) must not appear *too* appalling. The doctor held some instrument that might have come from one of Sebby's *Saw* movies, and Todd's heart palpitated.

"Be a man" could go fuck itself. "Er, wait, wait. Ah, wait."

The doctor paused.

"Sebby." Todd tried not to sound as desperate as he felt. "I'm afraid that at this juncture I require your presence. A bit, ah, closer than the opposite corner of the room."

Sebby was leaning against the far wall. He came forward a step, hesitated, and fell back against the wall with a thump. "Aw, what the hell ya want me to do, buddy—hold your hand?" he asked in a tone of affectionate derision.

Todd's mouth fell open and stayed open even as his hand closed into a painful fist.

"I'll hold your hand. I'm your mother," announced that personage. She eased up to the side of the bed opposite the doctor and folded the cold fingers of both hands around Todd's fist. The doctor leaned over him once again, bringing the sinister-looking instrument close enough that Todd could smell the antiseptic.

"Wait!" Todd cried, flinching away and blinking. He threw a look of mute appeal at Sebby, who gave him a tiny headshake. All three— Dr. Borne, the nurse, and Todd's mother—turned to look at Sebby, who waved an arm as if to say *Get on with it*. At this distance and once again without his eyeglasses, Todd tried in vain to read Sebby's expression, but his posture was one of affected casualness.

Squeamishness could not explain Sebby's reluctance to approach. In fact, Todd had half expected him to lean close and watch the proceedings with a glint of morbid fascination in his eyes.

"Sebby," Todd started, and then, to the doctor, "Sorry. Sorry. I wanted . . . I wanted . . ." His voice cut off as he was smacked by a flash of insight so brilliant it forced his eye shut.

"Did you want a sedative?" Dr. Borne inquired in his hypnotic baritone. "I was told you declined." He placed a hand on Todd's shoulder. "I promise it won't hurt much. You'll feel some tugging as the stitches come out, and soreness where the area is bruised and swollen. The psychological aspect of confronting your injury can be difficult, of course. There's still time for a sedative, if you want one."

Todd hardly noticed the kind words, lost in the revelation unfolding behind his closed eyelids: a vision of Sebastián lingering at the bedside of a male whose identity was rendered anonymous by bandages and contusions. The injured male's whisper quavered as he informed Sebastián that he could not see him anymore because he no longer wanted to be gay. Todd could mark by Sebastián's face the progress of the breaking of his heart as he let go of the male's hand, as he whispered back that he understood, that he would stay away . . .

Todd's eye snapped open. With trap-door swiftness, he drew his mother's hands to his heart, covered them with his other hand. "Mom."

"It's okay, Toddy. Be a brave soldier." With those words his mother had sprayed stinging antiseptic on his scraped knees and levered splinters from his fingers.

"Yes. No. I have to tell you something, ah, something you may not like . . ." Todd sensed rather than saw Sebastián twitch.

His mother's eyes flew wide in injured offense. "Why wouldn't I like it? You don't know what I like. I like lots of things."

"You're right." Todd swallowed and played with her fingers. "I *don't* necessarily know. Right, then." He forced himself to look his mother in the eyes, his one to her two.

"Todd . . ." Sebby warned.

It was difficult to resist the temptation to glance at Sebastián, but Todd was determined to hold his mother's gaze. The concern on her face was decaying into suspicion, and Todd spoke fast before she could have a chance to hazard guesses or accusations. "Mom, I'm gay."

Her expression wavered between suspicion and confusion.

"I'm gay. I am a homosexual man," he added in case she thought he was expressing giddiness.

Her lips parted and she leaned closer, turning her head as if to present her ear to a dying man's lips. Todd squeezed her hands in his, pressing them closer to his heart.

"You're not gay," she said. "He's not gay," she repeated, straightening and turning to the doctor as if for confirmation.

"We'll just come back in a few minutes." Dr. Borne's instrument made a musical clink as he replaced it on the tray, and there was a rattle as he stood and pushed the table aside. Nodding and smiling, he departed and his nurse with him, closing the door as they left. Todd, from the corner of his remaining eye, saw that Sebby had moved away from the wall and was hovering in the middle of the room, his hands clasped and pressed to his mouth.

"You're not gay," his mother said again. "I'd know if you were."

"Then you know," Todd said, "for it's true." Her lips pursed and moved from side to side as she ruminated, and Todd grew nervous. He pressed their joined hands still more tightly against his pounding heart. "I'm sorry, Mom. I mean, sorry to spring it on you like this. I'm not sorry for who I am." She was shaking her head, her eyes not meeting his, and Todd went on, hoping by words, by explanation and elaboration, to win her acceptance. "I am a gay man. Or queer, if you prefer." *I wish to submit exhibit A, may it please the court.* Todd let go with one hand long enough to gesture toward Sebastián. "Sebby . . . is my boyfriend. We share more than a house; we share a bed. Because we are in love." An unidentifiable sound came from Sebastián, and Todd eyed him anxiously.

"You're in love," his mother repeated. Her penciled brows knitted over her eyes, eyes that roamed back and forth over Todd's form.

"Yes," Todd affirmed.

"You and Sebby."

"Yes."

"With each other?" And she raised her eyes, her two to his one.
"Yes!"

She regarded him, consternated, and Todd returned her gaze, and then his mother's face broke into a smile. She burst into laughter, rocking back and forth in her chair and clutching Todd's hands till her fingernails drove hard into the flesh of his palm.

Todd stared. And he'd been so sure she was sober! "She's hysterical. Jesus." He had fucked this up royally, no surprise. He gave Sebby a rueful glance and was surprised to find him smiling.

"I'm not hysterical! Though I sure as *hell* need a drink. My land!" She rocked forward and planted a loud kiss on Todd's cheek before pulling her hands free and fishing her flask from her purse.

"Mom, don't. This is . . . I need you in possession of your faculties."

His mother tipped her head back and swallowed. Todd worried that she was draining the flask. He chided himself that he should have known she would respond by turning to drink; to what else would she turn? Her lips peeled back in the familiar postswallow rictus as she replaced the flask. With a long sigh, she surveyed the two of them.

"I'm sorry, Lois." Sebby shook his head at Todd. "I've tried *so* hard to civilize him."

"You'll never manage it. Nor me, neither."

"I beg your pardon!" Todd declared. "I contend that I've behaved in a completely civilized manner throughout!"

His mother pursed her lips, bunching them to one side, and her eyes met Todd's. "I thought you were breaking his heart. Not on purpose, but, my land! It was so *obvious* he loved you. I never thought you loved *him*!" She laughed again, slapping her thigh, but then her expression sobered. "Did you think I'd be mad?"

"Pop thought you would."

His mother drew herself up in indignation. "You told him but not me?"

"I meant to . . . to tell you both together. But he prevented me, and I realize now I shouldn't have allowed him to sway me from my purpose."

"Of all the . . ." Her mouth curled into a snarl. "I'm not mad. I'm not one of those mothers who disowns her child or tries to change you. I know you can't help it, and gay people are born that way. And I'm a good mother. And . . ." Her face softened, and her eyes brimmed. "I just want you to be happy."

Sebby made a noise of sympathy and stepped forward, but he halted and looked to Todd. Todd felt his own eyes stinging—the both of them. "I am happy," he said through his constricting throat. When his mother leaned toward him to pat his shoulder, he sat up to meet her and, catching hold of her arm, pulled her to himself, trying not to calculate how long it had been since his mother had hugged him. She stiffened and became all sharp bones, but he held on for several seconds before releasing her. Blinking, she sat back and cleared her throat, smoothed her hair, and got to her feet, not looking at him.

"I'll tell the doctor it's safe now." She backed toward the door. Sebby waylaid her with a tight hug, and Todd tried not to mind how she returned his embrace, but in the next moment Sebby was in his arms, and any resentment melted like ice chips in a dry mouth.

"Reckless, I said, didn't I? Todd, time and place!"

Sebby mashed his face into Todd's neck, and Todd tipped his head to bury his nose in the dark hair, inhaling the spicy scent, like exotic coffee. "I am a master of timing."

"What if your mother'd been upset?" Sebby fretted, his voice muffled.

"I don't know," Todd admitted. "But at that moment, your level of upset was of a higher priority to me."

Sebby snorted, which felt odd against Todd's neck. "You mean *your* level of upset."

"Perceptive as ever. I cannot claim complete altruism. Nevertheless, *cielito lindo*, I saw what a wreck you must have been." He kissed the top of Sebby's head. "I marvel at my own obtuseness."

"Brain surgery is a pretty good excuse for obtuseness, Toddfox." He raised his head to look Todd in the eye. "Are you happy, *querido*? For true?"

"I am." He paused. "Because it is so obvious that you love me."

Resting his head again, Sebby laughed shortly. "I guess my het act isn't as good as yours."

"Probably because it is so obvious that you love me."

Sebby *tsk*ed. "Don't gloat."

"It's difficult not to gloat when it is so obvious that you love me."

"*¡Dios mío!*" Sebby swatted half-heartedly at Todd's chest. "There'll be no living with you after this!"

"But you will. Because you so obviously love me."

The dialogue might have continued indefinitely in this manner but for the entrance of the ophthalmologist and his nurse. With his mother and Sebby at his bedside, the care of his eye socket was accomplished with less discomfort than expected. The worst moment occurred upon the opening of the eyelid when Todd, who had unconsciously been anticipating an uncomfortable brightness hitting the long-closed eye, instead experienced total darkness, and he felt an illogical certainty that something was covering his eye, blocking his sight. He reached instinctively to rub the organ and clear the blockage. No one prevented him. The flesh was puffy and tender, and it was still more disconcerting to be unable to see his fingertips as they explored the area. Closing his good eye and again opening the bad eye, he could not shake the expectancy of sight.

"I'm blind," he whispered.

"It'll take time to adjust," said the doctor, his hand a comforting weight on Todd's shoulder.

"It'll be okay." Sebby gently pulled Todd's hand away. Lips brushed Todd's knuckles and his remaining eye in turn, and the kissed eyelid sprang open. Sebby's face was very close. Deep-brown eyes looked into Todd's blue one. It seemed to Todd he had never seen anything so beautiful. He stared, determined to engrave the lines of cheek and jaw, the curve of nose, and yes, glint of eye under smooth brow, thoroughly into memory, against the possibility of losing the other eye.

Sebby smiled, bringing out his dimple. "See? Not blind."

"Half a loaf is better than none," his mother put in.

"And an eye in the socket is worth two in the bush," Todd agreed.

Chapter Fifty

Monocle

*T*odd had a great deal of time to himself in rehab, time to contemplate his life and recent events. Occasionally he found himself staring at *Vivid* on his cell phone. He ought to delete it. He decided he would. Right after one last text.

Vivian? Hello.

There was a short pause before the response came. *Todd! Hello, you.*

Hello.

You said that. So did I. How are you?

Fine. Well, recovering. I've had an injury. In fact, I am now a Cyclops.

Several heartbeats passed. *Are you employing hyperbole?*

Todd smiled. *If only. No, I have lost an eye and also a brain tumor. But rest assured that I am getting better, and all manner of things will be well.*

I don't even know how to respond! Could we talk about this? Can I call you?

Todd pursed his lips. He squeezed his eye shut. He called Vivian.

Todd related what had passed, how he had had an eye and a tumor removed, and after the initial exclamations, Vivian was uncharacteristically quiet during the telling. "Now we are both maimed."

"You're not maimed. You're scarred. There is a difference. And just imagine how rakish I look in an eye patch."

"Send me a pic."

Todd grimaced. "No, Vivian."

"I want to come to Denver; I want to see you. I mean . . . if you want me to."

"Viv—"

Vivian went on, speaking quickly. "You really, really are important to me. I don't know who I'd be right now if we hadn't been together, and I like that I am the me who loved you so much. I still do love you, and I really want us to stay, I don't know. Friends. That sounds awful."

"Not awful. I feel the same. But, Vivian . . . this isn't a good time. Truly. I am just recovering, and Sebby and I . . . we're together. That is, I have moved in with him, and I need time, time with him, time to settle, and time to recover before introducing an ex-boyfriend into the mix."

"Oh. Oh, of course. I don't want to intrude. Of course, I'll give you all the time you need, even forever, if you need it." He sniffled, and Todd winced.

"Love doesn't just . . . stop. But I am in love with Sebby. And he and I are well suited, whereas you and I . . . were always a turbulent mess."

"I loved that turbulent mess," Vivian said fervently. There was a pause, and then he went on wistfully. "But I ended it. It was my decision. And I think you're happy, there with Sebby and mountains and coffee. Even though tea is clearly superior and always will be."

Todd chuckled.

"Stay in touch," Vivian admonished.

"Take care of yourself," Todd said. "I mean it."

"I will. As much as I can. You know."

"I know. Good-bye, Vivian."

"Bye, Todd."

He stared at *Vivid* in his contacts. *Stay in touch*, Viv had said. *Stay in touch.* Todd bit his lip. His finger hovered over the delete selection. Finally, he drew a deep breath and set his phone aside.

Sebby was pleased when Todd was released after only one week in rehab. Sebby cared for Todd's eye, over his protests, but Sebby suspected that if he didn't take over the tasks of rinsing and applying ointment, Todd would neglect it. He followed each treatment with kisses, as Todd seemed self-conscious about the injury, and Sebby wanted him to know that he didn't mind it. He planned to talk Todd into getting a prosthetic eye, but each time he brought it up, Todd shuddered and went pale. When Sebby pointed out that a patch *with* glasses was like crazy overkill, and that if he didn't want a prosthesis he should get a contact lens for his good eye, Todd threatened to get a monocle.

Collin's cohort, when questioned, admitted that they had planned to jump Sebby's boyfriend, which established intent, which made the assault a more severe crime, and also established that Todd had acted in self-defense. Probation violation and commission of a new crime doomed Collin to hard time. There was plea bargaining for lesser offenses, and so nothing came to trial. The man who'd been actually responsible for damaging Todd's eye had an arrest record, and the judge was not inclined to be lenient.

Whether motivated by sympathy or a genuine interest in Todd's talents, the employer whose interview Todd had missed was willing to reschedule. Sebby nagged and cajoled and begged Todd to get either a prosthesis or a contact lens before the interview, but Todd was immovable on this point. He insisted that he'd be seen as colorful and eccentric, prized characteristics of an ad man. Off to the interview he went, wearing his eye patch under his glasses. Maybe he did know what he was talking about, because he was hired.

Sebby began to feel settled. There was no more pretending, no worries about being found out. Collin would never bother him again. Sebby had a job he enjoyed and a nice home. He had a boyfriend who was kind and who loved him. Todd's family liked Sebby, and Sebby's friends were Todd's friends now too. Even Ryan had started coming around. And Todd now had a "real" job, and that meant he'd stay.

Monogamy became a comfortable thing. Sebby had never appreciated before what it would be like, having just one person that you allowed so close to you. Instead of feeling anxious that Todd would be bored, Sebby found relief in Todd's promise of exclusivity, and it was a relief to have given the same. He worried about what Barry and

Lawrence would think, but they were happy for Sebby. He discovered that he didn't miss anything; instead, he'd gained something—a confidence in himself and his lover.

Chapter Fifty-One

Flaming Rum Punch

*T*odd was not much of a nightclub person, not since his college days anyway, but one evening he allowed Sebby to drag him to the bar where Barry and Lawrence tended. *One* of the bars, Sebby clarified, as there were apparently two or three. The boys moonlighted, always together. A proprietor could not get one without the other. Todd had to admit that he was curious to see how the two worked together.

They entered The Flaming Rum Punch and were greeted with squeals and over-the-bartop hugs. Barry and Lawrence wore identical fitted shirts, and short white aprons knotted around their hips over pants that looked too tight to move around in, yet limited their movements not at all. At one end of the bar, Hugh hunched, gargoyle-like, viewing his charges' flirtations with apparent wary tolerance. Men sat or stood or leaned, subtle touches and quick, eager glances speaking a language that Todd knew all too well. A few couples moved languidly on the dance floor, speckled with multicolored neon. A boy in shabby denim who did not look old enough to play varsity sports grasped the manicured little finger of a businessman, and drew him away from the bar and into the glittering dark. Todd suppressed the urge to reach out and rescue the young boy—he was probably older than he looked, he told himself. Sebby, noting the direction of his gaze, tugged on Todd's collar and whispered in his ear, "You can't save the world."

Todd shrugged off his unease and took the stool next to Hugh. "Hugh the Hero," he said, by way of greeting.

"Hey." Hugh straightened. "Sebby, you finally dragged him here."

Sebby merely nodded and seated himself on Todd's other side, turning away and leaning back against the bar. Todd thought that the whole Collin incident had made Sebby uncomfortable around Hugh, unless it was his continuing relationship with Barry and Lawrence that was the problem. The bartenders made their way over and said in obviously rehearsed unison, "Can we make you a hot toddy?"

Todd laughed—it was an old joke.

"We can make you a virgin hot toddy," Lawrence offered.

"I think that's impossible," said Barry.

"A priest can do it," said Lawrence.

"In point of fact, I am a virgin," Todd asserted. "In my left ear."

There was appreciative laughter, and drinks were lined up in front of them. "On the house!" they insisted, but Todd pulled out a five to slip into their tip jar. Sebby grasped his wrist.

"No!"

"What?"

"You don't tip someone you've slept with! 'S rude!"

Consternated, Todd stared pointedly at the stuffed jar and then allowed his eye to sweep the room. "In that case, money does grow on trees, and this container"—he knocked his knuckles on the side of the jar—"is an ecosphere."

Sebby sighed, tugged the bill from Todd's fingers, and added it to the jar.

"I tip them," Hugh said, his eyes following Barry, who blew a kiss in their direction from the other end of the bar. He hopped to sit on the counter, allowing a patron to slip a bill into his hip pocket before hopping down again.

"Martiniiis," Lawrence sang, scooping up a bottle of gin in one hand, a metal shaker in the other. Barry grabbed a bottle of vermouth. Mirroring one another, each poured into his own shaker and then tossed his bottle, unerringly plucking the other's bottle from the air and adding to his shaker. Back to back, they shook the martinis, wriggling against one another and evoking cheers and cat-calls from onlookers. Two martinis were dispensed. The tip jar sprouted new foliage. Sitting backward, elbows on the bar, Sebby sipped, his eyes roaming the room while Todd chatted with Hugh.

"Things must be going well." Todd nodded at Barry and Lawrence, who were pitching olives into the open mouths of patrons.

"Somehow." Hugh shook his head, looking dazzled. "God love 'em." The big man grinned, and for the first time, Todd noticed a resemblance to Hugh Jackman, though he doubted the likeness would have occurred to him if it had not been suggested. Hugh's expression sobered, and he leaned closer. "How's the eye?"

"Gone, thanks to our friend. Seriously, though, it's healing." He flicked at his eye patch. "Care to see?"

"Naw," Hugh said. "Wish I'd beat 'im better when I had the chance. Might still have your eye, then."

A hand touched Todd's elbow, and he turned his attention to Sebby. "I see someone I know. Kay?" Without waiting for answer, Sebby slid from the stool and glided away, hips swinging as he meandered between tables, skirting the dance floor.

"You did your best," Todd continued to Hugh. "And I did mine." He shook his head, still finding it hard to believe. "Who knew he had a friend?"

Evening wore on into night, and the mood changed as the place filled. Patrons had to shout into one another's ears to be heard as the music picked up and the buzz of conversation mounted. Subtlety was shed in favor of brazen advances. Todd lost sight of Sebby in the press of people.

Eventually, the bartenders opted for a break and tried to sweet-talk Hugh into dancing with them. "I don't dance," Hugh insisted gruffly. Barry and Lawrence pouted and wheedled, but Hugh remained as immovable as Colossus. "Get someone else."

They turned to Todd with such alacrity that he was certain this scenario had become habit—beg Hugh for the sake of politeness to dance, gain permission to find other partners, and move on. Todd attempted to glower like Hugh, but without success, and he found himself being dragged toward the sparkling space, the arms of a pretty boy wound around each of his own arms like duct tape. Over his shoulder, he shot Hugh a desperate glance. The man raised his margarita in salute, and Todd cursed him silently. The music thudded in his ears; the heavy bass pulsed in his chest. He felt out of place among the hipsters; though, if he were being honest with himself, plenty of older men like Hugh and conservative types such as himself were vying for attention alongside the more flamboyant. In vain, his eyes hunted the crowd for Sebby in hopes of being rescued.

There were bare-chested men sporting nipple rings, businessmen in ties, men dressed comfortably in jeans and tees, heavily made-up men in fishnet hose and heels, and a sprinkling of boys like the one Todd had spotted earlier who looked too young to be allowed. The crush of flesh and the pounding music heated his blood till he was caught up in the bohemian mood of the place, and gave in to the sheer pleasure of moving his body to music.

Smiling to himself, Sebby remained on the fringes, watching Todd's discomfort evaporate into enjoyment. As Barry and Lawrence returned to their work, other young men pressed forward to take their place. Sebby was proud of his man, whose infectious grin said, *I'm the most fun guy in this joint.* Todd was not the most handsome, certainly not the tallest, not even the best dancer, and he was even kind of odd looking with his eye patch under his glasses. But his smile and his charm, Sebby was sure, were unequaled. Sebby took pleasure in seeing other boys look into Todd's face, their own faces bright and eager, each one of them calculating how best to get Todd home . . . or at least into a dark corner. Clubby dance tunes gave way at last to a slow song, and Sebby made his way through the dancers to claim his own. With practiced dexterity, he shouldered aside the taller boy who clung to Todd's arm. Todd blinked, and his expression opened; the smile that bloomed was for Sebby alone. Sebby raised his arms slowly and gracefully and lowered them around Todd's neck. He pressed his whole length against him—not the first boy to have done so that night, but the first to do so knowing that Todd loved him.

Smug triumph buoyed him like helium; he smiled sweetly into the disappointed faces and, to send the point home, pressed his mouth to Todd's and thrust his tongue in deep. He felt Todd's startlement, felt that he pulled back a millimeter or two before returning the kiss with enthusiasm. There were jealous huffs as Todd's hands landed on Sebby's posterior, cupping it possessively.

"Mine," Sebby murmured against Todd's mouth.

Dear Reader,

Thank you for reading Laurie Loft's *Love and Other Hot Beverages*!

We know your time is precious and you have many, many entertainment options, so it means a lot that you've chosen to spend your time reading. We really hope you enjoyed it.

We'd be honored if you'd consider posting a review—good or bad—on sites like **Amazon, Barnes & Noble, Kobo, Goodreads, Twitter, Facebook, Tumblr,** and your blog or website. We'd also be honored if you told your friends and family about this book. Word of mouth is a book's lifeblood!

For more information on upcoming releases, author interviews, blog tours, contests, giveaways, and more, please sign up for our weekly, spam-free newsletter and visit us around the web:

Newsletter: tinyurl.com/RiptideSignup
Twitter: twitter.com/RiptideBooks
Facebook: facebook.com/RiptidePublishing
Goodreads: tinyurl.com/RiptideOnGoodreads
Tumblr: riptidepublishing.tumblr.com

Thank you so much for Reading the Rainbow!

RiptidePublishing.com

Acknowledgments

It would be ungrateful and hubris-y of me not to thank my NaNoWriMo friends for helping me with character development, among so many other things. Thank you, Callirhoe, Leeza, Baxter, Eli, Mittens, and especially Simon. We'll always have the Coffeehouse.

About the Author

Laurie Loft lives in Iowa, endeavoring to write stories to give you that *rush*. Her husband, cat, and dogs kindly tolerate this odd activity. Her first M/M novel came about because of a minor character in a straight romance who just took over and demanded his own book. Laurie enjoys NaNoWriMo (National Novel Writing Month) and other forms of writerly torture. She finds inspiration in her NaNo friends and her fellow Riptide authors. When not writing, or working at her mysterious day job, she can often be found screaming at tangled cross-stitch threads.

Website and blog: www.laurieloft.com
Twitter: @Laurie_Loft
Facebook: @laurieloftwriter

Enjoy more stories like
Love and Other Hot Beverages
at RiptidePublishing.com!